THE
EX
WIVES

BOOKS BY JENNA KERNAN

The Adoption

AGENT NADINE FINCH

A Killer's Daughter
The Hunted Girls

THE EX WIVES

JENNA KERNAN

bookouture

"Say it!"

She parroted his words. "I want a lawyer."

He glared and said, "I want a lawyer present for questioning."

Questioning? What was happening?

She parroted the entire sentence and he nodded, his brow furrowed. "Exactly like that. And *only* that!"

"Yes, Jackson."

Behind them, a man and a woman simultaneously exited the SUV.

"Here they come. Damn it!"

Elana's heartbeat throbbed in her eardrums, but she wasn't afraid. She was excited. Hopeful for the first time in months. What had Jackson done that could have brought these agents to their home?

Jackson clenched the wheel, his knuckles turning white. Was he sweating? He was! And his face had gone pink.

"Mommy?"

She reached back to take her daughter's extended hand. Phoebe still sat in her place, buckled in.

Jackson rounded on her daughter.

"Quiet!"

The sharp note in his voice made them both freeze.

Phoebe's eyes filled with tears. Unlike her mother, the child had never gotten used to him snapping at her.

Elana noted an unfamiliar expression on Jackson's red face. Was that fear? The possibility brought her up short.

"Not a word. You hear?" he barked at Phoebe.

"Yes, Daddy."

Jackson had insisted early on that her daughter call him "daddy," though he wasn't yet her legal guardian. It was one of those things he hadn't gotten to. The formal adoption.

Both she and Jackson stared out the side mirrors as the two

THE
EX
WIVES

JENNA KERNAN

bookouture

Published by Bookouture in 2022

An imprint of Storyfire Ltd.
Carmelite House
50 Victoria Embankment
London EC4Y 0DZ

www.bookouture.com

ISBN: 978-1-80314-024-7
ebook ISBN: 978-1-80314-023-0

For Jim, always

ONE

NOW

June 12, 2022, Sunday
Bald Cypress, Florida

Jackson Belauru swung his full-sized pickup truck into their driveway, glanced in his side mirror, and started cursing.

From the adjoining seat, his wife, Elana, pivoted, looking past her daughter at the large black SUV gliding up behind them. The tinted windows reminded her of the sort of vehicles used in presidential motorcades.

"What the hell do they want?"

"Who is it?" she asked.

"That's the fucking FBI."

Now how did he know that on sight?

Jackson slammed the gearshift into park, twitching. Were they here to arrest him?

She couldn't be that lucky.

Jackson pointed a finger at her. "Listen carefully. You don't say anything except 'I want a lawyer.' Understand?"

She stared, wide-eyed. The shock of his obvious panic had her gaping.

"Say it!"

She parroted his words. "I want a lawyer."

He glared and said, "I want a lawyer present for questioning."

Questioning? What was happening?

She parroted the entire sentence and he nodded, his brow furrowed. "Exactly like that. And *only* that!"

"Yes, Jackson."

Behind them, a man and a woman simultaneously exited the SUV.

"Here they come. Damn it!"

Elana's heartbeat throbbed in her eardrums, but she wasn't afraid. She was excited. Hopeful for the first time in months. What had Jackson done that could have brought these agents to their home?

Jackson clenched the wheel, his knuckles turning white. Was he sweating? He was! And his face had gone pink.

"Mommy?"

She reached back to take her daughter's extended hand. Phoebe still sat in her place, buckled in.

Jackson rounded on her daughter.

"Quiet!"

The sharp note in his voice made them both freeze.

Phoebe's eyes filled with tears. Unlike her mother, the child had never gotten used to him snapping at her.

Elana noted an unfamiliar expression on Jackson's red face. Was that fear? The possibility brought her up short.

"Not a word. You hear?" he barked at Phoebe.

"Yes, Daddy."

Jackson had insisted early on that her daughter call him "daddy," though he wasn't yet her legal guardian. It was one of those things he hadn't gotten to. The formal adoption.

Both she and Jackson stared out the side mirrors as the two

agents, one stocky male and one tall female, approached the truck. The woman hung back as her partner reached Jackson's side, flashed his badge, and told Elana's husband of one year to step out of the vehicle.

Jackson threw open the door and, slamming it behind him, left them alone in the running pickup as he walked back to the Escalade with the male agent.

She watched him in his side mirror as he transformed. With each step, her husband's public facade returned until he was again the mayor of their small town, showing nothing but a relaxed posture and easy smile.

Phoebe whimpered.

Elana squeezed her child's hand.

"We're all right, sweetheart." And she meant that. Both she and her daughter were safer with him outside the truck. "Just be a good girl."

Phoebe used her free hand to wipe her tears and stared back with the same green eyes as her mother's. Elana kicked herself yet again for putting her daughter under the roof of this abusive man.

The knock at the passenger window brought them both around. The female agent stood at Elana's side of the truck.

"Mrs. Elana Belauru?"

Elana stiffened; guilt at her anticipation that Jackson might be out of her life, and panic that she'd have to disobey him, collided like tectonic plates shaking her foundation.

The agent stared at her, unblinking. Elana returned the stare, seeing a slim face, a cap of short auburn hair, pale skin, and a mouth set in an expression of serious determination. Her intent, catlike eyes washed her cold.

The agent rapped sharply on the window with her knuckles again.

"Open the door, Mrs. Belauru."

She released her seatbelt and did as instructed.

From inside her home came the sound of hysterical barking. The three hunting dogs had heard them pull up and were baying as they always did upon any return.

"I want you to speak to my lawyer," she said, getting it all wrong. "I mean speak to me, or with my lawyer."

"You're not under investigation."

"Is Jackson?" Did she sound hopeful?

A quick glance at the side mirror showed her husband and the male agent were both out of sight.

"He can't see you. He can't hear you," said the woman, making an accurate guess at Elana's train of thought. "And I just want to talk."

"No," said Elana, clutching the straps to her purse, now on her lap, with both her sweating hands.

"How about I talk, then? And you just listen."

She hesitated and glanced back at her daughter.

"Stay here, Phoebe."

Elana hiked her bag onto her shoulder and slipped down to the hot concrete.

The special agent glanced through the open door at Phoebe. Jackson had left the parked truck running, the A/C blasting.

"We'll be right here, honey. You just sit tight." The agent closed the passenger door with barely a click.

"Mrs. Belauru, I'm Special Agent Inga."

She offered her business card, the FBI seal embossed on the corner. Elana held it before her like a lit fuse.

Inga was slim, fit, and had a pistol clipped to her belt. Elana was short, curvy, and packed only a designer handbag. She had to crane her neck to look at the agent's face.

The woman pointed at the monogramed charm, sheathed in fine leather and fixed to one of the purse's handles.

"You lose your bag a lot?"

"What?"

"You know that's a tracker, right? It's called an AirTag."

"A wha... Yes, it keeps me from losing my bag."

The woman gave her a dubious look.

"We are here to speak to your husband about the disappearances."

Elana's ears felt so hot. She knew Jackson's second wife, Shantel, had a young daughter who had been taken. But the abduction had happened after their divorce.

"Jackson told me all about that," she said, dropping the business card into her bag and knowing it could not stay there.

Her brows lifted. "Did he? I'd be very curious to know exactly what he said."

Something the agent said now registered in her mind.

"Wait. Did you say disappearances, plural?"

"Yes. Odd coincidence. Isn't it? Both his previous wives leave him and shortly afterward, each has a little girl go missing."

Elana had met Jackson's first ex-wife shortly after Jackson had proposed and he'd explained all about her daughter Grace.

"Well, Faith's daughter didn't go missing. She just left the Mennonite community where she was raised. Ran off. It's not all that uncommon."

"Is that what he told you?" The agent's mouth twisted in an expression of disgust, though whether at Jackson or at her was unclear.

Elana braced, feeling that whatever came next would be bad.

The agent's hands went to her hips, one resting just above her service pistol.

"Grace Collins went missing in 2013. She was five years old."

Elana's head snapped up.

The shock stole her breath away.

"That can't be right."

She gaped as the confusion constricted into anger.

You would think, when his second wife had crashed their rehearsal dinner screaming like a lunatic about her missing daughter, that one of Jackson's family would have said, "Oh, by the way, Jackson's other stepdaughter was kidnapped, too."

Someone *should* have told her.

They hadn't. Of course, they hadn't. Because his family never intended her to know. Might have changed her mind. Might still change her mind and divorce her tyrant of a husband.

In fact, she'd thought of little else recently. Just how and when to escape her terrible marriage.

Special Agent Inga's eyes were bright as she watched Elana absorb that punch.

"No one told me."

"I see. Well, we have two ex-wives and two missing children." She waited, letting that news seep into Elana's skin like poison before continuing. "And then you arrive, the third new bride, and what do you know? *You* have a little girl, too."

Elana could only gasp. For a moment she knew exactly how one of Jackson's game fish felt, hauled from the sea and tossed on the deck.

"Here's his first stepdaughter." The agent held out her phone.

Elana stared at the image.

The portrait was a professional one, judging from the mottled gray background. Grace's hair was coppery red and had a natural curl. Startling blue eyes, the color of summer skies, stared guilelessly out at the photographer.

"Only one we have. Her mother doesn't really approve of photographs."

Elana knew why. Faith was Mennonite and like many of her sect did not allow photographs or paintings in her home. Something about graven images and vanity, Faith had said.

"Religious objections," said Inga. "But she allowed this shot because her husband, *your* husband, wanted it. Grace was five then."

Elana swallowed, trying and failing to force down the horror that choked her.

"Snatched from Fort King Nature Reserve in April of 2013," said Special Agent Inga. "That's right up the road. Isn't it? You must drive by there."

She did and had taken Phoebe and the dogs walking through the trails in the cooler months. The kidnapper might have been there watching.

"Her fifteenth birthday's coming up. Her mother lives right here in town. Have you met?"

Elana nodded mechanically as she tore her gaze from the image on Inga's phone, then met the agent's hazel eyes. It was like facing down a mountain lion.

"Your husband's attorney said coincidence. But I don't believe in coincidences, Mrs. Belauru. Do you?"

She gulped down the lump of spiky panic expanding in her throat.

"Your husband is our prime suspect."

Elana used one hand to grip the back of her neck, a passenger taking the crash position, bracing as a wave of nausea threatened. She pressed her free hand to her mouth.

They thought he did this. Worse still, she believed it possible.

"Kidnappers often retain a keepsake from their victims," Inga said. "Something on their person when taken." From a note on her phone, she rattled off a description of every article of clothing each girl was wearing when taken. "Have you seen any of these items in your husband's possession?"

She shook her head and glanced back to be certain Jackson could not see her.

"We want your help to find evidence implicating your husband."

Was this woman insane? If what she said were true, crossing her husband was even more dangerous than she'd first believed.

The agent moved to another image. "This one was taken by a man at the reserve that day. That is his little girl in the foreground, but he also took the last-known photograph of Grace."

The image showed a toddler in a bonnet. Beyond her was a redhead, Grace, barefooted and kneeling on the bench of a picnic table in a simple purple dress.

"And these were aged by our people. Shows what she might look like at nine and thirteen."

Elana gaped, barely hearing as the blood pounded across her eardrums, staring at the age-progressed image of what might have been a girl and then a teen.

"So who told you that Grace ran away?"

"Jackson."

"I see."

"Still no leads," said the special agent. "She just vanished, exactly like Shantel Keen's daughter, Raelyn, snatched from her yard in 2018."

The agent used her phone to show an image of Raelyn at a birthday party, seated before a cake holding glowing candles. Would she ever blow out her birthday candles again?

"There she is. Around the time of disappearance. And here."

The image showed Raelyn, seated at the beach in a pink swimsuit. Her wet hair curled in corkscrews. She had a bright smile, chubby cheeks, and big blue eyes as she waved a sand shovel.

"She's been missing for four years. Would be eleven now, if she's still alive." She stopped talking then, watching Elana.

That's what Shantel had been trying to tell her when she'd crashed their rehearsal dinner one year ago.

At the time, Elana thought her a vindictive, embittered ex-wife.

Only after the knot was cinched good and tight, and had begun to choke the life from her, had the woman's words returned to haunt Elana.

One by one, the ex-wife's predictions had come true. Too many to ignore. Until she could no longer indulge in the comforts of dismissal.

She's still missing. Did you know that?

Shantel had been speaking of her daughter, Raelyn. She'd learned that afterward.

If Shantel hadn't turned up, would they have told her even that much?

Elana used her hands to bracket her nose and mouth, sucking in air through the gaps of her fingers.

Inga flipped to a shot of both missing children, side by side. "Kinda look like your little girl. Phoebe, isn't it?"

Elana cast a glance over her shoulder at her daughter still in her seatbelt, her eyes huge, tears streaming down her frightened face. That belt wouldn't protect her. That was Elana's job. The need to escape her marriage had just escalated like lava welling before an eruption.

"Why are you telling me this?"

"We need your help. Need evidence that Jackson did this."

"No."

"We could help you, too. Get you clear of him."

The temptation overwhelmed, glittering bright as sunlight on water. But the risk. Did they even consider... They had. And to them, it didn't matter because they couldn't make their case without evidence.

What this woman asked might get her killed. Or more likely, get Phoebe killed.

"I don't think so."

"How old is she now?" said Inga, staring at her daughter, who watched them from the rear seat of the truck.

"Seven."

"Same as Raelyn was... when she disappeared."

Elana said nothing, but she drew her own conclusions.

Jackson took those girls.

And, if she left, Phoebe would be next.

TWO

Special Agent Inga left Elana standing in their driveway beside her husband's truck, returning to her partner, Jackson, and their vehicle.

Elana retrieved the agent's business card from her purse, knowing better than to bring the contact information into the house. Instead, she slipped it under the floor mat of Jackson's pickup truck on the passenger side. Chances were slim that Jackson would search his own vehicle and if he did, she could deny knowledge. Meanwhile, she'd have an opportunity to retrieve it later.

Next, she collected Phoebe from the rear seat and helped her down to the hot concrete.

"Mommy, who was that lady?"

"Hush now."

If Jackson had really done this, had taken both his step-daughters, then Elana knew it was certainly not safe to help the FBI. Working with them would put Phoebe in even more danger.

She used the remote in the center console to open their garage door, then hustled Phoebe into their three-car garage, feeling Jackson's eyes on her. She had only a few minutes to compose herself.

Or a few minutes to run.

No. She would not do anything stupid. He was too smart and too dangerous. More dangerous than she had even realized.

But they couldn't stay here. For months, she'd thought of little else but leaving Jackson.

Her best idea had been to run during their upcoming trip to North Carolina. Their chances would be better. Jackson did not have his people there and she would finally be out of this rancid little town.

Had this new information changed everything?

If she left, and one day he found them... she shivered, thinking of Grace and Raelyn. It could happen. One day her daughter might not come home from school, or vanish from the yard.

The idea of helping the FBI made her insides tremble. Special Agent Inga had laid out what she wanted. Evidence that would get Jackson arrested. Convicted. Out of her life and away from Phoebe forever.

She let the idea steep like tea in hot water.

Looking for that kind of thing would be more dangerous than leaving.

Elana rejected the agent's request. Better to run. No divorce. That was obvious. They'd just vanish, and wherever and whenever they went, she had to be certain that Jackson could never find them.

The remorse at not helping find those missing girls twisted inside her, but protecting Phoebe needed to be her priority.

Were they alive? After so many years, she knew the chances were very small. But not looking for evidence to find their abductor felt like another tiny treachery to the girls.

Elana used the button on the wall to close the garage door, relieved to block out Jackson, even for a moment, but also to keep the dogs from pouring out of the house. They were friendly, but not so friendly that they might not perceive a threat.

Her mind flashed an image of Gunner, his favorite, taking a piece out of one of the agents. She opened the door to the house and the three German shorthaired pointers tumbled out, barking and tails wagging as if Elana had been gone for weeks instead of a few hours. They were more agitated than usual, likely because the trio recognized they had company.

Phoebe greeted each and they calmed somewhat. Elana ordered them back in the house.

Pointers were bred for flushing birds and retrieving them for their masters. Several of Jackson's trophy birds were stuffed and on display in the living room and his office, standing with artificial feet on driftwood platforms.

The three dogs were Jackson's constant companions. From the minute he returned home until he left for work in the morning, Gunner, Dash, and Chase left him only to sleep in the alcove beyond the master bedroom because he would not allow them past the door.

The dogs' toenails clicked as they danced about in the laundry room as Elana deposited her bag on the washer.

Jackson kept only purebreds and insisted they be walked twice a day. Of course, he didn't feed them, walk them, or clean up their messes. Those duties, along with vet visits and grooming, were Elana's. Despite her changing feelings toward Jackson, she did not begrudge his dogs, loving them and grateful for their apparent devotion.

For the moment, however, she needed more calm and less dancing enthusiasm at their return. So she shut the dogs in the laundry room between the kitchen and garage to give her and Phoebe a moment of peace.

Beside her, Phoebe clung to her skirts.

Elana stooped and wrapped Phoebe in a tight embrace,

unsure who needed comfort more. Her daughter sniffled against her shoulder as Elana stroked her hair.

Phoebe lifted her head. "Momma, who was that lady?"

It was difficult to pull away because her instinct was to gather up her daughter and run. But instead, she released Phoebe, kneeling at eye level, and meeting her direct stare.

"She's a very special sort of police."

"Why was she talking to you?"

How much had Phoebe heard through the window? She didn't want to frighten her daughter, but she wanted to explain anything she might have overheard. She also didn't want to furnish any new information that Phoebe might tell Jackson.

Her daughter was sweet, innocent, and honest. As a result, she couldn't keep a secret if she tried. And Jackson knew it. Exploited it.

He had a habit of interrogating the girl after any absence. In the early days of their marriage, Elana thought he was just taking an interest in Phoebe's day. That was until it became obvious that he used her own daughter as a monitoring system, rewarding her for revealing any change in their normal routine.

Phoebe was the dog flushing the birds from cover, and Elana was the duck.

"Did you hear what we were saying?"

"No. But it made you cry."

"Yes. She told me something sad. They're looking for someone who took something that didn't belong to him."

"A bad man?"

"Yes. Very bad. She just wanted to warn us. You know."

"Not to talk to strangers." Phoebe looked proud at knowing this vital bit of information.

At seven, Phoebe knew to avoid strangers and understood that evil existed in the world. She did not understand that evil and bad men were not always strangers.

"That's right. We're safe, Phoebe." *Were they?* "Everything is all right." *Was it?* "Go up to your room and change out of your dress."

Phoebe knew this meant getting out of the fancy clothing and into a casual dress. Never shorts or T-shirts, which Jackson hated and neither of them owned any longer.

"Yes, Momma."

Her daughter spun so that Elana could drag down the zipper. Then Phoebe trotted out of the kitchen and out of sight.

Elana stood and found herself shaking. She went to the sink and wet a dish towel, then wiped the sweat from her face and neck.

Finally, she hurried to the dining room window, her princess flats whispering across the hard tile. Outside, the agents returned to their SUV and drove away.

Jackson marched toward his truck and yanked open the door. A moment later, the rumble of the heavy garage door reached her.

Her heart pumped as his truck rolled inside and the door descended. She felt like a rabbit, frozen a few feet from cover and hoping a predator might not notice her.

Should she tell him that she knew about Faith's missing little girl?

Jackson came in, shouting at his dogs and slamming the door from the laundry room as he stomped through the kitchen without them. She hoped they wouldn't pee on the floor. Of course, they needed to go out after their absence. Now Elana needed to pee, too.

"Fishing expedition. Can't find who really did this, so they try and pin it on me. Of course. Look at the ex-husband."

"What did they want?" she asked.

He glared at her. "To harass me." Now he was peering out through the blinds. "Where's Phoebe?"

"Upstairs in her room."

"Hmm." He dropped the blind and swung around toward

her. She felt like a prisoner trapped in the searchlight just inches from the wall. "Did his partner speak to you?"

"She was watching you. I saw her in the driver's side mirror, standing behind your truck like she was covering him or something."

"Hmm," he snorted.

"That gun on her hip made me nervous. So, I took Phoebe inside."

"Nothing wrong with guns. Just who was carrying it."

The lies made her feel sick. She tried leaping to his defense. She'd seen her sister-in-law, Zoey, use this tactic successfully on several occasions. When Sawyer was upset, she'd immediately take his side, like his own personal echo chamber and guard dog, rolled into one.

"It's because they have no right to attack you—an innocent man. And at your own home. It's unconscionable. Shame on them. Grasping for straws is all. Desperate to solve a cold case." She scowled and made her best impression of an angry face. "Besides, you had nothing to do with any of that. Right?"

There was a slight pause before he said, "Right."

Was that his way of lying, a small gap for thinking time before the lie?

Elana tucked that information away.

"Are they trying to implicate you?"

"Damn straight they are."

"That's terrible. What can I do?"

"Don't talk to them."

"Yes, Jackson."

"You don't mention this, them coming here to anyone. Understand?"

"Oh, of course. That's very wise."

Flattery was one of the only currencies she had left.

"You finish the packing?" Now *he* was using a redirect, signaling he was done talking to her about their visitors.

"Nearly."

"Best get to it."

"What about the dogs?"

"I'll put them out."

She hoped he meant he'd bring them to the pen beside the house, the one she cleaned every day. That way they would be out of her way as she continued organizing for their upcoming trip.

"Thank you."

Dismissed, she headed to their bedroom, relieved to be away from him, if even for a minute. Still, each step seemed a chore, her feet nearly too heavy to lift as she trudged past Phoebe's door toward the bedroom she shared with her husband.

Elana had been organizing for weeks, helping with any tasks Jackson had prescribed her. The packing had begun in earnest.

He wanted to be in North Carolina before opening day of the week-long game fishing tournament to meet with the professional captain he used every year, organize the crew, and be certain his boat, *Reel Escape*, had made the journey safely from the Florida Panhandle to Dare Marina.

Elana wanted to be somewhere besides this clannish little backwater when she made her run from this marriage.

Some time ago she had determined that her best chance of escaping with her daughter would be in another state, as far from Bald Cypress, Florida, and Jackson's network of allies, as possible.

Here Jackson ran everything and everyone. She had believed she might be able to get them to her former in-laws in North Carolina where she could file for a divorce. But what would happen after that?

Jackson was the prime suspect in two child abductions, so she needed to rethink the decision to pursue a traditional divorce. Even if she succeeded, he'd know where they were and how to get to Phoebe. Both Jackson's other two ex-wives had divorced him. And both had lost their daughters.

If she left this marriage, Phoebe could be next.

She had been prepared to leave with nothing. But she was not prepared to endanger her daughter.

She paused inside the bedroom to press her back to the closed door, chin raised and eyes on the ceiling.

"God help me," she whispered, fighting the cold threads of panic slithering through her veins.

She had figured out long ago that Jackson was dangerous. Only now did she recognize the magnitude of the threat. Her forehead pressed to her hands as she rocked and prayed. But the only answers to her prayer were the three dogs, released from the laundry room, and charging through the door to find her.

Standing was the easiest way to avoid their slobbery greeting.

Elana sighed. She needed a new plan and she had little time to prepare. They'd be leaving tomorrow. Before her, on the bed, lay the neatly folded and stacked clothing she and Phoebe needed on the trip.

Jackson handled all his fishing and boat gear, but she was expected to pack all his clothing for all events and each day of fishing, plus anticipate any unexpected events that required an extra this or that.

"Get back at it," she whispered.

His hunting dogs followed her from room to room, getting underfoot and occasionally tripping her as she collected the rest of what was needed for their travels. She paused to give them an occasional pat and endearment, rubbing behind their velvety ears.

Chase, her favorite, was particularly anxious, even trying to climb into her open suitcase. Dogs could be so dumb, but occasionally they surprised her.

She paused to stroke Chase's soft head.

"You know I'm leaving. Don't you?"

Chase gazed into her eyes with soulful devotion as Elana pushed down the guilt and went back to sorting and folding.

She set another floral dress with the other items laid on their king-sized bed. Jackson would want to examine everything before she was allowed to place them in the suitcases.

It was a risk that he might remain to watch her pack as he had done in the past. Because this was a possibility, she knew that she and Phoebe would be leaving with very little. Now she was reconsidering her plan. When he found them gone, he would come after them.

She'd need to be fast and lucky to make it to her first husband's family and she could not stay there very long. But if they could reach Victoria and Braden Orrick, in Newton Grove, North Carolina, Gavin's parents would help her vanish. It was a chance.

Or would that only put Gavin's parents in danger? It was the obvious place for her to go.

Get to the tournament in Culpepper first. Then she and Phoebe would run.

Inga had asked Elana to help her find evidence. You might as well ask a monkey to kill a tiger. She wanted to help those grieving mothers discover the truth, whatever that might be. But it was impossible. If she touched his things, he'd know and what he'd do next was as unpredictable as a lightning strike. The potential for disaster overpowered her.

She was afraid of Jackson, and the FBI had only given her more reason to be.

Her first year of marriage had been a slow descent into hell. That wouldn't change with time unless it was to get worse.

They had to go, now.

Before her sat all the articles necessary for a lovely family vacation. Her engagement ring spun round and round as she examined the stacked garments, her nerves fraying like rotting nylon rope. From what she had packed, could he tell that she was never coming back here?

Jackson was a hawk, ever watchful for movement that might signal opportunity. He was clever, charming, and toxic.

He also was the first man she'd ever met who kept his eyes from dropping to her breasts.

She'd been told by the men she'd dated that her best features were her mouth and her boobs. Both were all natural, full, and overly large. Together they acted as the kind of lure that most young men found irresistible. As a teen, she'd been flattered by the male attention, as a young wife to her first husband, she'd been annoyed. Now she was more resolute.

Only women seemed to notice her green eyes or how hard she'd worked to lose her accent and speak as if she worked for the Weather Channel.

Jackson had noticed both. He even complimented her speaking voice, sure she'd been raised away from the piles of dirt and stinking retaining ponds left by decades of strip mining.

Now she knew exactly what he was. He was rich, successful, powerful, and cruel.

And he was not to be thwarted.

But that was exactly what she must do.

Elana turned to the mirror to check that her face did not reveal her rebellion. Her pale skin looked washed out and since he didn't like her "dolled up," she wore no makeup to cover the dark circles beneath her green eyes or blush to add a touch of color to her cheeks. Her straight, shoulder-length, golden-brown hair was still perfect in the chignon, as he preferred, wanting it loose only for bed.

The full-length mirror revealed her entire body, all five feet three inches of her, today garbed in a lavender A-line dress that dropped below her knee and resembled something seen on a 1950s sitcom. How had she ever found these outfits stylish?

Jackson liked her in simple, feminine clothing, so she wore

simple, feminine clothing. Modest. Nothing too short, flashy, or low-cut. Absolutely no wrap dresses. Shirt dresses and sheath dresses for workdays or a blouse paired with a skirt. Princess dresses and A-lines for church. Flowers were a perpetual favorite of his, while she'd grown to hate them.

How she longed for a pair of blue jeans, sneakers, and a T-shirt. Any T-shirt. Preferably with something unladylike or controversial on it. But those rock concert tees and shirts professing various causes were gone with her self-confidence. Replaced so skillfully she hadn't even noticed.

Then it was too late.

She lifted her chin and gave herself the look of defiance that Jackson had never seen. As she stared, the boiling sea of animosity rose. Despite her demure attire, her flushed face and glittering green eyes showed that she had not surrendered just yet. Elana gazed at her reflection. There was the face she could never show him.

Elana reached behind her back and drew down the zipper, letting the expensive outfit fall. Then she stepped on it before carrying it to her closet and changing into a white blouse and cotton box-pleat skirt with a matching cloth belt.

Dressed in her work clothing, she paused at Jackson's closet and thought back to the FBI request. She took one step and paused. The only time she was allowed in here was to put away his folded clothing after laundering them.

She backed out, finding her hands shaking. Elana smoothed her bodice, leaving one hand on her stomach in a useless effort to still the nervous acidy flutter. Then she went to find her husband.

All three dogs rose as she reached the door, trotting along, heads raised in what passed for a grin, hopeful for a treat.

She located Jackson in the garage, checking one of the many reels that all looked the same to her eye. Beside him was the wall of the large plastic bins she'd been ordered to "stay the hell out of."

The dogs charged down into the garage before she could stop them.

"Damn it. Chase, Gunner, Dash, go on."

He motioned them out and they reversed course, like the tiny tornado of destruction and exuberance they were, racing back up the stairs.

"Can't you keep them out of my workspace?"

He didn't like them "underfoot," but saw nothing wrong with them trailing at her heels all day.

His dogs were her responsibility, along with the house, her daughter, and providing him with a son. Three for four, so far.

Jackson's stormy expression told her he was still fuming over their visitors. This could go badly.

"What?"

He turned to stare at her with those dark, unreadable eyes. She'd made a bad start.

"You asked me to come get you?"

Her husband stood with hands on hips, glaring. Jackson wasn't especially tall, but he was striking.

She tried to remember the way he looked at her when she'd fallen in love with him, back when she'd been a critical combination of dazzled and desperate. Blinded by possibilities, she had ignored the warnings from his previous wife, Shantel. Why hadn't she listened or at least done a minimum amount of background checking on this narcissist she'd married?

Elana clasped her hands before her, knotting her fingers together. "I've got our things laid out."

"What things?"

"For packing." Her mind now raced. What had he said exactly? Had she not listened closely enough?

He scowled and she knew she'd made some mistake. He headed for the stairs leading to the house and she stepped aside to allow him to sweep past. Then she trailed him as he put the dogs out in the yard and then headed for Phoebe's room.

She wanted to redirect him, but fear robbed her of the words. Mutely, she crept behind him as he banged open her daughter's door, invading the child's privacy as he so often did to hers.

Phoebe sat on her bed, now in a simple powder blue polo shirtdress, legs folded, holding a stuffed unicorn with a rainbow mane. Phoebe's head swiveled as she gave a quick intake of breath. Then her eyes flashed to the outfit she'd worn to church that lay over her desk chair instead of hanging in her closet.

"Daddy?" she asked, lowering the plush toy. The way she said it, told Elana that her daughter felt insecure and uncomfortable with Jackson barging into her room.

For almost a year, Phoebe had witnessed many incidents where Elana silently accepted all the heaping piles of criticism when Jackson found her lacking. She wondered how much damage this had already done, seeing the way he treated her mother.

Well, not for much longer.

Until then, it was better to appear a whipped dog than to let him see that she was not defeated. Yet.

Jackson turned to her. "What's this? Where are her things?"

"They're all in the master," said Elana, keeping her chin tucked and her eyes down.

"Why the hell didn't you tell me that before I came all the way in here?"

She'd inconvenienced him. She apologized sincerely, but her words were for her daughter. Elana was weary of acts of contrition for his benefit.

"I'm sorry," she said again. And she *was*, sorry that her need to provide a decent home and good schools for her daughter had made her blind to any sign Jackson might have given to what he really was.

"Let's go." He reversed course and stopped short in the bedroom. His hands went to his hips.

"What's this?"

Some part of her wanted to yell the obvious. It was the latest task he'd set for her and the latest trap. She must have made some infinitesimal, insignificant mistake that would now become another weapon to illustrate how she couldn't even do the simplest job without his oversight.

Incompetent. Incapable. Useless.

He'd called her each of those at one time or another.

But then she remembered Shantel's warning that if she left him after they were married, Jackson would take her daughter. At the time, she dismissed the threat. But since their visitors today she believed every word.

So, she would act as if she were cowed and had no thought except to please him. He would not know she was leaving until he found them gone. If that meant abandoning her marriage, instead of the more conventional route of securing a divorce attorney, so be it. Safer was better.

"Well?" he said, turning now to face her.

"I laid out our things," she said, making a half-hearted gesture toward the bedspread laden with neat piles of clean, folded clothing. Nearby, on the floor, sat the empty luggage.

"I asked you to lay out Phoebe's things."

Instead of the compliment at going above and beyond, she should have expected the rebuke at overstepping. How many times did she need to be told to do exactly what he asked and no more?

"The trip is tomorrow." It was neither excuse nor apology.

"I know when the hell it is. I plan for this week all year. You think I forgot how long I have until the tournament?"

"No, I..." It was best not to finish. Just wait for whatever nasty way he meant to turn this terrible overreach of preparing the things she'd need on the trip before he told her to. She gazed at the formal feminine dresses and set her teeth, loathing them.

How was it possible that she even missed the synthetic navy blazer she'd worn at work? At least it included slacks.

"Put them away," he ordered.

"What?" She needed to be sure she understood what he meant exactly or risk making a second mistake.

She could not afford this. Not when they were so close to escape.

"Put *your* things back in the closet. You aren't going."

"You want us to stay home?"

That might mean she'd have a full week and a car to make her escape. Her heart raced, the hope pounding against the fear.

She was genuinely confused now, so it took a moment for the other possibility to seep into her conscious thoughts.

He couldn't mean just *her* things!

"Jackson? I don't understand."

He spoke slowly, as if to an idiot. "I'm taking Phoebe. You are staying home, which is why I told you to lay out *her* things."

He knew. Somehow, he knew what she was planning.

She stared at him, gaping, and blinking as if a shard of glass had lodged in her eye.

Fear morphed into fury.

She was not letting him take her daughter.

With skill born of practice she squelched the rebellion.

But now what? She couldn't stop him. Not with words. Nor with argument or outrage or logical conversation about the impossibility of him caring for a seven-year-old while game fishing.

"Who will take care of her?"

"Zoey can do it."

Her pregnant sister-in-law, with her boys to look after, was well-known for using the most minimal supervisory skills imaginable.

"Phoebe's never even been on an overnight. She's never been away from me."

Why was she arguing, knowing that didn't work?

"No time like the present."

He moved to the bed and checked Phoebe's clothing, flicking through the pile like a dealer checking a stacked deck.

"Swimsuits?"

"Four."

"Hat?"

"Two. Baseball and sunbonnet."

"No daughter of mine is wearing a baseball cap unless she's playing softball." He found the offending item and tossed it to the carpet.

Then he snatched up Elana's suitcase and strode out of the room. "Call me when her things are packed."

She watched him go, the unmasked hatred blazing like the blue flame of a forge fire.

She would not let him take her daughter anywhere without her.

Elana could not trail after him and beg him to change his mind. She knew this already from past failed attempts to get him to relent. They never worked. In fact, such hysterics would only decrease her chances of going with him and give him some awful unfathomable pleasure. Instead, she said nothing as he walked away with her suitcase.

She knew him. Had been studying him like a field researcher for nearly a year. He was enjoying her distress and would relish her unsuccessful efforts to earn his forgiveness for having the audacity to ready both their things without his instructions to do so.

Elana sat on the carpet beside Phoebe's ball cap. All the chores were done. Phoebe was playing in her room, and it was too early to start supper.

Jackson liked to select what she would prepare, and she'd

learned what foods to have on hand for his regular choices. It kept her from so often having to run out to the store. Though she thought he enjoyed picking things that would have one or two ingredients that he knew she didn't have. It was a game for him, making her life difficult.

The fishing trip loomed before her like an irrevocable deadline. It had been their chance at escape.

If he left her behind, to punish her, or because he sensed she was "up to something," Phoebe would be in danger.

She was already in danger. Elana thought of those other two missing girls. Raelyn. Grace.

Phoebe.

"I'll kill him and go to prison before I let him take her."

Her vow was just the merest exhalation as she mouthed the words, head down, face in her hands. He couldn't hear her and despite what he thought, he could not look inside her heart or mind.

She wondered if he'd be so brave or cavalier if he could?

She *was* up to something, but now it involved something terrible happening to him, likely as he slept. Jackson was a heavy sleeper, slumbering like an alpha wolf who had no fear of challengers.

After many long minutes, Elana rose stiffly from the floor and turned to the bed. She spent the next hour removing her belongings from the coverlet and returning them to various drawers and hangers. Then she packed Phoebe's little suitcase and the duffel.

She moved mechanically, all the while envisioning striking Jackson in the head or poisoning his food. She didn't expect to get away with his murder, but it was possible that a jury might understand and give her a lenient sentence.

Florida had the death penalty. She needed to be prepared for the worst. But he was not taking Phoebe out of this house without her.

Elana paused to place a hand over her racing heart. The queasiness reminded her of seasickness, but now the restless tossing came from within. She wasn't a murderer. Even considering this route as a fantasy made her sick.

There had to be another way to keep her daughter safe. She'd find it and follow it, whatever the cost to her. Phoebe's safety, that was all that mattered.

She looked at the packed luggage. The task was done. Now all she had to do was see that those bags never went anywhere without her.

She was taking Phoebe and making a run for it. She liked her chances from North Carolina better, but here and now was preferable to never.

"You done yet?" he asked, startling her.

Jackson stood in the doorway. How long had she been frozen over the bed, staring at her daughter's abandoned ball cap?

"Oh, yes. Just finished."

"I told you to call me."

"Yes. I'm sorry."

She flicked her gaze to him, keeping her expression earnest, while carefully ignoring the heat burning her cheeks.

Elana gave him the kind of smile she remembered offering in the days of their courtship, certain it did not reach her eyes.

He glanced to the two packed items resting side by side on the huge bed.

"I was just thinking about supper," she said. "Would you like meatloaf and macaroni and cheese?"

It was in that moment she noticed he held her suitcase in one hand. The air filled her lungs with the hope.

He tossed the hard-shelled case on the bed.

"Big news. You're coming, so pack your bags."

It was too much. Everything that had filled her whirling mind in the last hour came out in a sob.

"Oh, stop it. I was never going to leave you behind. All the guys bring their wives. What would it look like if I left you?"

A glance at the closet reminded her that she'd just put away every stitch. His timing was perfect. Had he been watching from the hall?

Now she understood the game. He had never wanted to leave her behind. He just wanted to remind her that he could.

THREE

THEN

April 2021, two months before the wedding
Bald Cypress, Florida

"I'm so nervous to meet your brothers," said Elana.

"Don't be. They'll love you as much as I do." Jackson's generous smile reassured her.

They had just concluded a tour of her soon-to-be hometown in his truck. Her fiancé had introduced her to several people, including the minister who would perform the service in June. After a wild, life-altering six-week courtship, he'd asked, and she'd said yes.

He really was too good to be true.

Tonight, she would meet his two brothers, Sawyer, the eldest, and Derek, the youngest, along with Sawyer's wife and their two young boys. But he'd thrown her another curveball, wanting to take her past a Mennonite community adjoining the wildlife preserve.

"That was my mother's church."

Both his parents were gone now.

Jackson slowed and Elana glanced out the truck window at

a small white concrete building with a tin roof. It didn't look like a church, more like a community center. Obvious in its absence was any sort of cross or stained glass. On the front, above the doorway, were the words: Madison County Mennonite Fellowship.

"Your mom was a Mennonite?"

"Yes. She left this community to marry my dad before Sawyer was born."

She glanced at her fiancé; his expression was wistful as he stared outward but also inward. Was he remembering the mother he had lost, missing her as a child always will, no matter their age? In his quiet reflection, she thought he'd never looked more handsome.

She reached across the distance separating them and took his hand. He cast her a sad smile and lifted her hand for a kiss.

Then he sighed and gave her hand a squeeze before returning his to the wheel.

Elana wondered if his mother had to leave the community because she'd gotten pregnant with Sawyer. But she didn't ask.

After all, she had been heading for community college until she'd discovered she was pregnant. Gavin had found work with the county, and they'd been married. College, money, careers—none of it seemed important. They had each other and a baby on the way. The bittersweet tug at the memory of Gavin saddened her, but she pushed it aside because thoughts of her first husband always stirred longing and regret. Longing for the love that had been snatched from her and regret that Phoebe would never really know her father.

She had a fresh start. Phoebe would be going to a private school and the kitchen of Jackson's house was bigger than her entire bungalow. She glanced at the unbelievably huge diamond solitaire. If she wasn't careful, the flash from that rock might blind a pilot.

Elana hugged the ring to her heart, so grateful to her fiancé.

He'd rescued them from poverty and all he wanted was to make her happy.

Jackson was the mayor of Bald Cypress. He ran several successful businesses, owned a cattle ranch, and he swore, drank, loved guns, and was an avid hunter and fisherman. It all seemed so exciting and masculine. As well as the opposite of a Mennonite, come to think of it.

"What do you know about them?"

"Not a lot. Keep to themselves. Strange clothing. Men with beards. Women with those white caps and too many children." She pulled up short. They were talking about his mother's faith. "Oh, I'm sorry."

He dismissed her apology with an easy wave of one hand, then returned it to the steering wheel.

"That might be Amish you're thinking of. Not all Mennonite men wear beards or even wear plain clothes. Though the sect here outside Bald Cypress is conservative with regard to dress. And the head covering is called a kapp. There's a lot of variety with those.

"As for the 'strange clothing,' the women here wear cape dresses. The bodice is loose fitting and made from a double layer of fabric to be modest. Mennonite women do not wish to repeat the sins of Eve by presenting a temptation to men."

"You're kidding."

"I'm not. Their dresses are practical and reveal their intention to embrace the will of God regarding their place."

"I see."

"They are Christian, but their faith comes from the Bible and not a particular church. Each community develops their own rules based on their interpretation of those teachings. The most important is an absolute rejection of physical violence. War for example. No Mennonite man has ever fought in one."

"How many in this fellowship?" The church looked very small.

"I don't know. Two hundred, maybe."

He got them moving again.

Jackson's mood brightened and his winning smile returned. He winked at her and she giggled, completely charmed by this wonderful man. He began to sing in a clear baritone voice, but not in English.

She didn't understand the words, but still her chest ached at the beauty of the music. Elana's smile widened. He was so talented and if she didn't love him already, this serenade would have made her tumble headfirst into wild devotion for him.

When he finished, she applauded. "That was beautiful. You have a lovely voice."

He blushed. "My mom taught me that one. It's in German. The words are about devotion to God."

He took them off the highway and down a paved road past a variety of modest homes that looked no different than the ones in town, except they were spaced more widely and many included outbuildings and livestock. Each house had a variety of outdoor seating under carports or porches. Many had pastures, barns, and farm equipment.

Elana spotted three small girls in long dresses feeding chickens.

Jackson slowed as they turned onto a dirt road off the state highway. The houses they passed here were prefabricated, with a few trailers sprinkled in. Most had small pastures and large gardens.

How long were they going to be out here? She needed to freshen up and change before meeting his brothers.

Elana glanced at the new phone Jackson had given her, checking the time and noticed the cell service had vanished.

"Dead zone," she said.

"What's that?"

"No service."

"This community doesn't use cellphones or computers, so

it's no problem for them."

She dropped her phone in her bag and had just returned her gaze to the road when he said, "I want you to meet someone."

"Who?"

"Her name is Faith. Her mother and mine were first cousins."

"I see." A second cousin. She was already so nervous about meeting Jackson's brothers and their families she felt sick to her stomach.

She spun her engagement ring again, gazing out the windshield at the orchard. Beyond appeared a double-wide trailer that looked exactly like the others on this road.

The solitary residence sat beside a large oak.

"Here we are."

He slowed the truck.

"Faith dresses simply, but she has a car. And she's devout, of course."

"I see." She glanced at the rope clothesline stretching from a pulley beside the home to the oak. On the line, women's garments flapped in a steady breeze. She saw no sign of male attire or children's things. "Is she married?"

"She's alone."

Jackson had never mentioned Faith before. The only family he'd spoken of were his brother's and his older brother's wife. He'd told her some information about his parents, but little about his mother. Until today.

Was this trip to fill in some of those details?

He pulled into the drive. The small, neat, cinderblock house looked well-maintained, nestled on freshly trimmed grass between a grove of citrus trees on one side and a huge, fenced garden on the other.

"How does she ever manage all this?"

"No television or radio. No books, either, except the Bible.

Leaves lots of time for work and prayer."

Elana looked about in wonder. "I guess so."

Beside the house was a sturdy-looking shed, enclosed on three sides with shelves bursting with the kinds of goods she'd seen at farm stands. Inside lay cartons of blueberries and bins of bright red and green peppers, cabbage, large cantaloupes, and stacks of sweet corn. On the opposite side lay rows of mason jars filled with pickles, preserved fruits, and jams. Between them sat a variety of baked goods.

"She sells fruits and vegetables?"

"Among other things. Anyway, I want you to buy your produce and your baked goods from her. Oh, and eggs. Can't beat them. She's very reasonable."

It was a good bit from town, but her job would soon be keeping his home and making him happy. If he wanted fresh eggs, she'd be delighted to buy them.

She grinned at him. "Of course. That sounds great."

"Wait until you have her blueberry muffins. They are out of this world."

"I look forward to that."

He made a sound of affirmation, eyes on the property in question as he slipped the vehicle into park. Then he was rounding the truck to open her door. Elana drew a breath and then slipped from the truck.

The only movement were the dresses on the line. All were pastel. All were covered with tiny flowers or plain synthetic fabric. Beside the dresses were black socks and white underwear.

A neat woman in a loose-fitting pink dress stepped from the house and onto the cinder blocks that served as a front step.

If her baking was as good as Jackson claimed, his cousin likely had customers coming and going all day.

Faith left the step and headed toward them. The bodice made it impossible to judge her figure and the bun and kapp obscured her hair color. His cousin gave the impression of a novice nun, in a seafoam-green dress and flat, practical shoes.

He turned to her. "Last stop before Sawyer's. Okay?"

Her smile came naturally. "Of course."

"You are just the best." He clasped her hand and gave it a squeeze. "How did I ever get so lucky to find you?"

She beamed. So happy and so in love.

Elana staunched her worries about making a good impression with Jackson's second cousin. Or was it his first cousin once removed? In any case, if Faith was at all like Jackson, she'd be charming, generous, and welcoming.

Her fiancé offered his hand as they walked together, bringing her to a stop before the plain little woman with the sparkling blue eyes.

"Faith, this is Elana."

"So nice to meet you, Elana." Faith nodded, but did not offer her hand.

"And you as well."

Faith aimed a sharp chin and intent stare at Elana. Whisps of her wheat-colored hair framed her face, but the rest was tugged harshly back and covered in a black kapp, tied behind her head.

"Won't you come in?"

"Outside, for now, I think," said Jackson. "It's too hot in there."

Faith nodded. "I'll bring out the iced tea."

Jackson motioned to a circular table covered with a spotless white cloth, surrounded by four chairs, and tucked in the shade of the mighty oak as Faith disappeared into the house.

Were they expected?

Faith returned with a tray holding a pitcher and three glasses. Why was Elana surprised to see ice in the glasses? He'd said she had electricity and a car, parked in the shade.

Jackson held Elana's chair and she settled, accepting a full glass of amber liquid.

"So you're the bride-to-be?"

"Yes."

"Lovely," she said. "And you're widowed. I'm sorry for your loss, Elana."

"Thank you." Elana wondered what else Jackson had shared.

"Was your husband a man of faith?"

"Yes. Gavin was a good man." Though not the churchgoing variety.

"A farmer?"

"No, not exactly. He worked for the county public works mowing along the highways."

"And he was killed in an auto accident. Is that right?"

Elana took the sharp stab of grief in stride, familiar now as her own face in the mirror.

Gavin had been killed by an uninsured driver who suffered a stroke that sent him onto the shoulder and right into her husband, who was operating his boom mower cutting grass.

Elana got hold of herself, pressing her lips tight as the loss settled in her heart.

"Yes. He was killed by an elderly man who experienced a medical emergency."

"What a tragedy."

"Yes."

"I'll pray for him."

Elana smiled and sipped her tea, which was so sweet she winced.

"You were married very young, I understand."

"I finished high school."

"I see. And worked outside the home?"

Was that a bad thing to a Mennonite? Likely, she thought. She assumed that their beliefs about a woman's place were different than hers.

"I worked at the Orlando Convention Center until my maternity leave." Elana had been an assistant to the events service manager and did not mention that she had returned to work as soon as Phoebe had been old enough to attend kindergarten.

She glanced from Faith to Jackson. This felt more like a job interview than a meeting with a cousin. Was Faith's approval important to Jackson? Why hadn't he mentioned her before?

"There is so much work here," said Faith, her smile still benign as a butterfly. "I don't have time for other things."

That felt like the gentlest of rebukes. Elana knew that the Mennonites had very definite beliefs about what was and was not appropriate for a woman's duties.

Faith motioned to the garden. "Cabbage is coming along. The chickens help with the caterpillars. Jackson still gets all his baked goods from me. Eggs too."

"He's told me."

"Wonderful." She beamed, hands still and folded in her lap in a rare moment of rest. "I know Jackson is eager to have children. Are you as well?"

She hesitated, glancing to Jackson, who held his smile.

"Well, yes. We would like children."

"I'll pray that God will bless your union."

"That's generous."

Faith grinned, looking pleased.

Elana tried to finish her tea, anxious to be gone. Jackson's glass was already empty.

Faith reached for the pitcher. "More tea?"

"I'm afraid we need to be going," said Jackson and Elana could have kissed him for stepping in and rescuing her.

They said their goodbyes and headed away. Once inside the truck, Jackson reversed them out of the drive.

"Your cousin is very sweet. Though not as sweet as her tea," said Elana, smiling at her joke.

"She's not just my cousin. She's also my first wife."

Elana stammered. "What?" Her mouth hung open as she stared at him. "I didn't know you had been married before."

"Yes."

"Wait. Did you say first wife?"

He nodded, looking terribly sad. He glided to the dirt shoulder and slipped the truck into park. When he turned to look at her, tears welled on his lower lids.

At the sight of his vulnerability and pain, she cried, too.

He choked out his reply. "I've been married twice."

Elana was thankful she was seated, but still needed to bracket her face in her hands as she absorbed these revelations.

"You should have told me sooner."

"Probably. But I didn't want to freak you out. See me as a loser. After all, if I've got two failed marriages, there must be something wrong with me. Right?"

"No." She was quick to reassure. "I would never have thought that."

"I waited as long as I could. Not telling you has caused me some sleepless nights and I've been so scared about what you'd do. But I owe you the truth. Elana, please don't leave me."

"Leave you! No, I'm not. I'm just shocked, I guess. Give me a minute." She pressed her hands to her mouth, staring straight ahead.

"I was really young when we married. Too young, I think."

Finally, her racing mind formed a question.

"Why did you leave her?"

"What makes you think it was my decision?" He sighed and stared out the windshield, silent for a long time.

The tea sloshed around in her stomach and she felt sick.

His brow etched and the corners of his mouth dipped. Finally, he blew away a long breath through his nose and spoke.

"Almost from the start, we clashed. She's got her beliefs and I can't abide all the rules. At first, I sneaked around. Drinking and partying with my brothers, like a teenager sneaking out of his parents' house. She wanted me to stop seeing them. She'd lost her family over me, so it seemed only fair. But I couldn't do it. Missed my brothers too much. Even missed my dad, if you can believe it. I was really unhappy, so she let me go."

That was an odd way of saying they had split up.

"Mennonites can divorce?"

"It's frowned upon. We broke up after she had a medical thing, premature menopause. She can't have any more children. But Faith says that God closed her womb."

"You have children?"

"She did. A daughter. That's another tragedy. She left the church. Ran away."

"Oh, no. What happened?"

"People leave the community all the time. A large percentage of young people don't want to farm cabbage and bake bread."

"How old was her daughter?"

"Grace? Not sure, exactly."

Elana imagined what she would feel if her daughter ran away as a teenager. She pictured Phoebe as a run-away in some cold, grim city. And her not knowing where she was or if she was safe. It would be such a constant stone in her heart.

How did Faith bear it?

"Anyway, she couldn't have children," he said. "I wanted them. I still have feelings for her. Mostly regret, but some obligation. Because of our marriage, she can't wed again. None of the men in her community will have anything to do with her."

"That's sad."

Jackson interrupted her musings. "I feel responsible for the failure of the marriage."

She could understand his feelings, but Faith's fertility problems and the alienation of his family seemed a terrible burden for any couple.

"Well, in any case. You'll likely see her in town and out here when you buy whatever you can from her. I'd appreciate it if you would buy from her. It's her only source of income."

"You should have warned me."

"No. It was less awkward this way. Better to meet her now when you have some privacy and confidence rather than being caught off guard, in town somewhere."

"Will she be at our wedding?"

"No."

He'd made the decision without her. Her face flushed.

"I feel so foolish."

"Why? She didn't know I never told you. Probably just thought you incredibly poised. Confident. And you should be. You're going to be my wife."

"I can't just avoid her?"

"Small town. And I told you, we need to buy produce from her. She and I are civil to each other. I hope you can be as well. She's a good person despite our differences."

"I didn't think they married outside their community."

"Rarely. Our marriage caused her problems with her fellowship, for sure. Many still won't speak to her."

"That's terrible."

Elana thought about Faith losing her friends, possibly her family over her marriage to Jackson. No wonder they split up.

"And your second wife?"

"The complete opposite of Faith. A party animal. Sexy, smart, and crazy. When Shantel got drunk and crashed the truck my dad bought me, he cut us off. No money. No job. Didn't take more than a month for her to pack her bags. I felt so stupid, realizing she'd married me for my family's money."

"Oh, no. That's terrible."

"It was. And she's even crazier now. We're not in touch."

That, at least, came as a relief. But what else didn't she know?

FOUR

NOW

June 20, 2022, Monday
Poseidon Offshore Open, Culpepper, NC

Elana had reached the end of her endurance. The effort of pretending her marriage was perfect had worn her thin as a Communion wafer. But she was *not* going to divorce him. He scared her too much for that.

She was going to take Phoebe and run. The FBI visit had made her even more determined.

If Houdini could make a full-grown elephant vanish, surely, she could pull off the smaller disappearing act for a woman and her young daughter.

Please, God, let this work.

She was here, out of state, with Phoebe, at the game fishing tournament that would keep her husband occupied for hours. And if he thought his sister-in-law was enough of a prison guard to hold them, he was dead wrong.

If she could hold on one more day, she'd have her chance to run. The day after the tournament ended, the boys went on a golf outing and her sister-in-law took the kids to visit her mother. It was the only day in the year that she could be assured privacy.

Elana waited on the dock of the Dare Marina with her daughter and her sister-in-law. Zoey was petite, blond with a perpetual dark stripe at her part-line despite bi-weekly trips to the salon. Her athletic build and devotion to both yoga and golf gave her a natural energy and glow that nearly overcame her thin mouth and sun-damaged skin. Being four months pregnant with baby number four did not seem to have slowed her down.

Zoey's two boys, Parker and Levy, spent their time running up and down the metal docking and creating a tripping hazard for all arriving vessels. As usual, Zoey seemed both blind and oblivious to the unruly pair despite being unburdened of her ten-month-old baby, Caleb, who was currently under the supervision of their housekeeper, who Zoey had insisted come along on this occasion.

"They've just boarded that boat," Elana said, pointing.

"They're fine," said her sister-in-law, making a dismissive gesture. "With luck they'll be shanghaied."

Elana gripped Phoebe's hand, for support as much as safety. At seven, her daughter was old enough not to be coddled, as Jackson called it. But Elana needed her daughter by her now more than ever.

Both Phoebe and Elana wore feminine dresses in pastel hues, as was Jackson's preference. Elana wore a belted apricot outfit with a square neckline and Phoebe wore a dressy dress in a solid mint green. Privately, Elana thought their attire was more appropriate for Easter Sunday than a fishing pier and the wind was playing havoc on their full skirts. They looked like a couple of melting scoops of sherbet as they batted down their hems with dexterity born of practice.

All she understood about the tournament was there were more levels than she could count, the entry fees added up to over twenty thousand dollars, and the payouts ran to the millions.

Jackson and his brothers were rich men. None of them needed to work, but all did, running the small town where they all lived like some ancient fiefdom.

The seventy-four-foot boat approached at idle speed. The crew would be famished because her husband's habit was to not feed them until they reached their berth as if they were a bunch of Viking Berserkers.

Jackson said, "A hungry crew is a motivated crew."

It was her job, and Zoey's, to be sure the caterers were ready with the spread served on the boat. But nothing chocolate because it gave Jackson hives. Even if she ate something containing chocolate, it would give him hives. As a result, she'd avoided every cake, cookie, and confection that contained her favorite flavor since well before their marriage.

What she wouldn't give for a bowl of chocolate ice cream covered in fudge.

The golf cart, laden with platters of shrimp, lobster, and crab, fruit, cheese, and crackers, rolled slowly by en route to the dock where the boat would be moored after the weigh-in.

She thought the men would prefer to eat somewhere out of the hot sun where there was no fish blood splashed on the deck, but it was one of many traditions she did not understand.

As soon as the fish were off-loaded and the contest results registered, the party would begin.

Tomorrow, she'd run like a hare and spend the rest of her life looking over her shoulder. Because Jackson would come after them. Shantel had told her that much.

Everything she believed about him had been a lie.

The tug of regret twitched again, the wish that she could do as Special Agent Inga had asked and help them locate those missing girls. Help her build a case to put the man responsible in prison. Perhaps that could lead to finding those precious children and bring some closure to those two grieving mothers.

But she wouldn't. She was too scared.

"Look at those fools," said Zoey, laughing at their husbands hooting and hollering as they motored toward the wharf. "They're just like little kids." This seemed to remind her that she was in charge of two actual children.

She turned in a circle, spotting her boys.

"Levy! Parker! Get off that man's boat."

Parker complied first. At six, he was agile, making the leap from boat to dock. His brother, two years younger, followed suit, but landed on all fours.

The youngsters clamored up the dock toward her. Parker had dark hair like his father, Sawyer, and the same narrow brown eyes. He had strong tanned legs and a freckled face that was showing some sunburn across his nose.

Levy had angelic features and a riot of golden curls. His pink cheeks and vivid blue eyes all but guaranteed he'd be a heartbreaker one day.

Parker made no indication of slowing on approach, so Zoey grabbed him by the shirt collar and Levy by the arm before they had an opportunity to charge right past. She lifted Levy to her hip and adjusted her grip on Parker.

"Your daddy's comin' in. He sees you bashin' about and he'll tan your hide for you."

Parker stilled and cast his gaze to the incoming sport fishing boats, interest shifting.

"They got fish?" he asked.

"Prize winner is what they say."

Levy stuck his thumb in his mouth, only to have it immediately batted away by Zoey.

"You're too old, Levy!"

Parker, suddenly free, made a run for it, but was captured

by one pumping arm and hauled back beside his mother. Zoey was quick and strong.

"Here comes your father. Look at that fish!"

The marlin was tied to the back platform of the vessel, behind the transom, and came into view as the *Reel Escape* pulled along the wharf. Once at dock, the mighty fish would be moved to the weighing station with the help of a crane. The marlin dwarfed the men. The protruding glassy eye and open mouth gave the huge fish a startled expression as if it could not believe this group of humans had managed to pluck it from the sea.

"It's a big one," said Zoey.

They waited as the fish was off-loaded and the vessel neatly tucked into its berth. The odor of diesel fumes made Elana cough. How Zoey could tolerate the cloud of exhaust and the stink of fish blood while pregnant was beyond her.

Jackson and Sawyer were first off the *Reel Escape*. Zoey greeted her husband with a one-armed hug and an exuberant kiss. Sawyer pulled back and tousled Levy's hair before lifting Parker. The four made a pretty picture of a happy family.

But Elana knew that appearances and reality were often strangers.

Sawyer was the tallest of the Belauru boys, but at five-eleven he was not really that tall. His position as city council president allowed the family to keep their hands in everything. But so much time in meetings and watching college football —*Go, Seminoles*—meant he was going soft and doughy around the middle and, though he had the thick wavy brown hair of all the Belauru men, his forehead was growing longer each year.

Sawyer lowered Parker to the dock and released him and the family headed after him toward the marina for the weigh-in of the great fish.

Jackson stepped to the dock next and stood with open arms, waiting for Elana to respond to his summons. She did not make him wait, but stepped forward with a faux enthusiasm she'd perfected.

"We are starving. How's the food coming?"

"All ready!"

"That's fine." He dropped a kiss on her mouth. He could be so loving and normal in front of other people. "What would I do without you?"

You are about to find out, she thought.

With the men gone to check the marlin's weight and the tournament rankings, Elana went to work, motioning for the caterer. Down the dock came another golf cart pulling a wagon laden with trays of shrimp, king crab, and salmon on ice, as well as filet mignon, rare and sliced. Much of the spread went into the kitchen area, or the galley, as Jackson called it.

Elana had never heard of a galley made of green onyx stone countertops, imported from Portugal. The cabinets had been fashioned from century-old logs of sinker cypress recovered from a river bottom in South Carolina.

Zoey took over setup of the drink station in the lounge as Elana orchestrated the placement of the heavy-laden trays of cheese, bread, and fruit on the counter, leaving the dinette clear for the men to dine. A folding table was erected on the cockpit as an additional seating space.

Meanwhile, past the sliding glass doors, the little boys scrambled up the stairs from the cockpit to the second helm above.

She and Zoey finished just in time to clear the decks for the arrival of the crew who attacked the bounty like a pack of wild dogs.

"Better step back so we don't lose a finger," said Zoey.

They watched the men continue to gorge. The gluttony and excess reminded Elana of some ancient medieval feast. After the men had been back for seconds and thirds, Elana and Zoey fixed a plate for each of their children.

Zoey watched her husband finishing a slice of pecan pie with an iced beer chaser.

"Is Jackson taking you out in the boat tonight?" she asked.

"Yes."

"He told Sawyer he wants to make a baby with you in the sound. Put the fishing bug in him right from the get-go."

Elana managed to laugh, then lied, "We are both anxious to get pregnant."

"But, Lanie, a year trying. Shouldn't you go see someone? Get some help."

"You sound like Jackson."

Zoey's latest pregnancy only fueled the contention in Elana's marriage because her sister-in-law had already produced three boys.

"I know he wants a son. All he can talk about around me," Zoey said and frowned. "All men want sons. Give him one and he's yours for life."

That was one of Elana's fears. So far, the spermicide had worked. But if her husband ever found out, there would be hell to pay.

"We'll just keep trying."

Zoey seemed happily married to a man who was only one step away from Jackson.

Was she truly? So many times, Elana had been tempted to ask, but Zoey was not an ally.

Her surrogate sister seemed to be a friend. But the risk that she would tell Sawyer every word of private conversations was too great.

Keeping her curiosity in check was safest for her and for Phoebe.

"Thanks for agreeing to watch Phoebe tonight, Zoey."

"Oh, Phoebe is no trouble. She's a little doll." She rested a hand over her still flat belly. "Wish I could get a girl. But all I seem capable of having is boys."

Elana suspected it was the other way around. Zoey seemed happy giving Sawyer what made Sawyer happy.

If she could just pretend for one more night, then tomorrow the men would play in the golf tournament. By the time they returned, she and Phoebe would be away from Jackson forever.

FIVE

THEN

June 2021, the day before the wedding

Elana had left the wedding rehearsal early, hurrying across town to the historic mansion where she and Jackson would host the small rehearsal dinner. She carried only her new designer bag, her makeup, and the outfit she would wear tonight, and was anxious to steal a few moments to change before the guests arrived.

Once through the main entrance, she paused to admire the grand old house, now an elegant country inn.

The mansion had been built by the city's first tycoon, who had made his fortune in lumber. It was three stories, brick and wood, with a second-floor sleeping porch, wide green lawns, and a gazebo surrounded by a picture-perfect rose garden.

The gathering and the wedding would be small and elegant. Both the ongoing pandemic and the fact that it was neither of their first marriages had made that decision simple.

Tonight, they would host the rehearsal dinner on the huge front porch. The outdoor location would be beautiful and helped them avoid the whole face mask issue.

Elana's emotions ran from elated to exhausted. The one emotion she didn't feel was nervous, because Jackson Belauru had come into her life like a gift.

Her groom had charm, means, rugged good looks, and a position that garnered respect as the mayor of the small, northwestern city of Bald Cypress, Florida. Most importantly, her daughter, Phoebe, loved him.

His previous two marriages had given her pause. If he'd made poor choices with his first and second wife, she knew she would be the partner he needed and longed for.

It was true that his wealth and position had played into her decision. As the mother of a young child, she needed to be practical, but she didn't know any single woman who would not have been thoroughly swept away by Jackson.

He was a force of nature. Bold and funny and charming. She'd fallen for him before she'd even seen his enormous home, the seventy-foot boat, or the family trust he managed. But the one-carat pear-shaped solitaire he'd offered was a clue. Simple, elegant, and so bright. He'd said, "You can use it to warn ships off the reefs."

It was that sense of humor that she found particularly charming. And he loved her laugh. He was the only man she'd ever known who noticed her manner of speaking and the correct use of grammar. He saw past her bra size and her current situation as a single mother working double shifts and living with a roommate in a tumbledown cottage that had not seen a renovation since before the installation of the avocado-colored toilet.

She was only sorry that her former in-laws would not be here. Jackson had not wanted the family of her first husband in attendance. She understood that Phoebe's grandparents might make her second wedding awkward.

He was right to remind her that they were at the start of new beginnings. It was a time to look forward. That was one reason she had not probed too deeply into his former broken marriages. Jackson had told her all she needed to know.

He'd been very young when he first married Faith. Flat broke, too, he said because his father cut him off when he announced his intention to marry a Mennonite woman, like his mom. Why he disapproved was unclear to Elana and so was the attraction.

Having met Jackson's first wife, she could not picture them as a couple, although the woman was hardworking, kind, and obviously devout.

Jackson hated farming and missed his family. The marriage seemed the mistake of a rebellious young man.

His second wife had apparently been the opposite of Faith in every way. Unpredictable. A party girl with a shopping addiction. Jackson told her that Shantel's out-of-control spending nearly bankrupted them. Worse still, her drinking had spoiled more than one family gathering. Shantel was lively, modern, and urban. Too urban to settle for life in a small town, it turned out. Bored and disillusioned that her reality did not match the fantasy, she'd run up an enormous personal debt and, too ashamed to ask for his father's help, Jackson had worked like a demon to pay it all off.

It was why he was now so crazy about checking all the spending for the wedding, and worried when she drank even a small glass of wine. It was just easier to give alcohol up, along with the chocolate. And being open about their finances seemed a plus to Elana.

"She'd never admit she had a problem," he'd said. "Mixed her vodka in everything. Coffee. Soda can. Hell, probably in her bathwater. She was a mess. Embarrassed me so many times."

Which explained why he was so thrilled that she had manners, didn't drink, and was an excellent mother. And he wanted kids. They both did.

Joann Halpern, their wedding planner, greeted her in the

downstairs living room and bustled Elana up the grand staircase to a room at the front of the house.

"You'd better hurry. They should be here in a few minutes." With that, she closed the door leaving Elana blissfully alone.

She exhaled. Then she draped the dress, still in the plastic bag from the store, over the spindle back chair with the cane seat. Jackson had helped her pick this lovely rose-colored cocktail dress and she could not wait to wear it at their rehearsal dinner.

Beyond the bed, past the antique glass-paneled doors, stood the sleeping porch where the photographer would take their photo tomorrow at sunset. Elana felt the butterflies of excitement flapping about and grinned, turning in a full circle. The room had been furnished with a vintage rolltop desk, rocking chair, and armoire. Braided rugs encircled a bed, with a brass headboard, like lily pads and the door to the chic bathroom gave a glimpse of a claw-foot tub.

"Get moving," she muttered. Their guests were likely already on their way over.

Their dinner included Jackson's two brothers—Derek, the youngest, and Sawyer, the eldest—along with Sawyer's wife and two little boys, Derek's girlfriend, and Elana's daughter, Phoebe, who was so excited to be the flower girl tomorrow and taking her responsibilities very seriously.

Derek, the baby of the Belauru boys, was the shortest of the three brothers and the most muscular. As an officer on the city's police force, he spent more time than Jackson or Sawyer in the weight room and on his physical fitness. When not working, hunting, or fishing with his brothers, he engaged in various iron man competitions throughout the state. He looked to Elana like a dwarfed bodybuilder, all bulging biceps and overtight clothing.

His girlfriend was Mennonite too, and of one of the less conservative fellowships. On the one occasion they had met, the woman had her brown hair tugged in a tight bun, wore no makeup or jewelry, and wore a white blouse and denim skirt. If Elana had not been told, she would not have known of her faith from Robyn's appearance.

Both Jackson's parents and hers had passed away. Due to the pandemic, Jackson had thought that inviting friends would be dangerous to everyone and she had to agree. So tomorrow the service would include only his direct family and her daughter.

She set her makeup bag down in the bathroom and had just draped her new dress across the bed when there was a rapping at the door. An unfamiliar woman peered in and then crossed the threshold without waiting for an invitation.

"Yes?" asked Elana, eyeing her.

The woman was masked so all that was visible of her face were two pale blue eyes set close beneath a broad forehead and thin brows. Her sandy-colored hair was tugged back in a bun, and she wore a dark pencil skirt, flats, and a crisp, white blouse.

"Hello, Elana," she said, extending her hand and then, thinking better of it, drew it back. "Joann asked me to handle a few things for the cocktail hour on the deck. Could you come with me?"

She was not leaving her dinner dress, purse, and jewelry in an unlocked guestroom.

"I don't have time. Joann knows what we've..." She lifted her attention to the stranger. Her words died.

Something about this intruder set all her alarm bells jangling.

The stranger now blocked the entrance, her back pressed to the solid door, her mask removed from her face and wadded in her fist. She looked so pale and frightened that Elana's breath caught.

"I don't have any money," she said, leaping to the conclusion that this woman was dangerous. Elana's eyes cut to the antique lead-glass doors that led to the porch beyond. If she could get through that ancient-looking door, she could call for help.

"I'm not here to rob you. The wedding announcement, I only saw it yesterday."

Jackson had insisted that they post the engagement announcement just prior to the wedding. She hadn't objected. Why should she?

There was no family to see it. Most of her friends didn't get paid leave and couldn't afford the day off. Even if they were invited and made the journey here, she didn't want to burden them with having to send a gift, not to mention risking someone bringing Covid to her wedding.

Now her ears were buzzing a warning. Elana backed away, stopping at the heavy velvet curtains drawn apart with a tasseled tieback. The only way out was past the woman blocking the door.

Her captor pressed a hand to her chest. "I'm Shantel."

Shantel.

She recognized the name.

"You're his other ex-wife."

The woman nodded. Why did she look more frightened than Elana felt? Tremors shook her like some internal storm. The woman had a drinking problem. Was that the cause of the shakes?

Her bloodshot eyes were watery, and red blotches covered her neck.

"What do you want?"

"To warn you. He's not what you think. He's a monster."

"What's wrong with you?"

"He can't see me." At this, she glanced at the door she had sealed and now guarded with her body. "I had to come. You can't go through with this marriage. He's pure evil."

Elana scowled as her fear fueled her irritation. She was not listening to insults from an embittered lush.

"He's the love of my life."

"Got your joint accounts yet? Keeping an eye on your spending."

"That's *your* fault. The debt you ran up took him years to pay off."

"That's a laugh. I never even had a credit card until he insisted I get one. Lets him keep better track of you. Where you go. What you buy."

They did have joint accounts. But naturally, they'd made several changes in preparation for merging their households. And as for keeping an eye on spending... Who didn't do that when planning a wedding?

Shantel stepped forward, advancing in a halting gait. "Get you a new phone? A new car? I'll bet he did. They've got software installed. He can see who you call, who you email, and track you with GPS."

"That's ridiculous. Get out of here."

She continued her advance, staggering slowly forward, arms outstretched like the walking dead.

"You have to believe me."

"I don't. I'm going to marry Jackson. You're crazy or jealous or both." Elana inhaled, trying, and failing to catch the odor of alcohol.

"I don't drink. Not anymore. Please don't go through with it. You have to trust me."

"I don't even know you. My wedding is tomorrow. And you come here with your ridiculous accusations."

The woman grabbed hold of her lapels and shook Elana like a rag doll.

The shock of this physical attack rocked her, and she lifted her arms in a gesture of surrender. The shaking stopped. Elana opened her mouth to scream, only to discover that her voice had abandoned her. All that emerged from her mouth was a strangled moan.

"You aren't listening! It won't happen right away. But over time. Leave right now! If you wait, you can't go. You can't ever go. Or he'll... he'll... I should have left him sooner before... When I did leave... and the divorce... It made him more danger-ous. I couldn't protect..."

"All right!" There was her voice, finally. Forceful, but shaking.

Her thoughts tumbled. Disjointed. Fragmented. *Run. Scream. Fight.*

She glanced toward the closed door, determining to run.

"I'm listening. He follows you. Keeps you under surveillance. Watches the finances."

Shantel nodded, her grip relaxing in slow degrees. "And he's a monster."

"I understand. Thank you for telling me."

The woman released her.

"I have to go and speak to the manager, call off the rehearsal dinner."

"Yes. Yes, that's right. And the minister. Call him, too."

Elana inched past her toward the exit.

"Thank you for warning me, Shantel. I appreciate you taking the time and trouble."

"You'll be grateful. Once you understand."

"Yes. It was a mistake." She was nearly to the door. "I can see that. And you're right. He did lease me a car."

"It's got tracking software."

"Yes. It does." They all did now and cameras. Shantel seemed more crazy than drunk. How could Jackson ever have married her? The woman obviously had some deep mental issues.

"You need to get away while you can. It might still be dangerous, but you have no choice."

Elana gripped the cold metal latch.

"You can't wait until after you are married to leave him and still protect your little girl. Phoebe, isn't it?"

Had she seen that in their wedding announcement?

"It might already be too late. I don't know."

At the mention of her child, Elana hesitated.

"What do you mean, 'too late'? Too late for what?"

"If you leave him, he'll take your daughter."

"Take her where?"

"I don't know. But you'll never see her again."

A cold shaft of fear bolted through her like a lightning strike. She stood there, staring at this wild woman as her thoughts ping-ponged between dismissal and panic.

"That's ridiculous."

"He'll do it," she warned. "Has done it, to my girl."

Elana tugged the door open, darting out into the hall and down the main stairs. Her feet pounding on the Oriental runner, fleeing from her husband's previous wife and the terrible prophecy, rejecting it even as it settled like a sliver of glass in her heart.

Behind her Shantel screamed and charged after Elana. But Elana had been a swimmer in high school and ran track, middle distance. She was fast as the wind. Before Shantel even reached the top step, she was down the stairs yelling for help.

Jackson darted off the first-floor porch and through the main double doors, followed by his brothers, Sawyer and Derek. All three pulled up short at seeing Shantel at the first landing gripping the thick oak banister.

She seemed frozen as the men advanced.

Elana continued her flight, running between the furniture grouped about the fireplace and the reading area and vintage gaming table opposite. She reached Jackson and cowered beside her fiancé.

He pulled her in, tight to his side.

"Did she hurt you?" he whispered.

She shook her head.

Derek stepped forward. The police officer used his commanding voice.

"You need to leave now."

Shantel ignored him, pinning her gaze on Jackson as she descended the final three steps, creeping forward with the caution of a cornered animal. She moved sideways down the final steps to the hallway that led toward the dining room, kitchen, and rear exit.

"No," Shantel whispered and then repeated it again and again as Jackson passed Elana to Sawyer and then advanced on Shantel.

Sawyer wrapped an arm around Elana's shoulder protectively as they watched Jackson clasp Shantel's upper arm and escort her firmly past the reception desk, across the room, and to the side exit door leading to the grand portico.

"What do you think you're doing?" he asked Shantel as he hustled her along.

"I came... I wanted to congratulate you." Her voice was different now. Shakier and more fearful. Elana could barely watch.

"Is that so?"

He held tight, reaching with his free hand for the brass knob.

"They haven't found her," she said to Jackson. "She's still missing. Did you know that?"

Elana's heartbeat drummed in her ears and she struggled to hear Shantel's words.

"Who's missing?" she whispered to Sawyer. Did Shantel really mean her daughter? Did she even have a daughter? Jackson had never mentioned a child.

He shrugged. "The woman's brain is missing, pickled. She's a mess. Worse than the last time I saw her."

"She's done this before?"

"Oh yeah. Set his old truck on fire. Showed up at political events. She's the poster child for crazy exes."

Beside him, Derek was on the phone to the police. Though not in his police uniform, Elana felt safer knowing he was here, armed and taking over the situation.

Jackson tugged the door open and stepped out with Shantel, followed by Derek, who firmly closed the ancient stained-glass door. The bang echoed in the silence as Sawyer's wife and boys appeared from the porch, gathering with them in the now-silent room.

"What did she say to you?" asked Sawyer, now standing at Elana's side. She pressed both her hands flat to her stomach as her insides continued to jerk, making her breath catch.

"She told me not to marry Jackson."

He snorted. "Anything else?"

Something about Sawyer's grip on her elbow and the hard glint in his eye made her cautious.

"No. Nothing." Why was she lying?

Zoey, Sawyer's wife, stepped up beside them.

"The kids," she said to Sawyer.

He glanced at his two boys, huddling with Phoebe in the open double doors leading out to the wide covered porch. Elana shook as the fear now exploded through her nerve endings. She rushed to her daughter and pulled her into the shelter of her arms. Thank goodness Phoebe had been safe here with Zoey.

She couldn't seem to catch her breath. Was it the physical threat she had escaped, or the one Shantel had insinuated that had her sputtering like butter in a hot pan? The woman was insane!

"Zoey, take them in there." Sawyer motioned to the breakfast room.

Reluctantly, Elana released her daughter to the protection of her sister-in-law-to-be.

His wife herded her boys, and Elana's daughter, in the

opposite direction that Shantel, Derek, and Jackson had taken. From somewhere nearby came the rising shrill of police sirens.

"Let's you and I get a drink," he said to Elana.

"I don't drink." Not anymore, though right now she was tempted. "And I have to get changed. I left my dress..." She pointed to the second level.

"Oh, right. Go on, then."

Sawyer headed out to join his brothers.

Instead of ascending the stairs, Elana followed as far as the glass side door to watch the three brothers walk Shantel to her vehicle. For a moment it appeared as if the men surrounding her were the aggressors, instead of the other way around.

Zoey drew up beside her, watching the unfolding drama.

"Did she threaten you?"

"Not exactly. She just said I couldn't marry Jackson."

"Well, she's wrong on that one. You absolutely can."

"What did she mean, she's still missing?"

"Oh, that. It's really sad. She had a daughter by a previous marriage. Few years back someone snatched her from her backyard."

"Oh, no!" Elana pressed her hands to her mouth. It was true, at least that her child was taken.

The poor woman. No wonder she was disturbed. But why did she think Jackson had anything to do with this?

"Why tell him? Doesn't he already know?"

"Of course, he knows. But since it happened, her drinking is worse. Sawyer told me Jackson tried to get her to rehab, even after the divorce. She wouldn't. Instead, she tells the police that Jackson took her child."

"Why would she do that?"

"Because she was drunk when it happened. Blaming him is easier than looking in a mirror."

"This is terrible."

"I'll say."

"But her daughter?"

"Gone. And well, she's torn up. Who wouldn't be? Disturbed. You know? The police questioned everyone. Even me. No suspects. No leads. Just poof, vanished."

Elana stared through the antique glass of the country inn, the ancient pane distorting the image of his previous wife into a disturbing, warped vision.

"She still thinks it was Jackson," whispered Elana.

Zoey waved her index finger at her temple, indicating exactly what she thought of the woman's accusations. "They investigated him, me, Sawyer, Shantel's first husband. Even investigated Faith, Jackson's first wife, as if she could. I mean she's Mennonite. They don't approve of violence of any kind."

"Yes, I know. He told me and that his mom was, as well. But none of the brothers were raised that way."

Zoey nodded. "That's right. Their dad wouldn't have it. Gun-toting billionaire and not about to be lectured by 'dirt farmers,' as he called them."

"You met him?"

Her eyes widened and she nodded. "Oh yeah. Intense. When those people turned their back on his wife, he wanted to chase that entire community out of the county. You do not want to piss off a Belauru. That's sure."

Elana wrapped her arms about herself, but could not shake off the chill that seeped into her bones. Jackson had told her that Shantel had problems. And she had lost her daughter? No wonder she was a mess. But seeing it with her own eyes was horrifying and very sad.

She understood a little better now what his second wife had put him through. Poor Jackson. And trying to get her help, even after the divorce. It was generous. Maybe some of those Mennonite teachings *had* rubbed off on him.

Finally, Shantel closed her door and the brake lights illuminated. She backed up and raced out of the lot as if chased by the devil himself.

Jackson raked a hand through his thick hair and glanced in Elana's direction. He was so handsome. Even with the high color in his cheeks and his square jaw set in annoyance, he took her breath away. Those fathomless black eyes pinned her, and her heart gave an excited leap as stress and fear melted away.

Derek remained outside as a police cruiser pulled into the portico. Sawyer entered first, moving to his wife, but his gaze trailed past her.

"Did your mama tell you to stay in that room?"

Both boys jumped off the sofa where they were standing and darted back the way they had come.

Phoebe appeared in the doorway to the breakfast room, staring wide-eyed at her mother, and Elana tucked her close.

"It's all right, sweetheart. Go on up to the sleeping porch. I'll be there in a few minutes." Phoebe hesitated and then did as her mother asked, pausing only to give her one desperate hug.

Sawyer and Zoey followed their boys as Jackson returned. He led her to the padded bench beneath the massive staircase.

"I'm so sorry, Elana. I should have realized she'd do something like this."

Was this the reason for the extremely late wedding announcement? Had Jackson been trying to prevent Shantel from creating a scene? How big a problem was this woman going to be?

"I'm all right."

"It's not the first time she's pulled a stunt like tonight. She tore a hank of hair out of the head of the first woman I dated after the divorce. We didn't even know she was following us."

"That's terrible."

"She's obsessed with me."

Elana glanced to the front door where Shantel had made

her exit, recalling the final words she'd overheard. *She's still missing. Did you know?*

"What did she say to you?" he asked, his words echoing Sawyer's.

Elana hesitated. "Nothing. It's not important."

"Please tell me. Do I have to press charges?"

"No. Oh, no, Jackson. Nothing like that. She just said I can't marry you. That I should leave right now. I had to agree with her just to get out of there. And Zoey told me about her daughter. Jackson, why didn't you tell me?"

He sighed, his gaze drifting toward the window. "I'm sorry. I should have. Did she tell you we were questioned by the FBI?"

"She said you were all questioned." Zoey hadn't told her it had been the FBI, however.

"It was awful. I was embarrassed. It was bad for my reputation. I meant to tell you and I should have. Forgive me?"

"Of course."

"We can't keep secrets. It's bad for a marriage." He glanced in the direction Shantel had gone. "Ruined mine."

She held his hand and he lifted hers for a kiss.

"Do you still want to get changed before dinner?"

She gasped. "My dress."

All of his family had arrived for cocktails, and she was still in the sheath dress she'd worn in the church rehearsal. She'd missed her grand entrance because of Shantel's intrusion.

"Is it upstairs?" he asked.

They hurried to the second floor together and found the garment in a puddle on the rug.

"Oh, darn it." She scooped up the delicate rose-colored fringed confection of a dress. "Is it wrinkled?"

He inspected the outfit. "Looks fine. Can't wait to see you in that!" He wiggled his eyebrows.

She giggled. Jackson was a generous lover and knew his way

around. Elana had nothing but anticipation for their wedding night.

"What did she say exactly?" he asked.

"Just what I said. I can't marry you. I need to call off the wedding and leave right now."

"That's all?"

Again, she omitted much of what Shantel had said about what Jackson was like. She didn't want to upset him.

"That's all. It was only a minute before I made a run for it." Elana lifted her hands. "Look. I'm still shaking."

The sound of a siren brought them both around.

"Finally," said Jackson.

"Is that the police?"

"I'm sure."

"Arresting her?"

"She was trespassing. She threatened you."

"Oh, but I don't want to press charges. It's bad luck."

He kissed her and then cradled her in his arms. "You are so good. You see? That's what I love about you. You're a kind soul."

"Just, you know. Keep her away from the wedding."

"I can guarantee that."

She heard an unfamiliar note of menace in his voice and wondered if they really would arrest Shantel.

"You okay?" he asked.

"Of course. You warned me about her. I'm sorry, you were right."

"She wasn't always like that. But I'm glad you see why I left her."

"Yes. I see."

He gave her another kiss and headed out of the room, leaving her to dress.

Funny. Jackson said he'd left Shantel. But his former wife said that it was the other way around. She'd said she'd left him and then divorced him and that made him more dangerous. As if he were dangerous already. It didn't make any sense.

And what had she meant when she'd said that Elana couldn't wait until after they were married to leave him and still protect her daughter? That was the sort of desperate lunacy that got in your head.

One of the reasons she was marrying *was* to protect Phoebe.

Gavin would want his child to have a good home and a father. And Elana believed that Phoebe was certainly safer in a stable home with two parents.

If Shantel had meant to raise doubts, she had succeeded. But that wouldn't stop Elana from marrying Jackson. From the moment they'd met she'd felt an instant connection. He was the very best thing that had ever happened to her and to Phoebe.

With him as her husband, she and her daughter would have a new home and a new start. She'd have love, respect, and never have to pull a double shift again.

Everything was going to be perfect.

SIX

NOW

June 20, 2022, Monday
Poseidon Offshore Open, Culpepper, NC

In less than twelve hours, Elana was leaving her marriage, Phoebe's friends, their beautiful home, and the man who terrified her. She had just one more night of pretending ahead.

Jackson summoned her by text just before ten in the evening. Phoebe was already fast asleep in one of the queen beds. She and Zoey had taken the kids back to the family suite at the resort. Her nephews looked angelic for a change.

"I just love to watch them sleep," said Zoey and then closed the door to the kids' room. "You better scoot. If he's like Sawyer, he does not like to be kept waiting."

"See you tomorrow, Zoey."

Elana walked out of the suite wearing a bright color for a change. Tonight, Jackson wanted her sexy, in a bubblegum-pink dress and hot-pink lipstick. He even told her to wear heels, though that made balancing on a moving boat more challenging.

She left the condo they were sharing with Sawyer's family during the tournament. Tomorrow, with nothing but her daughter, she would run—out of the marina, the city, the state. Far, far away.

Maybe if she was fast enough, smart enough, she might keep Phoebe from suffering the same fate as his former step-daughters.

What had happened to those girls? She didn't know. Might never know. But the possibilities were enough to send her fleeing with Phoebe.

Tomorrow. One more day and they'd run.

The landscape lighting along the walkways sent wide beams across the curving paths. Once off the pier, she stepped onto the long docks that led to the private berths of the bigger boats. The heels of her sandals rang on the metal dock like a percussion instrument. Many of the tournament participants slept on their boats and the music and noise made this seem more like a pub than a marina.

She hurried along. Jackson was not a patient man. And his lack of patience regarding her inability to conceive had added a new cruelty to him where she was concerned. Tonight, he'd feel invincible and be interested in two things, alcohol and sex.

And Elana hardly needed to act eager because she was full of anticipation, but not for Jackson. For him she had only terror. Would they make it to safety? How long before he began hunting for his wife and her daughter?

Elana's stomach heaved, sending up an acidy hint of her dinner. Her legs shook and she gulped, pausing on the dock to read the craft's name, stenciled on the transom in elaborate black script lettering outlined in gold. The *Reel Escape*.

Ironic, she thought.

Because it was possible that this vessel might just be *her* real escape. Tomorrow, she planned to pick up Phoebe and take the inflatable boat across the inlet to the town of Culpepper, where they'd take a bus to New Bern, North Carolina. From there she'd call her former in-laws who lived ninety minutes west in

Newton Grove. Phoebe's grandparents would help her get out of this city, county, and state. She couldn't stay with them long because he'd come after them. Would come after Phoebe. She knew that now.

"Permission to come aboard!"

Jackson emerged from the lounge through the rear sliders.

"There you are. Finally!" He stumbled forward and plucked her from the dock, swinging her to the stern and planting a sloppy kiss on her stained lips.

He drew back. "What took you so long?"

"It's only been a few minutes."

Jackson wasn't listening. He was already climbing up the exterior ladder toward the second helm to start the engines.

"Cast off," he called back to her, the order shouted as if she were one of the crew.

She stepped back to the dock and unwound the ropes at the stern and along the bow, tossing them onto the boat.

For a moment she fantasized of just staying right here and watching him motor off alone.

But then she thought of his retaliation and did exactly what he'd told her to do. Jackson was not to be disobeyed, not only because it might spoil her chance for tomorrow, but because the only way she'd ever succeeded in defying him was when he didn't find out.

Tomorrow would be different. The final defiance. A betrayal of everything she promised to do and be.

An obedient wife, faithful, loving, and there to stand by him in good times and bad. Outwardly they'd had only good times. But the things that happened behind closed doors were often invisible.

Was his brother Sawyer also a sociopath?

She didn't think so. Sawyer was two years older and Derek five years younger than Jackson. Her sister-in-law had told her that their father was a brutal man. And as for their mother,

Lydia? She'd learned from the mother of one of Phoebe's class-mates that, after leaving her religious community, her husband's mom had become a bit of a wild woman. Her drinking had impacted her third son, Derek, most greatly and he had many learning difficulties as a result. Lydia had overdosed and her youngest, then seven, had found her body. Her boys had spent their most formative years in the care and control of a woman so ravaged by mental illness that two decades later folks were still gossiping behind their backs.

Jackson's mother had chosen her own type of escape.

Elana should feel sorry for him, considering his upbringing. But it was hard to summon compassion for such a man.

The inboard engines fired, and Elana stepped through the transom door onto the deck of the cockpit. Before her sat the fighting chair where her husband strapped in to battle the big fish.

All she really remembered about the chair was it cost eigh-teen thousand dollars and she wasn't allowed to buy her daughter a slice of pizza without his permission.

Jackson turned to see her in the cockpit below him and they were off, headed out to the calm water of the sound, tucked behind the outer banks of the barrier island and the mainland.

She remained on the deck as they left the lights of the marina behind and threaded between the red and green of the channel markers. This watery marine passage was deep enough for all pleasure vessels and marked the fastest route to the Atlantic.

But Jackson left the channel to navigate to the stretch of black water between the two landmasses. There was a light, here or there, from a fellow boater, anchoring in deeper water of the inlet or still fishing.

The tournament drew thousands of game fishermen here. But there was still, and always, the commercial fisherman who had neither the time, nor the money, for such nonsense.

Once at anchor, Jackson wasted no time removing her dress.

Jackson lay now, semiconscious, sprawled across the narrow bed and tangled in the sheets. The musky scent of sex permeated the air and clung to her sticky thighs.

Her husband had charm when it suited him. Unfortunately, when they were alone or when he was drunk, like tonight, he sought to fulfill only his own needs. Not that she cared. Being satisfied by her husband had fallen far down the list of wants. It sat below protecting Phoebe and staying alive, then a few dozen other things, like staying out of his reach once she ran.

If only she could file a divorce, like a normal person, and endure a nasty legal battle to come out on the other side a free woman.

But that was not the game Jackson played. He didn't like losing fishing tournaments. Or wives. She'd had her suspicions, but the visit from the FBI had removed all doubt.

Jackson was their prime suspect in the disappearances of both his stepdaughters. Those precious little girls.

How could his first wife, Faith, even speak to him? The FBI must have told her about their investigation.

She couldn't understand the woman.

Elana rose from the bed and slipped into her sexy pink dress, leaving the difficult zipper unfastened. Then she headed out of the captain's cabin on bare feet.

"Where you goin'?" Jackson asked, managing to lift his head, his breath scented with bourbon.

"Meteor shower tonight."

He growled.

"I'll be right back."

But he wouldn't even let her have these few minutes alone to look at the stars. Jackson dragged himself up and tugged on his athletic shorts, a T-shirt, and that damned fishing vest. The man's lucky fishing vest was legendary, and he was never on board without it. He called it Vera, as if it were his transitional object. The back of the garment was mesh, but the front was multiple pockets into which he tucked all kinds of things. He carried extra hooks and lures, clippers for cutting line, forceps for removing hooks from fish mouths. There was sunscreen, insect repellant, and an energy bar. He even had one of those cheap plastic rain ponchos in there.

She'd once joked that if he ever went overboard in that thing, all that gear would drag him straight to the bottom. At the time, that had made him laugh.

She navigated the corridor past the three other cabins climbing the steps, emerging in the salon between the well-appointed galley, on the right, and the dinette, on the left. Beyond sat the L-shaped settee beneath which he stowed the various rods and reels.

Even in the dark, the large windows and the starlight gave her enough light to reach the slider and slip through the door to the cockpit, trailed by Jackson. She continued to the stern, sitting on the transom and staring upward. Without the moon, the sky glittered, and the hazy stream of the Milky Way painted a wide road across the sky.

She loved stargazing and craned her neck to look at the wonders above her.

"There's one!" She pointed at the momentary streak of light.

"Where?" He stared awhile and then said, "Get me a beer."

She retreated to the galley and returned with his beer, thinking he'd had plenty already, but wisely keeping that opinion to herself.

Jackson swayed from some internal alcoholic storm, his balance issues made more pronounced by his attempts to stare upward, searching for a falling star.

"Here you are," she said, offering the open bottle of icy beer already beading with moisture.

He took the brew and tipped back his head to drink, staggered, and fell heavily against the rear hull of the vessel. The bottle and his head struck the hard surface of the closed door.

Her stomach pitched in horror as instinct took her a step closer. He reached for her, gripping her shoulders as blood poured down his face. He opened his mouth, but no sound emerged.

His fingers turned to claws as they tore at her arms, cutting deep gouges. The sting came an instant before the blood. His hands slipped away, and he scissored his arms madly, catching the fluttering hem of her dress, rending the gossamer overskirt before sliding over the transom, across the slippery outer deck, and toward the dark water, still gripping her skirts.

His hold on her dress dragged her forward. He scrambled with his free hand as she hung, half overboard, folded at the waist and clutching a cleat upon which a rope had been neatly coiled. Jackson kicked at the water below, now at his knees.

He scrabbled with one hand to grasp anything on the outer deck. The narrow platform served as a landing spot where fish would be hauled onto the boat.

Jackson glanced up, her torn skirts in one fist, reaching with the other. She kept both hands firmly on the rail, straining with her legs to keep from tumbling over with him.

Her skirt tore away.

She heard the squeak of skin on decking, then a plunk, and he was gone.

Elana straightened, listening for his splashing, and was met with silence. The heartbeat pounding in her neck and temples seemed impossibly loud, deafening her to the wind and slap of the water on the hull.

Blood smeared along the transom, showing where he'd

struck his head and slipped along the outer platform before dropping into the inlet.

So much blood.

"Jackson!" She scanned the water and saw nothing but the glint of the cabin light on the dark water.

Blood trickled down her arms.

She ran across the cockpit to the ladder, clambering upward with sweaty palms, hand over hand, to the closest helm and radio. She lifted the handset trying to recall the channel for emergencies. Here she paused.

She needed to think.

Elana glanced at the wounds, seeing the marks left by his fingernails. Then she lifted what was left of the ruined skirts.

Everything she saw pointed to a struggle, with Jackson fighting for his life against... *her*.

Ripped clothing, his blood and hers. The scratches that could be interpreted as his attempt to fight for his life as she pushed him over the side. Without him here to explain...

"No one will believe me."

Look at all she had to gain by his death. She'd inherit the house, property, his wealth. And she'd be free of him finally and forever.

If she could get away with it, killing him was safer for her and her daughter than running.

Was it worth the gamble, the arrest, trial, and possible conviction?

She glanced at her arms. His nails had bitten deep. Blood coursed like scarlet veins over her skin to her fingertips where they fell in droplets onto the deck of the outer helm. There was a brilliant red smear across the spotless white vinyl seat. A glance showed the trail leading from the cockpit, past the centrally fixed fighting chair to this spot. Her blood even told how long she stood here, frozen in time.

Then she replaced the radio and sank into the captain's chair.

He'd fallen overboard and, despite his love of fishing, Jackson was not a strong swimmer and his ever-present lucky fishing vest would only add drag.

If he never came back... If she took Phoebe and ran now, they'd suspect the worst.

Would anyone believe that he slipped? *She* hardly believed it.

His family, his brothers, would not. The heaviness in her stomach settled like lead shot. They'd blame her and use every means to see her pay.

Elana hugged herself, her arms slippery from the blood oozing from the gashes on her bare arms. She flicked on the underwater lights and shouted his name.

"Jackson!"

She listened, but heard only the slapping of the waves against the hull.

What should she do?

SEVEN

THEN

June 2021, twelve months ago

Elana opened her eyes to find she wasn't dreaming. She really had married a perfect man who loved her desperately. She really was in their huge bed in the kind of home she'd only ever seen in magazines.

They'd returned from their honeymoon aboard Jackson's yacht of a fishing boat, the *Reel Escape*, happy and a little sore. With luck they had already started the family they both desperately wanted. Phoebe would have a little brother or sister. A brother, if Jackson got his wish.

She loved everything about her new home and new hometown. Bald Cypress was more like Tallahassee than Orlando, lots of good pastureland and plenty of lakes. Even the trees were different, heavy on the oaks draped in Spanish moss and tons of huge pine trees. Hardly a palm tree to be seen, but also no beaches.

It didn't matter. The drive to the shore from Orlando took two hours and the drive from this sweet little town to the Panhandle also took two hours.

In any case, this community was miles and miles better than the rusty, run-down town where she'd been raised. There, the highest elevation was on the top of the piles of earth scooped from the ground while strip-mining phosphate.

She smiled, sat up, and stretched. Beside her, Jackson made a growling sound in his throat. They'd been up late, with him showing her around and her familiarizing herself with her new home. Today they'd pick up her daughter. Her sister-in-law, Zoey, and Jackson's older brother, Sawyer, had graciously offered to watch Phoebe while they boated from the Panhandle all the way to Key West and back.

"Good morning," she whispered and kissed his cheek, rough now with stubble.

In answer he wrapped an arm around her and dragged her close for a real kiss.

Then he let her go and slipped naked from their bed. Jackson had a fine strong body, and she took a moment to admire his butt as he slipped into loose-fitting shorts.

"Coffee?" she asked Jackson.

His smile wavered.

"I heard coffee isn't good for women who are trying to get pregnant," he muttered.

Was that true? She had drunk coffee while she carried Phoebe.

"Oh, well, can I make *you* some coffee?"

He grinned, showing that sparkling smile. "Love some."

She thought of Gavin's face when she'd told him she was pregnant. They hadn't been married yet, but he'd been so thrilled. She wanted to see that same look on Jackson's face.

Would he be happy for them? She knew her first husband would want her to make a good home and find a father for his little girl. She just wished it could have been Gavin.

Elana pushed back the thought of her previous marriage with the covers. He'd been taken too soon. And she would always love him. But now she needed to focus on the future and her new husband, their new home, and their life together.

She returned Jackson's smile.

"I think I'm the luckiest SOB alive," he said. He held the new flowered robe he'd bought her in Key West. The pattern was all pink hibiscus and was satin soft. She thought of her old sleepwear, a nightshirt with "May Contain Wine" printed on the front. That, along with every other shabby piece of her old wardrobe, was now in a charity bin and she was wearing designer outfits.

"I'm a lucky girl," she cooed at him, stroking his cheek.

"I almost forgot. I bought you something."

"Oh, Jackson, you've given me enough."

"Never." He strode to his walk-in closet and returned with a shopping bag from a store she knew, but had never actually been inside.

Her eyes widened.

"Open it." He set the bag on the bed.

Beneath the bright tissue paper, she found a chic designer bag with a coordinated wallet. He'd even personalized the gift with a round, monogrammed charm fastened to one of the handles.

"Oh, Jackson!"

"Do you like it?" His dark eyes were big as he waited for her approval.

"I love it! I've never had anything so elegant."

"Now you can toss that tote bag and use this. Look like the queen of the county in that new car, new duds, and that designer bag."

"Oh, I can't believe it." She stroked the fine, soft leather. "Thank you."

She gave him a hug and a kiss. The coffee could wait.

EIGHT

NOW

June 21, 2022, Tuesday
Poseidon Offshore Open, Culpepper Inlet, NC

Peering out at the open water, Elana saw only the quiet water and the empty place where Jackson had vanished illuminated in the eerie green glow of the underwater lights.

Her shock receded, leaving her with this thought: she'd never have a chance like this again.

Elana stood at the helm station rocking in the light chop. The dash clock told her it was after midnight. An incessant breeze cooled her heated skin and the blood on her arms began to dry and itch.

She stood on the deck before one of the helm stations between the cockpit below and the lookout above. Beyond that, lay nothing but liquid blackness. She needed a better lookout.

Hand over hand, she scaled the steep ladder to the platform she called the crow's nest. This gave the best vantage of the water all around the boat.

Elana scanned the inlet as panic bubbled up like oil from the tar pits.

"Where is he?" she hissed.

The only answer was the whistle of the rising wind and the perpetual slap of the waves on the hull. She gripped the handrail, steadying against the rocking. The motion that seemed gentle as a cradle below felt more like a crazy carnival ride up here.

She had to be sure. Be certain he was gone.

Elana judged the moving water and tried to fathom which way he would travel. Was he moving in or out?

Down, she hoped.

It was so tempting to go check her phone. She could search anything she wanted now. The tides, the weather, the bus routes.

He wasn't here to monitor her search history, question each phone call, interrogate her after each outing. Catch her in the tiniest of deviations from the agreed-upon route.

But the police would check her phone. Especially if Jackson didn't come back. If he'd tugged her into the water at the exact same moment, there would be no calls or searches. He almost had. Elana resisted the urge to check which way the tide would take him.

The panic made thinking so difficult. Her mind felt drugged, slowed by circular thoughts that plodded past her consciousness with the regularity of an ox tied to a millstone.

Where is he?

Where is he?

Where is he?

And these thoughts were interrupted by ridiculous, irrelevant ideas.

Get to Phoebe.

Take the inflatable raft and search for him.

Throw out the life ring.

Remove the blood.

That last one stuck. She looked from her arms to the handrail, not seeing any blood, but knowing it was there.

She scanned the water.

There was no blood trail she could see. The darkness concealed that, too. The eerie green illumination beneath the boat and the restless breeze made her shiver.

He'd been bleeding. A head wound that gushed blood like a river.

Which way did the tides take him? She could not judge. The water seemed not to be moving in either direction.

What did Jackson call that? Ebb tide. The time when the rush of incoming current paused before rushing out again. He should still be behind the boat. Somewhere.

Unless, she speculated, he'd sunk like a bourbon-soaked bag of cement. All that muscle and malice dragging him to the sandy bottom. She scrambled around the lookout, searching for some glimpse of him.

No more time to waste. She needed to call for help or...

That last possibility gleamed like tinsel sparkling in the lights of a Christmas tree.

Or... she could do nothing. Pretend she'd been asleep or passed out when he'd fallen.

You have wounds on your arms. Your blood is all over the boat.

Or wait a bit longer and call for help?

Can they tell how long between when he went in and when you called from the drying blood?

Or call and tell them the truth?

And risk being charged with murder.

She hadn't pushed him, but who would believe her?

He'd grabbed her. Tried to pull himself back aboard. Had tried so hard he'd gouged her flesh.

It looked like a life-and-death struggle, even to her.

She'd been there and she scarcely believed what had occurred.

What if she claimed *he'd* tried to push *her*?

No one will believe that.

He could lift her over his head and throw her ten feet out and into the water. She knew because he'd done it once from this very boat.

Elana hurried down the exterior ladders to the decking at the cockpit to the stern. She opened the transom gate, designed to assist in dragging large game fish onto the deck. From here she watched the churning waves for some glimpse of that damned tan-colored fishing vest.

With all traces of Jackson gone, she looked at her ruined dress.

She pictured the police's questions.

Why didn't you call for help?

You saw him go over. How long before you phoned the coast guard or dialed 911?

She'd done neither.

Elana closed the transom door and crumpled into Jackson's fighting chair, which sat anchored to the deck. Minutes ticked by as she struggled with the various courses available to her.

The innocent lies that Jackson insisted on when it came to his family now rose in her mind. He'd changed everything about her. Had he known that would make her look like a more appealing suspect? At the time, he had said that he hadn't wanted anyone to know that she was poor and uneducated. Now everyone would know. Her entire background was a fabrication, from where she grew up to the fine college she never really attended. Only in this version of reality, they would all assume that *she* had lied about her roots.

He didn't want her to look like a gold digger.

Now she would appear just that. And if she'd been willing

to lie to marry Jackson, of what else might she be capable? Who would believe that this was Jackson's idea?

Nobody.

Oh my God.

She had no one in her corner. No one who would believe what had really happened. Instead, she'd have two angry and grieving brothers, hell bent on revenge.

They wouldn't want justice. They'd want their pound of flesh. Her flesh.

You do not want to piss off a Belauru. That's for sure.

Something moved close by. The splash unmistakable.

Was that Jackson? She stood, relief and panic flaring simultaneously, feet planted on the kickplate as she scanned the water.

More terrifying than any marine life, more frightening than the sharks that moved shoreward to feed at night, was the possibility of Jackson emerging out of the darkness.

From the stern, she scanned the murky water and tried to judge how long it had been since he'd slipped away from the boat. Time had gone funny. She had no sense of it. It might have been hours. But it was still dark. A glance to the east showed no sign of dawn. The lights twinkled from shore. They did not seem very far away.

If she swam to land, she could say that Jackson dragged her overboard. That they'd been separated in the inlet, and she'd been unable to return to the boat. The gouges, explained. He'd done that when he tugged her in. She'd tried and failed to hold him, haul him back aboard.

A martyr instead of a murderess.

Would his brothers believe that?

Perhaps not. The gouges were damning. But better than being found sitting alone on this boat.

Swept away, she'd swim for shore. Elana was a good swimmer. If she made it, she'd at least have a reason for not calling for help.

She spun in the chair, glancing up at the outer helm. That blood should not be there. And the third helm, far aloft, would not have blood unless she had climbed up there to look for him.

Unless she was on board after he went over.

Deciding on her course of action, she headed into the salon, filled a bucket with soapy water, added bleach, and then collected a flashlight and dishrag. She retraced her steps removing the blood she could see and realizing with a sinking feeling that in the dark, she would never get it all. But she tried, working from the third helm, back down to the second outdoor helm, scrubbing the ladder, knowing that every move added to the appearance of guilt.

Her father would have called it hedging her bets. Finally satisfied she could do no better, she threw the rag overboard and returned the flashlight and bucket to their place.

Back at the stern, she looked across the dark water for a long time. Then she climbed on the gunnel and dove into the inlet waters.

Cold stippled her skin as the gravity of her actions took hold, squeezing the air from her lungs.

She surfaced, sputtering. Salt water burned up her nose and stung her eyes. Here, only inches above the shifting surface, the previously gentle waves were churning and black. She could see nothing below her, but now recalled Jackson saying that bull sharks returned toward shore at night to hunt.

What had she just done?

Scissoring her legs, she turned in a slow circle and found herself already more than a hundred feet away from the stern of the boat. Alone in the dark water, she stared back at the *Reel Escape.*

A hitch of panic knotted behind her breastbone. She'd

underestimated the current that now dragged her along. As the tide tugged, she realized she could not return if she tried.

The *Reel Escape* sat anchored high in the water, seeming to levitate in the strange pale green spotlight.

She gasped, sucking in seawater. She'd forgotten to switch off the underwater lights. If Jackson survived, he'd know who flicked them on. He'd know she had not fallen overboard with him. He'd know and he'd make her sorry.

NINE

THEN

September 2021, nine months ago

Jackson and Elana were headed to a fundraiser alone. Zoey and Sawyer would have normally joined them, but her sister-in-law was due any minute and Sawyer didn't want to be so far from home and their hospital. They reached Jacksonville early, so Jackson had detoured to a residential neighborhood.

"My college roommate lives here. Maybe we can stop in for a few minutes to say hi. He's got a wife and... and he's got a son."

Jackson wanted children. They both did. They'd planned to get pregnant right away. But now, three months into their marriage, that hadn't happened. They were both disappointed, but trying was still fun.

He seemed to know exactly how to get to his friend's house, which surprised her. They turned this way and that until they were on a street called Quail. He slowed so they were just barely rolling along.

The roof on the house ahead of them was missing several

shingles and the neglected landscaping seemed out of place for the neighborhood.

He tapped the break, turning to look at this house.

Elana cocked her head. Surely a roommate of Jackson's would be doing better than this? The house was no more than a two-bedroom, cement box with a dirt drive and no garage.

In the yard, a lanky teenager threw a ball to a fleet German shepherd. The dog noticed them first, causing the boy to turn to stare.

"Is that his son?" she asked.

Jackson never took his eyes off the boy. At last, he said, "Yes." But nothing further.

The dog now sat beside the young man who paused to watch them roll slowly by.

"His car isn't here," said Jackson. "No reason to stop."

"Should we call him?"

"No. He's not here, so he's working."

She wanted to ask what he did. Nothing lucrative, obviously. The shabby home disappeared from her line of vision. It resembled the place she and Gavin had rented together. Except the landscaping. That had been perfect. A growing advertisement for what her husband could do with living things. He'd wanted his own landscaping business someday.

The sense of loss settled like a weighted blanket, and she hardly noticed as they sped away back to the highway and the city center.

This was her first political fundraiser banquet and an opportunity for Jackson to secure state funds for their town. The ticket price had made her blanch, but Jackson said it was worth every penny. She could once have paid her rent for a year with that much money, but that was the old days, before her second marriage. Before Jackson.

As they drove on, Elana began spinning her engagement ring.

"Nervous?" he asked, nodding toward her fidgeting hands.

"A little." Her clammy palms said otherwise.

"Don't be. You don't need to impress anyone but me."

That wasn't true. Jackson needed to gain the support of a state senator to get funding for their city. Her job was to help him.

And she wanted him to do well. Meet the senator and governor as he intended and make those contacts that were so vital to the health of their hometown. Elana smoothed her moist hand over the new dress that was unfortunately a pale pastel yellow and put questions about his friend, and his friend's boy, out of her mind.

Jackson was the one buying all her clothing now and she was grateful, though she secretly thought the pastels made her complexion look washed out and it meant no dark lipstick. In the month before their wedding, he'd taken her to Jacksonville on a shopping spree, buying her an entire new wardrobe, and when she'd gravitated toward the bright jewel tones, he admitted he hated those.

"Make you look like some femme fatale," he said. "Or a painted lady."

She did not equate vivid colors with prostitutes, but that *he* did was enough.

In any case, the buying spree meant discarding her old things, particularly her blue jeans, which Jackson hated.

At the time, she recalled him saying that both pants and denim were for farmers. Not his wife.

Throwing away all her "hideous" apparel had felt so freeing. A visible declaration of her leaving behind her old, tatty life of deprivation with those ragged things. But sometimes she missed the rock T-shirts she'd collected from Goodwill and her most comfortable jeans, of course.

Still, losing a few pairs of jeans and concert T-shirts that heralded a different time and place seemed a small price to pay for the lovely dresses, stylish skirts, designer blouses, and a dizzying array of accessories. A year ago, she only had one purse and one canvas tote bag, both now in the dumpster.

Now she usually carried a beautiful handbag that cost more than a month's salary at her old job.

Tonight, she carried an adorable, tiny crossbody bag that looked like a honeycomb, complete with applique bees. The compartment was large enough for her license, phone, comb, and lipstick. Jackson said she didn't need her debit card, as the meal was paid for and it was an open bar.

He'd even transferred her little stylish monogrammed tag, usually on her larger handbag, onto the narrow strap. She rubbed the smooth disc between her thumb and fingers as her husband pulled into the valet parking of the huge downtown hotel in Jacksonville.

The skyline reminded her of Orlando, and she was surprised to realize she missed the bustle of city life. Bald Cypress was charming, but tiny and remote.

She was glad she'd stopped drinking because the last thing she wanted was to be an embarrassment before so many important people. Though it would have helped with the nerves.

Her mind cast her a mental image of his second wife, Shantel, drunk and raving the night of their rehearsal dinner. The image lifted the hairs on her neck. The woman was a mess.

But who could blame her? Someone had taken her daughter. Elana could only imagine what that would do to a mother's mind.

Jackson pulled into a VIP spot close to the entrance, cut the engine, and flicked off the lights. He slipped out from behind the wheel of his fully loaded pickup truck and rounded the hood. He moved with a power and grace she found compelling. Dressed in a tailored suit and tie, he looked the picture of success. To her, he was the sexiest man alive, and she felt so darn lucky that he had chosen her. Because of him, everything had changed for her and for her daughter. Phoebe would have a good education, attend college, if she wanted, and Jackson promised to pay for her wedding.

Elana placed a hand on her flat stomach. Most women would be proud of their figure, but she was miffed she wasn't yet expecting.

She waited patiently for him to open her door and assist her out.

How lucky that she'd found someone to love her. After Gavin died, she thought she'd never find another man half as good as him. In many ways her two husbands were opposites. Gavin had laughed freely, was terrible with money, and stopped to pet every dog they ever met. He'd buy her little treats, like her favorite chocolate bars and a stretchy beaded bracelet that cost two bucks. Two bucks that they didn't have. They never had any money, and it didn't matter until Phoebe came along. Then they'd become expert yard sale shoppers and somehow got by.

Meanwhile, Jackson was successful, powerful, wealthy, and wanted a big family. Sons, lots of them, and she was glad to bring children into a world where she was safe and happy and there would be no struggle to provide for them.

She felt so lucky and smiled at Jackson, who now held out his hand to help her down. He always treated her like a lady. Some part of her loved this and another wondered if it made her feel uncomfortable, as if he thought her and women in general incapable or weak.

Silly. He was just a Southern boy, doing what his mama had taught him. It was part and parcel of his propensity to say "Yes, ma'am" and "Yes, sir" to anyone older than he was. It really was adorable.

He tucked her hand into the crook of his arm, and they walked together into the hall, pausing to speak to several people along the way.

Elana smiled as she effortlessly put names with faces,

feeling like the First Lady in her stylish dress. She was good at this. A natural extrovert, it took this evening out to recognize she missed parties and enjoyed visiting with her husband's colleagues.

Jackson wasn't tall, but there was an aura of power about him and an intensity that made him an excellent leader. People gravitated to him.

"You look very handsome in that suit," she said to him as they finally entered the hall.

The heels put her nearly at eye level with him and he gave her a warm smile at her compliment and patted her hand.

"And you, my lady, are stunning in yellow."

She secretly thought she looked like a pat of butter, but held her smile. Green would have set off her eyes. Red would have complemented her coloring. But he'd wanted yellow.

Her cheeks heated as she gazed at him. Marriage to Jackson had certainly been an adjustment.

Sometimes she had to pinch herself. Since their wedding, she'd moved from her shabby little rented bungalow into an enormous ranch house on a quiet private road. The property sat on a full acre of land, with a swimming pool. Phoebe had her own room and a play area indoors and a trampoline and tree house outside.

They both loved her new elementary school that had small class sizes, laptops for every child in the class, and a very sweet young teacher, Mrs. Fitzpatrick, who was a bundle of energy and was already planning several field trips. She'd recruited Elana as a chaperone and Jackson was pleased his new wife was engaging in community activities at school and at church.

They were the sort of charitable undertakings that helped his image as mayor and did real good for the public.

Inside, instead of heading to the table, he brought her to meet Senator Nicoletti and his wife. The senator had a full head of white hair, an engaging smile, and dark sparkling eyes.

His wife was fiftyish, with razor-straight black hair styled in a precision cut, a tanned weathered face, and was lively as a circus performer.

"Oh, so this is the new bride," said Mrs. Nicoletti. "Congratulations, my dear."

Did that mean they'd met Shantel? How did Elana compare? Shantel had appeared crazy the only time they'd met, but she was a pretty woman. She pushed down her insecurities. Now was not the time.

Elana shook hands with the senator, who was not wearing a mask. None of the guests were, despite the dire warnings from the CDC.

"So, here she is. I've heard a lot about you," said Nicoletti, turning to Jackson. "She's lovely, Jackson."

Her husband beamed and she felt several inches taller.

"We were so sorry we couldn't attend the wedding. The pandemic has made us curtail so much of our social schedule," said Mrs. Nicoletti.

Had Jackson invited them? They hadn't even invited any of her closest friends to the wedding because of the pandemic. She frowned and then forced herself to smile.

"I understand you two met in Orlando. Business conference."

"That's right. Elana was climbing the corporate ladder. Had to do some fast talking to convince her to marry me."

None of that was true. She'd been in a dead-end job and had needed no convincing to quit. But Jackson had asked her to amend a few parts of her past. He didn't want anyone here thinking she was some kind of gold digger. So, along with her new life as Mrs. Jackson Belauru, she now had a college degree in hotel management and had worked for a major hotel chain in their corporate offices.

That did seem more impressive than a staff position for the events service manager at the Orlando Convention Center.

It wasn't that he was ashamed of her modest roots, but he said they could do better.

"Yes," said Elana, uncomfortable, but ready with this reply. "We, my husband and I, were hoping to get some help with the planned industrial park back in Bald Cypress." She glanced to Jackson to see if she'd introduced the topic correctly, but his attention was on the senator.

Nicoletti smiled. "Corporate to politics, is it?" Then to Jackson. "Look out, she may run for mayor."

The two laughed as if this was funny and ridiculous. Elana held her smile, but sank a little in her shoes.

Jackson took over from there. She turned to the senator's wife at a loss. But there was no need.

Mrs. Nicoletti put Elana instantly at ease with her warmth and approachable demeanor, slipping her into a side conversation as easily as wading into warm water, seeming genuinely interested in every word and somehow steering them back into the main conversation as it drew to its natural conclusion. Then she sent them both on their way with such skill Elana hardly noticed until she was moving on and glancing back to see the senator greeting another supporter.

"She's amazing," Elana whispered, breathless now that they were heading off.

"Yes. He really picked a good one."

She cocked her head at the odd way of describing the senator's wife. She supposed you did pick a wife, but he made it sound like a cattle auction.

That thought made her smile.

Jackson gave her hand a little squeeze.

"So did I." He lifted her hand for a kiss.

She'd done well and he was pleased. Relief mingled with pride.

The only dark spot in her self-satisfaction was the lie about her background. Lying troubled her. She was terrible at it, for one thing. Jackson had commented early on that her face turned pink when she tried to pull off even a white lie. It was just a small thing, her work history. But the college degree, that seemed a bigger one.

Jackson said that since she wouldn't be working outside the home, claiming to have a degree and a career wouldn't hurt anyone—except maybe herself, she thought. And he wanted the citizens of Bald Cypress to respect her, in her own right. His insistence, and the very fact that he thought this necessary, made her feel as if she wasn't quite enough. Not educated enough or successful enough.

He didn't want her working in a traditional job. He had made that very clear before they wed. She didn't argue. Being able to be home when Phoebe returned from school seemed such a luxury, she felt very lucky. And leaving the afterschool keeper programs pleased both her and her daughter.

Your job is supporting mine, raising our daughter and any other children we are blessed with.

It wasn't until after they were married and she'd seen their new home that she truly comprehended just how wealthy Jackson's family was. She didn't know the exact figure because he didn't talk about the family trust he ran and she only kept the household accounts, while he did the earning, planning, and investing. But her sister-in-law had let it slip that Jackson's dad was a billionaire and she knew that her husband had purchased the seventy-four-foot tournament-ready fishing boat for one and a half million dollars, using just the profits from his stock market gains.

She couldn't conceive of a fishing boat worth that much, but she'd see it in the summer when they all traveled to North Carolina for a big game fishing tournament.

The MC stepped to the podium and asked the gathering to find their seats. Jackson took her to a place right up front at the senator's table. She was certain that cost extra.

Worth it? She didn't really know.

Jackson took the spot next to the senator, and she was seated beside a party official, a lank scarecrow of a man with a goatee that did not adequately disguise his cleft lip or bad front tooth. The brown stump reminded her of a rotting log, which he likely realized as he mostly kept his lips closed when smiling.

Never in a million years had she pictured a world where she sat at a table with a state senator. She felt like Cinderella hours before midnight and the thought made her smile. The happiness seemed to bubble up inside her like hot water in a kettle.

Elana placed her napkin on her lap. The salad, water, sweet tea, and dinner roll were already in place. She eyed the golden bun, but the butter, pressed into teaspoon-sized roses, was well out of reach. Before her was a large, glistening slice of chocolate cake.

Darn it. She loved chocolate, but it gave Jackson hives. If she ate it, he'd still get hives. He'd explained his sensitivity. Even brushing her teeth wouldn't help.

As a result, she hadn't had a piece of chocolate since before the wedding. And she missed it. That cake just seemed like an unfair temptation.

But Jackson got the waiter to take theirs away. She watched it disappear with the longing of a lover catching a glimpse of her departing beau.

The man beside her drew her attention back to her duties.

"It's so nice to finally meet you. Sawyer was right, you are a beauty."

She dropped her gaze and flushed. When she glanced up, she caught him staring at her breasts and wondered what her brother-in-law had really said. Since she turned fourteen, she'd heard all the jokes about her large chest and the comparisons to Dolly Parton. No one ever talked about how hard it was to find clothing that fit. If the top were sized correctly, the bottom swam on her and vice versa. No one ever mentioned the deep angry red marks left by the support bra scaffolding holding her breasts or the backaches she experienced from the weight.

"How long have you two known each other?"

Her smile flickered, like a light bulb in need of replacing.

"Nearly two years."

Jackson suggested that the whirlwind courtship might give people the wrong idea. He said that people drew unfair conclusions when they saw a beautiful young woman marry a successful older man. He wasn't that much older, only seven years. At thirty-five, he certainly wasn't old.

The last thing she wanted was to start off on the wrong foot.

"We met at a business conference," she said, repeating the lie as her hands repetitively smoothed the napkin on her lap as if stroking a pet cat.

The dinner was delicious and the speeches overly long. She tried not to salivate as she watched the senator's wife scoop the chocolate ganache from her slice of cake and pop it in her mouth.

By the time she finished her coffee her bladder needed relief.

Finally, the MC thanked them for attending and supporting the party ticket. Jackson helped her with her chair.

The night had been a rousing success. Every ticket sold, funds collected, and the party enlivened to the issues of the day.

She leaned in and whispered, "I've got to visit the ladies' room."

Jackson frowned and shook his head. "We're heading home."

That was well over an hour from this hotel. Her smile was more of a wince. "I really need to go."

Jackson turned to face her. When he spoke, his voice now held a sharp edge.

"I don't want my wife sitting on those dirty toilets. Who knows who has used them tonight?"

Was he teasing her? But the pinched lips and frown told her he was serious.

"Jackson, please."

She had meant her words as a light reproach. As in "Oh, please, you can't be serious." But she realized as he shook his head, denying her, that he had interpreted her words as an entreat.

She gaped. Had he just refused to let her go to the bathroom?

Her bladder pushed against the constraining garment giving her a sharp shaft of discomfort. The urge was all she could think of.

She glanced toward the exit and saw many other women hustling toward the restrooms.

He'd shown no germaphobia before this. Did he really think using a public toilet would somehow make her unclean?

"When we get home," he said, drawing her attention away from the bathrooms.

"No, Jackson. I can't wait."

Now his brows sank dangerously over his stormy gaze.

"My wife is *not* using a public toilet."

"Then we need to go home now."

He nodded, seeming to acquiesce, but then paused to speak to several of the gathering before finally bringing her to his custom Super Duty truck.

Climbing up into the vehicle caused her physical pain. She jiggled her legs in a vain effort to distract from the growing agony.

"Oh, sit still, Elana. You're not a child."

She pressed her lips tight, resisting the urge to cry. His treating her like a child made her feel like one.

Why was he doing this?

TEN

NOW

June 21, 2022, Tuesday—after midnight
Poseidon Offshore Open, Culpepper Inlet, NC

Desperately pushing through the water, Elana stared at Jackson's boat, now two hundred yards back. It seemed as if the anchored vessel was moving away from her, instead of the other way around. In a panic, she tried and failed to close the distance to safety.

The current was stronger, and the water colder than she'd expected. Cold and black. The light chop she'd seen from the deck now came in waves that lifted and dropped her back into the furrows. She was an unmoored float, cast about. Keeping the spray out of her mouth challenged and terrified. Already the salt water stole her heat away, making her fingers and toes tingle.

What had she been thinking? She'd never be able to keep her head above water until help came.

Phoebe needed her.

And she'd left the damned lights on.

With all her might, she swam toward the boat, kicking and

pulling with everything she had. Her mind raced with her beating legs and rotating arms.

He'd know. But no one else would. She could say he'd flicked on the lights earlier in the evening. If he survived, he'd know. They'd gone out to look at the stars, brilliant sparks of fire in the velvet sky. But the underwater lights would interfere with viewing. They'd left them off and Jackson, whatever his faults, had a very keen memory for detail. But if he drowned, then he couldn't contradict her.

She lifted her head to check her progress. The boat was the same distance from her as when she'd begun her return trip.

All she had managed was to expend useless energy to stay in one place. The moment she stopped kicking, the current dragged her away again. Her efforts accomplished nothing.

Elana stopped swimming and let the tide take her. The water dragged her along with a primitive power that awed and terrified. Keeping her head above the unpredictable waves took constant effort and despite her ability, she caught several choking mouthfuls of seawater.

Now she tread in both the water and her doubts, her dive from the boat looking more and more like a mistake with each passing minute. Was she really prepared for the marathon ahead?

She could not return to the boat. Some actions could not be reversed. You just had to deal with the consequences. Now she resumed swimming, changing from the crawl to a relaxed breaststroke as she cut across the current in easy, measured strokes, making for the shore. But as she swam, she discovered another harsh reality. The tide was carrying her away from the glimmering lights and toward the channel leaving to the open sea.

Panic beat against her breastbone as she struggled and kicked harder, trying to reach the shore. But the relentless current tugged her away.

The terror morphed into internal pleading. She begged God to help her, as if he would. At last, she stopped her useless flailing.

The current tightened its hold, sweeping her away.

Phoebe.

They'd never make it to her daughter's grandparents tomorrow. But Braden and Vic Orrick would raise her. And do an excellent job. They loved Phoebe and had missed seeing her since she'd married Jackson. Her husband had canceled the two planned trips to see them due to unforeseen circumstances and had made sure that they were away when her former in-laws visited Florida.

She'd begun to suspect he had made up the excuses just to further distance her from her daughter's only blood relatives and one of her last avenues of help. And she didn't wonder anymore. They were, and he had.

She slowed her swimming stroke again, easing back into the water.

It was hard to admit, but Phoebe would be better away from Jackson, even if it meant losing her mother.

A sacrifice, and Elana should be glad to make it. There would be no questions to answer if she drowned.

The temptation of that eventuality was so strong it almost dragged her down. There would be no police interview. No lies to tell. No Jackson to face. For the first time, her head dipped below the surface of the water.

No, Phoebe needed her mother. If she survived, they might both be free of him. And if he survived, she needed to be here.

She kicked, rising.

There was no retreat, and the possibility of rescue was hours away. They were supposed to be out overnight. Nobody would realize they were missing until sometime tomorrow.

She could not go back. She would survive or drown. As long as Jackson died at sea, she could accept either outcome.

She broke the surface, gasping and sputtering, still dragged along by the current, helpless as a jellyfish. Where she went was not up to her.

Elana changed tactics. She no longer swam. Conserving her strength, she floated along with the meagerest of kicks. The fishing boats would be out before dawn. Then, perhaps she had a chance of rescue.

Jackson was more muscular than she. Muscle sank in water. If she were struggling, surely Jackson was dead.

Please let him be dead.

Elana watched the lights from the hotels on the beach twinkling. The water was seventy-six degrees. That did not sound cold; in fact, she'd thought it refreshing when she and Phoebe had taken a dip in the inlet just yesterday. But now, only a few minutes after entering the water, she shivered.

She had not realized how quickly the cold would make her limbs clumsy.

A flash of light caught her attention. She spun to see the storm clouds, briefly illuminated against the sky. A chilly wind blew across the water, forewarning of the impending storm.

She recognized the signs. Soon the thunderstorm would be upon her, churning the water and summoning the wind.

Spinning again, she looked back, but could not see her husband's boat.

And then she saw something even more terrifying. A red light.

The channel markers! The tide was dragging her out to the open ocean.

She had become a leaf swept along the gutter, carried toward the storm drain.

Only her storm drain was the Atlantic. The gray, mighty, churning, merciless Atlantic.

Minutes passed and she had the sense of how tiny and insignificant she must look in this giant stream of seawater. She counted the markers until there were no more. The channel acted like a riptide, sweeping her out with dizzying speed to the open ocean and then releasing her to the rolling waves.

Elana concentrated on keeping her head above the shifting surface.

The shivering made it hard to breathe, as if some constricting corset cinched about her torso squeezing the air from her lungs. She dragged each shuddering gulp of oxygen through her windpipe, raw now from the burning sting of salt water. A whimper escaped Elana as she realized that soon the choice of living or dying would no longer be hers.

Her strength was gone. Her body did not obey her mind and the water washed over her head yet again.

The shivering grew worse, so she swept her arms out and back, bicycling with her legs to bring some warmth back to her limbs. The clattering of her teeth gradually slowed, but her muscles ached, weary and heavy as cast-iron. This drove her to stop her flailing and kicking and soon the shivering made her teeth chatter again.

That was when the first raindrops hit her in the face. Initially, she found the fresh water a godsend. She opened her mouth, trying to catch a few drops of the life-giving fluid to ease her dry mouth and throat. But the droplets kept falling, harder, faster. Stinging needles of pain struck her skin. She tipped her head down, now trying to keep the rain out of her airway. Breathing became a struggle. She flailed, trying to get her head farther out of the water, trying to shield her nose and mouth from the torrent of water pouring down in curtains.

Perhaps, she thought, she wouldn't survive another minute.

But she did. And the one after that. Then, as if some power beyond her understanding flipped some switch, the rain ceased. But she couldn't catch her breath. Exhaustion swamped her.

It was in those dark hours, before the hint of light leached into the eastern sky, that she realized why she had jumped into the sea.

She couldn't face the questions of the police, explaining to Jackson's brothers, or even the possibility of returning to a marriage to Jackson.

She hadn't jumped in a selfless act of sacrifice, martyring herself for her daughter's benefit. She had jumped from fear. An act of desperation by a coward. Afraid to stay with her husband and afraid to run. Afraid he had killed those missing little girls and afraid to tell anyone.

In that moment, when death was so close that it brushed against her in the cold, unforgiving sea, she decided. She would be a coward no longer. She might be afraid, but it would not keep her from finding a way to be free of Jackson.

Her resolve reinvigorated. She didn't feel cold.

The predawn light cast the wispy clouds in deep purple. By slow degrees, the color changed to pink, then apricot. When the beams of sunlight broke on the horizon, she could see only water.

How long before someone found the boat empty? And then, how much longer before they initiated a search?

When the sun finally broke the horizon, she was cursing the dazzling light. Her eyes burned from the saltwater and the blinding yellow-white glare. She was cold and hot at once, feeling her face burning, the seawater chafing away her skin and the thirst growing intolerable.

Where was Jackson now?

Dragging across the bottom, if there's any justice in the world.

A man who loved to fish would appreciate the irony of a fisherman feeding the fishes.

Elana caught glimpses of a fishing boat as she rose on the crest of a wave, then fell, sinking into endless valleys of the open

Atlantic Ocean. Unfortunately, they were far away from her current position.

Her stomach pitched as her body tumbled into the troth and then was swept up onto the crest of another swell.

They had to see her. She desperately tore a scrap of hot-pink fabric from her remaining overskirt of the ruined dress and tried to wave it above her head.

Her shivering was more spasm now and her limbs, flailing, uncooperative things. They seemed to belong to someone else because they no longer responded to her commands.

She was close enough to see men on one of the fishing boats.

Did they see her?

She waved harder, sucked in seawater, and choked. The wave rolled on, dropping her. She couldn't breathe and sank again, realizing she was going to drown within sight of rescue.

ELEVEN

THEN

December 2021, six months ago

Jackson set aside his empty coffee mug and glanced to Elana.

They sat at the dining room table crafted from Dade County pine heartwood, finishing breakfast beneath the antler chandelier. The elaborate light fixture looked like a weapon, but Jackson assured her that the support chain was sturdy, and it would hold.

Elana had her back to the living room with its magnificent fieldstone fireplace, cathedral ceiling, rustic hide rugs, and many mounted hunting trophies. She didn't particularly like the taxidermy creatures, which was why she sat facing away from the ducks flapping from the walls and side tables and the detached heads of buffalo, pronghorn, deer, and elk who seemed to follow her with glassy, reproachful eyes.

The worst was the bobcat that Jackson had taken on a hunting trip with Sawyer right here in Florida, and that now sat on the hand-hewn log mantel poised on a rocky outcropping. Though Jackson and his dogs gave it no notice, both she and Phoebe made obvious efforts to avoid its critical gaze.

She did, however, love the comfortable leather sofas, sheep-skin hides, beautiful Navajo rugs and pillows of the two-story, five-bedroom, ranch-style home. The combination of rugged architecture and rustic furnishings made her feel like she lived in a Western movie set or in some faraway mountain range in Wyoming.

"You sure you're okay driving there and back alone?" asked Jackson.

"We'll be fine."

Funny, this morning was the first time she and her daughter would have an outing alone together since before the wedding. Phoebe was on the winter break that would stretch until after New Year's and Elana was looking forward to spending more time with her daughter in this fun, festive season.

"You be careful."

"We will."

"What time will you be home?" asked Jackson.

"We meet the designer at ten and it's an hour back. So, I'd expect we'd be here for lunch."

The designer! He had hired a designer just to help her choose Phoebe's Christmas gift, an entire new suite of furniture for her bedroom.

Her husband was so generous. Such a good man, always looking out for them.

So why, with all that she now had, did she imagine Gavin when Jackson touched her?

She didn't like to dwell on it, but their lovemaking was better, when she just remembered what it felt like to be with Gavin.

After his accident, Gavin had been in intensive care for nearly a week. At the time, all she could think about was that this could not be happening. Not to him. Not to them.

How could her beautiful, funny, and sweet husband have been lying there, his skin chilled and his face slack? He needed to open his eyes and call Phoebe his honeybee and then tell her one of his awful "dad" jokes.

He needed to cup her face and tell her, as he had so many times, that everything would be all right.

She'd tried to convince herself that he'd wake up. Any moment, God would give him back to her. He'd open those beautiful blue eyes, spot her, and smile and ask her what a place like this was doing in a girl like her.

Then she'd know that they'd be okay. Because the thought of losing the man she loved was like losing a piece of her own soul.

But God hadn't given him back. Gavin's stubborn heart still beat, unaware that his brain had died the moment of the accident. He never opened those blue eyes and when she said goodbye, he didn't hear her because he was already gone. Not a coma.

Brain dead. Alive, but gone.

Modern medicine giving her false hope. She hadn't wanted a world without him.

Then she thought of their daughter and she knew what he'd expect. She'd signed the organ donor papers and hoped that some part of him, like that strong beating heart, would live on.

"I'll take care of her, Gavin. I will."

The outstanding medical bills had been insurmountable. It was like being waterboarded, that feeling of drowning and being unable to draw a breath. The wet blanket of debt suffocated.

The interest payments on the credit cards she'd used to handle the hospital bills just kept adding to what she owed until she couldn't even keep up with the interest.

Before the accident, Gavin had a job with the county public works as an equipment operator. He had regular hours and benefits. Medical insurance, too, though not as good as they had believed. It didn't cover everything.

His death had crushed her and set a bomb off in their

finances, sending them into debt. What twenty-four-year-old had a will and insurance?

Bankruptcy seemed the only way out. And then she'd met Jackson.

He'd paid off her debts before they were even married.

A man who could afford a million-dollar fishing boat had no trouble raising the twelve thousand that had seemed insurmountable to her.

His arrival in her life had been a godsend.

"Hi there. Do you work here?"

The name tag pinned on her ample chest indicated she did.

"Yes."

Instead of looking at her breasts, he looked at her left hand.

"Married?"

"Widowed." It felt so strange to say that.

"Oh, I'm so sorry." He seemed genuine.

"Thank you."

"How long ago did he pass?"

She'd told him, felt like she could tell him anything, everything. He was so interested in her, and she'd agreed to meet him for coffee before work. Then she'd agreed to meet him for dinner after work, takeout at her place, where he met Phoebe, who was uncharacteristically quiet. But she'd warmed up. They both had.

She'd gone from nearly losing everything to the sort of lifestyle she'd seen only on television. Private club memberships, holiday celebrations with his family, and being home with her daughter. It was all like a wonderful dream.

Elana was blissfully happy. Certainly, there were adjustments, some little foibles that she and Jackson had to sort out.

Jackson stood and she collected his dirty plate. He leaned to kiss her cheek.

"That was wonderful. Thank you, darlin'."

She beamed up at him.

"Remember, I'll be home late," he said. "Common council meeting tonight."

He left the table, leaving Elana to clean up the breakfast dishes and gather her things. Then she called Phoebe, who skipped into the kitchen, eyes bright and eager for their adventure.

At her SUV, he made sure Phoebe was strapped into her car seat and that she had not forgotten her bag or phone.

He was so thoughtful. She gave him a kiss and they were off.

Their first stop was a furniture store. This purchase did not need his okay, because Jackson said he didn't care what she and Phoebe picked for their daughter's room, as long as his designer green-lighted her selections. This was not Phoebe's only Christmas gift, but the bedroom set would be the largest.

Up until now, the furniture in her daughter's room consisted of an old dresser, mismatched side table, a horseshoe table lamp, and a twin bed on the cheapest frame imaginable.

At the furniture store, they met Gabby, their designer, who had fine, feathery blond hair, overlarge glasses, minimal makeup, and dressed in gauzy loose clothing accented with chunky jewelry big enough to double as body armor.

The woman led the way to the children's furniture.

"The inventory is not what I'd like. But there are shortages. No one wants to wait six months for their purchases, so I'm afraid there are only three in stock."

They moved from one option to the next, pausing at the final set.

"What do you think, darling?" said Elana to Phoebe.

Phoebe turned from one to the other.

"I'd recommend this final set. The bed can be later raised, and a desk unit placed below." Gabby motioned to the same set displayed in the mentioned arrangement. "Better for when she reaches secondary school."

"This one okay?" said Elana to her daughter, who nodded.

"My favorite color is red," said Phoebe.

Gabby frowned and gave her head a little shake. "Oh, sweetie, your new daddy specifically asked for only pastels. So... Pink?"

Phoebe wrinkled her nose and then looked to Elana who gave her daughter an apologetic look.

Gabby waved a hand. "Plenty of reds in the living room, along with the natural hides and antler."

Elana lowered her voice to speak to Phoebe. "He's buying this for you."

"So, I can't pick it out?" asked Phoebe.

Gabby took that one. "The furniture will be white. The accents can be any of these." She opened a book of swatches all looking like a box of macarons.

"Then white, I guess," said Phoebe.

"Well, that would be too much white." Gabby forced a tight smile. "What about this?"

She pointed an elegant finger tipped with a glossy blue nail to a pale green swatch.

Phoebe kept her chin down and nodded.

"Lovely. Curtains and bedspread in Mello Mint. Moving on."

A tiny piece of Elana's heart broke. Clearly, Phoebe was trying to please the designer and her mother and Jackson, instead of herself.

But it was Jackson's money and his gift to his stepdaughter.

Gabby steered Phoebe to pick the complete bedroom set that included bed, dresser, nightstand. All white with mint accents.

After making the purchase, Elana worried that her daughter would outgrow the white as she aged. But it was too late for second-guessing. She wished Jackson had allowed a bit more leeway on the color scheme.

"You need a lamp."

They found one for her bedside table that looked like a cheerleader's pom-pom for a pastel-themed high school, the Mello Mint Mustangs.

"Done," Gabby said to them. "The pieces are all in stock, which is a miracle, what with the supply chain issues. But your husband was very specific. Nothing that was not currently on hand. Limiting, but wise. I'll let you know about delivery as soon as I have the information."

Gabby waved and headed off toward the back of the show-room and out of sight.

Elana turned to Phoebe. "Where to now?"

"Bookstore?"

"For books or because they have cake pops in the coffee shop?"

"Books, Momma."

"Okay. Just one."

In the bookstore, she helped Phoebe pick out a picture book and then looked at several others, wondering if Zoey's kids might like any of them. She had seen Zoey's boys, Parker and Levy, wrestling, breaking things, or playing video games. What she had never seen them do was read.

Elana and Phoebe wandered out of the children's area, past the new releases and finally the gift section. Elana paused, finding a mug covered with images of various game fish. Billfish, Jackson called them, a specific class of fish, including marlin, swordfish, and she didn't know what else. He might like this.

They had already done their Christmas shopping together. Jackson liked to select his own gifts and she had done the same. That way, he said, they both got something they really wanted.

She'd selected new cookware for the kitchen and some small appliances. He'd chosen some special fishing reel that she never, in a million years, could have picked out.

Her husband was a fishing nut. Every free minute he was

out in the bass boat on the lake with Sawyer and sometimes with Derek, when his younger brother's shifts as a patrolman allowed. Jackson had the much larger boat docked in a marina in Destin. The three of them had begun preparing for some big annual championship in North Carolina. Jackson and his brothers took their entire families every June. According to her husband, the Poseidon Offshore Open in Culpepper, North Carolina, was the event of the season.

She replaced the display mug and selected one that came in a box, then moved to the magazines, flipping through various ones on country living as Phoebe stayed close by. Then she moved to the hobbies magazines and spotted one on fishing.

Jackson loved freshwater fishing nearly as much as open water. That was why their new home was on a large natural lake with a dock, so he could go out bass fishing whenever he had an hour or two.

Over the holiday, he'd have more free time. Her husband worked very hard, but rarely on Saturday and never on Sunday. He insisted they all attend church. Zoey had convinced Elana to help with the church school. Her sister-in-law worked with the minister on couple counseling and other various charitable endeavors. She also ran the summer Bible camp.

Before they reached the register, Phoebe had her hands on two more items, a children's nature magazine and a coloring book about fish. Elana wondered if it was worth the trouble to fight with her about the items she'd picked.

"It's reading," said Phoebe, sensing her mother's reticence.

"You should be a politician," said Elana.

"Like Daddy," she grinned, savoring her win. "This one is for him." Phoebe held up the coloring book on fish, waiting for her mother's approval, but preparing for objections. "For Christmas," she added.

Phoebe usually tried begging before she escalated to anger.

Her daughter was often more like a middle schooler than a second grader.

Elana already dreaded the teen years.

"Hand them over."

Phoebe did so with an excited little bounce at her victory. Elana gathered the purchases, checked out, and then turned to Phoebe. "I'm starving. How about some lunch?"

"Pizza!"

On a previous visit to the Pensacola area, they had discovered a shop that had a brick oven and today seemed the perfect time to try out the place.

At the restaurant, they chose a table by the window in a busy shopping plaza because Elana liked to people watch. The small community of Bald Cypress had its advantages, but she missed the buzz and blur of constant motion.

Phoebe had slipped one of her purchases out of the bag and now had her nose stuck in the nature magazine. Elana smiled. Her daughter had been right. It was reading.

Behind her, the television mounted high in the corner showed the news at noon logo. The sound had been turned off, but the subtitles were on allowing Elana to check the top stories.

The lead was tragic, which was par for the course. She read the scroll as images flashed by of police vehicles, on scene reporters, anxious neighbors, and firemen aiming hoses at a house completely ablaze.

The owner was not at home.

Elana glanced to her daughter and then out the window. When she looked back to the scroll, she gaped.

...cause yet undetermined. Homeowner, Shantel Keen, was detained for questioning regarding Friday's suspicious blaze.

Shantel.

Her mind flashed an image of the crazed woman who had

once trapped her in an upstairs bedroom. It wasn't a common name. Could this be Jackson's second ex-wife? Elana didn't know her last name.

"It's not her house," she whispered.

"What, Momma?" asked Phoebe, her attention now on her mother.

Elana forced a smile. "I'm starved. Where's that pizza?"

Her daughter set aside the magazine. "I'll go see."

Phoebe skipped to the counter and Elana's gaze flashed to the screen.

The video rolled of the homeowner, hand raised as she tried and failed to avoid the cameras. Elana thumped back in her seat.

That was the woman who had accosted her the night before her wedding. There was no doubt in her mind.

The woman suspected of burning down her own house was Shantel Belauru, or she had been once.

"Oh my God." Elana pressed her fingertips to her mouth as her body tingled with apprehension. She remembered Shantel's words.

He's a monster.

If she had set her own house ablaze, it proved everything Jackson and his family had said was true. Shantel *was* crazy.

She needed to tell Jackson.

That prospect had her fingertips sliding upward to cover her ears. She didn't want to.

But she should. Shouldn't she? After all, Jackson had nothing to do with the fire.

Of course not. The notion was ridiculous.

But the seed was planted. Jackson and his brother, Sawyer, had been gone Thursday and Friday buying an engine for the smaller fishing boat. Somewhere in Louisiana, they'd said.

Phoebe returned at a skip. "Five minutes," she reported and slipped into her seat.

"Oh, good." Her voice had a high, hysterical ring.

Phoebe pulled some napkins from the dispenser and then focused on her soft drink, a special treat for a special occasion.

Elana glanced at the television, but the story was gone as they moved to the release of wastewater from one of the leaking retaining pools of a phosphorous mine into the waters of the Gulf of Mexico.

She reached for her phone, planning to pull up the story online. But she froze, the device clutched in her cold, sweating hand.

What had Shantel said to her about her phone?

She'd said Jackson would get her a new phone. And he had.

It's got tracing software installed. He can see who you call, who you email, and track you with GPS.

She hadn't thought about those words since she'd heard them months ago. But now they rose with startling clarity.

If he could do all that, could he also see her search history?

She shook her head at the ridiculousness of her train of thoughts. She hadn't had any notions like this the whole time they'd been married. It was just seeing Shantel's name like that; it had made her twitchy. But she dropped the phone back in her bag. She'd need to check the news again. Maybe the five o'clock because Jackson would not be home until after his meeting.

This was stupid. Of course, Jackson had nothing to do with the blaze. What did she think—that Jackson and his brother had gone to Shantel's house and set it on fire? Jackson was their mayor. His brother was town council president, and his little brother was a cop, for goodness' sakes.

All his family did was public service and law enforcement. And Shantel had been crazy. Jealous. An alcoholic. It was sad that Shantel had felt she wanted to destroy Elana and Jackson's life together. And so sad that her daughter was missing.

"Pizza's here!" called Phoebe. "Can I have one, please?"

Elana mechanically delivered the slice from the metal tray onto a paper plate.

"Don't burn your mouth."

She wasn't going to think about this anymore.

But she did. All the way home. When they pulled into the drive, Jackson surprised them, back early from work and standing in the garage beside his truck as the door lifted.

She forced a smile, feeling unsettled at hearing about the fire. But it was good to be home safe. Should she tell Jackson?

No, that was not her job and she would not put that woman between them.

He waved as she rolled to a stop. Jackson opened the door for Phoebe, who slipped from the rear car seat carrying her purchases. Elana left the bag with the mug and magazine in the car, tucked in the wheel well beside her feet.

"You two have fun?" he asked her daughter.

"We had pizza!"

"Yes, I know, and a soda?"

Elana's smile faltered and the unease danced over her skin like the legs of a spider. But she brushed it off. He must have simply been checking the bank account on his phone and noticed what they'd ordered.

Elana left the vehicle and came to stand beside Phoebe, her protective instincts raised, though she didn't understand why.

"Bad for your teeth. You go brush them. Okay?"

Her daughter hesitated, holding her bag from the bookstore against her chest.

"Let's have a look at what you got."

Phoebe cast her mother a glance over her shoulder, brow furrowed. This was different. Her stepdad had never taken an interest in her books before and they borrowed books every week from the little town library.

Elana offered a forced smile and nodded. Phoebe turned over the bag and Jackson made a big show of asking her about the nature magazine, then lingered over the coloring book about fish. But she noticed he scanned for the price of each item.

"That one was supposed to be a surprise," said Phoebe, her voice hollow with regret.

"More like a secret, I think," he said.

Elana watched him, wondering why his actions disturbed her so. He was taking an interest in Phoebe. That was all.

He returned their purchase to the bag, dropping each separately so they made a sound striking the bottom. Then he handed them to Phoebe.

"Go up now," he said, giving the girl's shoulder a little push.

Phoebe took only one step, cradling the bag, then looked to her mother.

Elana nodded and she hurried away, seeming anxious to be gone.

Jackson lowered the garage door, setting off the hysterical barking from inside the house.

Phoebe paused at the top of the fourth step from the garage to the laundry room, hand on the knob, and glanced back at them.

"Don't let the dogs down here," he called after her.

Phoebe glanced to her mother; her expression registered worry, but the girl somehow managed to keep all three hounds inside before shutting the door.

Jackson waited as the sound of the dogs' scrambling toenails on the tiles receded and then turned to her. The stormy look he gave her told her that something was very wrong.

Was this about Shantel?

The high color in his face and the set of his jaw both set off alarm bells. She retreated a step, her hand going to her throat.

"Where's the rest of it?" he asked.

"What?"

"The rest of whatever you bought."

"Jackson, I don't—"

He cut her off, raising his voice, shouting in a tone and volume she had never heard.

"Don't lie to me!" Here he dropped his voice, and she found the menace even more chilling. "The book was nine ninety-nine. The magazines were seven ninety-nine each. With sales tax that's twenty-seven dollars and seventy-eight cents. But you spent thirty-eight dollars and forty-eight cents. So you bought something else. Didn't you?"

"Jackson, it's nothing."

"It's not, because your hands are empty. You're hiding something. Ten dollars and seventy cents' worth."

"Calm down. I'll get it."

"You told me you'd never do this. But you're doing it. Just like her. Lying! Hiding things in the trunk so I wouldn't see. She nearly bankrupted us."

Elana had heard the story. His second wife's spending now seemed the stuff of legends.

She tried for a calm tone, but her voice quavered.

"Jackson, it's only ten dollars."

"It's a lie. You swore to me. You swore to God that you wouldn't do this. That we'd be honest. Furniture for Phoebe. Not a pizza party and shopping at the bookstore. God! I thought I could trust you. That you'd be different. But you're just like her. Ringing up debt. Expecting me to bail you out."

"I didn't know we'd be gone so long. We were hungry and—"

"No more excuses. Give me whatever the hell it is right now."

Elana hurried around the car and collected the plastic bag. He snatched it from her hands.

"Hidden under your seat. I knew it!"

He was going to feel mighty foolish when he saw that this was a Christmas present for him.

"I just wanted to surprise you."

"No, you wanted to hurt me. Otherwise, you would do as I asked."

He reached in the bag and drew out the mug.

"It's for Christmas. I wanted you to have something that I picked out." She tried and failed to hold her smile, hands clasped before her in a mockery of prayer.

She felt shaky as a dead leaf clinging to a branch. Sweat beaded on her upper lip.

Jackson hoisted the box and flung it against the cement wall. The box hit so hard she heard the pieces inside explode on impact.

"I'll never be able to look at it without feeling betrayal. I can't believe you did this to me, to us."

Elana blinked, hardly trusting her eyes. Had she expected an apology? Yes. She really had. Or that he'd laugh or flush and say he felt foolish.

But this was escalating, and her heart now tumbled in her chest. He'd shut the door, trapping her. A glance to the stairs to the house showed them impossibly far. But the urge to flee continued to charge through her.

The house offered no escape. And her daughter was there. Whatever this was, she needed to face it here, alone.

He tore the fishing magazine in half. Not down the spine, but across the middle. The power of those hands terrified. He had nothing left but the fragile plastic bag that he crumpled in his fist.

"I'm sorry, Jackson. I didn't think—"

He didn't let her finish. Instead, he grasped her jaw with his free hand in a painful grip.

"That's right. Finally! You didn't think. We have rules in this marriage. I follow them and so do you. Not sometimes. Always. You don't get a break for the holidays."

"Yes. Jackson, you're hurting me."

He lowered his chin and loomed, only an inch from her

face. She could see the red veins in his eyes as he spoke through clenched teeth.

"Do you understand?"

"I do! I'm sorry." She was crying now, the tears coursing down her cheeks and her nose running. The tears shamed her, burning along her neck as she stood like a naughty child. The anger flared, but she stomped it down. Lashing out was the wrong move here. She felt that instinctually.

He held her there a moment longer. Then he released her with a thrust that sent her stumbling back against the side panel of the vehicle.

"Good. Now get inside."

The only time he'd ever spoken to her like this was when he wouldn't let her use the bathroom at the political fundraiser. She hated being treated as if she were a teenager breaking curfew. The humiliation at his words prickled like a fist full of nettles and that push made her gasp for breath. She didn't stop in the kitchen, but hurried to the main bedroom.

Only after retreating to this sanctuary, did she realize her mistake. He followed her, of course. And now he loomed in the bedroom door, as if deciding what to do next.

He's a monster. Shantel's words now held more merit.

The tears turned to sobs, making her shoulders shake.

"Here come the waterworks. I'll bet they worked on Gavin."

He'd never thrown her deceased husband's name into their marriage before. In fact, this was their first fight.

It's not a fight if he's the only one yelling, she thought.

Now she watched him glower and wondered if she was in physical danger. Gavin had never laid a finger on her. And every fight they'd had was over quickly and mutually.

This felt one-sided. More attack than disagreement.

She resisted the impulse to lift her hand to the bruised flesh on her throbbing jaw.

He cast a heavy sigh and then took one menacing step

toward her. Somehow, she kept from scuttling away like a frightened crab. Holding her ground was difficult, especially when he sat beside her on the bed and gathered her in his arms.

He was suddenly a stranger.

Did she know this man at all?

"I'm sorry I broke the mug, Elana. I was just so mad. I told you all about Shantel and her overspending," he said. "The drinking..."

She wanted to grumble that it was just thirty dollars. Instead, she rested her head on his chest and allowed him to cradle her in his arms. He rocked her like a child, and she closed her eyes, knowing that nothing and everything had changed. She felt dirty, debased, and still infuriated. But she remained still and said not a word in anger or defense.

Because now he frightened her. She'd never been afraid of him before.

"For a minute I just went back there. Finding the bills she'd been hiding. Kept them in a designer bag she only used when she was out without me. I couldn't trust her alone or even in the house. As long as she had that computer, she was shopping. It was an addiction for her."

Her heart swelled for him as he stroked her hair. Had his second marriage so damaged him, so broken his faith in women? If his last wife abused his trust, she had given him a very legitimate reason to be suspicious. Now she was angry at Shantel for making him like this. So unreasonable. This was absurd.

"I'm not her, Jackson."

"But you acted like her." Now his words were crisp and frosty.

"I need you to understand. To promise me. No detours. No lies about purchases. No more deception."

"I've never deceived you."

He gave her a look of such heartbreak. "You just did."

"It was a simple gift."

"It was a betrayal."

She gaped. His reaction was so surreal and disproportionate. His serious expression told her that he didn't think so.

"I saw that bag you hid in the car, and it all came rushing back. The lies. The debt. Her deception. I'm just so scared to go there again."

He was scared?

She pulled back.

Had this all been because of Shantel and not her? Had he really just been frightened? It seemed more like rage.

Perhaps this was some weird relationship flashback for him.

She held his hand and smiled, feeling slightly relieved, but still jittery inside, as if her stomach were filled with bugs.

But she lifted her chin and admitted her own feelings to her husband.

"Jackson, you frightened me."

"Maybe it will stop you from doing something as stupid as this ever again. No unapproved purchases. Do you understand?"

Now all she could think of was how grateful she was that she hadn't searched the story about Shantel on her phone.

She might have broken his trust today. But he'd broken something worse.

"You won't," he said, his words more pronouncement than query.

She shook her head.

Most couples surprised each other on Christmas. Sometimes they went too far and spent too much. That was normal. Wasn't it?

"I can't stomach this," he said. "So no surprises. Not at Christmas or Valentine's Day or my birthday. You can buy whatever you want for you or for Phoebe... if I know about it first."

Was the request that unreasonable? It didn't feel unreasonable, but his reaction certainly had been.

She needed to make this right.

"Yes, yes. Of course. I'm so sorry."

His entire demeanor changed. The frown lines at his forehead eased. The crow's feet at his eyes reappeared with his smile.

He blew away a breath in relief. Everything about him now seemed benign, normal.

She almost felt wobbly from the rapid transformation.

"Oh, thank goodness!" he said, relief evident as his shoulders dropped. "For a minute it was like Shantel all over again, her lies, the credit card debt. I thought you understood. I thought you were all right with us making all purchasing decisions together."

Obviously, he still carried the scars of a wife with an insidious addiction.

"Nothing I gave her was enough. She got some kind of thrill from the buying. Most of what she got, she didn't even take out of the boxes. Then she started hiding what she purchased. We fought all the time. It was a nightmare."

"Well, you don't have to worry. I will never do that to you."

He dropped his head back in relief, his gaze cast up. "Thank God!"

Then Jackson cupped her chin in his palm to study her face, his dark eyes scanning her expression, and she cast him a tentative smile.

"I don't want you agonizing every time I'm out. I'm so sorry I hurt you. I'll even take the magazine and coloring book back to the store."

He smiled and nodded, clearly pleased with this.

"Great. Go tell Phoebe to bring everything you two bought to me."

"We're going now?" she asked, surprised. It was over an hour to the chain bookstore.

"Right now. Get your purse and your daughter. Phoebe also needs to understand the rules."

"Yes. That's a good idea. But what about work?"

"This is more important."

Did he really think so?

Jackson pulled her in for a warm embrace.

"I knew you'd understand. I love you so much." He stroked her cheek and then kissed her, and she nestled against his chest, feeling relieved and happy. He really wanted what was best for their family.

He released her. "Let me get my keys. We'll take my truck."

He walked to the door, pausing there to smile back at her. "I'm so lucky to have you."

She thought of his wife, his second wife, the one right now in some police station, being questioned about a suspicious fire.

Jackson had been away all weekend. But coincidences happened all the time. Didn't they?

"Jackson?"

He met her gaze, waiting.

"I swear this will never happen again."

"I believe you."

TWELVE
NOW

June 21, 2022, Tuesday
Atlantic Ocean

Elana's shivering expanded into body-wracking spasms. She was not sure if she controlled her flailing, clumsy limbs or if it was the tremors. The uncooperative things seemed to belong to someone else, barely responding to her commands. The struggle to keep her mouth and nose above the water took all she had.

Why hadn't she remembered that the gentle waves of the inlet led to the Atlantic, before she dove in?

And cold? She had never experienced cold like this. The numbness grew to a bone-gnawing throbbing ache. Her joints stiffened, rusting like metal, seizing.

A wave washed over her face. She sucked in salt water that burned across her opened eyes. The swell tossed her above the surface where she wasted her chance to breathe on uncontrollable coughing.

Elana spotted the hull in short flashes as she rose on the crest of a wave, then fell, sinking into endless valleys of the churning water.

She waved the pink cloth over her head, praying the fishermen in the boat would see her and wondering if her hand had even broken the surface. Her strength had abandoned her hours after daybreak. The shivering shook her violently as the salt water stole her heat. The thirst tortured. Could they see her?

If they didn't see her soon, it would be too late. Likely was already too late. So many times, through the six-hour struggle, whenever she wanted to surrender, she'd thought of Phoebe. Was she still safe with her auntie Zoey?

She prayed they hadn't told her, hadn't frightened her. Elana kicked harder. Phoebe needed her. She couldn't give up.

Elana waved her arm above her head again. Shouting was pointless. They could never hear her over the engine. But this rosy strip of cloth, torn from her dress, might be bright enough to catch their attention.

The boat was like Jackson's, rigged for game fishing. There was a lookout platform. They would have a spotter up there. She sank again and held her breath, waiting to rise to the surface, fearing she never would. This time, on the crest of a wave, she saw the boat turn. Thrashing, she fought to see as the water tugged her down.

Yes! They were coming.

On the next crest, she made out the men aboard. Four stood on the deck pointing in her direction.

She sank. Her tired limbs proved nearly useless, her kick only a weak thrashing of a drowning woman.

They'd never reach her in time.

Where was her husband? Was he still alive?

She thought of her seven-year-old daughter, and squeezed her eyes shut against the burning seawater and the guilt.

I'm sorry, darling. I tried to save us both.

The rumble in her ears made her open her eyes. The hull of the boat blotted out the harsh sunlight. Something plunged into the water beside her.

A yank at the shoulder strap of her dress dragged her upward. She breached, vomiting up seawater.

"We got you, lady. Hold on."

"My husband," she gasped. "He's still out here."

The men hanging over the gunnels shouted to their fellow shipmate as he kicked them back toward the boat. At the stern, the others tugged her against the bobbing vessel. Slippery as a seal, they could keep hold of her only by grasping her tattered clothing to haul her aboard.

She slapped against the deck like one of the marlins they caught in the tournament, too weak to fight, too weak to swim. Easy prey for sharks and other predators.

She'd left one shark in the water.

The next thing she knew, she was vomiting seawater at the stern as the four men aboard scuttled about the cockpit like crabs released from the net.

"Blankets! Get her wrapped up."

"The wet clothes should come off."

"You can't take her clothes off!"

"Call the coast guard."

"Radio for help."

They lifted her through the fish door and set her down on the deck. She sagged against the gunnel. In a moment they bundled her in a blanket. It barely seemed to help. The waxy yellow color of her fingers alarmed Elana.

"Hot soup."

"No, just lukewarm water."

"No water. She might be in shock."

As the men argued and did their best to care for her, Elana realized she might still die from exposure. She didn't know much about core temperatures and hypothermia. It was not something a Florida girl ever needed to concern herself about. But she knew she had stopped shivering; her feet felt like chunks of wood, and she could barely see. Was that the salt water, dehydration, shock, or the cold?

She didn't know.

"Coast guard is on the way."

"Get her inside."

Someone lifted her and her head wobbled like those dolls with their head on a spring. They lowered her to a padded bench before a table. The galley, she thought, blinking her stinging eyes.

"Hold on, miss."

Someone gripped her shoulder. She tried to speak, but the raw skin of her throat made her words just a rasping whine. She had to tell them. Had to play the part of concerned wife.

"Say again?" asked one of her rescuers, leaning close to catch her words.

"My husband is out there."

"What's that?" asked one of her rescuers.

"My husband." She lifted a finger pointing. "Out there."

One of the men called over his shoulder, to the captain, she thought.

"There's another person out there!" He stood before her now. A blur in pale blue, haloed by the sun behind him, like a ghost trail of bioluminescent algae.

They didn't have to know her worst fear. That he might come back.

* * *

THEN

February 2022, four months ago

Elana sat with Zoey Belauru at a booth inside the shabby-chic restaurant across the Georgia line. The upscale eatery boasted urban Southern cuisine, which meant the shrimp and grits were twenty dollars instead of ten and the shortcake shared the menu with crème brûlée. Not to mention, this place had a reputation so good it traveled all the way to Bald Cypress. Above, the fans turned just hard enough not to blow around the mostly female clientele's hair. The chatter of conversations and scrape of silverware was a nice change from the shouts of the boys and the paper plates at the poolside dining they usually shared at Zoey and Sawyer's home.

The meal had arrived, and Zoey had tucked into her chicken and waffles and ordered a second white wine. Meanwhile, Elana pushed cheddar grits and quiche around her plate.

Elana was not here at her sister-in-law's invitation just to enjoy a ladies' lunch. She was here because she had finally devised a seemingly innocent way to check if what Jackson's second wife had told her about his tracking her movements was true.

Shantel had correctly predicted that Jackson would give her a new phone and new car, not as gifts, but to spy on her.

Since then, Elana had spent a great deal of energy trying to convince herself that the notion was ridiculous. But after eight months of marriage to a man who had incrementally exerted increasingly extreme measures to control every aspect of her life, she was no longer certain.

Since the incident at the fundraiser and the one before Christmas, when she and Phoebe had to accompany Jackson back to the bookstore to return her purchases, she'd done everything he'd asked and cleared every item she intended to buy. She'd strived to make him an elegant home and keep both him and her daughter happy.

But it was a façade.

Since then, she and Jackson had had several other altercations. He'd find her lacking, fly off the handle and the moment she apologized he transformed into the man she'd first met. The sweet, smart, loving husband she wanted. But that darker side was always lurking, putting her constantly on edge.

One of the most disturbing parts of this emerging pattern was that Jackson, after finding fault and bringing her to tears, after her babbled, blubbery apologies, would become so sweet and attentive, they usually ended up having sex. Jackson was always more energetic after her contrition, as if he found it sexually stimulating. That possibility made her physically sick, and their lovemaking had turned sour, for her, at least.

Shantel had been right. She should have called off the wedding.

Hindsight was a rascal.

Now she felt trapped, unhappy, and helpless. She'd considered a trial separation, but was too afraid to broach the subject.

She didn't even know where to begin.

When he'd originally told her she no longer needed to work, she'd been delighted and gladly resigned. She'd been overjoyed. Too good to be true, she'd thought at the time. And had been so right.

Had she really thought she'd be like those tennis moms at her daughter's school, the ones who came to PTA meetings dressed in athletic wear, had their nails done and their hair highlighted and styled, instead of tugged in a tight pony?

Why had she dismissed that bothersome inner voice that wondered why a man with Jackson's means and influence would choose an uneducated woman, with a child to support, as his wife? Elana had known since she was a teenager that she was only average in the looks department. Men, when attracted, appreciated her body more than her face or mind. But she had one asset irresistible to Jackson, much as she hated to admit it. She was easily intimidated.

Now she understood the bargain she had made when she'd accepted his proposal. Fewer friends, less autonomy, dependence on Jackson for everything that must be bought with money she no longer earned. Before their wedding, she'd willingly merged every dime of her assets into joint accounts, relieved to turn over her debt and credit cards to him. At the time, she had not realized that every woman needed a certain amount of hidden cash for emergencies, like the need to run from an unhealthy marriage.

She'd been warned.

"Girl, you are red as a strawberry. You allergic to something in that quiche?"

Elana glanced up, making brief eye contact. "I don't think so. Hot in here."

"If it's too hot for you now, what you gonna do when summer comes?" Zoey was studying her, her critical green eyes showing curiosity, like a cat catching movement.

"I'm all right," she said.

Another glance showed her dining companion arching a brow. She'd witnessed Zoey use that expression with her boys. It could mean irritation, skepticism, or signal impending action.

"You hardly touched your salad." She waved a fork toward the plate in question.

"Not very hungry, is all."

Zoey leaned forward, looking like a hunting feline. "You nauseous? Mornin' sick?"

"Oh, no. I'm not pregnant."

She sat back. "Hmm. Pity."

After delivering another baby boy in August, Zoey had told her they were again trying to get pregnant. Her short blond hair seemed impervious to heat or humidity. She wore a sheath dress in lime and pink by a designer Elana hated, but now owned, thanks to Zoey's gifts—no doubt approved by Jackson—on her birthday and Christmas. Both sat in tropical prints like a couple of tourists.

Elana fidgeted with the gold bangle bracelet Jackson had given her for her birthday, thinking how she preferred the one of plastic beads given to her by Gavin over this expensive bauble.

Zoey updated her on what baby Caleb could do. "Grabbed the dog so tight he yelped. And finally sleeping through the night, praise the Lord."

Elana reached in her designer bag to take out a pill bottle and her phone. The phone she slipped into the crack between the seat and the back cushion, pushing to make it less noticeable.

"What is that?" said Zoey, motioning to the pill bottle.

"Lactase. Helps me digest the dairy."

"There's no dairy in that salad." She glanced to the quiche. "Oh, heavy cream."

Elana took three chalky pills with water.

"Delicate little thing. Aren't you?"

It was the kind of insult that was just too subtle to call out, not that she would.

"If dairy bothers you, then order something without it."

Elana nodded. "Next time."

Was it possible that Sawyer ordered Zoey around the same way Jackson did to her? It would explain why she was so eager to boss Elana and anyone else she came near, whenever she was away from her husband.

Their server hovered. "Can I get you anything else?"

"Just some privacy," said Zoey, not even casting her a glance.

Sawyer's wife waited until the server retreated, then fixed her attention on Elana with the predatory gaze of a feral cat spotting a baby bunny.

"Okay, spill," said Zoey.

"What?"

"Something's on your mind. You're usually quiet, but you've barely said a word."

Elana wasn't stupid. She knew that if she denied being

distracted, Jackson would hear about it. And whatever she said next, he would also hear about. Better make it something that genuinely bothered her, she decided, or perhaps, something Zoey wouldn't be anxious to relay to Sawyer.

"Zoey, Jackson never mentions his dad. What do you know about him?"

"The great Simon Belauru, real estate mogul? Those boys never say a bad word about him, rest his soul. But I met him, and I can tell you I'd never leave my little ones with him."

"Why?"

"He used his belt. Sawyer still has marks. Oh, shoot, he doesn't want anyone to..."

Her words fell off and Elana realized she'd finally struck on a subject Zoey would likely never mention to her husband.

Her sister-in-law regrouped, gathering herself up. "Well, it's why you never see him without his shirt."

Elana hadn't noticed, but now, thinking of various pool parties, it was true. Sawyer never went in the water.

"He got the worst, being the oldest. But their dad licked every one of them boys. Turned them into hunters before they were even in kindergarten. Now I've got dead animals staring at me from every wall."

Just like Sawyer's place, Elana's home had several trophy heads mounted in the living room. She, too, found those glass eyes and reproachful expressions disquieting.

Zoey heaved a sigh, staring at a place above Elana's head, her eyes out of focus. "They'd never, well... How could anyone measure up? He was a real estate magnate. Entrepreneur like John D. and Carnegie. And he belittled those boys, even when they were grown."

The apples did not fall far from the tree.

"I heard something disturbing about his wife."

"Lydia?" Zoey went silent, her thumb nervously fiddling with the stem of her wineglass. "What'd ya hear?"

"Someone at Phoebe's school said she overdosed."

Zoey paused, mouth pressed tight, as if deciding whether to broach the topic of the mother of their husbands. Finally, she said, "I never met her."

"But the overdose?"

"I don't know." Zoey used an index finger to draw a vertical line in the beads of condensation on her wineglass. "Sawyer won't say, which makes me wonder. He did tell me that he was the one who found her. He was fourteen. Her obituary doesn't mention the cause of death except to say it was accidental. She was thirty-three and alone in the house."

"I see."

Zoey glanced up, her gaze now focused and sharp as the point of a dagger.

"Not surprised you heard the rumors. She'd tried before. This time with pills crushed up in her wine. I heard she left a note. Sawyer kept it. God knows why. So you can draw your own conclusions."

"You think she..." Elana leaned in. "But she was Mennonite. They can't. Suicide is forbidden."

"So is drinking and marrying outside the faith. But she did all three." Zoey shook her head like a dog hearing a siren. "At least that's what I heard, regardless of what it says on the certificate of death."

Elana thumped back in the booth, attention drifting toward the wall of paintings and mirrors in mismatched frames without really seeing them. That was one way out of a terrible marriage.

Then it occurred to her. Jackson's second wife, Shantel, was exactly as Zoey described his mother near the end of her life. Erratic and addicted. While Faith was as Lydia must have been as a young mother. Serene and steady. Predictable and poised.

The observation made Elana so sad.

"You didn't meet Simon." Zoey shook her head, then took a

swallow from her wineglass. "I'd have stayed drunk, too, if I were married to that man."

When Jackson spoke of his father, which was not often, it was to commend his business genius or his hunting prowess.

"How did he die? Jackson's never said."

"Massive heart attack at the shooting range. Only fifty-four. Sawyer says he died with his boots on and a shotgun in his hand."

Elana thought that sort of macho imagery ridiculous, but she appreciated the merits of a quick death.

"They mourn him, God knows why. Maybe death helps them forget the bad parts." Zoey drained her glass.

"Is it okay for you to have wine?" asked Elana.

"Not pregnant yet. Likely soon, so enjoy it while I can."

She knew there was no wine in Zoey's home, either, and wondered if that might be for the best.

Zoey lifted the goblet, noticed it was empty, and lowered it again.

"If you had boys, you'd know why I need it."

Elana said no more and turned her attention to her lunch as the corner of her cellphone dug into her backside.

She managed to eat a respectable portion of the meal.

"You want to have dessert? I'm in no hurry to get back to the kids."

Elana knew that Gabriella, Zoey's housekeeper and nanny, would be there to collect the boys from school as she did every afternoon.

"Lord, did I tell you I got another email from Parker's teacher? If she thinks Parker is a handful, wait until she meets Levy. That teacher and I are real pen pals. I told her he's her problem from eight to three. Deal with it. Also told her to slap him on his bottom anytime she feels the need. That'll take him down a peg. Better he be crying than her."

"But we should get back before they're out of school."

"Girl, you need to get a housekeeper so she can wait for the damn bus."

"Jackson wants me to handle the house."

"You give him a couple sons and you can get whatever you want. Haven't you figured that out yet?"

Zoey pushed away her glass, exhaling sharply, though whether in frustration at the topic of conversation, the empty glass, or at Elana, she didn't know.

"Create a showpiece." She waved a hand in a rolling motion. "Be an excellent hostess, a political partner, and listen to all their problems, while not having any of our own. Oh, and have babies. Preferably boys." She cradled her flat stomach. "That part I like."

Elana blinked at the realization that after knowing Zoey for more than a year, her sister-in-law had only now revealed something genuine and hinted that life with Sawyer might not be the domestic paradise it appeared. She barely had time to register her surprise at this when the server appeared and asked about dessert.

"No. Apparently we have a bus to catch."

"I'll get your check." The server motioned to Elana's plate. "Are you finished?"

Elana's face went hot at the attention this brought from Zoey.

"I am."

The server cleared their dishes and retreated.

"You know you're losing weight?" Zoey said. "I heard Jackson complaining to Sawyer. Said you've got bird arms. Hardly anything to grab hold of."

That revelation embarrassed her enough to cause a gasp.

"He said that?"

"You get pregnant, you won't have to worry about your figure for a while."

The server returned with the check and Zoey handled it.

"Ready?" Elana slid from the bench and blocked any view of her seat with her body until Zoey was up and out.

They reached the sidewalk and then the car, with Elana listening for the bang of a door, the call of a server.

Miss, you left your phone.

But the only sound was from the street and the car chime as she unlocked the vehicle.

Inside the blistering hot interior, Zoey buckled in as Elana watched the door and started the car.

"Phew, hotter than a thirteen-year-old with his daddy's girly magazines."

The air conditioning blew a blast of stifling air and then turned cooler by degrees. Elana held her breath and put the car in gear, gliding out of their parking spot and onto the road.

She glanced at the clock. It was ten minutes after one.

The lunch spot was forty-nine minutes from home. How long until he realized?

"You're very quiet," said Zoey as the clock turned to 1:11 p.m.

"That was a lovely meal. Thank you for inviting me."

"You didn't seem to enjoy it."

"Their portions are too big."

"Or your stomach is too small. We need to get you pregnant. That will fix that appetite. I swear I'm hungry all the time."

We need to get you pregnant? It was an odd thing to say. And it was a topic Zoey couldn't get enough of. Had Jackson told Zoey to encourage her?

Since learning of Shantel's house fire, she'd been less anxious for that baby. Some deep internal warning system told her she was not safe.

But obtaining birth control was impossible. Even a visit to a clinic cost money. Money she didn't have. Money that Jackson would see on a bank statement.

Another glance at the clock showed that eight minutes had passed. They headed out of town.

"I need to do that more often," said Zoey. "You want to go again next month? I'd like to try those pulled pork wontons."

"That would be lovely." Anything to leave her marriage, if only for a few hours.

Zoey went on to describe a place in Tallahassee where they served a fancy afternoon tea.

"They bring you a stack of food on those risers. Cakes on top and sandwiches in the middle. You don't have to drink the tea, either. And they've got mimosas."

Fourteen minutes now. She wondered if this would work or if it was just a way to upset Jackson by losing her phone.

He'd yell. He always yelled. He'd tell her she was careless and that if she wanted nice things, she needed to be more responsible. He'd say this even while throwing things, heedless of what broke.

This would happen without an audience, of course. Even Phoebe was protected from his rages. Jackson had control of himself all the time, all public times.

She alone was witness to his outbursts, his suspicions, and his malice. Until now, all this only took verbal form. But words could wound with even a near-lethal blow leaving no mark.

It was why she dreaded, in a gathering or at a party, when he would approach her and, in a pleasant voice, ask if he could speak to her a minute.

Elana, could I have a word?

No one but her saw the tight lines at the sides of his mouth or the flecks of ice in his eyes.

"You pick the sandwiches," said Zoey, continuing her description of the tea place. "They have all kinds. Serve them in little rectangles with the crusts cut off. I think I could do a fundraiser for church with a tea like that. Though maybe buttermilk biscuits instead of scones."

Seventeen minutes. Soon they'd be on the highway.

The tightness in her chest began to ease. Maybe Shantel had been wrong or just trying to scare her. That was exactly what she'd been telling herself. That reasonable, less hysterical part of her mind had cautioned that she was overreacting.

Maybe all the trouble she'd been through was for nothing.

Why would Jackson track her phone and car? She'd given him no reason. The idea was absurd.

But what about Shantel's claim that if Elana divorced him, Jackson would take Phoebe and she'd never see her again. That wasn't the sort of thing a person could get away with.

If he didn't call, she'd just forget the entire thing.

But if he did, she'd start planning how to get away from him. Even thinking the idea made her shiver as if dunked in cold water. Was she really thinking of leaving him? He wouldn't like it.

Not at all.

The sound of Zoey's phone ringing caused Elana to startle out of her seat.

"Oh, shoot, that's Sawyer's ringtone." She rummaged in her oversized leather bag and came up with her bejeweled phone.

"Hey, hon. What's up?"

Elana gripped the wheel as Zoey glanced in her direction.

"No. She's right here with me. Why?"

Her ears tingled and her neck burned, but she kept her eyes on the road.

"I didn't hear it ring." Zoey lifted the phone and spoke to Elana. "Says you're not answering your phone."

She pressed her lips together and kept her gaze straight ahead. Meanwhile the sweat popped out on her body like the beads of condensation on a water glass on a humid day.

He'd called. She'd not answered and so he'd called Sawyer.

Was that coincidence?

It was possible that Jackson really had just been trying to

call her. It was conceivable. How very much she wanted to believe that. But she didn't.

Zoey spoke to her husband. "Why were you calling Elana?" Another pause, presumably while Sawyer answered. "Oh. Jackson's calling her. It must be on mute or something."

She glanced at Elana and then to her bag, the look indicating she wanted Elana to check.

"Can't. Driving," said Elana.

Zoey was listening to something Sawyer was saying as she reached for Elana's bag and tugged it open.

"No, we left the restaurant. We're almost to the state line." Zoey continued to scrounge in the bag. "It's not here."

Elana blew out a breath and then slowly inhaled. It was an exercise that helped her relax and one that she'd had opportunity to perfect in recent months.

Zoey set aside Elana's bag and spoke into the phone. "All right. We'll head back. Gonna be late. Yes, I'll call Gabriella. Love you!" Zoey disconnected the call and turned to her. "Sawyer got a call from Jackson. He said you left your phone at the restaurant."

"How would he know we left the restaurant?"

A good guess, unless the phone finder told him exactly.

Zoey thought about that, elegant, manicured fingers wrapped around her phone.

"Sawyer said Jackson called him. So he must have called you first. Why, you think you left it home?"

Elana knew exactly where she had left it.

It was true. *Dear God, it was true.* She thought she might be sick.

"But me not answering... how would he know my phone is *at* the restaurant?"

"Used the find my phone app, I guess. When you didn't answer, I mean." Zoey now drummed her fingers on her knees as if playing scales on a piano. She stared straight ahead; her mouth pinched into a grim line.

Elana thought of confiding in her sister-in-law. For all she knew, Sawyer treated Zoey the same way. She thought back to what she'd said in the restaurant. *Listen to all their problems, while not having any of our own.* Elana was tempted to explore that hint of dissatisfaction, but she didn't trust her. The woman had been married to Sawyer a long time and Elana saw no indication that she champed at her bit or rattled her chains.

Zoey seemed... content. And that was of no use to Elana.

"Maybe we should try home first. Check there."

Zoey thought about that. "Better go back."

"Because that's what you think we should do or because that's what Jackson told us to do?"

Zoey gave her the first direct look she'd had, ever. Her smile was gone, and her brows lifted in surprise.

"I don't want to go home without that phone. Do you?"

Elana shook her head. She had her answer. Zoey understood and perhaps was dealing with the same kind of Jekyll and Hyde personality with Sawyer.

She performed a legal U-turn as she wondered what kind of hell Zoey's marriage might be.

Zoey's artificial smile returned, and she lounged back in her seat, appearing completely relaxed, if you ignored the relentless tapping of her index finger on the back of her phone case.

All the way back to the restaurant, Elana resisted the urge to ask Zoey about her marriage. But her sister-in-law was not her confidant. She might be a fellow prisoner, but prisoners knew to look out for themselves first and were very careful in choosing who to trust.

"I can have my gal pick up Phoebe from school with the boys."

"I'd appreciate that."

Zoey called her housekeeper, alerted her to the delay, and explained about the additional pickup.

"... Should be before Sawyer gets home. I don't know, plop them in front of the video games with a snack. Yes. Overtime. See you later."

At the restaurant, Elana dashed in to find her phone waiting behind the checkout counter.

"We found it at your table," said the hostess.

Elana accepted the phone, glancing at the screen. There were no calls from Jackson or anyone else.

There had been no coincidental call, because he hadn't phoned.

Instead, she forced herself to swallow. This was happening. It was real and she and her daughter might be in danger. Danger wrapped up in a nice house, good schools, a pretty life, and a tyrannical man.

THIRTEEN

NOW

June 21, 2022, Tuesday

The cabin stunk of cigarette smoke and diesel fuel. She rested on a bench and wondered why they didn't head for shore.

Her answer came with the coast guard vessel. As they boarded, she heard one of the men explain that this was the location of her recovery.

The sun was well up now. He'd been in the water for hours, weighed down by that stupid lucky fishing vest he insisted on wearing and enough alcohol to render him semiconscious.

It should be enough.

Please let it be enough.

She lost sight of him so fast, she couldn't be sure. All she knew was that she'd barely kept her head above. The outgoing tide had swept her from the protection of Bogue Sound past the red and green channel markers.

The man before her now introduced himself as Lieutenant Meng of the US Coast Guard, a gaunt, young, clean-shaven man with a black bristle of hair, dark eyes, and a somber expression.

"Your name?"

"Elana Belauru."

"Your husband is missing?"

"In the water! Yes!"

"Since when?"

"Last night."

He turned to a colleague and spoke in tones too low for Elana to comprehend. Was she losing her hearing?

"How?" he asked.

"We were..." She tried to remember it all. The salt made her throat raspy. "Stargazing at the back of the boat. He lost his balance. Fell. Dragged me over."

"Lost his balance?"

She nodded.

"Were you drinking?"

Another nod. "He was. I don't drink."

Did that make her look more guilty, falling without the excuse of alcohol to make her unsteady? But he'd dragged her in. That's what she'd said because that was what nearly happened.

But it hadn't.

"We are taking you off this boat and transporting you to the hospital in Culpepper. We didn't know you and your husband had gone overboard until you were spotted. But we're instituting a search for your husband now."

"Thank you." Elana began to cry again. "What about my daughter?"

"Was she aboard? I can send someone to the vessel."

"No, no, she's ashore with family."

"I'll see what I can find out."

"Tell her..." It was so hard to think and even harder to speak past her raw throat and swollen tongue. "Tell her, I'll be home soon."

"Yes, we will. You rest now. Lie back."

She did, her body surrendering to exhaustion.

They lifted her by stretcher onto the coast guard vessel. Once aboard they made a speedy trip to shore. Amazing how fast you could travel when you were not kicking to keep your head above the waves.

Had the tide taken Jackson out as well?

She pictured him, tossed about by the water, dragged down, and pitched back up again. Helpless as a cork, or possibly an empty bottle. She closed her eyes to savor that image and smiled.

At the hospital emergency room, they drew blood and started her on intravenous fluids. She was not allowed to drink anything, but was given ice chips until they ruled out other, more serious injuries.

The warming blanket did the trick, bringing her temperature rapidly back to normal. It wasn't really a blanket, but more like a light, plastic inflatable filled with moving hot air. Exhausted, she dozed until the nurse flicked off the blower and took her temperature. Satisfied, she replaced the warming blanket with the traditional kind.

She was dozing again when police arrived to question her.

A woman in navy slacks, a gray blazer, and a white button-up blouse introduced herself as Detective Denise Elmendorf.

Elana judged her to be in her mid-thirties, slender, and muscular, with brown hair cut short at the back and longer in the front. Her bangs fell over her forehead like the forelock of a pony. If she wore makeup, it was subtle.

This was why she'd jumped. To avoid questioning. But she'd survived. Elana tried to convince herself that was a good thing. But right now, the sick pitching in her stomach had nothing to do with her near drowning.

Elmendorf opened her notebook and drew out a cheap plastic pen missing its cap.

Elana was immediately intimidated by her aura of competence, but she gave the same account.

"He lost his balance. I tried to catch him, but we both went into the water. I heard his head hit the stern. When we came up, I was so far from the boat, and I couldn't see Jackson."

"Did Jackson make it back to the boat?"

"No."

"How do you know?"

"He didn't or he would have found me."

"Did you see him after you went in the water?"

"No. I couldn't see him."

"What time would you say this was?"

"I don't know. Late. After midnight, I think. We were celebrating his win."

"You were here for the tournament?"

"My husband was. He has a team. They won a trophy. Prize money. His brothers. We have to call Sawyer. That's Jackson's older brother."

The detective took it all down, her version of events, contact information. After she finished all her questions, she closed her black notebook and sat in silence for a moment.

"Jackson is strong," Elana said. "If I could survive this, he will, too."

The detective made no reply to this aspirational statement. Instead, she said, "What happened to your arms?"

Before Elana could reply, another man entered the room, dressed in business casual with a gold shield clipped beside his silver belt buckle, a handgun holstered at his hip. Elmendorf glanced to the new arrival.

"Mrs. Belauru, this is Detective Franklin Anderson."

"Did they find Jackson?" Elana asked him.

"Not yet," said the male detective. "But we did find your boat at anchor in the sound."

"That's good." She thought about the blood and imagined

crime techs crawling all over the boat like ants on a piece of toast slathered with honey.

"Mrs. Belauru, if you are correct that you both entered the water around midnight, your husband has been missing for twelve hours."

"Twelve?"

"I think you need to prepare yourself for the worst," said Detective Anderson gently.

Elmendorf scowled at Anderson.

Elana closed her eyes, absorbing the hard news delivered by the detective. This man had no concept of what the worst even was.

"But they're still searching?"

Detective Elmendorf nodded and swept her forelock of hair back from her face.

How long would they search?

"They have to find him."

The rest of that sentiment was that they had to find him dead. So she could be sure, certain as the grave, that he was not coming back. She would not be able to rest until then.

But what if they never found him? The cold water took bodies down. Once the air left the lungs, they sank.

"The coast guard is spearheading the search for your husband. No one is giving up hope. You hang in there," said Anderson.

Elana nodded.

A medical professional appeared. "I need a few minutes."

Elmendorf tucked away her notebook. "Thank you for your time, Mrs. Belauru. If we have any more questions, or any information to share, we will be in touch."

Elana watched through the observation glass as the detectives made their way out of sight. Meanwhile, the attendant checked her vitals.

"Can I wash?" she asked.

"Of course."

Elana was given a basin and washcloth. She used it to gingerly clean away the salt. She was safe.

But was she?

If the police find traces of blood all over the boat, they'd never believe she and her husband fell in together. Would they even call the police? Yes, if they didn't find Jackson, there would be an investigation. And no matter how carefully she scrubbed, some vestiges of his blood, and hers, would remain. Her jump into the sea now seemed no more than cowardice.

It seemed foolhardy. The police might find evidence of her lies. Then her story would decompose like tissue paper in water. It was almost enough to make her want them to find Jackson alive. Almost.

She had no proof of what he was or what she knew he had done. No proof of the hell she had been living through.

She could hear them now. *"Why didn't you just leave?"*

But I couldn't leave. He made sure of that.

If she left, he'd come for Phoebe. One day, when she dropped her guard or looked away, he'd be there, and her daughter would be gone.

What had he done to those poor innocent children? Had he killed them for their mothers' crimes of leaving the mighty Jackson Belauru?

She set aside the basin in favor of the lemon Jell-O and had finished drinking half a cup of black coffee when her sister-in-law arrived. Zoey Belauru flew into the room with arms outstretched.

"Oh, honey!" she said and hugged Elana.

"Phoebe?" asked Elana. She'd left Phoebe sleeping in the hotel suite in Zoey's care before joining Jackson for his little post-tournament celebration.

"She's with Gabriella," said Zoey, mentioning the housekeeper and nanny who had come along to help with the baby and the boys. "Scared, but fine."

At word that her daughter was safe, Elana's tears flowed. She hugged Zoey as she sobbed.

"Oh, Zoey, he's still out there!"

Zoey stroked Elana's head.

"Shhh, we know. They're gonna find him."

Zoey pulled back and gripped Elana by each shoulder, leveling her with a serious look.

The pale blue sheath dress emphasized Zoey's budding baby bump from her fourth child. Zoey, now in her second trimester, had admitted this was another boy, even though they had yet to have the official gender reveal party.

"I'm so glad you're safe. Little Phoebe, poor thing. After the police notified Sawyer that you were picked up offshore and that Jackson was missing, we didn't know what to tell her."

"She knows I'm okay?"

"Yes. I told her and that we're still looking for her daddy."

Phoebe's real daddy was dead. Maybe her stepdad was as well.

"We've been going crazy since we heard. How on earth?" She did not wait for an answer, but continued on. "Sawyer organized his own search. He's got all the fishermen still here from the tournament out looking." At this point Zoey gave Elana's shoulders a little shake for emphasis. "How in the Lord's name did you swim for all that time? Hours? I mean I've never seen you exercise, but my goodness, Elana!"

Here Zoey paused and Elana reminded herself that this woman was not her friend or ally.

"I kept thinking about Phoebe and that I needed to get help for Jackson."

"We're going to find him, honey. Sawyer won't quit until he finds him. You know he won't!"

The nurse, who had been caring for Elana since her arrival in the emergency department, entered the small room.

"We're not admitting you. I'll be back with the paperwork and then you can go. Now let's get rid of this," she said and proceeded to remove the IV.

Zoey stepped out of the ER examining room, which was hardly big enough to hold the bed and the nurse. But her sister-in-law watched them through the glass observation windows. In that way she reminded Elana of Jackson. Watching. Always watching.

The nurse finished and departed with the tubing and stand. Zoey swept back in, seating herself on the foot of the narrow bed, folding her limber frame to sit cross-legged and holding her belly like a statue of meditating Buddha.

"Tell me what happened," she demanded.

"I'm exhausted, Zoey."

"Sawyer sent me here to find out what happened. So spill."

Elana gathered herself.

"Well, you know that Jackson likes to celebrate after a tournament."

"Just the two of you on the boat. Yes. We know."

"Well, we were drinking. Too much, I guess."

"You don't drink," she said, accusation in her voice.

"All right, Jackson was drinking," Elana amended.

Zoey nodded at that. "So how did you both go in?"

Elana glanced at her bandaged forearms. The thought of how close her daughter had come to losing her mother brought the tears.

Weeping and using the bedsheet to dab her eyes, she said, "We'd been below deck and... well, afterward, we came on deck to look at the stars. He leaned on the transom, looking up. Lost his balance. I tried... He fell, grabbed me for balance, tore the skin off my arms." She extended her bandaged arms as evidence. "I couldn't hold him. Couldn't stop him from falling... but he grabbed my dress and pulled me in, too."

"Did his life vest deploy?"

"He wasn't wearing a vest. Neither of us was."

"He is always wearing a life vest. Every second he is on deck. It's built into the fishing vest he always wears."

"What?"

"There is a survival inflatable built into the lining. Sawyer has one, too. If it touches water, it self-inflates."

Elana blinked, trying to make sense of what her sister-in-law was saying.

"I don't know anything about that."

Zoey lifted her brows, incredulous. "He calls it Vera?"

"Yes, I know. But that's just a fishing vest."

"With a built-in self-inflating floatation."

Elana absorbed this bit of terrible news, blinking rapidly.

And suddenly she understood the joke. Why, all those months ago, when she'd suggested his fishing vest would drag him to the bottom, Jackson had laughed. Because among all that gear, it carried a personal floatation device that deployed automatically, regardless of whether the wearer was conscious.

Jackson might be alive.

That realization lifted all the hairs on her body. Her skin felt as if someone ran an electric current through it.

Oh, no.

"But if you were in the water with him, you must have seen it."

"I went in with him." Elana struggled to catch her breath. "But when I came up, I was alone. I called, but he didn't answer, or I couldn't hear him. And the current dragged me so far from the boat. I tried to swim back. But couldn't."

"Jackson didn't make it back, either."

"I know."

Her sister-in-law frowned. "How could you know that?"

"Because they didn't realize we went over until they found me. If Jackson were on board, he'd have called for help. Started a search."

Zoey looked Elana directly in the eye.

"You're right about that. But you said he grabbed you. And he'd never let you go, Elana. We both know it." Zoey gave her a long look.

"He did, though. He hit his head on the deck."

Zoey's eyes widened. "That's bad. But since he wore the vest, he *might* be alive."

Oh, God, he might still be alive.

Elana was now so grateful she'd jumped in after him. If he lived and found out she could have called for help, but didn't... She shivered.

"Sawyer will find him."

Speechless, Elana battled the rising panic as she pictured Jackson in the water. The yellow inflatable, secreted in his fishing vest, deploying with a tiny carbon dioxide cartridge. Jackson, sobered by the water, ducking his head through the opening, cinching the waistband around his middle.

If Jackson had a life vest, he might survive. He might remember. He was drunk, but was he that drunk?

He'd tell everyone what had really happened. Or worse, he *wouldn't* tell them. What would he do to her or to Phoebe?

In her distraction, she didn't see the police officer appear in the entrance to the doorway until he spoke.

"Mrs. Belauru?"

"Yes?"

"We found your husband. He's alive."

FOURTEEN

THEN

May 29, 2022, one month ago

Elana made the call with Jackson standing over her. They'd waited until Phoebe headed to a friend's house, happy as a butterfly as she danced and twirled her way to the classmate's family car, oblivious that her Mema and Pop-pop, as she called her paternal grandparents, were arriving in Florida today.

After trying for nearly a year to convince Elana to drive up for a visit, Gavin's parents had given up and announced they would be in Pensacola seeing an old friend and wanted to stop by Bald Cypress on the way. Though it was possible they were in the Sunshine State to see someone, she believed in her heart that they used this as an excuse and were here to see their granddaughter.

That made this all the more cruel.

It was Victoria's phone and she answered on the first ring, her voice bright and energetic as a middle school girl on a sleepover.

"Elana! We're almost to the state line! What time should we stop by? We could be there around lunchtime."

How early had they gotten on the road to make it to Florida already?

She swallowed, trying to choke down the lie. She flashed Jackson a pleading look. He cocked his head and rolled his hand in a gesture for her to get on with it.

"Yes, that's right, unfortunately we've had a death in the family. Jackson's aunt has passed away in Minneapolis."

"Oh, we're so sorry to hear that."

She'd said *we're* because she and her husband moved and acted like one unit. Elana couldn't imagine one without the other because they were just Braden and Vic. You said it together, as if they were one word and one individual.

"Yes. Jackson was very close to his mom's sister. The whole family is heading up there today."

"Today?" The despair was there now at the realization that they'd driven down here from North Carolina, more than ten hours away, only to be told they would not see Phoebe.

"Maybe we could swing by Phoebe's school and see her before you go? We have her birthday gift."

"We're already at the airport. I'm so sorry."

"When will you be back? We might be able to wait."

Jackson had taken care of that. Vic was a schoolteacher, but taught summer school. Braden was the manager of a quickie oil change place and had only the national holidays off. He'd also need to be back at work on Tuesday morning.

"The funeral is tomorrow at four. We'll be flying back on Monday..." She glanced to Jackson, her eyes pleading once more.

His mouth went tight.

"Late in the day."

"How late?"

"We'll be back by midnight."

"Oh." Vic's voice was now flat and lifeless as a corpse. "I see. That's very sad. Please tell Jackson how sorry we are." The hitch in her throat and the gurgling whine made it clear she was crying.

"Maybe we will see you..."

Jackson shook his head.

"Soon," she finished.

"We miss you and Phoebe so much."

"We miss you, too."

Jackson was rolling his index finger in a circle, signaling her to wind it up.

"I'm so sorry about this. Bye, Victoria." She disconnected while her former mother-in-law was still talking, knowing if she waited another second she'd be crying, too.

Elana set down the phone. Jackson switched it to mute.

"That was cruel," she said.

"I'm not sitting around listening to stories about how wonderful your first husband was."

"He was Phoebe's father."

"But I'm her father now."

No. You're not, she thought, but said nothing.

"We aren't required by law to allow them visitation. Next time they pull a stunt like this, I'm going to tell them point-blank. Stop sending gifts and stop trying to see Phoebe."

* * *

NOW

June 21, 2022, Tuesday
Culpepper Memorial Hospital, Culpepper, NC

"Did you hear him, Elana? They found Jackson alive!"

Zoey repeated the news the police officer had just delivered.

Elana's knees went to water, and she sank back on the bed in the tiny, claustrophobic room in the ER. She gasped like a catfish unexpectedly yanked from the water and tossed up onto the shore. The air in her lungs burned and a pain throbbed behind her breastbone.

Was she having a heart attack?

"I can't believe it."

This was the first honest thing she had said since the police began questioning her.

This was exactly why she'd jumped into the water, against this very possibility. Survived, against all odds.

Does he know?

"Where is he?" Her words came out high, like a reed instrument.

"Coast guard has him. They're airlifting him here."

Her skin burned, like Hercules after slipping on the shirt soaked in poison.

"Is he okay?" she asked the officer.

This question meant everything. Was he able to speak? Was he able to remember?

"I have no information on his condition. Alive. That was the message."

"Thank you for the news," she said, still feeling like an actress portraying some part, the anxious wife thrown a lifeline.

He nodded, scrutinizing her. The steady stare made her face heat.

"I want to see him," she said. It was what she should be saying, wasn't it?

From this instant onward everything would be different. She would need to convince them all that she was joyful at her husband's survival and grateful for a second chance.

Funny, the most important acting roles are never nominated for an Academy Award. This one, for instance, where she played an adoring wife, all grace and elegance, meek, loving, docile instead of a hostage.

You can do this, Elana. You must. Think of your daughter.

Think of Phoebe. Think of those other two girls, who Jackson made pay for their mother's betrayal.

He must not know she'd also betrayed him. Never, ever.

"They'll be bringing him here. I'm sure someone will come get you." With that, the officer withdrew.

Jackson was the only one who might remember that she had not gone in the water with him and that was the greater threat. His retribution would be worse than anything meted out by judge or jury.

She didn't fear the police. She feared her husband. And she didn't fear for herself, but for her daughter.

All Elana could think of doing was getting to her daughter and making a run for it. But what would that look like now?

"Is Phoebe okay with Gabriella? I'm sure she's scared. Maybe I should go get her. She'll want to see her daddy."

And they still might have time to run.

Zoey shook her head.

"Sawyer just sent Derek to watch her until we hear about Jackson. He'll bring her if her daddy is ready for visitors."

Zoey met Elana's gaze; her face impassive, but the threat was there. Jackson's family had her daughter.

"I brought you some of your things. Let me just pop out to the car and get them."

Elana sat on the gurney in the tiny room before the observation window that gave her a view of the comings and goings in the ER.

Zoey returned and passed her a tote bag with the tournament logo. Inside was a feminine flowered dress, formfitting with a scoop neck, pantyhose, and black shoes. This was just the sort of thing Jackson would want her to wear to visit him. Zoey had also included a pouch of Elana's makeup, which she applied with tasteful restraint, as was Jackson's preference, using the tiny mirror in the foundation powder compact.

She stared at the blue circles under her eyes, the ones the

coverup did not completely mask. Her gaunt, haunted image stared back. This would not do.

Elana swallowed down the bitter taste of fear.

She needed to appear an overwrought wife, desperate, hopeful, and now reunited with the man she loved.

Could she convince him that he had dragged them both overboard and that she still lived in the space beneath his bootheel?

Since February, she had planned to run, but had neither the courage nor the opportunity. And though she'd admitted to wishing all manner of horrors would befall Jackson, she was not the sort to murder a human being.

Not yet.

"Ready?" asked Zoey.

Elana nodded and together, they left her observation room. At the nurses' station counter Zoey did the talking, asking where to find Jackson Belauru.

Elana glanced at the large yellow sign with black lettering fixed to the front of the counter. It read:

Safe Haven
Safe Babies—Safe Place

Why didn't they have those for adults? she wondered. Why couldn't she just speak to that nurse and say she could not go back to her husband because she was afraid for her life and the life of her daughter?

Because you don't have your daughter, she reminded herself. Besides, it was too late for that now because, even if it were still possible, he'd send his brothers after her. She no longer had enough time to disappear. And if he ever found them, one day, months from now, Phoebe would be gone.

The buzz of panic vibrating over her skin had receded

enough for the calculating portion of her brain to reengage. He couldn't have figured it out yet.

Not yet. Because he'd been semi-conscious, unsteady on his feet. She knew from similar drinking bouts that he drank to the blackout stage and remembered little afterward.

Blind drunk, he called it. With luck, his memory would be spotty. But what about when he hit that water? What did he remember after that point? Would he recall that she had not been there?

Had he seen her looking down on him from the deck as she searched the dark water for some sign of him? Looking down, and not immediately calling for help?

"Elana?" Zoey stared at her with a puzzled expression. "You all right?"

She nodded. "Just worried."

"Here we go then." Zoey took hold of her arm, guiding her along behind a staff member, leading the parade of wife and sister-in-law outward to the ER waiting room.

"Isn't he in the ER?"

"No. Upstairs," said Zoey. "He's been moved from Critical Care to a regular room. Didn't you hear the nurse?"

She hadn't.

They headed down the hall, her heels ringing on the polished floor.

Once in the elevator, Zoey punched the appropriate button and up they went to seven.

"Is he awake?" she asked.

Zoey gave her an odd look. "Stable was all the nurse told us, whatever that means."

Walking down the long corridor to his room reminded Elana of many nightmares of such places. Lost in a maze of locked doors, she would run, pausing to pound seeking help, seeking the rescue that never came.

Finally, she had taken a tangible step to rescue herself. Why had she ever thought this would work?

Her only consolation was that she had nearly died. Her condition and the illogic of jumping into the sea might save her.

She thought of all the suspects found with self-inflicted wounds claiming some unknown attacker had shot them and killed their intended target.

How many had gotten away with it? How many had died of their injuries?

"Here we are," said Zoey.

No surprise, Detective Elmendorf stood just inside the door, watching Elana with cold, impassionate eyes.

If she had to judge, she'd say this woman had not made up her mind on the wife's role in the apparent accident. From what little she knew of the law, suspicion of guilt was not enough to investigate. They needed evidence of a crime. Like his blood on the helm of the *Reel Escape*. And since Jackson was alive, they would check his story, decide if there had been a crime committed, and, with luck, rule the incident a simple accident.

The room smelled of disinfectant. The next person she saw was Derek.

"I thought he had Phoebe," she said to Zoey.

"Where are the kids?" Zoey asked him.

"Gabriella has them. They're fine."

"Gonna have to give her more overtime," Zoey muttered.

Derek walked them in.

At her appearance, Sawyer rose from where he leaned on the window ledge, casting his gaze upon her. Judging. Derek stepped beside him, and paused, eyes on the bed.

"She's here," said Derek out of the side of his mouth.

Elana couldn't see Jackson because the white curtain hung between his bed beside the window and the empty one beside her. His legs were covered with a white sheet.

"Elana?" That was Jackson. Even with his voice hoarse and raw, she recognized it and found herself rooted to the floor.

She tried and failed to swallow, finding her mouth as dry as her gardens in the yearly winter drought.

Would she be able to tell at a glance what he knew?

Would he be able to tell at a glance what she'd done?

She felt the presence of the detective behind her.

Elana couldn't muster a smile. But then what came next was far better than a forced show of elation.

It only took that one step to see him there, large and imposing despite the bandage wrapping his head and the intravenous line snaking across the blanket to tunnel beneath the cloth tape affixed to the back of his hand. He looked as if he had stuck his head in a wasp's nest. His skin was an unnatural red, puffy, purple in places, and oozing in others. Skin flaked and curled like old paint from his ears and his eyes were swollen nearly shut.

"Oh, Jackson," she cried as the tears welled up like lava finding the closest vent to spill, hot and wet, down her cheeks.

She rushed to his side and threw herself across his body, letting the panic, terror, and horror of his survival ripple through her like the tremors forecasting a major earthquake.

"Sawyer told me they found you first," he said, his free hand coming up and around her in a possessive embrace.

She nodded, continuing to weep. "I told them you were still in the water."

Jackson spoke to his brothers as he stroked her head.

"Give us a minute. Okay?"

She heard them shuffling out and lifted her face to gaze at her husband. From the periphery of her vision, she saw Detective Elmendorf had not left her post and had been joined by her partner, Detective Anderson. The pair stood just beyond Jackson's line of sight keeping Elana in full view.

They had taken the gallery seats, but she was playing to the man seated front and center.

"I thought I'd lost you," she whispered, letting him hear the sorrow she was certain was there in her voice. He didn't need to know that her grief did not stem from the possibility of life without him, but from the reality that he'd survived.

"Why did you come in after me? If you'd stayed on the boat, you could have called for help."

The exhalation came as if someone had stomped on her back, forced from her in a gust. He thought she'd jumped in.

"I didn't come in after you. Jackson, you pulled me overboard."

His eyes narrowed as he absorbed this version of events. She could see the doubts swimming in his eyes.

"You shouldn't have done that," he said, his voice low, menacing.

The quicksilver flash of alarm fired automatically. She stiffened.

"Done what?"

"Fallen. If you'd kept your footing, none of this would have happened."

Of course. Even if he did get so drunk that he fell into the inlet and pulled her in after him, it was still her fault.

She wanted to counter that if he hadn't drunk to the stage where he could barely stand, none of this would have happened, either. Instead, she said, "Yes, Jackson."

This was a situation with which she was all too familiar. His tone and the stiffness of the arm encircling her gave her all the signals she needed.

Did he know they had an audience?

"I'm sorry, Jackson. I shouldn't have fallen, too."

He forced his eyes open to stare and she remained still, trying to summon nothing but docile, helpless regret. Jackson's attention shifted to the foot of the bed and his body stiffened.

"Who the hell are you?" he said.

She turned to glance at the detectives at the foot of Jackson's hospital bed and then rose to stand at his side. It was one of the rare occasions when she found herself momentarily in the superior position.

"I'm Detective Franklin Anderson, heading the investigation over the incident, and this is Detective Denise Elmendorf. I'd like to ask you a few questions, sir, if I might."

Jackson released Elana, who spun to a seated position, facing Anderson.

"Go on?"

"I'll need Mrs. Belauru to wait outside."

"Why?"

"Just routine. Questioning individuals separately gives us a clearer picture of what happened out there."

Jackson's body stiffened. Was he wondering why a detective was here at all? Was he second-guessing his memories?

She certainly would be.

The muscle at Jackson's jaw bulged as he locked his teeth. She hoped he was worried about something like operating a boat under the influence. Anything but the truth—that she'd watched him go over and done nothing to save him.

Elana hurried from the room. In the hall, she fought the urge to dart toward the emergency exit.

Turning, she spotted the three of them, Zoey, Derek, and Sawyer, all watching her.

They still had her daughter.

If she was getting out of this nightmare, this marriage, and their stinking cesspool of a town, she'd need to outfox them all.

FIFTEEN

NOW

June 22, 2022, Wednesday
I-95 Interstate Southbound, Georgia

Before sunset, Jackson drove Elana and Phoebe out of South Carolina crossing the Georgia line on I-95, ignoring the welcome center and the rest area that Elana already needed. Even without drinking anything this morning, her bladder was now complaining at each bump. Eventually, even Jackson would need to go, and she and Phoebe would have a chance to relieve themselves. This was how his hunting dogs must feel, always waiting for the go-ahead to pee.

Ahead, the heat on concrete created a mirage, appearing as a shimmering pool of water before vanishing, only to reappear farther up the road.

Midway across the state, as the sun set, he finally stopped, briefly. Too soon they were flying along the highway again, past Florida's welcome center, picking up the I-10 and heading west.

It was not lost on her that he'd chosen the longer route down a coastal highway, to avoid going anywhere near the home her former in-laws, and perhaps last allies, lived.

Phoebe slumped over in her seat behind them, the stuffed gray furry manatee toy loosely gripped in one hand, because Elana had left her daughter's favorite toy home on the possibility that the unicorn remaining in Phoebe's bedroom might help add to the illusion that she had planned for them to return with him.

Jackson had not waited in the hospital for the detective to come back the next morning, as he'd promised. After the police finished their questioning, he'd demanded his discharge papers and left the moment he'd received them, though they did state he'd been discharged AMA, against medical advice. At the hotel she and Zoey had packed to leave while Jackson and his brothers went to see about the departure of the *Reel Escape*.

However, his boat had to remain in Dare Marina until released by the police. That meant his captain would wait for access to then navigate south around the Florida Peninsula and the Keys, back to the marina in Pensacola.

Jackson seemed to be acting like the guilty party here, which came as a minor relief.

Her husband glanced in the rearview again. Perhaps checking on Phoebe or for some possible pursuit. Sawyer and Zoey were somewhere far behind them in the truck, hauling a travel trailer and their three sons after dropping Derek at the airport in Raleigh.

Jackson's head was no longer wrapped in gauze. He'd tossed that, soaking off the bloody gauze pad to reveal the stitches closing the gash on his forehead and temple. His attending physician had recommended a plastic surgeon. Elana very much doubted he'd do that. But right now, the laceration was an angry pink, crisscrossed with black thread on a blue and purple goose egg the size of an avocado pit.

There was no way Jackson was well enough to be driving, but she wasn't going to try and stop him. The fact that he was even upright was a mark of his stubbornness and tenacity.

Jackson kept tapping the blood-engorged lump and then checking his fingers. For blood or pus, she was uncertain.

He spoke without preamble. "How did you stay afloat all those hours?"

One of his methods of judging her true reaction was to spring questions on her. Another was to alert her that they needed to speak privately. This second one was her least favorite because it involved stewing as she tried to guess the reason for the talk, what mistakes she had made, and what he would do about it.

"I just rolled to my back and floated most of the time. Very little kick."

"Didn't you get cold?"

"Yes. And my eyes were burning from the salt water. I don't think I've ever been so thirsty. I kept imagining all the things I'd love to drink."

He nodded, outwardly satisfied.

"They said I lost eleven pounds," he said.

"Dehydration. Yes. Me too." She prayed that her decision to jump in might just be the single factor that kept him from suspecting. Though it was a funny thing to pray about, getting away with nearly killing herself.

She decided to say what she would have said, had this happened shortly after they were married.

"I don't know what I would have done if I'd lost you. It would destroy me."

"Because you need me."

"I *do*. But I also love you." Yes, that was just what she might have said, back when she didn't know what he had done. When she'd believed in absolutely everything she wanted to believe and stopped at face value, never questioning, or digging deeper. She was in this mess because she'd been too gullible to understand that brutes like Jackson prowled the world exacting vengeance on anyone who betrayed them.

"I've underestimated you."

She forced herself not to hold her breath when the impulse came.

He cast her a sideward glance before flicking his attention back to the highway, dark except for the beams of their halogen headlights.

"I didn't think you were that strong."

"I know. I–I'm surprised, too."

Here was hoping that he continued to underestimate her until she had another chance to be free of him.

"I kept thinking of you," she said, hands knotted in her lap, "swimming to shore and sending me help."

Of course, if she imagined him at all, it was picturing Jackson dragging along the bottom like a crab trap broken loose of its mooring.

"I'll always come for you." His pledge was unmistakably also a threat. She ignored it.

"I don't like to think how close I came to losing you." That was true after a fashion. Thinking of how close she came to freedom before the prison door snapped shut in her face left her crestfallen.

She decided to direct him away from dwelling on how impossible it was she swam that long alone in the dark.

"Should we get life insurance?" she asked.

He flashed her a look of fury. "I'm only thirty-six. I don't need life insurance."

She would have liked to remind him that he was a father and that he'd nearly died, but experience told her that when his face turned that shade of red and his mouth went tight, further discussion only made things worse. And she'd succeeded. He wasn't thinking of her narrow escape.

"Whatever you think is best," she said.

"Damn straight."

The silence stretched as they crossed the flat expanse

beneath glittering stars. The traffic had ebbed shortly after dark until now it seemed only them and the truckers rolling west. Their GPS indicated they were going eighty and had four hours and two minutes remaining until they reached their destination. The landscape was straight as a builder's level and perhaps twenty feet above sea level. Monotony and the steady hum of rubber on concrete lulled. Her head refused to remain up as her eyes drifted closed again.

His voice barked, causing her to startle awake.

"You need to keep me company so *I* don't fall asleep."

She forced her eyes wide as she spoke. "Yes, of course, Jackson."

"Talk about something. Tell me about falling overboard."

"Don't you remember?" Did she succeed in making that sound casual?

He glanced her way, giving her a cold stare. "I remember everything." Did he? Or was this bravado? A trick, perhaps, to get her to admit what she would never say to anyone, ever. "I just want to hear what you remember."

She had the sensation of sinking. When she saw the spots at the periphery of her vision, she knew she was about to pass out. She folded at the waist, getting her head down between her knees.

"What are you doing?"

"I feel dizzy."

"You sick?"

She opened her eyes and realized the spots had receded. Her heart thumped in time to the rubber that filled the gaps between the slabs of concrete.

Thump, thump, thump.

"Should I pull over?"

"No. It's fine." Now the thump of her heart slowed, not to resting, but close.

The constant tension under which she lived gave her hives, eczema, headaches, and a nervous stomach. Now, apparently, she could add fainting spells to a possible stomach ulcer.

She righted herself, slowly as if performing some yoga move.

She turned to check on Phoebe, still slumped and sleeping in the rear seat of the truck.

Swiveling back, she kept her gaze on the road, pretending to forget the topic of conversation.

"So?"

"Hmm?"

"Tell me what you remember."

"We were resting after, well, you know. And it was such a warm night, we wanted to see the stars." This was her first lie. She had gone out. There had been no "we." She paused to see if he would call her out on this. He did not, which either meant he accepted this as true, or he was collecting her mistakes for later use. "You put on your athletic shorts, a T-shirt and your lucky fishing vest. I slipped back into my dress and up we went to the cockpit. We were at the stern, looking up, and you were showing me which of the stars were planets."

"Jupiter," he said.

"Yes. You lost your balance and fell backward. You grabbed me, I tried to hold you, but we both went in."

"And?"

"And when I came up, you were gone and the boat was moving away from me, or it seemed to be. And I tried to swim back, but the current was so strong. I couldn't. No matter how hard I kicked, the tide took me out."

"That's not what happened."

She tried to remain still, but her hands were trembling, so she shoved them under her thighs.

"No?" she asked.

"*You* wanted to see the stars, but *you* fell in. I tried to save you. Hit my head. Blacked out. When I came to, you were gone."

She exhaled. "Is that how it happened?"

"The only thing you got right was the stars and the current."

"I'm sorry."

"Not surprising. My vest deploys when it senses liquid. So, I slipped it over my head and called your name. I searched for hours."

In this version, Jackson was the hero, risking his life to save hers. She could live with that. She glanced at Phoebe, picturing her heading to her grandparents right now while the search was called off and her mother declared dead like her father had been years earlier.

Would she be safe if her mother had died? Or would Jackson still be a threat?

Her husband kept talking, but it seemed more for himself than her benefit, as if he were working out the story that he would relay to others.

"I tried to save you. I searched for you. You are the reason we almost died. Wanted to go on deck to see the stars."

"I'm sorry, Jackson."

"You nearly killed us both. You know that, right?"

On that, at least, they could both agree.

Back at the house, Elana roused Phoebe and helped her to bed, unpacked the car and started the laundry, before finally dragging herself to the bedroom for a few hours of sleep. Seemingly only a moment later, Jackson roused her, wanting a hot breakfast before heading into town hall to check on business. Even battered, bloodied, and bruised, he wanted the citizens of Bald Cypress to see that nothing, not even his near death, could slow him down. And as the mayor of this city, he oversaw every department, knew every police officer, hired every city employee, nominated every school board member, and approved every fire and ambulance corp volunteer. With his brothers, they had their fingers in every pie.

She cracked eggs into a bowl and whisked them with milk that smelled a little suspect. While the oven heated for the corn bread, she ducked into the laundry room to move another load of their things to the dryer.

"Do that after I leave," he said, eyeing the overladen basket of laundry. "Then go pick up Chase, Dash, and Gunner from the kennel."

The three pointers had spent the past ten days in a very nice kennel, which they hated. Upon their return, they would be more clingy and hypervigilant than usual.

"Yes, Jackson."

"Don't forget your phone."

"I won't. May I bring Phoebe?" The ridiculousness of having to ask permission to take along her own daughter was not lost to her.

"Yes, take her. No ice cream. They use that same scoop in all the flavors. Gets chocolate on everything."

She nodded her understanding and lowered the basket to the floor.

Every time she got behind the wheel of any vehicle with Phoebe, she imagined just driving away. Fill the tank with the debit card and she and Phoebe would go.

Where hadn't mattered, only that they would be away from here. Away from him. She'd had a plan. Get to her former in-laws, then escape to a place where Jackson could not find them.

But that was before the FBI had visited and explained exactly what happened to the children of the women who had done just that. You didn't leave this man. At least not in the conventional way.

"Don't leave the laundry here in front of the garage door. Someone might trip and break their neck."

If only.

"Yes, Jackson." She lifted the basket and moved it to the top of the machine.

He pushed her up against the washer. For a moment she thought she was under attack. Then his voice grated in her ear.

"I want us to get pregnant."

It was only luck that he had her flattened with her back to him. It kept him from seeing the momentary flicker of fear change to resistance. He lowered his mouth to her neck and whispered, his breath hot against her nape.

"I want a son. A child of our own."

And with a baby, he'd have yet another tie to bind her.

"Yes, Jackson," she said as her mind screamed objections.

"We've been married over a year." He drew back and spun her toward him. "Sawyer's already having another baby. Four so far and I'll bet a silver dollar it's another boy."

It was not Sawyer but Zoey who was "having another baby." But she did not voice that opinion.

"Do you need to see a doctor or something?"

Of course, it would never occur to him that he might be the problem. He wasn't, as far as she knew, but if he ever discovered the real cause of their "problem" getting pregnant, there would certainly be hell to pay.

Jackson was careless with his loose change. Never counted it and simply dumped it into a bag in the truck or in a bowl in the drawer at the entranceway. It was an oversight by an otherwise vigilant watchdog and how she got everything she needed that he wouldn't allow her. Important things, like spermicide.

The trick was making sure he never saw what she'd purchased.

It had been easy to dump out all the cream from her lavender stress relief body lotion. Harder to suck the spermicide back into the container. But it worked. He never touched her perfumed products and she had it handy to administer before and after they had sex.

It was a technique that worked to date. She could only imagine the fury he'd unleash upon her if he ever discovered what she was doing.

"I'm sorry, Jackson."

It was like her mantra. Her fault, anything, and everything, always. She had become the perfect apology machine.

"I don't want 'sorry.' I want a son!"

"Yes, Jackson. I understand."

He nestled her tight and she forced herself to relax against his embrace.

"I love you so much, Elana. If you ever left me, I'd kill myself."

She closed her eyes against this emotional blackmail. Jackson was a master at this. But this threat was new.

He leaned close and bit her earlobe hard enough to make her jump. Then he said, "But not before I killed you."

Then he laughed and pushed away, harder than necessary, before striding from the room, whistling. She remained, shaking with anger and fear. The combination played havoc on her body. She could feel the hot tingle of the hive already forming on her upper lip. She lifted a finger to the growing hard spot in the soft tissue.

From the kitchen, the oven indicated it was up to temperature for the breakfast he clearly no longer wanted.

Was that true? Would he kill her? Up until this minute she'd believed it was Phoebe's life she risked. But even the great Jackson Belauru couldn't get away with making three step-daughters vanish.

Her death seemed preferable, but not if that left her daughter in the hands of this monster.

She loaded the dryer and started the cycle before heading to the garage to find Jackson's vehicle was gone. Only then could she breathe again.

SIXTEEN

June 26, 2022, Sunday

They had been home four days. Elana made a small breakfast, since they would be going to Zoey's for brunch after services, as usual. Jackson disappeared to get dressed and she cleaned up the kitchen and let the dogs out in the pen beside the house.

The time in the water had damaged her skin and several places were raw and oozing. Despite her sore body and raw wounds, she put on her best dress and a hat to cover some of the damage to her skin, got Phoebe ready, and off they went.

She moved through the day robotically: services, accepting the outpouring of concern from the congregation afterward, brunch at Zoey's, and the inevitable chaos of when you combine children with a swimming pool. Home at last, Jackson settled to watch baseball in the den and she retrieved the dogs for their walk.

"Phoebe, do you want to go to the park with me and the dogs?" It was one of the places Elana did not need permission to visit because Jackson approved of any exercise his dogs could get.

"Yes!"

"Then into a play dress."

Phoebe skipped away.

A few minutes later, Elana walked three dogs toward the park accompanied by her daughter, riding her bike. Once on the empty soccer field, Phoebe chose a stick and Elana released the dogs from their leashes. The three exuberant pointers leapt before her daughter as Elana settled on a bench, sweating in the shade, as storm clouds billowed threatening rain.

Despite the restriction of the tight bodice of her dress, Phoebe could really fling that branch. The stick spiraled out and away. The dogs tore after it, Gunner in the lead and Chase and Dash close behind.

A woman sat beside her. Elana turned to smile and nod.

But the smile fell away, dropped like a glass bottle on concrete. There beside her on the bench was FBI Special Agent Inga.

"Hello, Elana."

"I can't talk to you."

"Of course, you can. It's just a conversation."

"Not without a lawyer." Elana fixed her eyes on Phoebe and the dogs, hopping and frantic for another throw.

"I see. Well, I'll talk then. We found Raelyn. Shantel Keen's daughter."

Hope exploded like a bursting firework.

"Alive?"

The agent glanced away. "No. Unfortunately, no. She's dead. A homicide."

Elana folded at the waist, both hands tight over her mouth and eyes squeezed shut.

"Oh, no," she muttered. She thought back to the photograph Agent Inga had shown her, of a little blue-eyed girl smiling broadly at her birthday party.

"Yes, I'm afraid so. Killed shortly after her abduction

according to the ME. My partner and I are heading over to inform your husband and to see if he might have anything to help us find Raelyn's killer."

Killer.

She's still missing. Did you know that?

"I thought you might want to know before you head home."

Oh my God! Jackson would be livid. Enraged.

"You're certain you found her?"

"Positive ID. One curious detail. Her body was fully dressed, minus the one flip-flop recovered from the scene of her abduction. But two items were missing, the red sequined headband she wore and a woven friendship bracelet." The agent used her thumb and index finger to encircle her wrist. "You know the kind? Girls make them for their friends. This one was a rainbow of colors. Embroidery thread, you know?"

She did know, because she'd seen them on the wrists of some of the older children in Phoebe's school.

"Yes, I know what you mean."

"The point is that Raelyn Keen was wearing that headband and bracelet when abducted, but neither item was recovered with her body. Which means that her murderer might have kept these things as mementos."

Elana didn't try to keep the revulsion from her face. She turned to the agent.

"Who would do such a thing?"

The agent smiled. "We think we know. And if you find either item, it will likely contain Raelyn's DNA. If your husband is in possession of either of these articles, we'd have enough for an arrest warrant."

Elana stiffened. The agent was asking for her help, but she was also asking Elana to risk both her and her daughter's life.

"So tragic. Her abductor just plucked her from the grass like a daisy." The agent watched Phoebe retrieve the stick dropped at her feet by Dash. "You would think a child would be safe in her own backyard."

The first rumble of thunder sounded. The storm was building.

"Mrs. Belauru, which of Jackson's wives have you met?"

"Well, Faith, of course. She lives right outside town."

"In a home your husband provided."

Elana did not respond to that.

"And Shantel Keen?"

"She crashed my wedding rehearsal dinner."

"Why would she do that?"

To warn me, she thought. "She seemed to have mental illness issues. Perhaps she was drunk, too."

"I see. You know that, in December, Shantel's home was destroyed in a suspicious fire?"

Elana looked straight ahead, neither affirming nor denying. But perhaps her silence was answer enough.

"Arson. And the odd thing is that the fire started in her bedroom, on her bed, using an accelerant. Gasoline. Not many people have that lying around their bedroom."

"That's very sad."

"Your husband was hunting that December weekend. Both his brothers and the hunting reserve verified his alibi."

Here on the bench in the shade, her breath seemed to be coming through a straw now, making it so difficult to catch her breath. Meanwhile Phoebe cast the branch again for the eager dogs.

Everything looked so benign. So safe.

"Elana, do you have anything that might help us?" asked Inga.

"Anything... no. I'm not helping you." The cloud that had been majestic and soaring now had a dark gray underbelly. The rumble came again.

"I see."

"I have to get Phoebe home before the storm." Elana stood.

Inga remained seated.

"We heard about the boat accident. Anything you'd like to tell me?"

"I'm sure you've read my statement to the police there."

She nodded.

"So you know everything."

"Funny you both going over. Happens, I suppose."

Elana set her jaw, refusing to say another word, wanting to call Phoebe. Not wanting her daughter to see her talking to this agent.

"Did you know, Elana, that when a woman is about to leave an abusive relationship, violence escalates?"

"Why tell *me* that?"

"Just a warning. Be very careful. This man, your husband, is dangerous and we don't think you have the resources to get far enough away to protect you and Phoebe. He'll come for you. Find you."

The agent's words echoed her own deepest fears. Elana turned her back on Inga, staring at her beautiful, precious girl.

"If you help us, we can help you."

She looked over her shoulder. "How?"

"I could take you and your daughter to a domestic violence agency right now."

"He'd find us there."

"Well, then your best option might be to provide incriminating evidence against your husband. If you furnish us with evidence that will help us build a case, for that kind of help, we could refer you to WPP."

"What is WPP?"

"Witness Protection Program. US Marshals would take you somewhere safe. Give you and your daughter new identities. A fresh start."

The glimmering possibility of that stopped her breathing. But then the rest of her deal hit her like a moving vehicle.

Trial? Testimony? Elana's skin crawled at the thought of what he'd do if he even heard a word of this conversation.

"You're going to get us killed." But Inga was right.

Her best chance, perhaps her only chance, was to find something the FBI could use to prove Jackson took either of his former stepdaughters.

"I'll think about it."

"That's wonderful. You have my card?"

"Yes."

Elana watched the agent head back toward the parking area.

Jackson had two ex-wives and two missing stepdaughters. The internal wave of wintery frost stippled Elana's skin as she realized that one of the girls was no longer missing.

Raelyn was dead.

And Raelyn's mother was the one who'd had the audacity to try and warn Jackson's bride that her nuptials were a terrible, dangerous mistake. He'd burned Shantel's house down. Elana had no evidence and yet no doubt.

How could she ever have been so fooled by this man?

He needed to be locked away where he could never get his hands on another little girl. *Her* little girl.

Elana couldn't run. Couldn't register her daughter for school without a birth certificate and inoculation records, school progress reports, and the like. And the minute she asked for those, Jackson would have them.

He had handpicked the school board president and sat in on the interview for the superintendent of schools. He did that with all branches of government in his boondocks of a town.

She'd once been impressed with the power he wielded. Now it terrified her.

Jackson had done what he promised. He'd cleared her debt.

Given them a beautiful home, reliable vehicle, and gotten Phoebe into a good school. And all at the price of her sanity and peace of mind.

Special Agent Inga had asked her for assistance implicating Jackson. They suspected Jackson, but had nothing to prove he'd done any of this. Accepting the offer to get her to an agency that could help her escape her marriage was tempting. But it was an illusion. Jackson was relentless. He'd find them eventually. She understood that nothing would be as secure or have the best chance of delivering them from his control than joining witness protection. And it was an opportunity to get justice for those poor missing girls. Closure for their grieving mothers. She could help if she took the path Agent Inga offered.

But that course was also the most dangerous.

Could she be brave enough? Certainly, she was in the right place, inside the monster's cave. She might find what they could not, because she lived with this fiend.

A red headband.

A friendship bracelet.

She'd start searching tomorrow.

SEVENTEEN

June 27, 2022, Monday

Elana was anxious to search for any evidence that might help Special Agent Inga, and enable her and her daughter to escape Jackson. Early on, she'd recognized Jackson was a tyrant and she had suspected worse. Now she knew he was evil right down to his dark, controlling soul.

Her grand act of defiance began with mundane chores. They'd been gone a week and she had little food in the house. Once she dropped Phoebe off at Bible camp, that meant a trip to the grocery store and one to Faith's farm stand. She did this every week, a normal part of her routine, because Jackson loved Faith's breads, cakes, and jams. Jackson provided the cash; Faith provided a receipt. Elana made certain there was never any discrepancy.

But today she felt nervous because she knew that Faith's own daughter had gone missing at Jackson's hands. He'd let her believe that Grace had been old enough to leave their church and run away. But she had only been five years old. Had she met the same fate as poor Raelyn?

Elana parked, noticing that Faith had only a few items out in her stand, so she headed to her house and knocked on the door.

She braced, preparing, and cautioning herself to behave as she had always done since first meeting Faith. But she could not understand the woman's unfailingly pleasant demeanor. She seemed to bear Jackson no grudge for their failed marriage or any perceivable grief at her daughter's kidnapping. Rather than being grief-stricken and miserable, Faith exuded joy.

Unnatural, she thought.

The screen door creaked open and there she was, dressed in blue today and sweating and smiling, as usual.

"Well, hello, Elana. You are early today."

"Too early?"

"No, no. Not at all." Faith's smile wavered. "What happened to you?"

Elana knew she looked a fright, with a swollen puffy face and the bandages on her forearms. Her muscles still ached, and her throat felt as if she had the worst case of strep ever.

She explained about their ordeal in a rasping voice.

Faith looked past her to her vehicle, one hand over her heart. "Is Jackson all right?"

"Yes. He struck his head and has stitches on his forehead, but the doctor cleared him to come home."

Faith looked past her, searching the yard. "Where is he?"

"Work."

Her shoulders sagged. "That's a blessing." She returned her attention to Elana. "God was watching over you both."

Elana forced a smile.

"What can I get for you today? You've been gone a week. Larders must be empty."

"Nearly."

"Just finishing up the baking. I like to get that done before it gets too hot." She swiped a dishrag over her flushed face. "Would you come in?"

Judging from the heat pouring from the interior, Elana sensed it was already too hot. Faith did have electricity, but only a window fan and no air conditioning.

"Do you have any bread?"

"Yes, yes. Just a minute. It's cooling."

How anything could cool in that sweatbox was beyond her.

Elana waited in the shade of the house. Faith emerged carrying a brown paper sack.

"Too hot for the plastic," she said, handing it over.

Elana gave her the exact amount in cash.

"I put in some cookies for Phoebe and Jackson."

"Thank you."

"And I made you some tea," she handed over a smaller bag filled with dried herbs. "Just seep it in some hot water. It's to help with conception."

Elana's brows rose. "Oh, well that's very kind. Thank you."

She tucked the bag in her purse and glanced toward her vehicle, eager to be gone.

"I told Jackson that perhaps you are like Hannah, mother of Samuel. She was barren for many years, but God granted her prayers and gave her a son. And Elizabeth, mother of John the Baptist, was an old woman and barren until she conceived. Both devout. You are praying?"

"Ah, yes."

"Do you read the Bible?"

"I do." She didn't like the way this conversation had turned. The topic and speaking about it with Faith made her uncomfortable.

"One of my favorite passages is the story of Tamar. Do you know it?"

Elana shook her head, wondering what was in the tea. No way to tell from the bits of dried leaves and twigs.

"When Tamar's husband died, it was her right to marry his brother. But his father denied the match. Yet, she knew her duty was to produce a son by her husband's line. So, she dressed as a prostitute, went to her husband's father, and conceived a son by him. In doing so, she did her duty to her husband."

Elana tried and failed to keep her expression from showing her disgust.

"I'll have to look that up."

Was Faith suggesting Elana sleep with one of Jackson's brothers? That thought made her flesh crawl. Something was wrong with this woman.

"Genesis," said Faith.

Back at home, Elana put away the groceries and baked goods and dumped the tea Faith had made down the drain. Then she cut open several ordinary teabags and refilled the packet. That task complete, she prepared for her search for the evidence the FBI believed Jackson had retained, the chilling keepsakes. Reminders of the depth of his evil.

She thought of Shantel's little girl and shivered, knowing that Jackson's second wife might be the only person alive willing to help her implicate Jackson.

Shantel had divorced Jackson. And paid for it with her daughter.

But Elana never would, because she was doing whatever it took to get herself and Phoebe into witness protection.

Fueled by black coffee and a banked rage at how any human could commit such evil, she prepared herself. At the garage door, she hesitated. Her emotions seesawed between indignant fury and terror for her child. What she was about to do, it could not be undone. And if Jackson had even the tiniest suspicion of what she was up to, both she and her daughter were in grave danger.

Elana released the knob and retreated to safer ground. Start small, she thought, and then she'd build to searching the things she'd been told never to touch.

The first item she found was in her own things. Elana kept a paper calendar because it helped Phoebe, who earned stickers for completing certain chores and her schoolwork. She already knew that Jackson and Sawyer had taken an overnight hunting trip on the December weekend when Shantel's home had burned. She'd made a note of it in her calendar. This wasn't evidence, exactly. The FBI had already said he had witnesses to his whereabouts from the hunting party.

"His brothers," she muttered, knowing they could not be trusted. She kept looking.

Jackson kept large plastic bins out in the garage on the wall of shelving. She checked methodically through hunting things, fishing gear, car-washing implements, tools, finding nothing that seemed to belong to a little girl. She searched the Christmas decorations and paper, the familiar garlands, a stuffed polar bear in the red sweater. The glass ornaments for each of the twelve days of Christmas. Stockings, just three, and the ones for the dogs, of course.

Nothing.

The boxes of documents interested her the most. She went through everything but the fireproof lockbox. Breaking into that would certainly be noted, eventually.

Below the locked box was another smaller cardboard container and inside that were photographs.

Jackpot.

Elana opened the box, memorizing how the stacks of images were arranged and which ones were on top.

Then she sat on the cement floor, upturning the contents before placing them back in the box in the same order.

She had similar boxes. Images taken back when cameras had film and were developed in the drugstore. She didn't recall

exactly when the world had switched to all digital, but knew her
wedding photos were mostly digital, as were Phoebe's baby
pictures.

All the photos from her childhood and teen years were
printed. She scanned through Jackson's memories. Most of
them were of his family. His older brother, Sawyer, and kid
brother, Derek, at the lake, at the theme parks, at the ocean, and
somewhere on a farm with tractors and an older couple. Grandparents? The background looked like the Midwest.

There were ones of his father, the man who had made
billions in real estate, duck hunting with his three boys and dogs
that, except for the markings, might have been Dash, Gunner,
and Chase. Lydia was there, too, her smile the same in every
image and haunting in its familiarity.

She found one of Jackson in a tuxedo standing beside a thin
girl with dark red hair and huge brown eyes. Her lavender dress
was a shade darker than the paint beside Elana.

The next several photos were of football games. She
assumed one of the players was either Jackson or Sawyer. Then
one showed Jackson with that same girl, now in a cheerleading
costume. Red and white, the small white pom-poms were huge
on her narrow hips. She seemed curvier than in the prom
photo.

The next series of photos showed why.

The girl was pregnant. In the next image her stomach
bulged, threatening to topple her birdlike frame.

And then came a photo with Jackson holding a pink
newborn wrapped in a blue blanket and wearing a tiny
blue cap.

Did Jackson have a son?

She flipped the first of one of three boxes of photos and was
frustrated again that there was nothing written on the back of
any of these prints. Elana continued to search, coming upon a
professionally made birth announcement. There was an image

of a fuzzy-headed newborn in a blue cotton top. Beside the image it read:

Welcoming our BABY, Wyatt Benjamin
October 8, 2005 at 11:05 p.m.
6 pounds 4 oz. 17 inches
Proud parents,
Marlo Sullivan & Jackson Belauru

Jackson had a son!

He had gotten a girl pregnant during high school. Had the teens married? The mother had kept her maiden name. So perhaps not.

Elana calculated the years. At eighteen, Jackson had gotten an underclassman in trouble.

She studied the image of Marlo. Was she even fifteen?

Marlo had dark red hair, tanned freckled arms, and a hopeful expression. Twig legs stuck out below the short white pleated skirt of her cheerleading uniform. She looked like a middle school student with no curves yet in evidence.

She went back to the photos of the football games, looking at the uniforms of the cheerleaders on the sidelines and noting that Marlo's was different. Junior Varsity? Frosh football?

Yes, she suspected so.

She continued to search, but found only graduation photos with Jackson looking older. But both the girl, Marlo, and his son, Wyatt, had vanished from the box.

Where had they gone?

Clearly, Jackson was in high school when Marlo got pregnant.

Elana stared at the baby's photo. This boy would be almost seventeen. Older than the age Marlo had been when discovering herself pregnant.

"Marlo Sullivan," Elana said, staring at the image of the fragile girl with the bulging stomach. "Where did you go?"

Elana put everything back on the shelves with trembling hands, returning to the house to call to make the appointment with her gynecologist, as Jackson had insisted. As a bit of bad luck, they had an opening on Thursday, which she took, afraid to do otherwise.

Was that enough time for the spermicide to leave her body or would some trace remain? Worse still, that meant that if Jackson slept with her, she'd be unprotected.

One thing was certain, she was never having Jackson's child. The very idea of sharing his bed, after learning what he was, made her physically ill.

It was the one place she feared he would notice a change. How did she keep from showing him with every touch that she feared and despised him?

Gavin. Her husband who was taken too soon. Even though he was gone forever, he could still save her, because she would close her eyes and see his face, feel his warm body. Memories of Gavin might just be enough to fool the monster in her bed.

She'd missed lunch, but saw it was nearly time for Zoey to drop Phoebe off from camp. And, since it was Monday, she knew Jackson would miss dinner because of the weekly common council meeting that kept him late, usually well past ten in the evening.

So, after her daughter returned, Elana took Phoebe to the library, as usual. But unlike most other visits, she left Phoebe with the other children, on the colorful rug in the children's section of their public library. The afternoon story hour had just begun, and she wondered if she might find the addresses and phone numbers for Marlo Sullivan and Shantel Keen.

She wanted to tell Shantel how terribly sorry she was about

her daughter's death and how committed she was to helping the FBI find Raelyn's killer. Maybe Shantel herself had information that could help her. She was also very curious about Marlo Sullivan. It disturbed her, to the point of lifting the hairs on her neck, that no one in town or Jackson's family had ever mentioned her. It was as if she were also dead. But the FBI would have mentioned that, surely. How could Jackson, his family, and every member of her church and this town have failed to mention to her that Jackson had gotten a girl in trouble during high school, and she had delivered a son? The entire omission seemed like a criminal conspiracy.

She dove into the reference material with determination. Unfortunately, she did not find any listing in the directories for either Shantel or Marlo.

Frustrated, she pushed the volume back in place and glanced about. Several of the kiosks had people hunched over laptops. The tables before the circulars had three visitors and an unattended computer.

She had her own computer at home, but didn't dare use it for this.

Elana inched closer, becoming a thief. Should she just take the laptop and go to some private place in the library? Or use it right here?

She stood beside the table now, her eyes flashing here and there as she searched for the owner and then dropped to the object of her racing pulse.

The front of the small laptop was covered with stickers of musical groups and environmental activism. She frowned at the Darwin fish, knowing that her sister-in-law would not approve. Zoey was very religious. Asking after Elana's religious convictions was among the very first inquiries she'd made. Zoey had informed Elana that she did not approve of divorces or second marriages. Marriage was forever, she'd said. Elana had been so taken aback that she had failed to ask if that was true for Jackson as well, or just for her. And, in conjunction, what about second marriages after your husband was killed by a motorist who should never have been driving?

She spotted the laptop owner now, there by the circulation desk, leaning over the counter, chatting with a pretty young woman who smiled and twirled a strand of tawny hair about her index finger.

That was something that would draw a young man away from even the temptations of the digital world.

Elana slipped into the seat before the computer. At a single brush of her finger on the touchpad, the screen roused to a familiar internet browser.

She typed: Marlo Sullivan, address.

The results populated immediately. But they each wanted money to give her the information.

The boy's backpack sat beside his chair. Heart racing, and keeping one eye at the circulation desk, she rummaged and found his wallet and credit cards.

Who had she turned into?

She knew if she was caught, the police would do nothing, because of her position as the wife of the mayor and her husband's influence over such things. Unless Jackson wanted to make an example of her. Thoughts of what Jackson might do had her stomach jump like a trampoline performer.

Her clumsy fingers fell on the wrong keys as she entered the card information. She tried again and then flipped the plastic to get the three-digit code.

In a moment she was back at the search. There were twenty-one M. Sullivans in the state of Florida. But only one listed an association with a W. Sullivan.

She tore a sheet of paper from the young man's spiral note-book and scribbled down the information. Marlo Sullivan and her son lived all the way in Jacksonville, Florida.

Her mind flashed her a memory of a warm September day.

Before she'd realized just how bad things were. She and Jackson had been on their way to a fundraiser when he took a detour.

She frowned, recalling the trim little street and the modest home where he'd slowed to stare at a boy and a dog playing in their front yard.

"An old friend, was it?" she whispered. "Or was that your son, Jackson?"

A better question was: how was *she* going to get to Jacksonville?

Elana was unsure what she would learn, but she determined to follow this thread to discover all she could about Jackson's past. In addition, she was worried about Marlo Sullivan's safety. If this woman had abandoned him, her child might be in danger. Though she acknowledged there were key differences between the boy and the missing children. The girls had been abducted soon after their mothers and Jackson had divorced. Also, Wyatt was male and he was Jackson's biological son. Was that enough to protect him? She didn't know, but was determined to warn his mother of what the FBI had told her.

But Jacksonville! It might as well be on the moon. Jackson tracked her mileage on the car, overtly to check the gas mileage, but also to record how many miles she went each day. He had the pattern down and would notice a detour of several hundred miles.

A bus? Would take too long. And tickets cost money.

Shantel's search was easier. She learned Shantel Keen lived in Tallahassee near where she and Phoebe had picked out her daughter's bedroom set.

A glance to the circulation desk showed the pair still engaged in conversation.

She hurriedly jotted down the contact information, thinking this a fool's errand. How would she ever even access a phone to contact them? Perhaps a letter?

But what if they replied?

The postman, a friend of Jackson's, delivered their residential mail to city hall. He'd see it.

She abandoned that notion, closed the search engine, and glanced back to the desk. Feeling eyes upon her, she noticed the girl at the far end of the adjoining table watching her, her mouth pressed into a tight expression of disapproval. A flash of guilt heated her face and Elana's neck prickled. Setting aside the pencil, she watched the girl who had been staring leave her spot and head toward the circulation desk.

Elana lowered her head and hurried toward the children's section. A backward glance showed all three in a group, the girl pointing in her direction. She ducked her head and fled around the bookshelf.

He'd check his computer first. Had the girl watched her use his credit card? Oh, God, that had been stupid and dangerous. What if his webcam was on?

She pictured her name in the local paper.

Mayor's wife arrested for petty theft.

In the children's section, Phoebe sat with legs folded, attention on the storyteller, who read an elaborately illustrated fairy tale.

Elana gave her shoulder a brief touch and then motioned her to come. Her daughter's face fell. She loved stories and reading.

But Elana hadn't time to argue. She extended her hand and the moment she had a hold on Phoebe, they hurried toward the rear exit. She paused at the sign that said that an alarm would sound.

"Mommy, I didn't get a book yet," said Phoebe.

Elana drew a breath and pressed the panic bar. She and her daughter were well down the sidewalk when she realized that no alarm sounded, and no one pursued them.

At the SUV, she opened the rear door and told Phoebe to hurry.

Something in her tone caused her daughter to scamper up into the car seat.

"Where are we going?" she asked as Elana buckled her in.

"Home."

Was that a momentary flash of disappointment on her daughter's face?

She swept into the driver's seat and started the engine, popped the gear into reverse, and hit the accelerator. They were out of the lot in seconds. Elana glanced in the rearview mirror, but saw no one. That didn't mean they had not called the police or that no one had recognized her.

How stupid was she? That was super dangerous. She'd have to be incredibly lucky not to get caught. Her mind flashed a montage of grizzly images of the actual fate that befell those missing children. What had he done to them? What had he done with them?

He had killed them and had done so without a moment's remorse. If anything, she believed he'd find the prospect of having one of his ex-wives completely in his control empowering. Did he get a thrill from taking her only child?

And why did he protect Faith? Demand Elana shop with his ex-wife and treat her... and the answer came to her. Faith was family. A second cousin, blood relative, just like Wyatt.

But she and Phoebe were not.

She had nothing to fight this man. He was a wild cat with fangs and claws, and she was a field mouse. Her only choice was to run and hide.

In the back seat, Phoebe was crying.

EIGHTEEN

June 30, 2022, Thursday

Eight days after returning from North Carolina, Elana's body was healing and the bruising on Jackson's forehead had spread under his left eye in spectacular fashion. The colors from the internal bleeding had traveled across his brow and to his cheek, making him look like a surly raccoon, but the stitches were out.

Jackson arrived back at the house in time to accompany her to her doctor's appointment. Since Monday, she had searched the house and all of Jackson's things, but found nothing to implicate him in the abductions. Though that lockbox in the garage tempted, she'd resisted, because, sooner or later, he'd notice.

They left home well before the appointment and after arrival and check-in, Elana bounced her leg restlessly as she worried about the spermicide showing up on something. Jackson would be livid. He thought they were trying to have a baby, and the last thing she needed was for him to learn exactly why they hadn't.

Thus far, he had not tried to bed her since Monday. Whether that was because of his preoccupation with the police investigation of the accident or because his body, like hers, was still suffering the aftereffects of the battering they had received, she did not know.

But it was a rare stretch of good luck. Elana sighed, knowing it would not last.

What would he do to her?

"Mrs. Belauru?" The nurse standing in the partially opened door called her name. She was stick-thin with russet-brown skin and hair piled in an imposing tower on her head.

Jackson stood up. "We're here."

The nurse gave him a silent stare. "You'd like to join us?"

He nodded.

"Just a minute, please."

She left them both standing there. Elana gritted her teeth to keep from whimpering. Perhaps she didn't have the constitution for this, sneaking around, deceiving Jackson, hunting for clues.

And that was precisely why he'd picked her as a wife. It wasn't because she was capable. It was because he thought her easily cowed, overly anxious to please, and in desperate need of providing for and protecting her daughter.

Jackson found her exactly the opposite of capable.

How could she ever have been so naïve?

The nurse returned and showed them into an exam room. Jackson took a seat, and Elana was told to take off everything, including panties, wear the gown with the ties in front, and place the paper wrap over her lap.

She did as she was told and sat on the white paper wrapped in more paper.

Jackson paid her no attention as he checked his phone. But she felt his intrusion here, keenly.

He stood when the doctor arrived and then resumed his place.

Elana had met her new gynecologist only once. The woman was mid-forties, with a solid, squarish body and brown hair in a simple pony. Today she wore purple scrubs and a matching stethoscope looped over her neck like a scarf. She lifted the laptop, glancing at the information there and then set it aside to wash her broad, sturdy hands. As she scrubbed, she asked preliminary questions and then went right to work, beginning with a breast exam and moving south from there. Her husband's presence cast a pall over the appointment for Elana, and she could barely relax enough for the physician to be able to complete the pelvic exam.

"Nothing wrong that I can see," the doctor said, stripping off her gloves and tossing them into the trash. "I'm referring you to a specialist." She turned to Jackson. "He might want a sample from you as well, but you can do that here."

"A sample?" Jackson's face flushed. "There's nothing wrong on my end."

"Well, my assistant will set up your appointment." She turned to Elana. "Best of luck to you, Mrs. Belauru."

"Thank you."

The way she said it made Elana sure down to her naked toes that the doctor had examined both the previous Mrs. Belaurus, as neither of them had given Jackson a son.

But Marlo Sullivan had.

The door closed, leaving her alone with Jackson, who was red-faced and puffing. Back out at reception, they stood side by side in the outer office, across the counter from the physician's assistant, who consulted her computer monitor.

Jackson declined to set up an appointment and so the receptionist turned to Elana.

"So... just the consult for Mrs. Belauru with Dr. Zelden at the fertility clinic in Jacksonville?"

"That's right," said her husband.

Jacksonville!

Marlo Sullivan lived in Jacksonville. The thrill died as she realized she had exactly zero chance of ever finding herself alone in that city. Zero chance of learning if Marlo had suffered some tragedy as a result of leaving Jackson. She longed for answers, anything that could bring her closer to finding the evidence the FBI needed to send Jackson out of her life forever.

"Oh, wow. Lucky you," said the gaunt assistant, who seemed to have either an eating disorder or a tapeworm, judging from her decaying teeth and sunken cheeks. "They had a cancelation. So you can get in this Wednesday. That's July sixth."

Miracle of miracles, that date overlapped with Jackson and his brother's long-planned fishing trip to the Panhandle, and they'd already paid the two-thousand-dollar entrance fee.

Elana realized instantly and a spark of joy ignited. She kept her expression blank as the ember burned bright as a bonfire in a mine shaft. Giving away her desire to go without him was a certain way to crush the possibility. Jackson enjoyed seeing her hopes dashed. It was one of the ultimate thrills. So, she deferred to him.

"What do you think?" she asked.

He scowled at her, then shook his head.

"Pensacola International Tournament," he said. He turned to the assistant. "When is the next one?"

"Not until the third week in October, I'm afraid. They are booked pretty solid. Of course, they can put you on a waiting list. Something else might pop up." She shrugged and then chewed on a ragged nail as she waited.

October was duck hunting season. Elana staunched a smile.

He glanced at his wife. "You be able to drive down there alone?"

"I think so." She sounded uncertain when she felt like dancing an Irish jig. "Maybe Zoey can watch Phoebe. It's about two hours, right?"

"The way you drive, maybe."

"Well, I can make it there and back in a day."

He hesitated and she stilled the mad jiggling of her foot.

Her knee was bobbing like the needle on her sewing machine, relaying her anticipation at the possibility of being alone in a city where Marlo and Wyatt Sullivan resided.

Jackson snorted out of his nose like a horse clearing dust from its nasal passages. Plainly, he was less than thrilled by this situation.

"God damn it. Fine. Book it. Maybe Zoey can go along."

But it turned out, her sister-in-law had a church leadership conference in Seacrest and was unable to go.

Independence Day weekend had meant a church picnic on Sunday with sparklers and games for the kids and a potluck lunch, of course.

The Fourth landed on a Monday. Jackson and his brothers left early for the Pensacola International Tournament that ran through Wednesday. She and Phoebe spent the day at Zoey's for a poolside barbeque and to watch the city's fireworks display on the lake after dark.

On Wednesday, the 6th, Elana stole the spare key to the coin catchers from Jackson's closet and headed to the laundromat he owned. There she filled a sandwich bag full of quarters. She'd need them to get to her destination once she reached Jacksonville. After an uneventful drive, she parked in the medical facility garage and took the pedestrian walkway to the offices.

She was early, and they were running late. A dilemma. It felt like an opportunity, but if she left and missed her appointment, Jackson would know. If she waited, she might not have time to visit Marlo.

"How far behind are you running?" she asked the sullen-faced blonde behind the reception counter.

"About forty-five minutes."

"I see."

The receptionist's phone buzzed, and she took the call.

"Yes, I'll take care of it." Lowering the handset, she rose to her feet and spoke to Elana and the three women waiting in the reception area. "That was the hospital. Dr. Zelden has been called in for an emergency surgery. I'm afraid we will have to reschedule your appointments."

There was a groan from everyone but Elana. Had she just caught a second break? Jackson wouldn't know if she'd been waiting an hour before they canceled.

The others shuffled to their feet. Elana realized she was first in line.

"I, um, I have to check with work before I can make another appointment." Amazing how easily the lie came. But saying she did not dare make an appointment without first checking with Jackson was too embarrassing. So, she covered for her situation instead. "Could you phone me a taxi?"

"Certainly." Elana waited as she made the call.

"It will be here in three to seven minutes."

Elana smiled. "Lovely. Thank you."

She was free. Free to find Marlo Sullivan and learn what she could.

Her only stop was the bathroom, where she dropped her phone in the garbage, hearing it land with a soft thunk, cushioned by all the wadded paper towels. Then she removed her monogrammed tag and tossed that in as well.

There was a risk he might call or be angry that she did not reply to a text. But worse would be if he knew where she was when she was supposed to be at the doctor's.

Elana hurried to the portico, her silver princess flats beating against the sidewalk and her stylish dress, adorned with pink poppies, flapped against her thighs with the rhythm of her stride. The taxi waited and she swept inside. She reached Marlo Sullivan's home in nineteen minutes.

As she neared the location, the hairs on her neck lifted. This was the street Jackson had taken them to, on their trip to the political fundraiser.

The buzz in her ears and twist in her gut told her that she knew the house. And sure enough, Marlo's home was the one with the unattended landscaping where the boy and dog had stood. She'd been right. Jackson had been stalking his old flame.

Marlo was in danger.

Elana paid the cabby in quarters and skillfully ignored his look of disgust. Money was money and that was the best she could manage.

She stepped from the vehicle determined to warn Marlo of exactly what the FBI believed Jackson was capable. She could not save Raelyn or Grace. But she could help Marlo protect her boy.

She hurried along past the scraggly, overgrown landscaping to the modest white house that seemed neglected, but the grass had been recently mown. At the walkway, she paused to note drawn curtains filling every visible window. Elana walked beside the guardrail that stretched from the carport to the front door with more confidence than she felt.

The video doorbell gave her a moment's pause, but she pressed it and was rewarded with the ominous barking of a big dog.

The door swung open and the barking grew louder. The huge dog made a lunge for her, but was blocked by both a leg and a hand on his collar.

"Sit!" The voice was so like Jackson's, Elana staggered back a step.

The German shepherd complied instantly, pink tongue now lolling as he looked benign and peaceful as a grazing sheep.

Elana swallowed, making an involuntary sound in her throat before directing her gaze upward.

There stood a boy not much taller than Jackson, with the same brown eyes, slanting downward at the corners, and the same square jaw. The resemblance ended at his hair, which was the color of polished copper. Beside him the canine watched with interest, tufted brows lifted.

The boy glanced to her vehicle and then drifted back to sweep over her.

"Can I help you?"

"I'm here to see Marlo."

"Oh yeah? She expecting you?" He also had his father's expression of skepticism and suspicion.

"She's not. But it's important."

He hesitated, hand on the door. Then he turned his head and shouted over his shoulder.

"Ma! Somebody wants to see you."

The dog's ears perked, and he darted away, back into the house and out of sight.

"Coming." The voice was lyrical.

The sound of footsteps and the click of the dog's toenails on the tile floor heralded her approach.

"Who is it, Wyatt?"

"I don't know. Said she was here to see you. Important." He turned to Elana. "Right?"

She nodded.

"Are you from social services?"

"No. I'm from, ah, Bald Cypress."

"Bald Cy...?" The female voice trailed off and she slowed her approach.

The dog leaned against Marlo's leg as she moved forward. It took a moment to understand what Elana was seeing. The face of the woman before her showed a fine lacework of puckering white scars. The pigment around her forehead and temple was gone, bleached white.

The reason for the dog, its behavior, and her son gently taking his mother's arm all collapsed on her with the realization that Marlo Sullivan was blind.

NINETEEN

The woman stood with one hand in the crook of her son's arm and the other gently brushing the top of the German shepherd's head. Her milky eyes stared upward and in opposite directions. Her smile was gentle and welcoming and untouched by the scars that covered her forehead and eyes like a cobweb. Her long red hair lay in a braided plait over one shoulder.

"Hello, may I help you?"

Elana finally recovered herself over the shock of seeing the evidence of some dreadful accident, but didn't know how to introduce herself without alerting Wyatt who she was as well.

"Are you from Bald Cypress?"

"Yes."

She nodded. "What is it you want?"

"I wanted a chance to speak to you, Ms. Sullivan, about a mutual acquaintance. My name is Elana..." Here her words trailed off and she drew a breath before adding the rest. "Elana Belauru."

Marlo Sullivan sucked in air through her nose as if she'd been slapped. Her entire body stiffened.

"Belauru?" asked Wyatt.

The note of menace in his voice was so like his father's, it sent a zing of terror straight up her spine to the base of her skull.

Judging from the sinking of his brows, he knew the name.

"Let her in, Wyatt. Bring her to the living room."

Marlo dropped her hold on her son and reversed course, fingers on the dog's head as she walked confidently away. Clearly, she knew her way around her home.

Wyatt now regarded Elana as if she were a venomous snake he'd just discovered in his sock drawer.

"You're related to him." His words gritted out through clenched teeth, an accusation.

"I'm Jackson Belauru's wife."

"We read his wife's house burned down."

"That was his ex-wife. One of them."

He made a growling sound in the back of his throat.

"Bring her in, Wyatt."

He never took his eyes off her, but motioned her forward. She stepped across the threshold, the vampire willingly invited into the victim's home.

Wyatt waited until she'd cleared the threshold and then locked the door behind her.

Marlo turned her head in the direction of her son, but seemed to be staring at the ceiling.

"Introduce her to Justice," said Marlo and pushed the dog's neck. "Say hello, Justice."

Wyatt motioned the dog forward and Justice advanced, nose up and sniffing.

"Put out your hand," Wyatt said.

She did and the canine sniffed and then licked her palm, his tongue warm and wet.

"You can pet him," said Marlo.

She did, tentatively. Justice closed his eyes and seemed to smile.

"Heel, Justice." The dog moved to Marlo's side, and she collected his collar. "Chair."

The dog walked Marlo to an overstuffed, comfortable seat. Once collected, she told her dog to lie down.

"Won't you have a seat, Elana?"

She did.

Marlo turned to the place where Wyatt stood and spoke to her son.

"Get us something to drink, please, Wyatt."

Wyatt reversed direction to the kitchen and opened the refrigerator, retrieving bottles of water.

The dog curled in a ball in his bed and closed his eyes.

"Would you like some water?" Marlo motioned to the table, which she must have known the position of by memory, and the three bottles left by her son.

"Thank you." Elana picked one out and drank, thirsty after the drive.

Silence stretched as she struggled with where to begin.

"It's started again, hasn't it? You wanting to leave. Him wanting to keep you," she asked.

"Yes."

"Do you have any children?"

"Yes, one. My daughter by my first marriage. Her name is Phoebe."

"Ah. I see. And if you leave, you're afraid that he'll hurt your daughter."

"Yes."

"Does he know you want to leave him?"

She shook her head and then told Marlo about the boat, but in her retelling, Elana left out that Jackson had fallen in first and alone and that she had jumped in hours later to avoid the appearance of blame for his mishap. Then she told Marlo about her meeting Jackson's second ex-wife before her wedding.

"I heard of the disappearances, of course. And we read

about Shantel's house fire. I wondered if he was responsible. The police said the blaze was suspicious. Now I understand why he came back for her. She betrayed him twice. Once in leaving and once by warning you."

"I should have listened."

"On the eve of your wedding? I'm sure you thought you were the luckiest woman alive. A real Cinderella."

"Yes." Elana capped the water and rolled the bottle restlessly in her hands, feeling both stupid and naïve.

"But midnight has struck?"

Elana nodded and then realized Marlo couldn't see her.

"Yes. Most definitely. Marlo, I came today to warn you. The FBI has been to see me. Jackson is the prime suspect in the abduction of both of his stepdaughters. They think he killed them."

"I've held that suspicion for some time."

She knew. Marlo seemed to have already learned about the missing girls and had drawn her own conclusions. Elana absorbed this and then ventured on.

"Have you... I mean, do you have anything that might implicate him? Any evidence?"

"Oh, no. Just my experience with him. You will never find a man more charming or vindictive."

Elana nodded at that and then, recalling Marlo's blindness, murmured her agreement.

Marlo's brows lifted. "But the FBI contacted you? Really? Don't let Jackson hear about that."

"I won't."

"They haven't been here yet."

"Maybe they don't know about you."

"They will, if they are looking into his past. I wish I had something for them, but Jackson is very clever. And dangerous. How did you get away from him today?" Marlo asked.

"He thinks I'm at a doctor's appointment. I have one, but the doctor canceled. I needed to make sure you knew to be extra careful. So I took a detour." Elana fiddled with the bottle.

"You came all this way to warn me?"

"Yes. And because I'm looking for evidence to help them convict him."

Marlo sucked in a breath. "That's very dangerous."

"So is staying with him. So is leaving him. I need to get my daughter to safety and the FBI has promised to put us in the Witness Protection Program if I can find something to help them make their case."

"I understand. Well, I appreciate the warning, but I think Jackson is through with me."

"He came here last September. Drove us right by your house."

Marlo straightened at this revelation. "That's disturbing to hear."

"He saw Wyatt. Slowed to look at him." Elana repeated the lie Jackson had told her about an old classmate.

"Did you hear that, Wyatt?" Marlo asked, raising her voice.

"I heard," he said from his sentry spot in the kitchen. His eyes glittered dangerously, and Elana was unsure if the malice was directed at her, the messenger, or Jackson, the threat. "And I remember seeing that guy. He gave me a bad feeling."

His mother nodded and spoke to Elana. "The boy has good instincts. As for your search, I wish I had something, some proof. But he's very careful. I've never known him to make that kind of mistake. The fact that the FBI can't find anything speaks to that. Doesn't it?"

"I suppose. But they think he's retained keepsakes from his victims." She explained and Marlo listened.

"Are you certain you want to do this?" asked Marlo. "He's very dangerous."

"I'm afraid. All the time. Afraid to do this. Afraid not to."

"Yes. He can be very intimidating." She ran a hand over the raised scars on her cheek. "You know that Wyatt is Jackson's son?"

She stared at the boy, who watched them from the kitchen, so close to a man. What kind of a man? she wondered.

"If I didn't, I would have known after meeting him. They are very similar in appearance."

"That's unfortunate. I'm glad I can't see that."

Wyatt frowned and lowered his gaze, his cheeks flushing pink.

"How did you find me?"

Elana told her about the photos and the clipping.

"Let me fill in the blanks then. I was thirteen when I lost my virginity to Jackson in the bed of his father's pickup truck."

"Um, Wyatt is in the kitchen." Elana felt she needed to let Marlo know that her son could hear everything she said.

"He knows this already. Has known since he was old enough to understand."

Elana met Wyatt's gaze and saw the same burning menace in his eyes as in his father's. But in the boy the hatred and malice seemed to be for someone else. Jackson?

"As I was saying, when I realized I was pregnant, I was still in middle school. I told Jackson first. He was eighteen at the time and wanted to elope. Mostly, I think because he was afraid of what his father might do to him if he found out. Instead, I told my parents. They threatened to have Jackson arrested. Statutory rape."

Elana made a little yelping sound. She'd suspected, but here it was.

"Jackson's father got involved. He was very well off. Owned half the Panhandle, I was told. No, not just well-off, rich. Very, very rich. My folks were blue collar. We got along, but nothing fancy. You have to understand, Jackson was handsome, charming, an upperclassman, and had his own truck. At the time, I felt special."

"I do understand." Perhaps more than Marlo could imagine.

"Hard to believe, but I was younger than Wyatt is now. And I was angry at my parents. At first, anyway. Thought I was Juliet, or something. A settlement was offered. Money. A lot of it. Enough to send me to college and set up a trust for Wyatt. Enough to make the charges go away. But my mother insisted that Jackson relinquish all custody rights. Somehow, she knew what he was. So, a restraining order and a few forms later and Jackson went off to college while my family and I left town. I never saw him again."

"He hasn't bothered you or Wyatt?"

She gave a sad little smile and touched the scars at her temple.

"He hasn't bothered Wyatt. And as I said, I never saw him again. But there was the accident. I was a painter. Quite good, so I was told. Making some splash and one of my pieces sold to the Jackson Museum of Art." She motioned over her shoulder to a large canvas. "That one over there is mine."

The subject was tropical foliage, done all in blues with yellow highlights as if painted under a rising moon. The shadows for the leaves and branches wove interesting patterns on the garden wall beyond.

"That's..." Heartbreaking, she wanted to say. Such talent and promise, stolen from Marlo before she'd even begun. "Lovely," she said.

Marlo smiled. "I've had offers. But we don't need the money. I can still see it. And I still paint, but now only in my mind. Imagine, you know?" The wistful expression dissolved by slow degrees.

"What happened, Marlo?"

"I was at the gallery, setting up for my opening. I'd stepped out back to have a smoke and someone threw something at my face. It was dark in the alley. I never saw him. I remember the splash and the sensation of wetness for just an instant before the burning pain took over. One of the owners heard me screaming. He said he found me alone rolling on the ground. He got me inside and rinsed my face. Kept cold water running until the ambulance got there. But there was nothing anyone could do."

They sat in silence. Elana had no doubt who would do such a thing. It wasn't random, yet as far as she knew, Jackson had not even been questioned about the blaze. For a moment she wondered if she should call that special agent and voice her suspicions about Shantel's fire and Marlo's accident.

"I can practically hear you thinking," she said. "I thought it was him as well. The police investigated. Jackson was working with his father at the time. They produced witnesses. Affidavits."

Elana had no doubt that they had done so. But that didn't change her conviction.

"He did this."

"Yes. He did. I refused to marry him. I took his son, and he took my sight. It seems to me he takes whatever you hold most dear. The daughters of his ex-wives and my ability to paint. He couldn't take Wyatt. And he'd never harm his own blood. So he took what was second most important. My eyes."

"He threatened me," said Elana. "He said if I left him, he'd make me sorry."

"I have no doubt. And he will."

"He also said he'd kill himself, but not before killing me."

"Hmm. I believe the last part."

Elana swallowed back the hard knot of panic in her throat. Had she expected reassurances?

"Jackson is like a male lion. First thing he does is chase away other lions. Then he kills the cubs from the first litter. Finally, he breeds the new lioness."

Her skin prickled as Elana thought of Jackson's determination to get her pregnant and her subterfuge to avoid the same.

"He chose you for a reason. Mothers are easier to control. He finds women with few resources and then cuts what little they have away."

"I don't have any money or family."

"Which is why he chose you. I got free with my parents' help. And all it cost me was my sight. Worth the price to be rid of him."

"Any price." She had to agree.

Marlo turned toward the kitchen. "Wyatt. Get my checkbook, please."

Her boy moved out of Elana's sight as his mother turned back to face her.

"I think he took both of those girls and that they are long since dead and buried. I have nothing but theories, of course. And, frankly, I'm surprised Shantel risked speaking to you so publicly. She must have known such a step would rekindle his fury."

She *had* known, which was why Shantel had posed as an employee at the historic inn and cornered Elana at the first opportunity. Then Elana had raised the alarm. Jackson knew Shantel was there, because of her.

Guilt washed over her like warm blood.

Marlo's musings drew her from her own.

"I fear he's not done with her yet."

A sharp jolt of realization tore through Elana as she realized she might have done it again. If Jackson learned of this meeting, she'd done more than put herself in jeopardy, she might also have dragged Marlo back into Jackson's sights.

She rose to her feet.

"I shouldn't have come. Marlo, I'm so sorry."

Marlo nodded, accepting the apology with a grim expression.

"Listen carefully. You're in danger. More danger if he knows you plan to leave him. So, when you do run, be prepared. He *will* come after you."

"He won't."

"Why not?"

"Because when I leave, Jackson will be in handcuffs."

TWENTY

Marlo insisted that her son bring Elana back to the clinic. It was a silent journey, but Wyatt was a good driver and assured her he did have a license.

A little over an hour after she left, she stood on the sidewalk before the medical facility. Elana thanked Wyatt and then returned to retrieve her cellphone and bag. She found them easily, at the bottom of the bin in the lady's bathroom.

Jackson had texted her four minutes ago. She suspected that meant the tournament was winding down.

You done?

She typed her reply.

Still waiting.

Doctor is running late.

She answered him.

They just canceled. Emergency surgery.

Should I reschedule?

She waited there in the bathroom for eight minutes before the reply arrived.

No. Come home.

Before leaving the building, she called her husband and explained.

"Why did it take so long to text me back?"

Was this a trap? She didn't know, but she played the hand she was dealt.

"I was speaking to the receptionist, trying to understand what was happening. There was a line." She'd been ready with that lie.

"When will you be home?"

"I'm leaving the lot now." She crossed the sidewalk, headed for the elevator. "How's the fishing?"

"Great. Where's Phoebe?"

"I asked Zoey to see to her today."

"Come straight home."

"I will."

Elana made it back to Bald Cypress before five.

Marlo had written her a check for two thousand dollars to support her efforts to find evidence or, if she changed her mind about crossing Jackson, "to make a run for it." If anyone had reason to want Jackson behind bars, it was herself and Marlo.

The banks were closed when she reached Bald Cypress. So, her final stop was the library, where she hid the check in the reference section under a collection of three tomes on the history of opera, right beside the paper holding the contact information she'd uncovered for Shantel and Marlo.

What was the expression about reading about music being like dancing to architecture? She hoped so. The plan was to get back here tomorrow, pick up the check and make a deposit.

It was tempting to cash the check, grab Phoebe, and run. But she had abandoned that plan as a pipe dream. Running was not an option. The only way to be certain he wouldn't find them was to see that he was locked up in prison.

Jackson had burned down Shantel's home, attacked Marlo, and was responsible for the kidnapping of both his stepdaughters and the murder of at least one. Two little girls, gone. There had to be evidence.

Now she was afraid, not only for her daughter, but for Shantel, Marlo, Faith, and Grace, who would now be fourteen. Or she might remain always and forever the age she had been when she had reportedly wandered off.

Forever five.

Elana set her teeth and vowed she would not let that happen again. Protecting Phoebe was her job, but she now added Marlo and Wyatt, Shantel, and Faith to the people under her protection.

It felt empowering to be a protector instead of a victim. She wanted that and she was ready to fight.

It was past Phoebe's dinnertime when she picked her daughter up from Zoey's place.

"I fed her lunch. Hot dogs and fries. She only ate the dog and potatoes." Zoey stroked Phoebe's head. "Finished her brownie, though."

Phoebe grinned.

"Brownie? We can't have chocolate. Jackson's allergic."

"Well, Jackson didn't have a brownie. Phoebe did and it was hours ago."

Neither she nor Phoebe was allowed chocolate. Her daughter knew that.

She cast her daughter a hard stare and Phoebe's lip began to tremble. She knew exactly what she'd done. If Jackson got one single hive, it would make everything harder.

"Jackson won't know." Zoey turned to Phoebe. "Will he?"

Her daughter shook her head. Zoey stuck out her manicured little finger and extracted a pinky swear. Phoebe's solemn promise.

Elana relented. The last thing she wanted was to become like Jackson, dictatorial and vengeful. She blew away a breath. Seeing Marlo today had shaken her, shown her the cost of opposing her husband. She needed to be careful. But she also needed to love her daughter.

Her arms went out and Phoebe stepped in for a hug. Then Elana rubbed her back and turned her to face Zoey.

"Thank your aunt for taking such good care of you."

Her daughter piped her thank-you and then skipped to the car.

When they finally pulled into the garage Elana let her shoulders sag, allowing the weariness and stress to drag at her tired muscles.

The dogs barked frantically from the fenced area, having missed their regular dinnertime. She used the remote to open the garage and collected Gunner, Chase, and Dash and in they all went. Even if Jackson didn't figure out where she had been, the dogs knew. From their sniffing and attention, she realized they smelled Justice on her skin.

Elana hurried the dogs inside, thankful Jackson was not here to witness their abnormal reaction to her.

In the kitchen she paused to think. She was back. Jackson would be here tomorrow. Could he tell by looking at her where she had been? The strangling fingers of dread closed at her throat.

"Mommy?" Phoebe was staring at her.

"It's okay, dearest. Go put your bag away."

Phoebe lifted her backpack and headed from the kitchen, casting one worried glance over her shoulder. Elana held a fragile smile until she disappeared. Then she filled a glass of water and guzzled the liquid, choking and sputtering.

The dogs danced at her feet, stomachs rumbling and drooling. She got their food ready and set it on the floor beside the kitchen island. The three wolfed down the offering and began licking the bowls until they spun.

The dogs danced with her, getting underfoot until she collected their bowls and ordered them out.

"Calm down, calm down, calm down. He won't find out." She chanted the mantra as her heart continued to flutter and the dizziness grew worse.

"He won't. If he does, just..." What? She had no explanation.

What she should be thinking about was what else she could discover in Jackson's things before he returned, and how and when she could search his truck for a girl's headband and a friendship bracelet.

TWENTY-ONE

Jackson was preoccupied when he returned home late on Wednesday evening. He barely spoke to her and kept checking his phone, texting with someone. His brothers? Work? The FBI?

It was like getting a stay of execution.

Unfortunately, her thorough search of Jackson's closet had yielded nothing. If he had kept a keepsake, it was in that lockbox or somewhere beyond these walls.

"I rescheduled," he said, barely glancing at her. "October, so I can come along. Damn doctors wasting everyone's time."

"Yes, Jackson."

"Should have him pay for the damn gas. How about you send Phoebe up to her room and we see if we can solve this fertility thing between us?"

Jackson obviously now felt recuperated from his ordeal, at least enough for sex with his wife.

She did exactly as she was told. There was too much at stake to raise his ire or alert him that she was no longer willing to abide her prison sentence.

Upstairs, Elana used the spermicide and then returned to

the bedroom to find Jackson stretched out on the sheets naked and ready.

The next morning, Jackson called her and told Elana to meet him at his office before noon. No explanation or reason was offered, and she knew better than to ask. As a result, her stomach produced so much acid with her worrying that her insides ached when she left the house earlier than necessary to reach him at midday.

She stopped at the library, collecting the check Marlo had given her. It was time to prepare for whatever came next. Having some available cash made a small security blanket. She left her bag in her vehicle and carried only her ignition fob, the check, and her wallet, walking to a bank they never used to open an account. There she deposited the check, collecting her receipt. Then she used some of the cash she'd taken from the coin catchers in Jackson's laundromat to open a safety deposit box. Finally, she returned to the library to hide the deposit box key in a reference book that looked as if it had been untouched for decades.

The process of filling out paperwork for the account and renting the box took longer than anticipated, but she had made her first deposit. Unfortunately, the check would take four days to clear. She hurried to the SUV knowing better than to keep Jackson waiting, arriving at city hall with only three minutes to spare.

Sweat trickled down her back as she hustled through the long corridor toward the mayor's office.

She worried that his reason for summoning her had something to do with her visit with Marlo. But he couldn't know. Could he?

Elana reached Jackson's office at noon to find his assistant gathering her purse.

Ilene Adams had a fondness for loose-fitting gauzy tops and chunky oversized necklaces. Working for the city for more than thirty years had given her a weary carriage and streaks of gray in her upswept black hair.

At Elana's appearance her open, earnest face fell, but she recovered quickly.

"Good morning, Mrs. Belauru."

"How are you, Ilene?"

"Knees are aching me. Must be due for some rain." She groaned to her feet and showed her into Jackson's office. "He's still out inspecting the proposed site for a water treatment plant."

"Oh, I see."

Ilene glanced at the clock, which showed her precious lunch hour was ticking away. "You okay waiting here? I have to lock the outer door during lunch."

Elana tried to staunch the spark of hope that flared.

"Perfectly fine." She crossed her fingers like a child and prayed for a miracle.

"I'm sure he'll be right along. Would you like me to wait?"

"That's not necessary. I'll just check my email." She sat at the conference table in Jackson's office and drew out her phone where she had no email account.

How long would she have to search his office? Ten minutes? Fifteen? And there was his desk phone. Did he have access to outgoing calls made from this line? She would take the chance. Call Shantel's number, which she had memorized.

Ilene stood in the doorway, with one foot in the outer office and one hand on the door. Elana settled in a seat at the conference table and glanced to her husband's desk, upon which a phone lay.

Ilene hesitated, one hand at her throat.

"No need to wait. Really. I'm fine." Elana smiled up at the assistant, benign as a butterfly.

"I'll just be in the staff room. But I can eat at my desk."

Oh, no, that would be bad.

"Let me see what's keeping him." She needed Ilene to be away and not sitting in the outer office. "I'll just text him to see when he'll be back."

"Oh, no. Please don't bother."

His assistant was waving both hands at her. Elana noted the flash of concern in Ilene's gaze. Was she afraid of him as well?

"He's expecting you. I'm sure he'll be right along," said Ilene. "And I'll be back in a few minutes."

"No need to hurry. Have a nice lunch."

Elana sat and pretended to be engaged with her phone until she heard the outer door click.

She would not have a chance like this again.

On her feet now she opened each of his desk drawers and rummaged through the objects and folders, finding nothing but what one would expect. Office supplies, pens, a dish of rubber bands. On his bookshelves, she checked each book for a bookmark made of embroidery thread. In the coat closet she found a locked floor safe. Skipping that, she peered into file boxes and binders.

Breathing fast and sweating, she finished her wild search in the tiny bathroom, disappointed to see only what the mayor of a small town would have on hand.

A sound brought her racing out of the bathroom, but there was no one in the outer office.

Elana turned in a circle, checking that nothing obvious seemed out of place. Then she snatched up the phone to call Shantel.

This woman, at least, had already reached out and tried to help. Whether to help Elana or as some payback for her daughter, Elana was uncertain. But there was a chance she might have some suggestion on where to find evidence against Jackson.

A sound from behind her caused Elana to slam the handset back onto the cradle.

She dropped into the chair at the conference table as two men walked down the corridor, glancing in at her with no apparent interest. The moment they were out of sight, she rushed to Jackson's desk phone.

The call connected on the first ring.

"Who's this?"

Elana recognized the voice, even after all this time.

"Shantel?"

"Who's askin'?"

"It's Elana Belauru. Jackson's wife."

Silence.

"I wondered if you could meet me."

Another long pause caused Elana to glance at the wall clock as the minute hand swept forward.

"When?"

"Tomorrow?"

"Where?"

She gave Shantel the place.

At the jingle of keys, Elana's head snapped up.

"Have to go. See you soon." She punched the disconnect and replaced the handset. Then Elana darted across the room and into her seat. A moment later, Ilene limped into sight carrying a bag with the logo from the sandwich shop next door.

The assistant ducked her head inside Jackson's office.

"Thought I'd better keep you company. Mayor Belauru doesn't allow anyone in here alone. You understand."

"He's wise. Lots of important papers and things here."

"Exactly. I'll be at my desk." She retreated and sat in such a way that she could watch Elana without being overt about it.

They had only a few minutes' wait before Jackson appeared. Elana rose.

"You ready?" he asked.

"For what?" She tried to keep her voice calm, but it still came out higher than usual.

"I'm taking you out to lunch and then we're going to buy you something nice at the jewelry store. I'm proud of you, taking care of that appointment, hopefully getting some answers to why there is no bun in that oven." He patted her stomach proprietarily and she repressed a shudder.

She had become familiar with this pattern. First the explosive outburst, then the vindictive wrath, and later, no apology. Never that, but a gift of some kind as a way of indicating he was, if not remorseful, ready to move on. She now hated every trinket he'd offered her.

"And if we can get you pregnant, I'll buy you whatever you like."

Elana held her smile at the obvious bribe. This was what he did, something terrible and then something sweet. It kept her always unsteady and ever bracing for what came next.

But today, this Jackson was the man she had fallen in love with. Sweet, attentive, and kind. The difference was now she knew it was a lie. This was the nectar that drew the unsuspecting insect into the Venus flytrap.

Elana fawned. "Oh, Jackson. That is so sweet!"

Ilene glanced up at them, a dot of mayonnaise at the corner of her mouth. "You're a lucky woman, Mrs. Belauru."

"The luckiest," she said and took Jackson's offered arm, wondering if she could pawn whatever he bought her.

That afternoon, on her way home alone, she pulled to the shoulder of the road, removed the flashlight from the glove box, exited her vehicle, and hit the windshield with the butt end of the light with everything she had.

A spidery crack threaded in two directions across the glass. It grew on the drive home and when Jackson returned from work, she showed him the damage and told him a bit of something, maybe gravel, hit the glass.

His face reddened as the anticipated inquisition commenced. Finally, still angry, but seemingly satisfied, he said, "I told you not to follow construction vehicles, especially dump trucks."

"I'm so sorry, Jackson. You don't have to do anything. I can see fine through the glass."

"Until it breaks in on you. I'll call the dealer."

Elana smiled.

When she picked a time to meet Shantel, Elana counted on two things. Jackson had told her he had a very busy Friday. And her car was in the shop.

Normally she would have brought Phoebe along with her on errands, but Phoebe would never be able to keep a secret about her meeting with Shantel, and Jackson would know.

In May, Jackson had coaxed Phoebe into revealing that she'd made him a paperweight for his birthday. At the time, she and Jackson had laughed. She wasn't laughing now. He'd turned her daughter into a surveillance operative and there was little she could do about it.

Friday morning, Jackson left for work as usual.

She drove to Zoey's in the unfamiliar loaner car furnished by the dealership and dropped off some cookies for tomorrow's church bake sale. Zoey was organizing these frequently as fundraisers for the church's youth group.

"I'm going to run to the store. Need anything?"

Zoey made out a list.

"Mind if I leave Phoebe with you?"

Her sister-in-law gave her an assessing look and then agreed.

After telling her daughter to be good, she intentionally left her purse in Zoey's foyer, with her phone on mute, whispering a prayer that Jackson would not phone or text. He rarely did so during work hours, but he did sporadically make some excuse to check in on her.

If Jackson checked her location, it would appear she had spent the morning with Zoey preparing for the bake sale.

Then she headed to the nature reserve and parked by the picnic area as prearranged with Shantel. Only one car was in the lot, a very old economy car with a crumpled rear fender and a string of shiny plastic beads looped over the rearview mirror.

Shantel's car resembled the one Elana had been driving when she'd met Jackson. Until he'd presented her with the keys to a new SUV with all the upgrades. It was hard to remember how happy and hopeful she'd been back then.

Elana fidgeted with the gold chain Jackson had picked out for her. The heavy braided rope reminded her of a dog collar. He was back to treating her like a princess. She knew that wouldn't last long. The ups and downs had become predictable as a roller-coaster ride. Until now, she'd never done anything to provoke him. But now, she would.

Just beyond, in the picnic area, a familiar woman stood at her approach. Shantel had lost weight, that much was clear even from this distance. Since their first meeting, the FBI would have delivered the news. They'd found her daughter's body.

Elana hurried toward the picnic table in the shade of the ancient oaks' interlocking branches. The area gave a view of the marsh where butterflies floated from one cluster of yellow flowers to the next. The bees' droning could not drown out the mad thumping of her own heart.

Shantel remained standing in the shadows of a large oak draped with cascading gray-green strands of Spanish moss.

"You alone?" asked Shantel.

"Yes."

"Where is he?"

"Work."

"Your daughter?"

"Not here."

Shantel stepped from cover. "Your phone?"

Elana explained about leaving her phone with Zoey.

"That one. No friend, I can tell you. How many kids she have now?"

"Three boys and expecting again."

"She's smarter than either of us. And Sawyer isn't allergic to chocolate, so she can have all she wants."

"That's true."

"So can I now."

Elana thought that would be small comfort compared to everything she'd lost.

Shantel stared toward the parking lot. "He can track your car."

"He can. But that's a loaner car. Mine is in the shop."

Shantel's brows lifted and a slight smile flickered over her mouth.

This woman had warned her. Little had Elana known that Shantel's warnings were as serious as the Old Testament. Gospel, full of fire and brimstone and predictions of doom.

If you leave, he'll take your daughter.

"Thank you for meeting me."

"I'm taking a risk being here. You know that. Right?"

"I do." She stepped forward. "You were right about everything. I should have listened."

Elana gripped the braided gold chain, Jackson's latest outward show of devotion, and frowned. Her skin had made the metal warm. She resisted the urge to tug it from her throat.

Shantel stared up at her with big blue eyes. Her cheeks were sunken, and the dark circles and haunted expression made her look older than her years.

"You hear about my girl?" asked Shantel.

"The FBI told me. I'm so very sorry for your loss."

Tears filled her eyes as her entire demeanor changed. Her hands balled into fists and she glared with bloodshot eyes, tears streaming down her cheeks.

"He wanted to send her to a private school. Residential, you know? Get rid of her. I should have let him. Let her go. Stayed. She'd be alive now."

Elana was at a loss for words. Watching this mother tortured by guilt and wracked with pain and the loss of her child tore at her heart.

"He did this. I can't prove it. But I know." She beat her fists against her thighs and then used them to dash the tears from her cheeks.

"I agree."

"You need money? I can lend you a hundred bucks."

"No," Elana said. She'd given up on that idea. She was fully committed to getting what the FBI needed to convict Jackson and showing the world what this man really was. "I'm not running. He'd find me and Phoebe."

She left the rest unspoken, but Shantel nodded her understanding.

"I'm not about to divorce him."

"You gonna stay?"

"No. I want to find something, evidence, implicating him in any of these crimes."

Slowly, Shantel began to smile. It was a hard smile, full of malice.

"Dangerous. But yeah. Good."

"I've searched his things." She told Shantel about Marlo. She looked stunned as Elana relayed her visit. "Did you know about her?"

"Absolutely not."

"I wanted to warn you. She believes that Jackson isn't done with you yet."

"She's probably right."

"The FBI told me that Raelyn's bracelet and headband were missing from—from her. I've been trying to find them in the house."

Shantel dropped her gaze, sniffing. Elana paused to absorb the bone-deep grief radiating from Shantel like the gravitational field of a black hole. The pain and loss overtook her, and Elana bowed her head.

They stood like that, heads lowered, carrying together the weight of one lost child on their backs.

Finally, Shantel reached out and squeezed Elana's hand.

"Thank you for trying to find her. I look everywhere. In the faces of strangers, at parks, shopping centers. I know she's gone. I'm certain he killed her. But I can't stop looking. I can never stop."

"If we find either the headband or bracelet in Jackson's possession, the FBI will arrest him."

Shantel's eyes glimmered bright. "Yes!"

"Do you have any ideas where else to look?"

"You're assuming he kept them."

"If he took them, he still has them."

Shantel gave the briefest of nods. "He won't have them in the house. Has a safe at work. Maybe on that fishing boat or his truck? I don't know."

"I've searched what I could of his office. Been trying to get into his truck. It has that big silver gear box."

"He keeps that locked."

Elana nodded. "And he has a lockbox in the garage."

"The firebox? I've seen it. Never seen what's inside, though. Not allowed to touch it." She gave Elana a hard look. "He'll know if you break the lock. No hiding it. So if you do and you come up empty, you best be prepared to run unless..." Her eyes rolled upward, seeming to study the tree branches overhead.

Elana leaned in. "Yes?"

"Unless you get an identical one and swap out the keys. Don't know where he keeps them, though."

That was a very good idea. "If I can find the key."

"And get away to buy another and have the money to buy another."

Shantel understood her situation all too well.

"What do you know about his first wife, Faith?"

The woman's mouth twisted. "Odd, that one. Don't know if she has a phone, but she does drive, I think, and has electricity, unlike some. She dresses plain and wears that doily thing on her head, that, or a white head covering, little triangular veil pinned to her bun. Not sure what it's called.

"Had to buy all our vegetables from her and that awful white bread. I know she used to go to the Mennonite church for services, but not since she married Jackson."

"She left the church?" asked Elana.

"No. They won't speak to her."

"They're shunning her?"

"That's right. I've seen them look right through her. That's why she lives all by herself outside their community."

That, she had not known.

"Can only have gotten worse since she left him."

"She left?"

"I think so. Couldn't have his children. Blah, blah."

"Do you think she'd help me?"

There was a long pause. "Not sure. Might not be worth the risk."

The pause marked the natural end to their conversation.

"Thank you again for meeting me."

"Sure. Thanks for the warning." Shantel spun her ring of car keys on her index finger. "Cover your ass, okay? He's dangerous as hell."

"Yes. I will. Please take care."

"Yeah. Think I'll move again. Nothing for me here

anymore." Shantel stared at Elana's loaner vehicle, a shiny black SUV, the newest model. Her mouth twisted. "Mine was gray."

"Mine is, too."

Shantel blew away a sigh. "Like nothing better than to visit that man in prison."

They left the lot, heading in similar directions, Elana going home, Shantel back to the highway and on to Tallahassee. When they passed the turn-off to Faith's place, Elana spotted a small woman walking on the shoulder under the shade of an umbrella.

As she passed her, Elana recognized the Mennonite woman as Faith.

Hopes that she hadn't been spotted died as Faith made eye contact and lifted a hand in greeting.

TWENTY-TWO

Before the time to leave for the bake sale, Elana headed to Zoey's with the groceries and to pick up her bag and phone. Her meeting with Shantel had been both hopeful and discouraging.

She couldn't search the boat or the safe in his office. His truck would be an enormous challenge, but the idea about switching the lockbox was brilliant.

When she swung into Zoey's drive, it was to find Jackson's truck parked before the garage. Her heart shot to her throat blocking her breathing. The wave of nausea contracted her middle as she realized what this could mean.

The front door opened, and Zoey hurried out. She met Elana beside her vehicle and pressed something into her hand.

"Take this. You paid cash that I gave you."

Elana's husband appeared around the truck.

"Jackson, is everything all right?"

He growled his annoyance deep in his throat.

"Did you get it?" he asked, his voice laced with irritation.

Elana's mind went blank. "Did I..."

Zoey interrupted, "The medicine for Phoebe's stomach. I gave you cash."

Had her sister-in-law just lied for her?

"Oh." She glanced at the object in her hand. It was a children's over-the-counter liquid medication for stomach upset. "Yes, right here."

"What took you so long?" he growled.

She glanced from Zoey to Jackson.

"Wasn't that long," said Zoey, collecting the bags. "Look, she didn't even have time to unpack my groceries."

"Then how'd her purse get inside your house?" he asked Zoey.

"Phoebe had to use the bathroom. Because she was sick. I sent Elana right out again."

"Without your purse," Jackson said, eyes on Elana. "Driving without a license."

Zoey cut in again. "I hardly think anyone on the force would dare pull your wife over."

That comment caused Jackson to make a sound in his throat that wasn't quite amusement, perhaps acknowledgment of the truth in that. But he was not deterred from his verbal chastisement.

"If she's got a stomach bug, I don't want it. Why would you bring her here? Infect all Sawyer's kids."

"It's no problem," said Zoey. "We've got her in the guest bedroom, private bathroom. She won't infect anyone. And you can't leave her alone in the car or drag a sick little girl through the pharmacy."

Was Zoey covering for her?

"Thank you, Zoey." She meant it. She'd never expected this from her sister-in-law.

Zoey had made up this entire story. She was so smooth, Elana nearly believed her.

"Come on, we can finish packing up the baking and get you home."

They headed inside to the foyer where Jackson collected

Elana's bag and followed them into the kitchen. Zoey put the grocery bags on the floor beside the granite island.

"Careless." He growled less deeply this time, his irritation fading. "Couldn't reach you."

What terrible luck that Jackson tried and failed to reach her. Thank the Lord she had left her bag and was not driving her vehicle. But none of that would matter if her sister-in-law hadn't calmed the beast. The only reason he didn't know for sure was that Zoey was actually in her corner.

Elana's mind flashed a perfect image of Faith, under that umbrella, waving at her. That country road was nowhere near their pharmacy. She swallowed the chunk of panic lodged in her throat.

In the kitchen they paused. Zoey handed Jackson an oatmeal cookie. He scowled at the offering.

The smell of baking cake filled the air. At the chime of the oven timer, Gabriella stooped and lifted the chocolate sheet cake from the oven.

He backed away like the Scarecrow before the Wicked Witch's fiery broom.

"We can finish up here, if you want to take Phoebe home." She turned to Elana. "Let's get some medicine to our girl."

Jackson stood there, one hand on his hip and the other on the unwanted cookie, looking as out of place in Zoey's warm, welcoming kitchen as a hyena.

"I'm not watching a sick kid, so you can't help Zoey at the bake sale."

"Yes, Jackson." She turned to Zoey. "I'm so sorry."

Zoey's mouth twisted, some of her fury leaking through the façade. When she spoke, her calm voice revealed nothing. "That's for the best."

"Don't forget your purse," he said, already heading toward the door, still barking orders. "And wipe down everything she touches. I'm not getting stomach flu."

"Yes, Jackson."

"Hurry up and get home. I'll be waiting."

He snatched up his keys, then stomped out of the house. There would be no goodbye kiss after her lie of omission. It almost made it worth his ire.

But she feared this was not the end of it.

Today's departure from her usual routine had triggered Jackson's instincts. What if Faith told him she had seen Elana out on the highway at the same time she had claimed to be in town at the pharmacy?

What if he already knew?

What if he was just giving her enough rope to hang herself?

From behind the counter a small, dirty hand reached toward the rack holding cooling cookies.

Zoey whirled. "Parker, you want a lickin'?"

The hand disappeared.

"You tell your aunt you hope she and Phoebe feel better."

The boys rose in unison and called a chorus, repeating their mother's words.

Zoey spoke to her housekeeper. "Gabriella, take them out back. I'll come get them after we pack up all this." She waved at the kitchen island loaded with cooling baked goods.

Only after the door closed behind them did Zoey turn on her. When she spoke, her voice was the hiss of an angry snake.

"Where you been, girl?"

"I... I..." She had no answer and was terrible at thinking on her feet.

"You weren't home. That's sure."

"Zoey, I'm sorry. Had to—"

"Stop right there. Do not tell me anything. Jackson knew your phone was here and that you weren't where you were supposed to be."

"Zoey, you don't understand."

She lifted a hand to halt Elana. "And I don't want to. You're putting me in a pickle. You see that, right?"

"I do. I'm sorry."

Zoey exhaled like a fire-breathing dragon.

"You listen to me." She aimed her index finger at Elana, like a cocked gun. "You listening?"

Elana nodded.

"You were gone too long to pick up medicine. He asks again, and he will, you tell him you left Phoebe here because she got sick, and I sent you for medicine. My suggestion. Understand? But they were out of that medicine, and you were going to head back here, but a delivery truck came in and the pharmacist told you to wait."

"Where's Phoebe?"

"I sent her upstairs and told the boys if they went in, they'd all get so sick their little pee-pees would fall off. And you best know they believed me."

"You did?" Elana blinked in confusion. "Zoey, thank you. I don't know what to say."

"Here's what you say. 'Whatever I'm doing, I'm not doing it again.' You hear?"

"Yes. I hear."

"Fine. You be sure Phoebe knows what to say. That gal is too sweet and innocent by half. Too young to understand. Sweet Jesus, watch over us."

Zoey aimed the finger at her again, leveling her eyes on Elana.

"Don't you ever drag me into something like this again."

"But, Zoey, I think Faith saw me."

A look of panic flashed on Zoey's face.

"Where?"

"Out on the highway near her place."

Zoey's face went pale. "Lord, protect us."

TWENTY-THREE

Elana stopped en route to pick up her repaired car. When she got home with Phoebe, Jackson was waiting. He watched them as she took her daughter off to bed in her room and, at her return, ordered her to wash her hands.

Now she'd discover if he believed any of the lie that Zoey had concocted.

"I need to speak to you."

Elana nodded and kept her expression placid as a sheep chewing its cud. But her body trembled, and she clasped her hands together before her to prevent the tremors from exposing her terror.

What would he do if he knew she'd met Shantel?

Without meaning to, she glanced back upstairs where Phoebe now lay safe in her bed. But was she safe?

"Why did it take so long to get Phoebe a simple bottle of over-the-counter medicine?" he asked. "Did you stop anywhere else?"

She paused, wondering if he already knew, and if he did not, how long until Faith revealed she'd seen his new wife in a place she was not supposed to be.

"I only stopped at the pharmacy. Just there and back to Zoey's."

"If she hadn't given you cash, you would have been up the creek. You have to be more organized."

"Yes. You're right. I'm sorry."

Jackson held her gaze so long she could feel the sweat trickle down her back. Finally, he released her from his scrutinizing stare.

"I've got to get back to the office." He headed out the door, preoccupied and without his usual farewell.

Jackson went fishing early Saturday but was home by mid-afternoon. That evening, he was unusually quiet during dinner and then went to the garage for several hours.

She wondered if he was simply fiddling with his fishing gear.

When he came up, he gave her no answers and she could tell at a glance, he was stewing over something.

Elana knew what this was. Retribution for not answering her phone, for allowing Phoebe to get sick, and for forgetting her purse. Making Phoebe suffer was the surest way to hurt his wife.

So Phoebe and Elana missed the Saturday afternoon church rummage sale that included Zoey's bake sale because of her daughter's made-up stomachache.

His spite only increased Elana's determination to keep looking for evidence. Long after he'd fallen asleep, she'd crept out of bed to check on Phoebe and then retrieved Jackson's keys from his master closet. Jackson kept keys, wallet, and change in a box inside a built-in bureau. She lifted the ring with painful slowness, trying not to make any noise. But the dogs heard her and rose from their beds beside their master to see what she was doing.

Elana hurried out with the keys, retreating to the bathroom, shooing the three hounds out and closing the door. There she exhaled and panted as if she just finished a strenuous run instead of walked a few steps. There she waited, back pressed to the wall, key ring gripped in her hand, listening for any sound that might alert her that the dogs had woken their master.

Finally, she flicked on a light and examined the ring. If he found her in here with his keys, what would she say? She could think of nothing. No reasonable explanation.

Hurry then. Don't let him catch you.

One small tubular key seemed the right size to open that lockbox. On one side was the manufacturer's name and on the other was a serial number, stamped into the silver-colored surface.

Elana memorized the number. Finally, she crept back to his closet, returned the keys, and slipped back into bed. It was a long time before her heart slowed its desperate pounding.

On Sunday, he sent them to church without him. The change unnerved Elana. Jackson never missed church. The only good thing about this deviation was that she did not have to spend brunch and the afternoon with Sawyer's family.

When they returned, it was to find Jackson gone. So after the lunch dishes were cleaned and put away, she told Phoebe to bring the dogs outside, so she could take another look at that lockbox. She would need the exact make and model if she was to buy a duplicate, and thanks to the new bank account she now could.

In the garage she paused. Something felt different. He'd moved some of the boxes. She glanced about and saw the reason. On the shelves before her was the glowing red eye of a security camera.

Her body tensed as she stared. The implications pressed the air from her lungs.

She moved slowly to the gardening supplies as her mind galloped backward over to the day she'd found Wyatt's birth announcement, hidden in a box. A little humming sound escaped her, the sound of a scream, stifled by her fixed smile and busy hands. She gathered the grass seed and her clippers and then stooped behind her car, as if to gather something from the bottom shelf.

There her knees gave way and she landed hard on her seat. Hidden from any motion alarm or camera surveillance, she allowed herself to tremble and the tears to fall.

Had that camera been there when she'd rummaged through those bins? She would have seen that glowing red eye, triggered by her motion.

He didn't know. If he did, he would have confronted her. But he was suspicious. Suspicious enough to install webcams down here. The answer to what he was doing in the garage yesterday was clear. He was installing surveillance *inside* their home.

Her skin prickled as the shock turned to fury.

How dare he treat her like this?

Camera or no camera. She needed a look at that lockbox.

But first, she needed to block that camera.

Elana rose to her feet, gathered the twine from the bottom shelf, and stood, leaving the garage by the side door.

Outside, she checked on Phoebe and the dogs. The sprinkler system took care of most of the watering, but the seedlings needed more care than the hardy agave, banana trees, and broad-leaved traveler palms that grew beside the garage. At the street hot-pink bougainvillea cascaded over the front wall in a colorful carpet, and neat impatiens, in white and purple, exploded with color in the pots beside the entrance.

Elana seeded two bare patches and her daughter watered

the same. Finally, they tied up some sagging jasmine vines with bailing twine. Inside, she noted the new security camera clipped to the blinds on the kitchen window.

In the living room, she found another beneath the flatscreen. Another fixed in the corner of the laundry room above the dog's leashes.

They were everywhere. All over the inside of the house.

Jackson didn't trust her.

Did he think she was planning to leave him?

She wasn't. She was planning for him to leave her, on a prison bus.

Monday morning, she asked Phoebe if she'd like to paint her bedroom.

Of course, her daughter was enthusiastic.

"Let's ask Daddy when he comes down," said Elana.

"Yeah!" piped Phoebe.

Jackson took one look at Phoebe bouncing in her seat and said, "Feeling better?"

"Yes! Daddy, can we paint my bedroom?"

He glanced to Elana, who smiled. "I told her that we'd have to ask you."

He nodded his approval of this. "Let me see the color first. Nothing too dark. Maybe peach or pink?"

"I was thinking lavender," said Elana.

"What's that?" he asked.

"Pale purple. Very light. Feminine."

"Fine."

"Hurray!" shouted Phoebe.

Jackson winced at the shout and Elana told Phoebe to eat her breakfast.

"I can pick up the paint today," she said, bringing him his coffee.

"Fine."

Jackson finished his meal and watched Phoebe eating her toast.

"Your stomach okay?"

"Yes, Daddy."

"Want to go on that field trip today?" He was talking about the Bible camp outing to the local farm.

"Can I?"

"Not going to puke on the bus?"

Phoebe shook her head.

"You can go." Then he turned to Elana. "But you can stay home and start that painting job."

With that order delivered, he left the kitchen. Elana drummed her fingers on the table waiting for the sound of his truck engine. Jackson thought by keeping her from chaperoning the trip, he was meting out some punishment, when he'd left her exactly where she needed to be.

Once he rolled from the driveway, she went about her normal morning cleanup, exactly as always, aware she was now under surveillance.

In Phoebe's room, Elana carefully checked for cameras and was extremely relieved not to find any; however there was one in Elana's walk-in closet.

Once she'd dropped Phoebe at camp, she headed to the local hardware store and purchased what she needed. Back at the house, she made a show of unloading and placing all the necessary supplies on the garage floor. She peeled off the wrapping from the paintbrush and the plastic from the three-pack of rollers, located a screwdriver to open the gallon of paint, and set it in the pan with a new roller, the brush, and paint stirrer. Humming a tune, she retrieved the ladder, resting it right before the red eye of the camera. Then she grabbed two bins, set them on the floor, and quickly opened the one holding the lockbox. The manufacturer's name was stenciled in white on the black plastic and matched the name on the barrel key on Jackson's key ring.

The serial number also matched.

Jackpot!

She wrote down all the details from the bottom of the box, then measured it with the paint stirrer as a gage. Finally, she replaced the lockbox to its bin and returned both plastic containers to the shelving.

She carried the ladder up first and then the rest of the supplies. Once safely in Phoebe's room, she laid out the drop cloths and went to work, relieved that there was no camera in this room, at least.

By the time Zoey dropped Phoebe off at the door, Elana had only the rolling to complete.

Phoebe enjoyed brushing while Elana rolled. They had the job finished and were all cleaned up before Jackson returned home to admire their work.

He nodded his approval. "Nice color."

"Like Rapunzel," said Phoebe.

Elana was secretly regretting the color that, combined with the Mello Mint bedspread, curtains, and lamp, made the room look like the inside of an Easter basket.

But she had the necessary details on his lockbox. Now she needed to figure out a way to switch both the box and the key on Jackson's key ring.

On Wednesday, Elana needed to bring the dogs to the vet for their annual appointment. Jackson took her SUV and left his truck for this outing.

The plan was to bring the dogs to the vet, drop Phoebe at camp, then search Jackson's truck.

Zoey, as always, would bring Phoebe home, after camp.

Handling three hunting dogs on leashes was challenge

enough, but somehow, she'd gotten them into the rear seat of the pickup.

Gunner tried to get out as she loaded Dash. The oldest of the three, he'd become suspicious, perhaps realizing that when Elana drove, they were heading to the vet.

Phoebe tried to comfort the trio from the rear seat.

Beside her, the pack's alpha was now on his feet, bumping and tumbling into the others as they tried to crawl between the bucket seats. That behavior got Chase barking and Dash was so scared he shook.

"Momma, Dash just peed," said Phoebe.

Elana groaned, knowing she'd need to clean that up before returning the keys to Jackson.

Gunner hung his head between the seat, slobbering on Elana's sleeve and making that sound that indicated he was going to be sick.

That made the youngest, Chase, begin to drool. Past experience meant Gunner would shortly vomit in the back seat of Jackson's truck.

Which would mean she would have to clean up that mess as well. She stepped on the accelerator, looking for a place to safely pull over. And immediately the patrol car behind her hit the lights.

She exhaled through her nose as she glanced in the rearview mirror, recognizing Derek, Jackson's youngest brother. He had not advanced from patrolman, mainly because he had failed the test required to be promoted to detective three times.

She put on her directional and pulled to the shoulder. Derek seemed surprised to see Elana and Phoebe in Jackson's truck, judging from the blank expression followed by the sudden confusion. His bewilderment grew when she hopped down and jerked the bucket seat forward. All three dogs tumbled out. Gunner hacked, then puked up his breakfast on the sandy shoulder. The other dogs lowered their noses to investigate.

In a panic, she grabbed Gunner's and Dash's collars, blocking Chase with her leg as she ordered them up into the truck. Chase made a run for it, but Derek, now out of his vehicle, grabbed the dog's collar and walked him back.

"What's wrong with them?"

"Going to the vet and they just make themselves sick."

"Nerves. They'll do that."

Yes, I'm aware.

He guided Chase up and slammed the door. Inside the truck, Phoebe petted the hound, trying to calm the nervous dog.

Elana held on to Gunner and Dash as she turned to her brother-in-law. "Everything all right? I got a taillight out or something?" She tried for a confident smile, but police, even in the form of her brother-in-law, made her nervous.

"Thought it was Jackson."

"Anything you want me to tell him?"

"No. Just a question, it's about the next exam."

Inside the car, Chase slipped from Phoebe's grasp and leapt out the window onto the road.

"Chase!" Both she and Derek shouted in unison.

But the dog had the scent of something and took off at a run across the road and down an alley.

A sharp jolt of terror zipped through her at the possibility that Chase might be struck by a motor vehicle. Only secondarily did she realize that Jackson would be furious at her for losing hold of one of his prize hunting dogs.

The beads of sweat on her forehead had little to do with the summer heat.

"Don't worry. I'll get him," said Derek.

"We're heading to the vet. Could you bring him?"

"Will do."

Derek held a hand over his service pistol and the other over his radio and trotted off, calling the wayward dog.

She'd never had a problem with Derek. He seemed oblivious to Jackson's darker nature and, as far as she could determine, had not been invited on the hunting trip that corresponded with Shantel Keen's house fire.

Derek headed off the opposite shoulder and disappeared into the brush. Elana waited a few minutes, but then feared she'd be late for her appointment and left Derek searching for Jackson's hound.

Elana climbed back in the vehicle. Behind her, the two dogs panted and danced from one side of the rear seat to the other, bumping into each other and toppling over Phoebe.

She knew exactly how they felt. She wished they could trade places. She'd get the shots and they could search for evidence.

Gunner rested a head on her shoulder.

"You'd do it, too. Wouldn't you, boy?"

Elana started the vehicle and pulled back onto the road. Her stomach ached. It reminded her of when she was in the school play. That feeling she had just before stepping onto the stage when she felt certain she would forget all her lines and possibly trip or be sick. The risk of humiliation seemed so huge back then.

But now she risked so much more.

Once the remaining pair was with the vet, she asked the receptionist for something to clean the truck. Outside, Phoebe sat on the bench in the shade, her nose in a book, while Elana scrubbed away the mess in the rear seat. As she worked, she conducted a fruitless search of Jackson's vehicle in a place her husband could not watch.

Back inside, Derek appeared with Chase. Her shoulders sagged with relief at seeing her favorite here and safe. Dr. Trumble took the dog for his check and shots. The delay made her late to drop Phoebe off at camp. Other than that slight inconvenience, there was no harm done.

With the dogs and her daughter back in the truck, she drove them to Phoebe's camp.

The dogs continued their constant motion, moving as if they needed to run all the way. Finally, Phoebe got them all to sit, using a very authoritative voice. The tone and firmness reminded her of Jackson. With all the hounds finally still, Phoebe posed a question.

"Momma, will Daddy be mad about Chase running away?"

TWENTY-FOUR

Jackson stormed in just before dinner on Wednesday with an expression that told her unquestionably that he'd discovered about her meeting with Shantel or Marlo or both. She held her breath and froze as if playing the child's game of freeze tag until he spoke.

"Where is he?"

Elana's panic morphed into confusion. Phoebe was seated in one of the stools at the center island, a purple crayon suspended above her drawing.

She carefully retrieved the cutting board and knife, setting them on the counter before collecting the vegetables needed for making a salad. But really, it was about having the knife close at hand.

His eyes were bloodshot, and his murderous expression had her muscles bracing.

"Who?" Was this about Derek?

"Chase!" he bellowed. "Had my brother running all over town. Wouldn't come when he called."

"He doesn't like the vet." As she said it, she wondered why she was defending his dog when it had been an opportunity to take his side. "He's out in the pen with Dash and Gunner. They all got their shots."

He stomped past her toward the master suite.

"Mommy? Why is daddy so mad?"

She shook her head. "His dog was naughty today."

"'Cause he ran away?"

"Yes."

"And he disobeyed." Phoebe's pronouncement was grave.

"Disobey," "disobedient," "unruly," and "disrespectful" were all new vocabulary words for her daughter. She'd learned them all watching Jackson and her mother.

Jackson returned carrying a rifle.

"Jackson! What are you going to do?"

Normally she knew never to question him, but she couldn't help it. He turned toward her, eyes bulging, and mouth twisted in a grim sneer.

"I don't keep disobedient dogs."

She took a step forward to argue, thought better of it, and retreated.

"Mommy?"

He headed out the back door as Elana gathered her crying daughter in her arms. She stroked Phoebe's soft hair and cradled her close. Her daughter was too big to be picked up, but Phoebe needed her.

The crack of the single shot made them both flinch.

"Mommy, did he hurt Chase?"

It wasn't a large leap for Elana to see the correlation between her behavior and that of his dead hunting dog, killed for the infraction of disobedience. For the sin of running away.

Whether he'd made the point intentionally or coincidentally, the message was clear as a lightning strike.

She was that dog.

. . .

The next morning, Elana busied herself cleaning up after breakfast, trying to ignore the fresh dirt on her kitchen floor beside the three dog dishes. Last night, after the rifle shot, Jackson had returned for his shovel. She'd watched him dig a grave on the property for Chase, but couldn't bear to watch him bury her favorite dog. They were rambunctious and got under her feet, but they were so goofy and loving. Her nearly constant companions. She hated him for hurting that beautiful, affectionate dog.

With his terrible task complete, he returned, tracking soil and sand through the house, and announced he was going out.

She wasn't sure when he came back, but he was up and dressed when she came downstairs to make his breakfast.

Elana had just returned to the kitchen after delivering Jackson's plate of runny eggs, crisp bacon, and lightly browned toast before him when her phone rang.

She didn't understand why, but the feeling of dread was so great she couldn't answer it. In her mind it was Shantel, disregarding her wishes and using her phone number to contact her. Whoever it was, Jackson would know.

Elana stared at the offending device as it rang again.

On the third ring, she finally retrieved her phone because a missed call still registered. He'd know who called, whether she did or not.

"Hello?"

"Hi, Elana, it's your former father-in-law, Braden Orrick."

The shock at hearing his voice slapped her in the face like an open palm.

She had not heard from him or his wife, Victoria, in months. They had sent a wedding gift with their congratulations at her wedding to Jackson and had tried on several occasions to convince her to bring Phoebe for a visit. This past spring, they'd attempted to come here. The guilt and pain over Jackson's refusal to allow Phoebe to see them, and her inability to stop him, made her throat close.

If Vic wasn't teaching summer school, she would now be on break.

Were they trying for another visit?

That possibility filled her with dread.

"Hello? Elana? You there?"

Had it been only a month ago she had thought to run from her marriage and to them for help? It would be the first place Jackson would look.

"Yes, I'm here. It's so good to hear your voice." She gripped the phone tighter as she imagined their house in flames.

I don't keep disobedient dogs.

Elana leaned against the cool stone of the granite island.

"I just wanted to let you know that Vicky died last night. Complications of the diabetes."

The shock hit her like a jet from a fire hose, knocking her off her feet. She slid along the kitchen island and folded to her seat on the tile as her knees gave way.

"Oh, Braden. I'm so sorry. I didn't know she was ill."

She gripped the phone as the sound of weeping reached her.

"Health's been declining for several years."

He didn't shout reproach or remind her that they'd driven ten hours to see Phoebe, only to be turned away for a funeral for a person that never existed. If Jackson had an aunt, she didn't know of it. They'd spent that Memorial Day weekend on the *Reel Escape*, just offshore far enough that the Orricks could not reach them. Jackson, she recalled, had been in a particularly jubilant mood that further darkened hers.

The guilt twisted inside her like a black snake.

"She was so s-sick at the end. They'd taken her feet. But the wounds just got worse and worse. Wouldn't heal. She got sepsis."

"Oh, how terrible."

"It was. A horrific way to die."

She'd been so preoccupied; she didn't hear Jackson's approach. Suddenly he was there in the kitchen, glaring.

"Who is that?"

She muted the phone. "It's Braden Orrick. His wife just died."

Jackson absorbed this news with no change in expression, just the slightest lifting of his brows. The scowl remained.

"Send flowers. You aren't going to the funeral."

Elana nodded. "Yes, Jackson."

Braden, unaware of the side conversation, continued.

"We're planning the service for this weekend. I sure hope you and Phoebe can make it. I'd love to see Phoebe. You know we missed her at Christmas last year."

She unmuted the phone and spoke to Braden. "We'd like to be there, but Phoebe has Covid."

Jackson nodded his approval.

"Oh. That's too bad. Is she all right?" His voice sounded small and so far away.

"Minor symptoms, but we wouldn't want to expose you."

"Maybe after things get settled, I can drive down there. Sooner would be best. Doctor says I've got COPD and macular degeneration. Not sure how much longer I'll be able to safely drive."

The last thing a man whose son was killed by an elderly driver wanted was to be another such driver.

"Maybe we can come up there this summer."

Jackson was shaking his head.

"Really? Oh, I'd love that. Well, I'd better go. Got some more calls to make. Give my love to Phoebe and to you. We miss you. I mean, well, I miss you."

There was no *we* any longer for her father-in-law.

She set her teeth together. One way or another, she was

getting Phoebe up to see her grandpa. As it was now, she barely remembered him. And she suspected that was exactly what Jackson wanted.

"Thank you for calling."

"Sure thing."

"And we are so sorry for your loss. Vic was a wonderful woman."

"She was that. Bye-bye." He ended the call.

She met Jackson's hard glare.

"You aren't dragging Phoebe to Georgia for a funeral or for any other reason."

Yet he could drag them to North Carolina for a fishing tournament each year, while carefully avoiding the city where the Orricks lived. She studied the tiny red pepper flake stuck in the grout line of the kitchen floor. Silent. Defiance rising like the hackles on a dog.

Jackson loomed forward until his nose nearly touched hers. His voice was low and forced through clenched teeth.

"You hear me?"

She thought of Chase, killed for his disobedience. Buried in the yard. She thought of little Raelyn, her bracelet and headband taken as a reminder of the depths of his brutality.

"Yes, Jackson."

TWENTY-FIVE

The ramifications of what her former father-in-law had told her took a while to sink in. Besides her momma, Braden and Vic Orrick were Phoebe's only living relatives. More importantly, they were her designated legal guardians in Elana's will. She had specified that should something happen to her, Phoebe would be placed in the custody of her grandparents.

But Grandma Orrick was dead, and Grandpa Orrick had COPD, vision issues, and was a cancer survivor.

If she died, what would happen to Phoebe?

But she knew and the realization terrified her. She was not leaving her daughter with that man.

She wondered why he hadn't insisted she change her will, while they were changing everything else. And then it struck her. He didn't care anything about Phoebe or what might happen to her if Elana died. Phoebe was a bargaining chip, a vehicle to keep Elana from running off or filing for divorce. As long as protecting her daughter was more important than her own happiness, he knew she would stay.

She folded in half as if kicked in the stomach by a horse.

For several heartbeats she considered just giving up.

But then she remembered Shantel's fire, Grace's disappearance, and Raelyn's murder.

I don't keep disobedient dogs.

Or wives. No. She had set her course. One way or another, she was finding the evidence to make Jackson pay for what he had done to his stepdaughters. What he was doing to her and Phoebe.

Elana pulled into the drive before Faith's farm stand on Friday afternoon. In the summer, when the growing season was mostly finished, she sold eggs, butter, cheese, and a variety of baked goods. Her sandwich bread was amazing.

If she hurried, she'd have time to see Faith and get home before Zoey dropped Phoebe off at their house.

Behind Faith's place, a swaybacked horse and donkey stared back at her. From inside the dwelling a dog barked. Chickens pecked and scratched from their enclosure, safe from coyotes, bobcats, and eagles.

The windows of the double-wide were all open and the screens in place. The day was unbearably hot, and she could just imagine the temperature inside of an insulated box with no air conditioning.

The dog continued to bark, but frantic now, driving itself into a frenzy. It sounded big. Faith shouted something in the unique language used by the Mennonites here, speaking to the dog, who ignored her. A door slammed and the sound seemed more distant.

Footsteps slapped loud on the flooring and then the door swept open.

She appeared in a peach-colored cape dress with a high-scooped neckline and fitted waist. Her stockings, kapp, and hairstyle were identical to the first time they had met and every time thereafter.

"Elana. I missed you last week."

"Yes. I'm afraid Phoebe had a stomach bug."

Faith's smile wavered. "That's too bad. But I saw you on the road. Different car."

Elana exhaled out of her nose, keeping her teeth firmly set. After leaving Shantel, Elana remembered passing Faith on the road. She had deeply hoped that Faith offered a friendly wave to no one in particular. But it appeared that Jackson's first wife had recognized her even though she drove the dealership's loaner car. Instinctively, Elana dropped the idea of asking Faith to keep that sighting to herself. Lying would be against her beliefs and asking would raise suspicion.

Finally, she said, "Broken windshield." Then she waved a hand toward the car. "But as you can see. All fixed."

"That's good."

"We missed your bread."

"Well, I have plenty and sticky buns and whoopie pies."

"Chocolate?" Most whoopie pies were two chocolate cookies with a fluffy white frosting or whipped cream between to make an irresistible sweet sandwich.

"No. I have both lemon-blueberry and molasses."

Elana realized then that Faith never sold anything made with cocoa or chocolate. Odd. It was as if she still followed Jackson's rules, though she no longer lived under his roof.

But Faith actually did still live under his roof, because Jackson had admitted he had furnished this house after they had separated.

Elana made her selections, along with eggs and a container of potato salad.

She tried to sound casual as she asked the question that had brought her here.

"Faith, did you see Jackson recently?"

"I see him often. He came here on Saturday, and I asked him where you were heading on Friday."

Elana felt herself sinking in sand. Jackson had been here after confronting her at Zoey's. Then he'd installed those web cameras all over the house. And on Wednesday he'd shot Chase. He knew she was up to something.

"It's ungodly to deceive your husband."

She had her answer. As Shantel had suspected, Faith was obligated to Jackson and no friend to Elana.

"You must be mistaken. I wasn't out this way on Friday."

Faith did not recant or contradict. She simply stared at Elana as if she were a worm on one of her cabbages.

"How much do I owe you, Faith?" she asked.

That afternoon, Jackson came home early again. The two remaining dogs heard him first, thundered out to the laundry room, barking madly. He let them into the garage, but didn't come up.

Not for a very long time. Sweat soaked under Elana's arms and trickled down her back as she tried and failed to convince herself that his delayed appearance had nothing to do with her or the bins she searched.

"Honey? Could you come down here?" Jackson called from the garage, and she knew she'd made a mistake.

But what?

Her stomach muscles contracted. Something in his voice gave her goosebumps.

She inched down the steps, slinking around her vehicle to find him standing, hands on hips, the Colossus of Rhodes, waiting to face her, the dogs seated on either side.

"What is it, Jackson?" she asked, pleased that her voice sounded musical and relaxed. Her wringing hands told a different story.

She resisted the urge to wipe her sweating palms on her

skirt, instead taking one deep breath before forcing a pleasant smile.

"Where were you on Friday morning?"

"What?" Her fingers went icy.

"Friday. You weren't at the drugstore."

"I was."

"You were on the highway, outside of town."

She shook her head.

"Who were you meeting?"

"No one."

"What's his name?"

"Jackson, I was getting medicine." She repeated the lie about the delivery truck and the wait.

Her husband's narrowing eyes told her he did not believe a word.

If he told her that Faith had recognized her, she'd just suggest that the woman had made a mistake.

But he didn't. Instead, he slipped a hand into his pocket and withdrew a bit of wadded plastic. Carefully he pressed it flat, revealing the thin transparent packaging that had protected the bristles of the nylon brush she'd purchased to paint Phoebe's room.

"Know where I found this?"

"The floor?"

He shook his head.

"Between the plastic bins. Right there."

He pointed to the two clear containers holding photographs, newspaper clippings, the birth announcement, and the lockbox. The plastic packaging must have stuck to the bottom of one of the bins when she'd put it back. She hadn't even noticed it was missing when she'd thrown away the wrapping from the rollers.

How on earth had he spotted this so quickly? She'd triggered some trap. It was the only answer. There had been something, like a matchstick, shoved in a closed door, some little detail that he'd seen was different down here.

Oh, God.

"You were in my things." He cast a glance back at the bins, neatly stacked behind him.

"I—I wasn't." The denial came naturally as breathing.

"Then how do you explain this?" He waved the clear bit of garbage. "Wedged between two of the boxes I told you never to touch."

Elana glanced away from the damning evidence.

"You were snooping."

She shook her head.

Think, you idiot.

Her first notion was to blame her daughter, much to her shame. But what would he do to Phoebe if he thought she was playing with his belongings?

The risk was too great.

"I was putting the painting things away when the ladder fell over. It knocked the top tub from the shelf, so I put it back. The static must have made the brush wrapper stick to the bottom."

"And you didn't think to tell me?"

"I—I forgot. I'd been painting and I just put that away with the rest."

"Or... you didn't want to get in trouble. Or... you were snooping and are lying to me now. How long did you look through those photos for?"

"I didn't."

She couldn't let him hurt her daughter.

"I'm so sorry, Jackson. I put it all back on the shelf, just the way it was. The container is fine. I checked."

He stood there, staring. She forced herself to stand still, eyes downcast, cheeks flaming.

The silence deafened as the panic dropped over her like a

shroud. Did he know what she had found? About her visit to Marlo? About her plans to break that lockbox? That the FBI had promised her witness protection if she helped them convict him for murder?

The urge to gather her daughter and flee overwhelmed her. But she remained where she was because Elana knew where that choice would lead. Sooner or later, he'd come for them and then Phoebe would be on the website for missing children right beside Grace and Raelyn.

She waited for him to confront her about her lie about the medicine. The fact he didn't only added to her anxiety. She knew that he was aware and the next time he saw Faith, he would know she knew.

"No more painting," said Jackson.

Her ears were broken. She could hardly hear past the rushing sound of water.

"You're careless. Falling off the boat, it nearly killed us both. And driving behind a dump truck, breaking the windshield and forgetting your license at Zoey's. I don't know what's gotten into you lately, but I don't like it."

"I understand."

"No more. You hear? No more lies or ladders and the only thing you touch in this garage is your vehicle."

"Of course, Jackson. That's fine."

She peeked at him and found him scowling down at her, clearly furious, but possibly accepting her explanation of what had happened.

"If I find out you're snooping in my business, Elana, it will be bad. You do not want to go there."

"I understand, Jackson. Really. It was just a careless accident." That was her story and she would stick to it now and always.

"No more accidents," he said.

"Yes, Jackson."

He opened the passenger door of his truck and pointed. "Up," he said.

For a moment she thought he meant her, but the dogs bounded into the cab and scrambled into the rear seat. He cast her an inscrutable stare. "I'm getting Phoebe from camp today."

His declaration touched off a cascading rockslide of panic nearly knocking her off her feet.

Jackson never picked up her daughter. There was no need because Zoey ran the Bible camp and dropped Phoebe off every afternoon.

"Zoey drops her off," said Elana.

"Not today."

He left her there, arms wrapped around herself like a straitjacket. As he pulled out of the drive, she debated calling the police.

Who would she ask for? His brother? And what would she say—that her husband was picking up his stepdaughter?

Instead, she paced, in the empty garage, while the camera's red eye recorded her panic. It was taking too long. The round trip shouldn't be more than ten minutes. They'd been gone nearly thirty.

She felt like a cat in a microwave. Every hair follicle hurt as she cooked from the inside out.

Finally, Elana decided to take Phoebe's bike to town and use the payphone in the laundry to call Braden, Gavin's father. But just then the garage door lifted, and Jackson's truck rolled into sight.

Elana tore down the drive, spotting Phoebe's face in the rear window with the dogs. Her daughter waved as Elana pressed a hand to her mouth.

The truck rolled past her, into the garage. Elana brushed away the tears as she rushed after the vehicle.

At the truck, she tried and failed to open the rear door. It was locked, of course, until the vehicle went into park. But still she lifted the handle again and again, repeating the useless motion until her gaze finally shifted from Phoebe, removing her seatbelt, to Jackson who stared at her with fixed, predatory eyes and a half smile.

He wanted her to know he was the one in control.

Only when she stepped back did he release the lock.

Phoebe pushed open the door. Both dogs sprang out, dancing and getting underfoot, as her daughter struggled with her backpack to scoot across the rear seat where she'd ridden.

"Hi, sweetheart." Her voice trembled with the rest of her as she reached and lifted Phoebe out and to the ground.

"We got ice cream!" said Phoebe, the evidence clear on her face, smeared with a ring of vanilla and one green sprinkle.

Jackson never allowed food in his car. But he'd allowed this sticky little one to sit inside, just to prove a point. He was her stepfather and could take her anywhere at any time.

"Did you?" Elana grabbed Phoebe's backpack and took firm hold of her hand.

Her daughter jabbered about her day. Once inside, Elana mopped off her daughter's face and sent Phoebe to her room.

Phoebe was here and she was safe. For now.

When she turned, she found Jackson standing in the kitchen.

He motioned with his thumb toward Phoebe's room. "You think I can't reach her in there?"

TWENTY-SIX

Jackson left with his brothers to fish on the lake before dawn on Saturday, thank the Lord. Elana got Phoebe up and dressed, trying not to let her daughter see the stress on her face as she readied her for a playdate with Marielle, a friend from camp.

After discovering that paintbrush packaging in the garage, her husband knew she had been in his things. And that was very dangerous.

She dropped Phoebe at Marielle's then returned home, where she spun in her usual cleaning circles. She had not been home even an hour when the dogs leapt up barking and charging for the laundry room. A moment later, the rumble of the lifting door reached her.

Elana gripped the kitchen counter for support, bracing.

Why was Jackson home so early? It was a deviation and that scared her. She tried and failed to control her trembling and the painful thumping of her heart.

In the laundry room, Dash and Gunner barked, tails wagging. The pair knew exactly who was on the other side of that door.

Had they forgotten Chase so quickly?

In the laundry room entrance, he greeted his dogs by name, offering them each a thump on the ribs before telling them to "go on now."

Jackson's smile dropped when his eyes found her. His jaw clenched tight as he waved a piece of paper before him like a fan. What was that in his hand?

"Stopped by the office to pick up our mail. Missed it yesterday and missed this." Another wave of the page. "It's the report of our rescue from the coast guard out of Culpepper. Want to know what they said?"

Not waiting for a reply, he advanced. She backed away. Whatever it said, she knew she was in trouble. If she could get to the kitchen, she might pull a knife out of the block on the counter. She had never dreamed of being violent toward him before. But everything had changed.

"Says that we were found at *opposite* ends of the inlet. You were rescued first, exactly three hours before me, out in the open ocean, causing the search to move outward from your position."

She wanted to say that her rescue *triggered* the search for him, but the spit flying from his mouth as he spoke kept her mute. She reached the counter and gripped the cold stone, waiting to see if she needed that knife to survive.

How much did he know and how much did he guess?

"Meanwhile I was spotted by a kayaker in the other direction, still in the sound, washed up on a salt flat, unconscious, hypothermic, dehydrated."

And likely still drunk, she thought.

"I kept wondering how you swam for nine hours. We went out after midnight. Fell in. You were rescued at..." He glanced at the page and read. "Nine o-six a.m. Me at twelve nineteen p.m. You're a good swimmer, but in the open ocean? That's

where they said they found you. While I was within sight of the
Hammock Island Bridge, not even a mile from the coast guard
station. Not where they were searching in the open ocean—
because of you. Still in the damned inlet. Why weren't we
found in the same general vicinity? At least the same direction
from the boat?"

She splayed one hand on the counter, determined not to
disappear without a trace. If nothing else, she'd leave physical
evidence of whatever he planned to do to her.

"How does that happen? You lost your balance, I tried to
save you. We both went in. That's what I told them."

Her voice was as fragile and brittle as she felt. "I tried to
save you, but my dress tore."

"Is that right?" His words dripped with cynicism. "So how did
we go in opposite directions? Doesn't make any sense."

She calculated the distance from her hand and the speed
with which she could grab that knife. It would be close.

"Tides don't work like that. They pull everything in one
direction. Then it struck me."

She remained silent as her skin went damp with sweat.

"Only explanation is that we went into the water at separate
times. But that would mean you didn't fall with me. Didn't try
to save me, or that you did, but I went in and you didn't. But
that can't be, because you didn't call for help. You just... what?
Waited? Waited so long the tides turned before you jumped in
to avoid anyone finding out?"

"It happened just as I said."

He raised a hand to stop her. "I know those waters, the tides,
the currents. I've been fishing them for years. Yet you thought I
wouldn't figure this out."

She'd hoped so, anyway.

"Did you push me or just watch me go under?"

"Jackson, we went in at the same time. There has to be some other explanation. The life vest." She was grasping for straws. "It could have changed things."

"That's what they said. It doesn't work. I might have been taken farther than you were, but still in the same direction. I don't know why the coast guard didn't raise a red flag. They had to believe every word you said. *They* did. I don't."

"That's what happened." It was her only choice at this point, hold the lie. Repeat it until it became true or, at least, cast doubt on the truth.

"I think it happened this way. You asked me to come look at the stars. When I got to the transom, you pushed me overboard." He fingered the raised pink scar, showing where he'd struck his head. "Then you waited a few hours, enough time for the tides to turn, before you panicked and jumped in."

"That's ridiculous."

He leaned in so she could feel his hot breath on her face.

"Is it? What did you do while you were on that boat? Did you go through my things? What were you looking for?"

"I didn't. I went overboard with you."

He snorted his disbelief.

Then just like that, he moved away, leaning casually on the island, collecting an apple from the fruit bowl, and tossing it repeatedly up before catching it in his hand. "As far as the Culpepper Police are concerned, the matter is closed. Just an accident on the water. Two survivors, so no reason to investigate. But I thought maybe you had a little help from the boat. Took something, a seat cushion or cooler. Keep you afloat until rescue. Wouldn't have time to do that if I pulled you over. Would you?"

She hadn't taken anything. She had thought about it, then decided against it for this exact reason. If he survived, it would be the proof he needed. And she had cleaned everything she'd touched. Then the rain had come and washed away anything she'd missed. She'd left no trace. Except the lights. She'd turned on the underwater lights.

They'd been off when they'd come on deck and off when he'd gone overboard. Would he remember that?

It was the one definite fact that sank her alibi. But maybe someone would have been aboard, to clean or check the boat. Maybe the lights were already switched off.

But perhaps they were not. Perhaps he would discover her lie.

"It happened just as I said, Jackson. You fell, grabbed my dress. I tried to pull you back onto the deck, but we both went over and when I came up, you were gone."

"Why not swim to the boat? You being such a strong swimmer."

"I couldn't. I told you. I tried, but the tide was too strong."

The apple landed in his palm with a slap and then he closed his fist, crushing the fruit. Juice and pulp squeezed between his curling fingers.

"I went in during an ebb tide. No current," he said.

He dropped the apple on the spotless floor and lifted a dish towel. He meticulously cleaned each finger before tossing away the cloth. Finally, he folded his arms over his wide chest.

"You're up to something. I can feel it."

"Jackson, please—"

"The *Reel Escape* is back at dock in Pensacola. I'm going down there. I find one thing missing or out of place and I'll make you sorry."

"I don't understand. I didn't do anything." That was true. She'd had the chance to do something, call for help, call 911 or radio the coast guard, and she'd done none of it. If she had known about his inflatable fishing vest, she would not have been so daring.

"Jackson, please. This is absurd."

He snorted. "I hope you run. Nothing I like better than flushing birds and shooting them out of the clear blue sky."

TWENTY-SEVEN

Despite Jackson pretending that nothing had changed, everything *had* changed.

He'd shot his own dog to demonstrate, with deadly accuracy, exactly what he was capable of. Now he had suspicions about what she had been up to in the garage and over the boat accident.

The chill and menace emanating from her husband had her as anxious as a hare before the hounds.

After accusing her of trying to kill him and vowing to find some proof of that version of events, Jackson had taken the dogs out in the pen. When he didn't come in, she headed to the window in the kitchen to see him chatting with their next-door neighbor as if everything was just as it should be. The conversation lasted several minutes and ended with laughter and a wave before Jackson headed to the garage.

From the dining room she saw him stroll down the drive to fix the flag on their unused mailbox, pausing to speak to a couple from up the street and stroke their golden retriever.

She imagined the police questioning the pair.

"Did he seem agitated or upset? Was he angry?"

No. Jackson was, as always, charismatic and smooth as ice on a pond.

Shortly after, he returned to the house whistling.

He was plotting something terrible. She felt it in the soft center of her bones. Her plan of helping the FBI shifted to one of immediate survival. He would not be taking her somewhere to disappear and she was not leaving her daughter unprotected. If he forced her. She would fight.

Elana moved to the kitchen and the cutting board, taking the melon she'd purchased from Faith's farm stand and using her longest, sharpest knife to cut it into bite-sized pieces. The front door opened, and she waited to see what he would do next.

Once inside the foyer he lifted his keys from his pocket and spun them. He said nothing as he watched her work the knife in and out of the thick green rind and into the soft pink pulp.

She paused to glance up at his hand, turning the keys. On that ring was the barrel key she needed to replace. The check should have cleared by now, so she could buy that lockbox.

He smiled as he watched her, as if memorizing what she looked like, there working in his kitchen. A picture he could keep long after she was gone.

He opened the cabinet in the foyer, the one where he kept his loose change, sunglasses, and wallet. But not his side of the cabinet.

Hers.

Jackson scooped up her purse. Then he removed her phone and slipped it in his back pocket. He cast her a malicious smile, dropped her purse, and reached for the doorknob.

"Where are you going?"

"Out," he said.

"To Derek's?"

He snorted and swept through the wide double doors, leaving them open. Behind the house, he retrieved his dogs, then headed for his truck. Gunner and Dash clambered beside him.

It was quite some time before she closed the front doors.

He'd left her key fob.

I hope you run.

His words echoed like a shout from the bottom of a well.

Where would she run without her daughter?

A creeping dread began in her gut and spiraled upward to her lungs until she gasped for breath.

"Phoebe!"

She didn't remember the drive to her daughter's friend's home, but she arrived, winded, and dashed to the door. She knew this family, of course, as they attended the same church, and Connie's daughter, Marielle, and Phoebe were best buddies at Bible camp.

"Hey there," said Connie, who seemed confused at Elana's early arrival. "Is everything all right? Phoebe forget something?"

"Forget?"

Her brow twitched as the first sign of concern flashed on Connie's face before the smile returned.

"Yes. Your husband picked her up a little bit ago. Did you get your wires crossed?"

Elana swallowed down the dread, struggling between the need to act normal and the urge to scream that he'd stolen her child.

"Yes, that must be it," she said in a voice that seemed too high and shrill to be her own.

"Elana? Is everything okay?"

"Yes. Why?"

"You've gone pale."

"Excuse me," she said and wobbled down the path. She just made it to her SUV before sprawling into the bucket seat.

The voice in her head screamed like a noon whistle.

She was too late.

He's taken her. Where?

Should she report her daughter missing?

Call the police. Call them! Call Sawyer and Derek. Call the FBI.

She scrambled for her phone and then paused. He'd taken her phone.

Elana sat back, finally thinking.

Jackson had picked her daughter up from her friend's. If Phoebe went missing, he would be the last one with her. He'd never be so reckless. That meant he'd done this for some other reason.

She lowered her head to the steering wheel and sobbed in relief.

Why had he taken her? To scare Phoebe or her mother? Both, but also... Oh, God! The interrogation. He could be questioning her right now.

Phoebe didn't know anything.

Except that she didn't have a stomach bug. Had her daughter seen her searching Jackson's truck?

Elana got hold of herself and drove home. When the garage door trundled up, she saw that Jackson's truck was not in its usual place, so she reversed course and drove to Derek's home, but no one answered her pounding.

Next, she went to Sawyer's. Zoey and the boys were out shopping for bathing suits, and he claimed not to know where Jackson might be. A call to his wife yielded no answers.

Bald Cypress was not very big. So, she drove the streets, rolling slowly past the pool, park, skate park, riverwalk, and down the main street twice. She tried city hall, finding it locked up tight. She scanned the parking lots for his truck at the library and the arcade in the strip mall, the pharmacy, the ice cream hut, the vet's, and both fast-food joints in town.

Then she stopped at Jackson's laundromat and used the payphone to call Zoey.

"Have you seen Jackson or Phoebe?"

The pause stretched endlessly.

"No. Sawyer already called and asked me. Is everything okay?"

"I can't find them."

"Not at home?"

"No. Not when I checked."

"Call him."

"I can't. He took my phone."

Another long pause. "Then how are you calling me?"

"I'm at the laundromat. Payphone."

"I'll have Sawyer try."

"Thank you."

Elana drove home with her heart in her throat.

Jackson's truck was in the garage.

She jerked the vehicle into park and ran under the rising door, then up the three steps into the house. The dogs greeted her, barking, and leaping as they did every time she returned home.

She ignored both and hurried on.

"Phoebe!"

"We're in here," said Jackson.

She charged through the kitchen and skidded to a halt in the formal dining room where Phoebe sat before a melting bowl of vanilla ice cream topped with caramel in a Styrofoam cup. Beside the bowl, her arm rested, encased in a pink cast.

Their eyes met and her daughter looked on the edge of tears.

"Oh, God! What happened?"

Jackson lifted a hand to halt her, and she stopped, conditioned, it seemed, to follow his hand gestures.

"Calm down. She just had a little accident. I picked her up from her friend's."

"I know! I went there."

He shrugged a shoulder and cast her a half smile.

"Should have called first."

"You took my phone."

"*My* phone. I bought it. My phone..." He thumbed over his shoulder at her SUV in the driveway, not bothering to look as he continued to speak in a chant. "My car... My house...."

Then he rested an arm about Phoebe's narrow shoulders, making her daughter wince. The threat was clear. He had gotten to her child and could get to her anytime, anyplace. Elana's notions of protecting her daughter were just a fantasy. He was too strong and too smart.

Elana rushed to her daughter.

"What happened, baby?"

"She fell off the climbing wall at the park."

The climbing wall was only seven feet tall and surrounded with a rubberized surface to reduce the chance of scraped knees or broken bones.

She met his gaze and saw the challenge in his eyes. He expected her to call him a liar or ask Phoebe if what he said was true.

Elana hesitated. He'd done this on purpose. Every bone in her body told her he had hurt Phoebe. She could pretend she believed him, speak to Phoebe's doctor, and talk to Phoebe privately, or she could confront him.

She recognized that this might be a trap. But try as she might, she could not see it.

Be smart. You can still do this.

Find that evidence. Then he'll never be able to touch Phoebe again.

Or was it already too late? To find proof of guilt, she needed access to his house, his things, his life. She needed his trust and that was already gone.

She had placed her daughter in danger... and she had found nothing.

Instead, Jackson had beaten her again.

This was a power play.

She knew it.

Elana dropped to a knee beside Phoebe, who looked miserable. Her untouched ice cream melting before her.

"Does it hurt, baby?"

She nodded.

"I'll get her some Tylenol." She rose.

"I already gave her some."

Had he? She doubted that.

Her daughter lifted her gaze to her mother and big fat tears rolled down her face.

Something in Elana snapped. She felt herself veering from her plan, changing course like a drunk driver losing control of her vehicle, swerving dangerously across lanes.

Why had she ever thought she could find anything that might put Jackson behind bars?

Her need to be free of him had jeopardized Phoebe. But he couldn't take her. Not three. Even Jackson wouldn't be able to make three stepdaughters vanish and face no consequences.

Could he?

She wasn't taking that chance.

Heedless of the inner voice shouting caution, she extended her hand to Phoebe.

"Come on, Phoebe."

Phoebe slid off the chair and took a tight hold. Together they left the dining room with Jackson in pursuit.

The words of Special Agent Inga popped into her mind like a bad dollar bill from a vending machine.

When a woman is about to leave an abusive relationship, violence escalates.

"Where are you going?" he asked, now at her heels.

She gave the answer he'd given her more times than she could count.

"Out."

"You're staying right here."

She nudged Phoebe behind her and faced him.

"No."

His brows shot up. He was a bully. Bullies didn't like hearing the word "no."

"I have some errands."

It wasn't what she planned. But she would not let him touch Phoebe again.

She was going. Right now, with nothing but her purse, Phoebe, and a copy of the key to the laundromat coin catcher.

Jackson smirked, his dark eyes twinkling. He seemed to be anticipating what came next and that scared her.

Elana walked Phoebe out of the front door and to the car parked in the driveway. Jackson followed as far as the front stoop and paused. The dogs darted after Elana, determined to ride along wherever she was going.

With every step, she expected his attack.

She got Phoebe strapped into her car seat.

From the front steps, Jackson called the dogs and then called to her. "You better turn around."

She waved. "See you in a little while."

Inside the car, she drove out of the upscale neighborhood and down Main Street.

"Where are we going, Momma?"

"Away from here."

Phoebe's eyes were huge in her tiny, tear-streaked face.

"Phoebe, baby. What happened to your arm?"

Her daughter lowered her gaze to her dirty knees.

"Daddy pushed me."

Jackson had hurt Phoebe.

That was that. She was never going back. How far could she get on a tank of gas?

She could go in any direction. Stop at the grocery and use that Coinstar kiosk to turn the change into bills.

She'd ditch the car in an airport and take a taxi to the train station. Then catch a westbound train. Nashville. No, Denver maybe. She'd never been anywhere but the Keys on Jackson's boat. But she'd always wanted to see the Rocky Mountains and those red rock formations in the Southwest deserts. It was a big country. Big enough, she hoped, for a little girl and her mother to get lost.

She could not risk the time it would take to retrieve the deposit box key and get her debit card. She'd come back for them or get a new card later because she was not giving Jackson one more minute to rally his troops.

And she'd always have to look over her shoulder. Never enter an alley without thinking of Marlo. Never fall asleep without wondering if the smoke detector was working.

It didn't matter. One tank of gas was enough. She'd drive over the state line. She'd call Gavin's dad. Ask Braden's help.

Jackson had hurt Phoebe. Finally forced her hand.

Elana set her teeth and stepped on the accelerator, racing toward the city limits of Bald Cypress. If she never saw this town again, it would be too soon.

Her mind flashed an image of the way Jackson had looked at her when she left. She almost thought she was making a mistake. But he'd made the mistake hurting her child.

Should she drive to the urgent care clinic in town and report the child abuse, call her pediatrician's service, or head to a larger city to report him?

Jacksonville. A little over an hour. Reachable on a tank of gas. They had a major hospital and she knew where it was.

Phoebe could tell them that her stepfather pushed her. After that, Jackson would be arrested, lose any parental rights.

"Phoebe, I'm going to take you to a hospital. I want you to tell them what happened."

She glanced at her little girl, who looked small and vulnerable tucked in her car seat, cradling her injured forearm.

"I already did that, Momma. Just what Daddy told me to say."

Elana dropped her voice to a whisper and still the words stuck in her throat. "What did he ask you to say?"

Phoebe spoke to her lap. "That you... you pushed me and I fell." She lifted her chin, her eyes now wide and earnest as she hurried on. "But it was a-a accident."

Elana's heart stuttered like her antilock brakes, vainly trying to avoid the imminent crash of her world.

His smirk. It suddenly made sense and she could finally see the trap he'd set. But too late because she was already falling into his bear pit.

"Oh my God," she whispered.

The flashing red and blue lights in her rearview mirror had her sitting up straight.

"No," she whispered.

Behind her, the police cruiser hit the siren.

TWENTY-EIGHT

For just a moment, Elana considered making a run for it. Even if she only got as far as the county limits, she might stand a chance. If the sheriffs were involved or the Florida Highway Patrol. Any organization that her husband did not have firmly in his pocket.

Then she glanced at Phoebe, one hand cradling her cast, and her eyes wide as she looked to her momma for rescue.

Elana put on the directional and rolled to the shoulder, sand and gravel crunching beneath her tires.

The cruiser pulled in behind her and Derek Belauru stepped from the vehicle.

Elana watched him in her side mirror as Jackson's younger brother adjusted his belt and made a leisurely approach. He stood at the window, and she turned her head, eyes on the road that she would not be taking, and window rolled up.

He knocked. She pressed the button to lower the window.

"I want to speak to social services," she said. It was a weak play, especially if he'd gotten there first, but it was all she could think to do.

"Hi, Uncle Derek!" said Phoebe, her voice bright as sunshine.

"Hello, peanut. Where you heading?"

Phoebe shrugged.

Derek turned to Elana. "I'm going to ask you to step out of the vehicle."

"Are you serious?"

"Deadly," he said.

"Why did you stop me? Other than because Jackson told you to, I mean."

"You were driving erratically. Now please step out of the vehicle."

"Mommy?" Phoebe now looked and sounded worried.

"Wait right there, peanut." And to Elana, "Turn off the engine."

She did and stepped out of the vehicle and onto the pavement, radiating heat through the soles of her princess flats. Derek took her through all the sobriety tests as vehicles slowed to stare at them.

Her cheeks burned with shame as he drew out the Breathalyzer.

"I don't drink," she said.

"We'll see. Won't we?" He held up the contraption.

"I'm not breathing into that."

"You refusing to comply?"

She hesitated. It was a no-win choice. If she refused, he could arrest her. If she took the test, he could fudge the results.

"Is your body camera on?" she asked.

"Not working." He smiled.

"I'm not taking the test."

He spun her around so fast she had time only to gasp before she found herself folded over the hood of the SUV. The hot metal burned her cheek. She yelped and struggled, but found herself handcuffed.

From inside the vehicle, she heard her daughter's screams.

Her brother-in-law marched her back to his police cruiser as another car slowed. She glanced to the SUV and saw Connie, Phoebe's friend's mother, roll slowly by, her mouth hanging open in shock.

Elana reflexively dropped her gaze to the cracked concrete, barely aware of the rear door opening until Derek had his hand on her head as he forced her into the cruiser.

The shock of landing in the rear seat jolted her out of her embarrassment.

"Phoebe!"

"We've got her. I've called Jackson."

"You mean he called you."

Derek cocked his head and smiled. Then he slammed the door. She watched through the metal grate separating the front and rear seats as Derek returned to Elana's vehicle, leaning into the compartment to retrieve her daughter.

Elana screamed and kicked at the door, then at the grate, her rage at being so easily subdued exploding from her like lava.

He knew she'd run. Knew that the one thing she could never tolerate was him hurting her little girl. So that was what he had done. He'd broken his own stepdaughter's arm, then waited for her to run.

But what choice did she have? Just stay and let him hurt Phoebe?

She could call Agent Inga for help. But what would she say? She had no proof that Phoebe broke her arm while with Jackson. He'd made sure this was a "he said/she said" situation. And what mother wouldn't deny that she'd hurt her child, especially if she really had? Her denial would ring hollow.

And she had not unearthed what they wanted in exchange for protection. She had no evidence to deliver and so Inga would offer only what she already had, referral to an organization that helped women of domestic violence. It would not be enough to stop Jackson from hurting Phoebe.

Suddenly she was like Marlo Sullivan. Suspicions, but no proof of guilt, because Jackson was too clever to leave any.

She thought of Marlo and her admission that it was worth the cost of her sight to be rid of him.

What would Jackson take from her?

But then she knew. He'd take Phoebe from her. That would be pure hell. Knowing he had her daughter and that she could do nothing. And she saw it now. Her every mistake and his every move.

Derek returned and opened the rear door.

"Do you want to explain this?" He held up a baggie. Inside was a needle, a blackened spoon, and a smaller packet of white powder.

An icy dread rolled like mercury down her spine.

"What is that?"

"You tell me. I found it in your vehicle."

"That's impossible." She shook her head, realizing it was happening.

Right now. Right here.

It was happening.

They were making a case.

Unfit mother. Did Jackson plant that, or had Derek?

It didn't matter.

"Looks like heroin to me. Several grams. You're looking at felony charges. And this?" He held up another bag of white tablets. They were thicker than aspirin. "Looks like oxycodone. You selling to afford your habit, Elana?"

"You know I don't do drugs."

He smiled, a confident man holding every card in his stacked deck.

"You are under arrest."

TWENTY-NINE

She waited in the police car, expecting Jackson to appear and tell her he'd take her home if she was a good girl. But instead, two more cruisers appeared. One held the single female officer on the force who helped Phoebe from the rear seat, took her to her cruiser, and placed her in a car seat there.

"You can't take her," she said to the empty vehicle.

But they did. The car holding her daughter drove away and the remaining officers searched her vehicle, tearing out every car mat and removing every item from the trunk and glove box.

Derek finally returned. "Taking you to the station now for processing."

"Processing? This is a joke. Right?"

He glanced at her in the rearview and for a moment she saw the same cold stare of her husband looking back at her.

"You shouldn't have gone through his things, Elana. That's none of your business."

They knew. Of course, they knew.

"How can you help him do this thing? He took those two girls. He's killed at least one child. And now he's taking Phoebe. Please, Derek, you have to help me."

"I am helping. Jackson reported abuse earlier today and we've called social services. They'll get someone to look after Phoebe and find out just what kind of a mother you really are. And..." He lifted his brow. "Get you the treatment you clearly need."

"Treatment!"

"Rehab, then."

"Those drugs aren't mine! You know they're not."

He snorted. "If I had a nickel..."

"And I'm a great mother!" But even as she said it, she knew it was a lie. If she were even a good mother, she would have left as soon as she realized what kind of a man Jackson was. Instead of making the same mistakes as Faith and Shantel, she'd tried to outwit him. And made different mistakes. Dangerous mistakes.

Finally, she'd simply stepped into another type of trap.

Of course, he couldn't make Phoebe vanish. Not after his last two stepdaughters were both missing. That would be a bridge too far, even for him. Especially now he knew the FBI was onto him.

But he could make *her* vanish.

Suddenly she was freezing cold in the back of Derek's cruiser, icy from the inside out as she contemplated all the scenarios that might now be in play.

At the station she was searched, fingerprinted, and photographed. Then a female officer led her to a holding cell. There she waited and waited.

Jackson didn't appear. She asked to see a lawyer.

She considered using her phone call to contact Special Agent Inga, but that would alert Jackson that she was working with the FBI. Would that make him more cautious or more volatile?

Sometime after dark she was taken to a windowless, drab little room where she waited again. It was hours until the door opened and in strolled a short, pudgy man, with slicked-back black hair and a fringe of a beard, meant to outline his nonexistent jawline. He introduced himself as Detective Cudden. Elana regarded him as he stared at his clipboard and then his prisoner.

She demanded an attorney. But he ignored her and took the seat opposite her at the little table.

"Your blood alcohol level was three times the legal limit. Additionally, narcotics were discovered on a routine search of your vehicle. You are looking at serious charges."

"The results of the test were wrong. I don't drink alcohol. And those were planted."

"Is that right? Who planted them?"

She repeated her demand for an attorney.

"Your husband was here. Picked up your little girl."

That sent a jolt of terror right to the pulsing marrow of her bones.

"No."

"How did she break her arm?"

"I want to see Jackson."

"Is that right? Well, he's refused to post bail. Said you're an unfit mother."

"He pushed Phoebe. Broke her arm."

"He claims that *you* pushed her and left the injury unattended for two days. Upon returning from a fishing outing, he discovered the injury and took her to the hospital for X-rays where they found the break. Hospital staff called child services. Took down his statement. Then when he confronted you, you ran."

"That's not what happened."

"So, what did happen?"

Detective Cudden had the audacity to look bored. Meanwhile, sweat beaded on her brow and her bladder sent a sharp stab of pain across her middle with every breath.

"I want to see an attorney."

· · ·

Sometime, hours later, after she'd given up speaking all together, she was returned to the holding cell where she was allowed to use the steel toilet in plain sight of the matron who had escorted her back.

There was no bunk. Just a long concrete bench built into the wall and the toilet. She sat staring at the bars from the cold seat in the musty cell, surrounded by cinderblock walls painted a ghastly, dirty pink that reminded her of liverwurst. She was the only person in holding.

Sometime in the wee hours, she paced, lay on the concrete bench, stretched, and stood a long while with her hands curled around the black bars, shiny from so many layers of paint.

Breakfast arrived on a cardboard tray. A cold, soggy egg sandwich and black coffee.

"I want to make a phone call."

The matron just snorted, set down the tray, and left her.

She told the officer delivering her next meal that she wanted to see an attorney and he said he'd pass along her request. Lunch was an egg salad sandwich, a fruit cup, and more coffee. Dinner was cold pork and beans, seemingly from a can, and served in a paper bowl with a plastic spoon. The matron collected the untouched dinner, as she had done the lunch, without comment.

The day wore on to night.

As they flicked off all but the hallway lights for the second time, Elana began to feel as squirrely as a drug addict. How long could they keep her here without providing an attorney?

Sunday evening gave way to a long dark Monday morning as Elana realized she'd missed church for the first time since arriving in this town. By now, everyone in Bald Cypress knew exactly where she was. Jackson must be delighted.

The flick of a light switch now marked night from day. The

rattle of the outer door told her someone approached, but instead of a public defender, the next person to visit her cell was Jackson.

"Good morning," he said, as if they had just awoken in bed together. His voice held no malice. There was no need. He had her where he wanted her.

Panic and rage collided like a bird striking glass, making her momentarily reel. But she rallied because this man fed on weakness.

"I want to speak to an attorney."

"Yes. I've heard you are quite the mynah bird repeating the same thing all night. You aren't going to see an attorney. But you will be seeing a judge for an arraignment."

"I'll ask the judge for an attorney."

"Fine. Do that. And they'll charge you with felony drug possession, dealing, and reckless endangerment of a child."

He stopped talking and let that sink in.

"The evidence is overwhelming. You'll be convicted, Elana."

"The planted evidence?"

"You'll lose. Or..." He let the possibility hang as she clung to the steel bars, her index finger rubbing over the chip in the paint repetitively, as if stroking one of his hounds.

"Where's Phoebe?"

"Home. Where you should be."

"Is my daughter all right?"

"Misses her mommy."

He used her daughter's fear like a blade, slicing into her causing physical pain. The ache inside her pulsed and throbbed like a bloody tumor. She needed to get to Phoebe.

"I've asked for an addiction specialist to help you with your problem."

"The only problem I have is you."

"I'm not your problem. I'm your solution because I can post bail and get you home."

"What about the charges?"

"That's up to you. Are you ready to come home?"

"What about the drug charges?"

"First-time offender. They have some leeway."

"They found quantity to deal."

"That didn't go in the record, yet. Whether it does, depends on what you do right now." He left that remark to hang in the air like the choking black exhaust spewed from a diesel engine. "You ready to come home and stay home?"

"What do I have to do?"

He passed a tube of rolled papers through the bar to her.

"It's a plea deal. Rehab, counseling for the drugs, and you get to come home."

"Rehab?" The anger leaked into her voice and he smiled.

"And you get to come *home*," he repeated.

He stopped talking, waiting for her to decide.

He had to think he'd won. Who was she fooling? He *had* won.

She signed the papers. Anything to get back to Phoebe.

Jackson collected the documents and left her.

"Wait. What about the bail?"

"Working on it now," he said and gave her a victorious smile.

She sank back to the bench, wondering if she'd just made another terrible mistake.

The answer came before noon, at her arraignment when she met Jackson and her public defender.

But in the courtroom before a judge, she learned the price of Jackson's help. The judge demanded she undergo mandatory rehab, mandatory counseling, and supervised visits with her daughter until such time as the court could "reasonably deem she was no longer a threat to her daughter."

"In addition," said the judge, "Mrs. Belauru will maintain a separate residence from her daughter who will reside with her stepfather for a period of four months after which the matter will be reexamined."

Separate residence. Supervised visits.

She hadn't agreed to that. But she'd signed the papers and they'd cut this deal.

By admitting to possession, she'd given the courts cause to deem her an unfit mother.

An elderly court guard led her away.

"Where's Phoebe?" she called to Jackson.

"Zoey's got her. She's very disappointed in you. We all are."

That afternoon she had another visitor.

Braden Orrick appeared before her cell. Her former father-in-law was so gaunt that it took her a moment to recognize him. His skin had an unhealthy gray cast and the puffy bags under his eyes were scarlet. His arms were covered with purple bruises beneath papery skin.

"Braden?"

"Hi, honey. I'm so sorry to hear about what happened."

"It's a mistake. No, actually, Jackson did this to me."

"Jackson is the one who called me. I'm here to aid all I can. Encourage you to seek the help you need."

"I'm not using, Braden. It's a trick to take Phoebe."

"He said you'd say that. I wanted you to know that I'd take Phoebe if I could. But with Victoria gone and my medical issues, I just am not capable of raising a young child, knowing, you know... I won't be there for her."

She gripped the bars with one hand and reached out to him.

"It's back?"

"Yup. It's moved around. They found it... well, everywhere. In my lungs now. I'm like a tree all filled with termites. They're gnawing away at me. It's terrible."

"I'm so sorry, Braden." She gripped his hand, feeling his dry, cold skin.

"I guess I'll be with Victoria soon. I already told Jackson that I wouldn't dispute his custody for Phoebe. I only had custody if something happened to you and no court would give me guardianship, anyway. Just look at me." He tugged at the belt into which he had punched several more holes. The pants bunched around his narrow waist looking as if they belonged to a much bigger man.

Hopelessness choked her as she recognized that Jackson, and the cancer, were taking her last ally.

"Braden, you can't let Jackson have Phoebe."

"I'm afraid I can. You're in here and I've got chemo twice a week. I met Zoey. She seems nice. Gonna help out all she can."

"Will you at least make a phone call?" She was now desperate enough to call Special Agent Inga. She knew she had nothing to offer, had failed to find any evidence against Jackson, but perhaps the imminent threat to her daughter might bring her here.

"Your dealer?"

"The FBI."

"The FBI?" He retreated a step, releasing her hand. "Why?"

"Jackson's trying to lock me up and take Phoebe."

He shook his head. "He told me the withdrawals would make you irrational."

She thrust her hand through the bars and he staggered back out of her reach.

"Branden. Please. I need to hire an attorney and fight this. A good one. Can you lend me some money?"

He glanced away.

"He said you'd ask for money. Told me you've been stealing from him to buy drugs."

"I haven't. I never..."

"Have some friends with kids with just this problem. They've been through hell. I'm going to do what I can. Visit Phoebe as long as I'm able. But I won't give you any money. I will give everything I have to Phoebe. It's already in my will."

"Jackson will take it."

"I hope so. Not that he needs it, but I hope it will go to her schooling or maybe a wedding one day."

"Braden, please. Everything he's telling you is a lie."

His expression turned hard.

"I heard about Phoebe's accident. The broken arm. I can't be a part of that, Elana. I'm sorry."

He turned and shuffled away.

Checkmate, she thought. Jackson had successfully cut off her last avenue of help.

Her husband would have his revenge. What he'd done was worse than killing her. He'd ruined her reputation, had her declared an unfit mother, and separated her from her child as neatly as a surgeon with a scalpel.

What was he doing to her daughter right now?

Images of Raelyn and Grace rose before her.

Elana burst into tears, letting the wracking sobs echo off the walls as she held her face in her hands.

That was where Jackson found her, crying alone in the holding cell.

"How was your visit?"

Her head jerked up and she saw the triumph in his smug face.

"Where's Phoebe?"

"With Zoey for now. She'll have her until I get home. Then I'll be the one to raise Phoebe. Already hired a live-in nanny."

He snapped his fingers. "Replaced you in just over twenty-four hours. Might be a record."

"You're going to make me vanish. Aren't you?"

"Don't be so melodramatic. Just follow the judge's orders. Visit your daughter with the court official watching your every move or break the agreement and run.

Then you'll go to prison, and I'll have your daughter. Your choice."

THIRTY

THIRTEEN DAYS LATER

Elana watched out the dirty kitchen window inside the upstairs apartment for Jackson's truck.

After completing the ten-day mandatory residential drug rehabilitation program, she'd moved into this little firetrap the last week of July.

The window air conditioning unit in the main room roared like a failing jet engine as it tried and failed to cool the living space that included the main room, eating area, and galley kitchen. But the dilapidated appliance could not keep up with the combined summer temperatures in Florida and the rising heat on the second floor above the laundromat.

Since Jackson had arranged for this hellhole, she knew he'd made the choice of accommodations to punish her and to remind her of what she'd lost.

And since he surely had keys, she kept the deadbolt locked when inside and searched everywhere upon each return to be certain he had not planted any drugs or drug paraphernalia on the premises.

Bald Cypress was not meant for walking. But he'd kept her vehicle and phone, so much of her time was spent walking to the grocery and hauling home whatever she could carry. Each footfall on the hot pavement struck a drumbeat, reminding her she'd faced Jackson and lost. She hadn't been able to protect her own daughter. And she hadn't been able to find justice for two other lost little girls.

Seeing members of their neighbors and people from her church meted more chastisement as they hurried away, pretending not to see her, or cast her reproachful glances. Keeping her chin up was no challenge because everything he'd done only kindled her fury and gave her time to think.

Without Phoebe to feed and bathe and dress, pick up from camp, without her daughter's playdates, back-to-school shopping, the dogs, the car, the big house to care for, and her husband's errands to run, she turned her mind to the chessboard of her life and how to outplay Jackson.

She moved the faded curtain away from the kitchen window and peered out at the rear parking area again.

Two thousand and seventy-one dollars against millions. She almost wished she were Marlo Sullivan, free and happy in her home with her son and that ferocious dog.

Almost.

Any minute, he would bring Phoebe and the dreadful woman who sat as still and silent witness to everything she said or did with her daughter.

How could Elana protect her child?

A familiar roar of the special muffler Jackson added to his truck caused her to lean forward for a better view of the lot as his vehicle pulled up.

The woman from social services would next emerge from her silver sedan, which had been parked for fifteen minutes, and she'd collect Phoebe and escort her up the narrow back stairs to Elana's meager living space.

On the initial two supervised visits, Elana did not speak to Jackson and saw him only from her tower. Today, he exited the truck and looked up. She looked down. Phoebe was ferried from his truck to her apartment without a word exchanged.

Usually.

So, when he walked with her daughter toward the rear entrance to her upstairs apartment, she dropped the curtain and backed away until she collided with the small refrigerator.

Jackson was making his next move.

Elana cast about as she searched wildly for a place to hide. Seconds ticked past before she got hold of herself. The social worker, Mrs. Graham, would be with him. She wouldn't be alone.

Anything he said or did would be witnessed. This time away from Phoebe had been hell, but being away from Jackson was paradise. It gave her a glimpse of what her life might have been if she had not reached with greedy hands for the security he offered.

Before she'd met Jackson, she and Phoebe did not have much, but they did have a safe place to live. Friends and some of the less expensive pleasures, like the freedom to come and go as she liked when not working nights.

Being working class, struggling financially, having a picnic in the park because the landlord refused to let them have a barbeque grill.

All that now seemed like paradise.

His footsteps sounded on the stairs, a slow, rhythmic strike, each foot falling heavily on the wood steps. He didn't knock, of course, just called to her from outside the door.

The urge to set the chain in the lock overwhelmed.

Instead, she lifted her chin and opened the door, as if she had expected him all along.

He regarded her with an expressionless face, sweeping over her body from head to toe. His face reddened as he noticed her jeans and T-shirt. His gaze cut to hers, narrowing his eyes. Did he wonder how she afforded them?

They'd been free, discards from charitable folks at the food pantry where she volunteered.

"Mommy!" called Phoebe and pushed past Jackson to hug Elana.

She wore her best clothing, having just come from the church Elana no longer attended. The pink arm cast now bore the names and well wishes of many people, but the cotton batting around her hand was dirty and ragged.

Elana crouched and gathered her daughter to her, resting her cheek on the top of Phoebe's head, still warm from the sun. Her daughter smelled of soap and cinnamon. She sent a silent prayer of thanks to whatever woman was seeing to Phoebe's care in her absence.

"Have you had lunch, baby?"

"I'm not a baby!"

She squatted before her. "You most certainly are not. But you'll always be *my* baby."

Almost a third grader and the first day of school was only three weeks away. Where would they be then? Back with Jackson?

Elana's stomach squeezed and she fought the queasiness.

Movement caught her eye as Mrs. Graham reached the landing, out of breath. The woman was years past retirement and had little to no chance of keeping up with a seven-year-old.

Jackson stepped into her apartment and turned in a slow circle. He smiled now as he took in the shabby surroundings, eyeing the dilapidated furniture, dull Formica breakfast table, and faded carpet. Finally, he rested a hand on a metal chair with a cracked vinyl seat, spun it, and sat backward as if he owned the place. Likely he did, as rental properties went hand in hand with his real estate business.

"Mrs. Graham, take Phoebe for a walk."

"Well, I've just..." Her words trailed off at the look he cast her. "Come here, Phoebe."

Phoebe glanced to her mother, eyes round with worry. Elana's skin tingled a warning and her heart sped, but whatever Jackson wanted to say, she did not want Phoebe hearing.

Mrs. Graham, however, was a different story. She could provide testimony in court of whatever dirty little deal Jackson was going to propose.

Who was she kidding? Her foolish fantasies of speaking to detectives, having her day in court, and getting away from Jackson were finished. That day had come and gone. She'd lost.

"Go on," Elana said to Phoebe. "Mommy will be there soon."

"Ten minutes," he said to Mrs. Graham.

And out they went, closing the door behind them with an ominous click.

Jackson motioned to the chair opposite him.

She did not offer him anything before taking the place he indicated.

"Phoebe misses you."

There was no question here, so she said nothing.

He folded his arms and leaned on the chairback. "I want you to come home."

"That's up to the judge."

He snorted as if she could not be more naïve.

"Do you want to come home?"

She didn't. But she did want Phoebe.

"Yes," she said.

He reached behind him and for an instant she thought he'd brought a gun. She pressed both hands on the table, fingers splayed, and teeth set tight.

He withdrew several folded papers, stapled at the corner. He dropped them between her hands, now ringed with the vapor of her own sweat.

"Sign those and we'll get you before that judge."

She unfolded the packet. "What is it?"

"Adoption papers. I want to legally adopt Phoebe."

She sucked in a breath, but remained still, eyes on the application. Taking this step meant that he'd have her daughter should anything happen to her.

She flicked her gaze to his.

He had warned her that if she tried to leave him, he'd make her sorry. And she'd done just that.

Was he planning to send her to prison, institutionalize her, or kill her?

Elana didn't know. What she did know was that Jackson wouldn't tolerate a disobedient dog.

Rest in peace, Chase, she thought. Signing these papers would be signing her own death warrant.

If she didn't sign them, he'd still have Phoebe because Grandpa Orrick was terminally ill, and she was Phoebe's only other blood relative.

She pushed them away, but kept one hand on them, realizing that the game was on again. And, this time, he would not catch her unprepared. She had the debit card in her safety deposit box and the key, still secreted in the library. She knew because she'd been there yesterday and still thought that old reference book a safer hiding spot than anything in this apartment. The bank statements would be coming to a new email address she'd set up from the library computer. Paperless, so he'd never see one.

And he wouldn't do it right away. He'd want time to control the optics before he killed her. That was obvious or she would have been found dead in that jail cell.

Elana pulled the pages before her and accepted the pen he offered. Then she signed the application.

Everything happened quickly after that. Her court date. Clearing her of all charges and her return to the beautiful home she once thought she wanted.

On the third Monday in August, just over two weeks after she'd signed the adoption papers, Jackson welcomed her with uncharacteristic grace, reminding her of the charming, charismatic man who had duped her into marriage.

Phoebe and the hounds were near hysterical with joy.

And the live-in nanny had left no trace except a variety of cleaning products under the kitchen sink with which Elana was unfamiliar.

The change in Jackson's behavior had her on edge. He didn't touch her. Made sure they were seen in public and that his behavior was nothing but exemplary. A textbook performance of a husband trying to bring his fallen wife back to the fold.

She still didn't know what he planned to do with her.

Perhaps he hadn't made up his mind yet.

But she knew which one *she* needed him to choose.

It was tempting to give up. Let him do whatever he wanted. Get it over with. But those two lost girls deserved better. And Phoebe.

She had to protect Phoebe.

Elana didn't have enough money to get away from him. But she had enough to stay and expose her perfect husband for the monster he really was.

If she could show them what he would do to her, if others could see, then Phoebe would be free.

If Elana survived, they both would be.

That, she realized, would be too much to ask. But it wouldn't stop her. Marlo had lost her eyes. And she knew that any of them, Shantel, Faith, or Marlo, would have died to protect their children.

And that meant she had to compel Jackson to choose murder.

She had to let him kill her.

THIRTY-ONE

It wasn't hard, really, to give him the reason. Motive, they'd call it. She closed her eyes and prayed that, afterward, they would come for him and work it all out, motive, means, and manner of death.

Easy.

Once Jackson knew, instead of just suspected, what she had done on the boat, he'd act.

She only needed to admit he hadn't dragged her overboard. That she'd been on his boat for hours and had not even considered calling the coast guard when he'd fallen into the inlet in a drunken stupor. Instead, she'd prayed to God for him to suffer and drown.

Once he was sure, then he would get rid of her. No question. And he would not be satisfied with her incarceration. He'd want her dead.

Her daughter's grandfather was ill, but was not gone yet. She might have signed the adoption papers, but if Jackson was incarcerated for Elana's murder, Phoebe would become Braden's responsibility. He'd find a suitable caretaker and a place for Phoebe to grow up. She knew that with every fiber of her being because Braden Orrick was the exact opposite of her husband.

First, she needed to prepare her own trap. Dig a bear pit, deep and strong with high, inescapable walls. Then cover it so perfectly, he'd never see the loose fronds and branches until they tumbled with him into the void.

Before that, everything must be in place. That meant getting the necessary equipment, stretching the money she had, and taking whatever else she needed from those coin catchers in the laundromat.

The FBI had interest only in solid evidence. Evidence she hadn't been able to find. The police here were firmly in Jackson's pocket.

But out there in the Wild West that was social media, there were a billion eyes watching. She just needed to direct the lens to her private hell.

That third Thursday morning in August, she dropped Phoebe off at school and then purchased groceries, took her husband's suits to the dry cleaner, and picked up Jackson's repaired bowling ball. Errands complete, she stopped at the box store and used her new debit card. She bought the same brand laptop Jackson had purchased for her, along with as many web cameras as she could afford.

The following morning, she placed the cameras in the house, covering their glowing red light with black electrical tape. With her new email service, she opened her first social media account, setting every option to public. She entered her high school and former places of employment. The algorithm immediately furnished several potential friends. She sent requests to all of them, even the ones she did not recognize.

Her first post was a live video of the dogs running and tumbling after a tennis ball in their morning game of fetch. By eleven in the morning, she had twenty-two friends.

After lunch she connected all the cameras to her new home

security account, funded with her checking account. The cheap, voice-activated assistant would turn on all cameras to livestream on her verbal command.

She practiced all Friday afternoon, recording herself in the kitchen, drilling until she knew how to use the cameras on the live feed. She posted the video in real time on her new feeds, getting odd comments from voyeurs, accepting every friend request and sending out many more.

The cameras were only black and white because they were so much cheaper than the color versions. But they did record sound.

She worried that he might attack her when she was too far from the device to start the livestream or when she was in the car or away from the house. But it was a chance worth taking.

Unfortunately, downloading the social media accounts to her phone was impossible. Jackson would see that, as he controlled her phone account, and she did not have enough to buy a second phone.

That evening, when Jackson returned from work, he found Phoebe gone to a friend's house for her first sleepover. Elana had arranged that without consulting him and his brow descended at the news.

She waited until he retrieved a beer from the refrigerator and settled in his favorite chair, beside the dead, mounted mallard duck.

Then she straightened and drew a full breath like a woman preparing to dive headfirst into a shark tank. When fear nearly closed her throat, she thought of the missing girls and her daughter. All of them needed her bravery.

"You know, you were right." She had his attention. "That night on the boat. I did push you overboard. Then I stood on deck while you flailed like a cat tossed in a bathtub."

His mouth tightened and he set aside the beer bottle.

"Watched to see you sink right to the bottom. Should have,

drunk as you were." She had never spoken to him like this in her life.

Jackson's eyes blazed, the tiny blood vessels pulsing red. He gripped the arm of the chair and rose.

"Didn't call for help either because I hoped you'd drown. Waited hours. Right there next to the radio planning the trip I was taking in that stupid boat. The Bahamas maybe. Then I'd sell it along with your precious house and every one of those hideous dead animals."

She pointed at the duck.

"That one especially."

It was like she had left her body, floating above herself, watching some other woman take charge, a strong and brave woman who would do anything for her child.

He advanced, silent as a stalking panther. The beast that had been inside him all along finally out in the open now.

"Would have worked, too, but for that damned lucky fishing vest."

Jackson took a menacing step forward and then paused, seeming to recall where they were.

"That's right. Neighbors saw you come home. You waved to that couple with the retriever. Remember? They were right there at our mailbox."

She'd bet her life that he was aware enough to realize he had no alibi here and now. If he attacked her, killed her, there would be no way to deny that he was home.

But Jackson had never been rash. Calculating, yes. He stared at her, his breathing heavy and his eyes red as the blood on the deck of that stupid boat.

She gathered her courage and forged on.

"And I've been stealing from you. Fifty dollars a week from the coinboxes at the laundromat. I've got enough money to leave you and where I'm going, you'll never find us."

His reply was growled through clenched teeth. "You aren't going anywhere."

"You can't stop us."

"Can't I? You had nothing when I met you and you have nothing now, except a criminal record for drug possession and you just admitted to theft. I could have you declared an unfit mother like that." He snapped his fingers.

"I'd like to see you try."

The smile was full of menace. Once upon a time that look would have sent her scurrying to please.

Not anymore. Now she wanted him to attack her and lifted a defiant chin in challenge.

"You think you can beat me?" he asked.

"I think you're a coward. A bully and a fake. Wait until I tell everyone exactly what you are. I'll ruin you, Jackson. You won't be elected dogcatcher in the next election."

That threat had him stepping backward. She couldn't have been more shocked if he had dropped to his knees to apologize. Jackson Belauru looked scared. His red face had gone pale and the vessels at his throat throbbed.

He was afraid of her. How was it that she had never realized she wielded some power after all? That satisfaction and sense of triumph were short-lived, replaced with a deep pulsing fury at herself for tolerating this. Why hadn't she challenged him before?

But she knew the reason. Jackson was a coward and a bully. But he *was* dangerous.

"I know you took your stepdaughters. I know it was you and I'm going to call the FBI and tell them so."

"You've got nothing but theories."

"Maybe, but I can tell them you pushed Phoebe off that rock wall."

His eyes narrowed as he scowled.

"Your word against mine. I already told the doctor that she

was with you and that I was worried when you wouldn't bring her for an X-ray. Seemed you had something to hide. And then the drug arrest. I've legally adopted her. Elana, I'm three steps ahead of you. Have been since day one."

Was he?

They'd soon see.

"I'm sleeping in the guest room," she said. That way she could record him if he followed her. "Tomorrow I'm taking Phoebe."

Jackson stormed to the foyer and grabbed her purse, rummaging.

"They aren't in there."

His head jerked up. "What?"

"My car keys. Not there."

Her husband grabbed her phone and dropped her bag. Then he stormed through the house to the garage, retreating.

He needed to plan how best to tackle this new problem.

Have her pulled over for drug possession again or DWI? She hoped not. Besides, Phoebe was safe with Marielle's family until tomorrow, so she didn't need to use the car and wouldn't. She was staying right here, under his nose, waiting for Jackson to make the move she knew he could not resist.

Flushing birds and shooting them out of the clear blue sky.

On Saturday morning, she rose early to find her SUV in the garage beside Jackson's truck with the hood up. Closer inspection showed he'd removed something, because cables were sticking up, attached to nothing.

The appearance of the dogs gave her a jolt of panic. Jackson was up and he'd find her here, too far from the voice activation device and cameras. Her insides contracted as she hurried to the house, too late.

Jackson blocked her entry into the laundry room.

"I'm taking a few days off. Heading to Georgia. Do some squirrel hunting."

He held a duffel bag in one hand and his keys in the other.

She almost wept with relief.

Jackson never hunted anything as small as squirrels. He was after something bigger.

"Get the dogs in shape for duck season."

"I see. Is there something wrong with my car?"

"Yes."

He tossed his bag in the truck bed and ordered Gunner and Dash into his vehicle. She stepped back into the house, closing and locking the door.

It was happening.

He'd leave. Be seen wherever they were shooting squirrels and then sneak back here in the night. When he did, he wouldn't find Phoebe here. Just her, waiting.

Connie stopped before supper to drop Phoebe off; but at a safe distance on the doorstep Elana reported she'd tested positive for Covid and asked the woman to keep her one more night.

Marielle's mom looked unhappy and suspicious, but she agreed.

"Is Jackson sick, too?" she asked.

"He left to go hunting with his brothers, but he seemed fine. He said he'll grab a test up there in Georgia."

"Should you be home all alone?"

Was Connie concerned about Elana's drug problem?

She almost laughed. "I'll be fine. Don't even feel sick, really." If you didn't count heartsick.

Elana blew air kisses at her daughter and watched her drive safely away.

As evening gripped the quiet neighborhood, she sat up well past dark listening for any unfamiliar sound. The alarm was set, but, of course, Jackson could deactivate it. But he could not deactivate *her* security system.

She waited, ready to activate her camera. Ready for his attack. And then she realized there was no longer a reason not to break that damned lockbox. It was there, in the garage. Breaking into it now would make no difference in what Jackson intended to do to her.

But if she did find something, some evidence of his involvement in the disappearances, she could call Special Agent Inga.

"It's worth a try."

Without the dogs following her everywhere or Phoebe here with her, the house seemed empty. The only sound was the lock turning in the garage door and her footsteps descending into Jackson's domain.

She walked straight to the bin holding the lockbox and opened it. Then she dumped the contents on the floor. The lockbox thumped heavily to the concrete.

He had a wide variety of tools. Prybars and hand sledges. But she tried a simpler method, lifting the awkward container above her head and dropping it on its corner. The box cracked open like an egg.

Papers and documents spewed across the floor, some floating along before coming to rest. She knelt to study the contents.

Insurance documents were closer to the top. Fire, flood, car. All the normal policies. Phoebe's adoption papers were next. Seeing it made her blood heat, making her face blaze.

"You will never get my daughter," she promised, staring at her shaky signature, and remembering the day she had signed this.

Elana set it aside with the others and lifted a large manila envelope. Inside were passports, old identification, birth certificates, discharge papers.

"He was in the army?"

She studied each one. The notarized marriage certificate to Faith Collins, one for Shantel Keen, and the final one with her name on it below Jackson's. She exhaled her aggravation at seeing it had taken only fourteen months for everything in her world to fall to ruins.

"But I'm not done yet."

She glanced at the divorce papers for Shantel, tucked in a legal envelope with the other important papers, and thought of the cost of her betrayal.

If she had known Jackson would take her daughter, would she still have left him?

At the bottom of the fireproof box sat one large white envelope, wedged so tightly it had not dislodged with the others.

Elana used her fingernail to get under one edge. The contents were stiff, like cardboard, and the twelve-by-nine envelope had been sealed with blue painter's tape.

She peeled it away and upended the contents into her open hand.

Photographs. A stack of several, all the same size.

The first was very familiar. It was an eight-by-ten glossy of Grace Collins Belauru, the very same one the FBI had shown her. Faith's daughter. Grace was five, in kindergarten and wearing a bright turquoise dress. Elana paused to stare, lips pressed tight against the twisting emotion seeing the happy, smiling little girl.

"Where are you, Grace?" she whispered.

Elana flipped to the next photograph and gasped.

The photo was of Grace again. Only she was bigger. Older.

She shook her head in confusion and flipped to the next image.

Grace again, missing her front teeth, as all second graders did.

"She's getting older."

Elana gathered the photographs and jumped in her vehicle, only to recall he'd disabled her SUV. She poked her head under the hood and lifted the wires, noting the places where they seemed to connect. She pushed each clip back into place and closed the hood. Then she tried the ignition.

Her vehicle started and she frowned, realizing Jackson thought her too stupid to know how to clip the cables back to the spark plugs. Underestimating her had become a bad habit.

If she wanted, she could still collect Phoebe.

She ignored the urge and instead raced through the night toward the home of Faith Belauru. Beside her on the passenger seat were nine photos that showed her daughter in kindergarten through eighth grade, each dated on the back. The last photo was taken this very year.

Faith's missing daughter was alive.

She reached the house and pulled into the narrow twin tracks that served as a driveway, raising dust, and leaning on the horn. It was only a little past eight in the evening, but the house was dark. On one side of the manufactured home a light flicked on, and a large dog barked.

Elana snatched up the photos and ran to the house, pounding on the door.

"Faith. It's Elana. Are you in there?"

The porch light flicked on. Elana glanced at the photo before her. Grace, older, clearly thinning out as she approached her teens, but still in a simple, plain dress. She was alive. Jackson had taken her and... and she didn't know. But Faith needed to hear this, right now.

She'd found it. The evidence that Jackson had taken Grace. Together she and Faith could go to the FBI.

An interior light glowed, illuminating the screen and closed blind.

A female voice told the dog to be quiet. Then a door slammed, muffling the barking as she shut away the vocal canine.

The front door creaked open. Faith stood in a high-necked white nightgown of cotton. Around her shoulders she held a knit gray shawl. Unlike every other time Elana had seen her, she wore no kapp and her wheat-colored hair lay in a single thick braid draped over one shoulder.

"I found her! I found Grace!" Elana held up the photo and Faith leaned to peer through the screen. "We can go to the FBI. Have Jackson arrested and find your daughter."

Faith opened the door.

"Come in."

Elana swept into the house. From down the hallway, toward the bedrooms, a dog whined.

"Hush up now," said Faith, then turned back to Elana. "I'm sorry about the noise."

"Look at these." Elana extended the portraits. "They're your daughter. All of them. She's getting older. That means she's alive."

And instead of the shock and joy Elana expected, Faith methodically flipped from one image to the next until she had stared at the last. Then, without a word, she turned to a cabinet beside her sewing machine and withdrew the exact same photo.

Elana stared, trying to make sense of what was happening. And then the possibility struck like a pneumonic hammer.

"You already knew."

Faith nodded, blue eyes steady and clear. "Jackson gives me one of these every year on Grace's birthday."

"So she's alive? Where is she?"

"I don't know where. But she's safe and look how happy." Faith turned the image, now on the stack with the ones Elana had given her.

"Is she a captive? If he's intimidating you with the threat of injuring your daughter..."

Her words fell off at Faith's musical laugh. The sound was so unexpected it might as well have been a slap. Her mirth sent a chill over Elana's body.

"No, no. My dear, nothing like that. Early in our marriage,

before I knew God had closed my womb, Grace was a distraction. She can't help it. She has special needs. But she was always crawling into our bed at night and demanding so much attention. I couldn't fully focus on Jackson."

"You couldn't focus..." She gaped. This was impossible. "But she's alive. He took her."

"I asked him to send her away so I could be a better wife. He's a good husband and he knows his duty to me and to God."

"You asked him to take your child?"

"Yes. And, after God closed my womb, I asked him to take a second wife. But she was not a godly woman. Not like you."

She was talking about Shantel.

"She's still his wife as well. A marriage is until death. You can't renounce a vow you make before God. So, I told him to be God's vengeful hand."

"To do what?" But she knew. Even before Faith spoke, she knew.

"To take her little girl."

"You... you told him to do that?"

"She is a bad mother and a bad wife. She couldn't bring him a son. It is her duty to be fruitful and multiply. Not forsake the vows she swore before God and abandon her marriage."

"Faith, this is crazy."

She moved back to the stove, dropped the photos on the burner, and turned on the gas.

"No!" Elana rushed forward as Faith lifted a wicked carving knife from the wooden block on the counter.

Elana stopped. Faith glanced back at the photos, burning now, the smoke coiling upward. She flicked on the exhaust fan, drawing away the smoke and making the flames leap higher.

"I shouldn't have kept these. We are not allowed to have photographs. They cause vanity and sinful pride. 'Thou shalt not make unto thee any graven image, or any likeness of anything that is in heaven above, or that is in the earth beneath, or that is in the water under the earth.' Exodus 20:4. The Second Commandment."

A glance told Elana that Faith had no photos or pictures of any kind on the walls of her home. Then she looked back at the knife in Faith's left hand, the simple silver wedding ring now obvious.

"He still comes to me, though I can bring him no children. And I comfort him, welcome him into his home."

"You're still married?"

"The Bible says a man may have more than one wife."

"I don't think it says that," said Elana.

"'And Lamech took two wives. The name of one was Adah, and the name of the other Zillah.' Genesis 4:19. It was my idea."

That's why she had not seen a divorce settlement between Faith and Jackson. They were still married.

"God intended for a wife to produce a son of her husband's line, so even if that means he produces one through you, I do my duty to him and to God. And I am, and shall ever be, his first wife."

"It's illegal."

"It's God's will," said Faith simply.

Elana backed toward the door. But she stopped, realizing the evidence she needed to prove Grace was alive had burned to ashes on her stove.

"He is getting impatient with you. We expected children by now." Faith continued to grip the knife. "We have been very patient. But I fear I must agree with Jackson. Your time is up."

"My time?"

"Until death do you part."

Elana's skin tingled a warning, relaying the danger like the whiskers of a cat conducted movement on the currents of air. "He was here?"

"Earlier. Gone now. I do not know exactly, but I do know

that he is not where you think he is. I'm sorry, Elana, that you have not preformed your duties to him or to God. We were so hopeful. And I really wanted us to be friends."

"Faith, don't you want Grace back?"

She shook her head with a chilling certainty. "I do not, because I fulfill my duties as a wife. Though I fear it is fire and brimstone for you, my dear."

"You know what he's planning?"

Faith's thin brows lifted and she nodded.

"And your faith allows for him to murder me?"

"You have eaten the fruit from the tree of knowledge, Elana, and God said, 'You shall not eat of the fruit of the tree lest you die.' You have chosen your path. Now you must walk it."

Faith crept forward, a look of delight on her face as she raised the weapon.

Elana ran out the front door, leaping the three steps and springing over the ground. She reached her vehicle, her heart thumping painfully in her chest. She didn't have the photographs because Faith had destroyed the evidence.

She could still alert the FBI, but with nothing more than accusations, what could they do? And even if they found Grace Belauru at some point, it would not change what Jackson had planned tonight.

Faith had already made the pronouncement. Like Shantel, she was not a godly woman, or a good wife, and she'd had long enough to give Jackson children.

She drove toward home. Jackson was coming for her, and she planned to be there to greet him.

Her last duty as a good wife.

Back in the garage, she stepped over the ruins of the lockbox and the scant evidence it now provided. Only the absence of a divorce settlement from his first wife. Because they were still married. Jackson was a bigamist. She doubted that crime even carried jail time.

Once back in the house, she undressed and slipped into her bed in the guest bedroom where she'd slept since telling Jackson she'd pushed him overboard.

Damn that fishing vest.

Then she blew out a breath and closed her eyes.

She didn't have long to wait.

In the early hours, when the house was still dark, but faint light from outside silhouetted the palm trees against the charcoal sky, Elana heard a click. The sound reminded her of a cocking pistol. She sat up in the dark.

On bare feet, dressed in only her cotton nightshirt, she opened the door to her room, listening. The sound from the entry had her dropping to the ground.

Someone was in the house.

THIRTY-TWO

She could not see if it was Jackson, but she knew it must be. He had not even waited the night.

Likely he and his brothers had checked into the ranch in the reserve up in Georgia. Squirrel hunting. That was a laugh. The property was created for the sole purpose of allowing men like the Belauru brothers to blast away at wild animals raised in captivity. Killed for sport.

It was a perfect pastime for Jackson.

Still in the guest bedroom, Elana called out to the device, saying the name that activated the system.

She had time to flick on the light and tap her computer awake to see the feed appear on her social media account. The red box beneath the video said: LIVESTREAM.

Then she crept down the hall, flicking on the lights in the living room and then again in the kitchen.

He stood just inside the door from the laundry room, dressed in black, his eyes bright with the kind of bloodlust she'd only seen when watching him gaff a tuna on the *Reel Escape*.

"Jackson," she said.

"Surprise!" He held his hands out to the side, revealing nothing but his open palms.

"What do you want?"

"Phoebe for a start. And you, gone."

She backed away. He actually stepped aside to let her flee. She ran toward the front door, making a genuine attempt to escape.

She never made it. He had her by the hair, yanking brutally as he dragged her kicking away from the box. Her scalp burned.

"Quit now or you'll wake your daughter. You don't want her to see what comes next."

But he didn't know that Phoebe wasn't in the house.

He tossed her to the ground and she landed hard on her knees.

"What are you going to do?"

"Seems obvious. I'm going to make you sorry. Then I'm going to kill you."

"Like you killed Raelyn?"

He smiled. "Just like that."

And there was the first admission of guilt, picked up by the microphones in the security camera not two feet from where she now knelt at his feet.

"You took those girls," she said, not revealing that she had visited Faith and knew Grace was alive, somewhere.

"So what?"

"How could you?"

He advanced. She scrambled away like a crab, scuttling backward toward the front door.

"And you burned your wife's house to the ground," Elana said, the accusation clear in her voice.

"Shantel was my *ex*-wife." He hissed his words. "And she *left* me. I told her. I warned her just like I warned *you*. Why can't you be happy with all this?" He waved his hands at the hunting lodge of a home. In the living room, a taxidermy duck seemed to be attempting an escape from a side table. From the walls, mounted heads stared back with glassy black eyes.

And from the potted fern, the new security camera stared with a single gleaming black lens.

"You had nothing! And look at this place. It's a damned mansion. You're a queen in this town. Why aren't you happy?"

"I'm not a wife. I'm your prisoner."

"Please."

"It's true."

He smiled. "Well, you won't have to worry about that much longer."

Jackson grabbed her by the collar and yanked her to her feet. His release was so abrupt, she staggered.

Who was up at this hour to witness this domestic tragedy on her webcams?

What if the whole world was sleeping?

Without any warning, his fist flew out and collided with her eye socket. The blow dropped her to the ground. Stunned, she found herself on her hands and knees, staring at the tile.

What was she doing here? She blinked at the tiny, perfect, russet-colored oak leaf on the grout line.

Then she vomited on the floor.

"Get up."

Her face throbbed and her mind cleared. She got one foot between her hands and pushed off, rising.

"You were the prettiest of all of them."

"Marlo was pretty," she whispered, her face throbbing with her heartbeat. "Before you threw acid in her face."

He didn't deny it.

"How could you do that to the mother of your only son?"

"I offered her marriage. I offered to be a father to that boy. They treated me like a leper. Threatened to charge me with rape. Me!"

"So you blinded her."

His sinister smile made her stomach pitch.

"She said she never wanted to see me again. I just gave her what she asked for."

THIRTY-THREE

Elana opened her eyes to find herself staring at the dog's water bowl. Where were Gunner and Dash? Would they help her? But he'd taken them with him. Even if they were here, they'd always followed Jackson's orders exactly, all except poor Chase, and her, of course.

And where were his brothers? Was Derek out in the driveway in his cruiser? Was Sawyer readying the getaway car just down the block?

Or were they both at the reserve in Georgia, asleep in their beds?

That was when she realized she was face down on the kitchen floor lying in something sticky and warm. Had he hit her again?

"Get up."

That was Jackson's voice. A command. But she couldn't get her arms underneath her body. They seemed to have turned to rubber. They flopped around like Phoebe's pool noodles.

Phoebe!

That thought got her to lift her head off the tile. She made it to her elbows and drew her legs under her torso, the hard knobs of her kneecaps jammed tight against her ribs.

What would he do to Phoebe if she blacked out?

Again.

It had to be again because she didn't remember how she had gotten to the kitchen.

Wait, her daughter wasn't here. Was she?

Elana didn't know. Her brain was all fuzzy.

She turned her head and saw a bloody smear streaking the stone tiles from the entranceway to her spotless kitchen. One of the island stools lay on its side.

That blood would be hell to get out of the grout lines, she thought. Then she slowly shook her head, trying to clear her thoughts. More blood dripped from her face to the floor.

"Cameras," she said. Were they on? How long did the livestream have to run before some stranger out there in Cyberspace figured out that she needed help?

Her profile had all her private details, all set to public. City, address, phone, marital status, though that last one was changing by the minute.

"They're off," he said. "The entire system is off because you don't know how to set it. Never turn it on when I'm gone. Remember?"

He meant the main security system. He'd refused to teach her how to use it or share the password. She could turn it on, but not off again. She'd learned that the hard way, locking them in and unable to open a door with the system active.

Had he said something else? The buzz in her ears grew louder, reminding her of the hum of tires on the interstate.

Maybe help was on the way. But she doubted that she'd be alive to see the rescue.

She pictured Derek in his squad car blocking the entrance to their road. Keeping help from reaching her.

Up at last, she staggered, bent in two like a rickety, hunched old woman. But she was staggering in the right direction. Jackson followed at a leisurely walk.

She reached the alarm box in the entranceway, leaving a bloody palm print on the wall beside the system controls before he grabbed the back of her nightshirt and hauled her away again.

Setting the scene, she realized, making a pretty picture for the murder investigation. A break-in, burglary. Such a shock in this quiet little town.

He dropped her beside his favorite chair in the dog bed that both Gunner and Dash used. In the spot he doubtless believed she belonged.

All this time, he'd never hit her. Not until tonight. He could have finished her anytime. Used a lamp or his fists to crush her skull. But he seemed content to stretch out her pain. And why not? In his mind he had all the time in the world.

"Phoebe," she whispered.

"Not here. I checked. Where is she?"

Elana lifted one hand to her throbbing jaw and winced.

"She can't hide. I'll get to her eventually. But she'll be livin' with her stepdaddy for a while. When she disappears, it will be at college. Dangerous place for girls, you know? All those eager young men hungry for sex."

She felt sick. She found it challenging to focus on him through the swelling now sealing shut one eye.

"I won. You lost. You lost my trust, your daughter, your life." He spat on her, the glob of saliva warm and wet as it glided over her neck.

Would her husband's DNA even be questioned? No. His DNA was on her body because they lived together.

Who was she kidding? There would not be some team of CSI techs, dressed in white jumpsuits, scouring her home or a careful medical examiner collecting samples from her autopsy for a murder investigation. It would be Jackson's police force

and Jackson's coroner. They'd find a break-in, a robbery interrupted by the mayor's wife. Thank goodness his daughter was
away.

"Such a brave man, raising her alone," she whispered to the
padding of the dog bed.

"What?"

"Had her cremated."

"Stop mumbling."

She blinked one eye open, trying to focus on Jackson. He
squatted before her, forearms resting on his knees. His fists were
scraped raw and bloody. Mostly her blood, she thought.

A fleck of it dotted his cheek, like a red birthmark.

She smiled and felt her swollen lip crack. A tentative
motion of her tongue showed one of her front teeth shorn in two
and the other rocking in its socket.

There was no warning before she vomited on the dog bed.

She'd need to clean that up before Jackson got home.

Something took hold of her leg and yanked her backward.
Her cheek dragged across the rough carpet fibers. The dander
made her sneeze, which caused her to cry out at the sharp stab
of pain through her nasal passages. She used her index finger to
wipe her nose and then lifted her hand to stare in fascination at
the bright red blood streaking her skin.

Her foot thudded to the carpet. She crawled between the
coffee table and couch, pressing her back against the reassuring
solid surface of the upholstered furniture.

Where was Jackson?

With great effort, she pushed up on one elbow peering over
the surface of the table between the antique wooden duck
decoy with the red glass eyes and the scented candle they never
lit. He stood at the vertical stained-glass window beside the
double-door entrance.

What was he doing?

She glanced to the camera on the mantel, praying it was

recording, transmitting... Was she waving? Yes, she was. Waving at her silent audience.

He turned and ran half the distance to her.

"What did you do?" he growled and glanced back over his shoulder, then jerked his attention to her. "Who did you call?"

"What?"

"Where's your phone?"

Where was it? She didn't actually remember.

Jackson charged away in the direction of the guest bedroom, returning with her laptop, roused from sleep mode by his jostling. Of course, she didn't have a passcode.

"What the hell is this?"

He thrust the device in her direction. On the screen was a live image of the back of his head. He turned and ran toward the artificial ivy, cascading from the hearth mantel, and spotted the camera. In one violent tug he ripped it from its hiding place and jerked the power cord loose. Then he threw the web device.

"What is this?" he bellowed.

"They're watching," she said, drawing to a seated position. Everything hurt. But the swelling was slowing the bleeding. "Livestream. Broadcasting since you came in."

And there it was, the expression she'd imagined and longed to see.

Fear. Gut-twisting terror. He went stiff as an opossum confronting one of his hunting dogs. In an instant, his color went from pink to ghastly gray. His vision glazed as he viewed some internal nightmare. His life flashing before his eyes?

She hoped so.

Or perhaps he saw his future.

She heard it now. The rising wail of police sirens. Not police. Likely sheriff or highway patrol. The cacophony rose like the screaming whistle of a freight train nearing the crossing.

"They're coming for you, Jackson."

He backed away, staggered, and fell into the wall, indenting the Sheetrock.

"Now you see what *I do* to anyone who threatens *my daughter*."

He ran toward the kitchen and out of sight.

She used the armrest to gain her footing. Then with slow, painful, dignified steps, she walked erect to the front door.

Jackson didn't like her rushing around like "a chicken with her head cut off."

He wanted an elegant wife. One who would do him credit.

She hoped she'd made him proud.

Elana reached the entryway, threw back the bolt, and opened the front door in time to see Jackson making a run for it across their lawn, his escape clear in the landscape lights that shone on the ornamental palms and the mailbox.

The first unit up the street pursued him as he reached the road and darted in the opposite direction. He ran well. She'd give him that. All that fishing and hunting had honed his body. But he was no match for the vehicle in pursuit. She could read the lettering on the side of the sedan now.

Sheriff.

The second vehicle pulled to a stop. The officer exited the vehicle and opened the rear door. She saw a streak of movement and realized he'd released a dog. A big black canine as fast as a greyhound.

Above the siren's wail, she thought she heard a man scream.

That would be Jackson, meeting the sheriff's dog.

His county tax dollars at work.

A second unit followed the first, fanning out beside them. The road was a cul-de-sac. Jackson was trapped against the expensive homes of the neighbors who had elected him mayor.

Several of their community now stood on their porches and entranceways. Huddled together as they watched the drama unfold.

She hoped they saw it all and appeared in court.

A third vehicle screeched into their drive, tires smoking and lights flashing red and blue. She reached the bench tucked beside a potted fern on their porch and thumped to the wooden slats.

A man in a forest-green uniform jogged in her direction.

"Mrs. Belauru?"

"Elana," she said. She didn't think she'd be using Belauru again.

"Are you alone in the house?"

"Yes. My daughter is at a friend's tonight." Her words were muffled by the swelling of her upper and lower lips.

"Any dogs?"

"He took them." She lifted a hand, pointing.

"Your husband?"

She frowned and it hurt. Then she aimed a finger in the direction of the other officers scuffling with a man and a dog.

He used his radio, calling for an ambulance.

Another vehicle pulled up, this one black with a gold emblem on the door. She recognized the Bald Cypress police vehicle.

"I'll take it from here," called the driver, only half out of his squad car.

"I don't think so," said the sheriff.

"This is my jurisdiction," said Derek Belauru, but his voice relayed strain.

"My brother-in-law," she muttered.

"Get back in your vehicle," said the sheriff, his hand moving to his sidearm.

Derek raised his voice. "You're inside the town limits. This is *city* jurisdiction."

The sheriff placed his hand on the grip of his gun and faced Derek, his expression grim. "We've notified the chief of police. We've contacted federal authorities."

"Not their jurisdiction," howled Derek, but he came no closer, remaining there gripping the top of the open door like a medieval shield.

"Patrolman, I'm placing you under arrest."

Elana set an elbow on the armrest and cradled her throbbing cheek in one palm, thinking that Sawyer would soon also be under arrest. Accomplices and accessories. Maybe worse.

Jackson had told her that he and his brothers were meant to be hunting in Georgia right now, but miraculously two of the three of them were here. Was Sawyer up north using his brother's credit cards and creating alibis or was he also here?

And then she saw Sawyer, illuminated in the dome light of Derek's squad car.

His little brother slipped back behind the wheel.

They reversed as far as the end of the driveway where a large SUV blocked their retreat.

The ambulance appeared, looking more like a small fire truck and parked behind the law enforcement vehicle. A man and woman darted out, both lugging heavy bags and hurried up the driveway toward the motioning sheriff.

She turned to the door and the web camera she'd mounted in one of the two large pots of white impatiens flanking the front entrance. Then she waved. She'd taped the glowing red light here as well. But she now knew they were watching.

"Thank you, everybody. Thank you for sending help."

The EMTs took over as the sheriff stepped aside to allow them access. They offered an ice pack wrapped in a paper towel, which she cradled against her eye socket, the cool gel bringing welcome numbness.

"Is there anyone you'd like us to call?"

She mentioned Marielle's parents. And then she said, "FBI Special Agent Inga, in the Jacksonville field office. Tell her I got the evidence she wanted."

THIRTY-FOUR

Three days later, Elana lay in the hospital bed here in Tallahassee, eighty-three miles from Bald Cypress. Until her release she was under the protection of the Federal Bureau of Investigation, who had detained three persons of interest in two missing persons cases.

She had been transferred here, away from Jackson's family and his corrupt little town. The nest of vipers was scattering, pointing fingers, and slithering away from the bright light cast by the FBI's investigation.

And most importantly, Phoebe was safe. Safe where Jackson couldn't harm her.

This morning Elana lay, slightly inclined, thanks to the mechanical hospital bed, answering a few more questions from Special Agent Inga who held her notepad open and a slim silver pen in her manicured fingers. She looked tanned and relaxed as she scanned the damage Jackson had wrought, then frowned.

"How are you feeling?"

"Like the loser in a prizefight."

"I'm sorry." She cleared her throat. When she glanced up again, the special agent had a firm hold of herself. "Your husband is being held in the county jail and I'm handling the murder case of Raelyn Keen and the abduction case of Grace Collins. Jackson Belauru remains our prime suspect and the focus of our investigations."

Smiling still hurt and Elana was self-conscious about her broken front tooth. Until she saw a dentist and her swollen lip healed, she got on with nodding when possible.

"And Marlo Sullivan's attack?"

"Not our case, but it will be reopened along with the house fire."

It was gratifying that she'd outmaneuvered Jackson, using his main weapon, secrecy, and throwing a brilliant spotlight on the monster he really was.

She couldn't quite believe she had survived it.

"Sawyer?" she asked.

"Also under arrest. An accessory. He's being cooperative. His attorney is working out a deal to insure he avoids the worst of the charges if he testifies against your husband. We'll drop the murder charge, though we are firm on the kidnapping charge. And here's a shocker. He claims that Jackson killed their mom. Put the pills in her drink and forged the suicide note."

Elana's eyes widened, but both the swelling and the pain stopped her.

"That true?" she whispered.

"He gave us the note and we're looking into it."

"Why?"

"Sawyer says she made their life hell, especially his younger brother, who, we feel, has some developmental issues."

Jackson had killed his mother and his stepdaughter Raelyn.

Two murders. Elana felt the weight of that squeezing at her chest, making it hard to draw a normal breath. If this was true, Jackson had already been a killer at twelve. And Sawyer had been his accomplice.

"Why keep the note?"

"Says initially he feared that if things went south, Jackson might pin the crime on him, being the oldest. Later on, he claims it was to protect his wife and his kids. A little insurance policy."

Elana thought about that. Jackson removing a woman, his own mother, who did not meet his standards. Sawyer being so afraid of his little brother he needed protection.

Yes, she believed it. All of it.

"And before you have to ask, Derek Belauru has been relieved of duty. Inquest pending. My opinion, no way a man with his IQ could pass the exam to get his badge in the first place."

Elana had no doubt he'd had some help from his brothers.

Someone was finally bringing the Belauru boys to heel. Past time. The relief brought the tears seeping from her eyes and dribbling over her raw skin, the salt water making it burn.

"You find Grace?"

"That's the good news. She's alive. Her mother took her to a community in Ohio. Traveled there a few weeks before they claimed Grace was abducted. She told them that the child was orphaned. Her little girl was adopted by a family who had no idea the child was abandoned."

"She all right?"

"Child services is checking into that."

Elana wondered if they'd let Grace remain with the family who had adopted her.

"Her mother, however, is in our custody. Charges include kidnapping and confinement."

It was baffling how a woman of faith, literally named Faith, could do such a thing. She struggled to wrap her mind around what Special Agent Inga had told her.

"But she's Mennonite," said Elana. "How could she desert her daughter?"

"She's no longer Mennonite, or at least she is not welcome

in their community. We were told by the men who would speak to us that she has not been permitted to worship with them since her marriage to Jackson and has been largely ignored by her former fellowship. Prior to Jackson, her interpretation of the Bible troubled the elders. I've spoken to her. She has keyed in on some very obscure and specific references."

"Tamar," said Elana.

"That's one of them. In any case, after recent events, they are unwilling to let her live even at their outskirts and they own the land upon which that house sits. They have asked her to leave. Her house is for sale, and she'll need all of that for her defense."

"How sad."

"Her decision to marry Jackson cost her everything."

And still it wasn't enough.

"I'm happy Grace is alive." Elana's jaw throbbed at each movement. She panted with the exertion at the effort this conversation cost.

"Me too. We expected the worst. Case like this... it's rare."

The agent fell silent as her eyes drifted up and Elana wondered what horrors were in her case files.

Faith was a very strange cautionary tale.

Elana thought about Jackson's unlikely first wife. She appeared Mennonite, but now the house, set near but outside the community, and the photographs of Grace made more sense. Faith had broken the tenets of her beliefs. Of course, her people could not permit that.

Inga scowled as she moved her hands to her hips, sending her blazer flaring out like the cape of a superhero.

"As for the Keen abduction case," she said, referring to Raelyn's murder. "We found some interesting items on Jackson's boat. The very ones I mentioned to you, the headband and a woven bracelet. Both were on the child's person when abducted and both were recovered from the safe in the master suite of the *Reel Escape*."

Elana gasped. "Shantel said to look there. Never got into that safe, though."

"We drilled it. And Shantel positively identified both items. He's claiming they left them behind when he and Shantel separated. But she had said that her daughter was wearing the headband when she vanished, and that Raelyn never took off the friendship bracelet. We're checking both for DNA and are very hopeful, but results are still pending."

Elana closed the one eye that was not already swollen shut and said a prayer for Shantel's little daughter, Raelyn. But she did not offer one for Jackson. He would be judged here by a jury of his peers. Hopefully he'd have to answer to an even higher power when his time on earth was done.

She thought about all the stories she'd heard as a girl about the devil waiting at the crossroads, just south of the graveyard on any midnight a person was foolish enough to go seeking his help.

For reasons too disturbing to explore, she imagined Jackson filling that role, appearing from the mist in his jacked-up pickup truck and asking the seeker if he wanted a lift.

She now knew that any crossroads, real or metaphorical, would suffice and that the devil didn't wait for midnight. Anytime would do.

"We've been through your house and have released the scene. Much of Jackson's belongings have been seized. Your new laptop, too, I'm afraid, and the cameras and digital footage."

"S'okay," Elana muttered. "The dogs?"

"Who?"

"His dogs."

"Jackson's?" She consulted her notepad. "Three male dogs. With his sister-in-law. That sit okay with you?"

"Three?"

"Yes." She glanced at her notes again. "Two recovered from Jackson's truck. The third was collected from the home of Faith Belauru after her arrest." She ran a finger over her notes. "Yes, according to your sister-in-law, the two recovered from the vehicle are called Gunner and Dash and the one recovered from the home of Faith Belauru was named Chase."

"Chase." She closed her eyes and let the tears come. Chase was alive!

"Elana?"

She met the agent's worried stare.

"I thought Jackson shot him."

"The dog? I'd like to hear about that."

"He took Chase out and we heard a gunshot. Then he was in the backyard digging a grave. Did he do all that to make us believe he would kill Chase?"

Inga scribbled something in her notepad.

"You'll need to show me where this happened."

"Of course."

"As for that stunt you pulled... that livestream? It was incredibly dangerous. And brave. You could have been killed."

Elana smiled and her lip cracked. The agent offered her a tissue for the blood.

She'd learned that upon broadcasting her livestream, calls had flooded the 911 call centers all over the country. Her public social media settings had allowed authorities to quickly find her.

The local police had initially been unresponsive, but the county and state agencies had mercifully stepped in.

Now the Bald Cypress police force was cleaning house.

They'd soon need a special election to fill two more recently vacated city posts. She expected more were to come.

Elana closed her eyes, thinking she might finally be able to rest.

"You know, Jackson's attorneys are trying to sell the house and contents for his defense, but we've frozen his assets."

"Don't need it," she said and neither did she want anything that had been his.

She was healing. Her doctors said that the bruised kidneys would mend. She'd already met with a plastic surgeon about the facial injuries. And the protective armor replacing her skin seemed as strong as chainmail. Soon she'd be impenetrable and free.

"We can help you collect any personal items, and you can be sure you will be receiving your fair share of your husband's assets. Wouldn't be surprised if a jury gives you all of it."

Elana shook her head, not wanting his money or to endure Jackson's trial. But knowing she'd have to face both.

"Your personal items?"

"Don't have any. Never did." He'd picked her clothing, right down to her underwear, and she was not wearing any of it. Never again. Then she recalled one thing. "Can you grab Phoebe's stuffed unicorn? It has a rainbow mane."

Inga nodded, making a note.

"Your sister-in-law has tried to see you."

Elana hunched and then remembered she was safe. Then she thought of Zoey and her children, wondering what would become of them.

"We've told her, and anyone else who tried, that we are not allowing visitors."

She hadn't seen her own daughter yet and didn't want Phoebe to see her like this, though her child was safe at last.

Braden Orrick, Phoebe's grandfather, had taken charge of Phoebe and the pair was temporarily residing in an actual safe-house here in Tallahassee. By all reports, granddaughter and grandfather were having a marvelous time getting reacquainted.

Not that she wasn't aching to hold Phoebe and tell her everything would be different now. Answer all those unanswerable questions that a nearly eight-year-old was bound to have. But she didn't want to scare Phoebe. And seeing her mother so beaten and bruised would certainly do that. Elana *had* glimpsed her own reflection and that was reason enough to keep her daughter away. Instead, she spoke to her several times each day by phone. And for the first time in months, she felt her little girl was protected and with someone who loved her.

"Who's come?" she asked, curious.

"Many of your husband's colleagues. We're keeping a list."

Because anyone willing to drive over an hour to try to curry favor with her after Jackson's arrest might be worth investigating, she thought.

"A woman from your daughter's school, Fitzpatrick."

That was Phoebe's second-grade teacher. She would be sorry to have missed her.

Inga continued. "Wives of your husband's political party associates."

In other words, no one she ever wanted to see again. Most of them hadn't suspected the hell she'd been living. How could they? Jackson was clever, charming, and bold.

He was also a grade-A sociopath and a narcissist of the first order. Or he had been. Would prison change him?

She could not keep the smile from curling her cracked lips.

The bear pit worked. It caught that bear.

"You've got one visitor coming today, from WPP," said Special Agent Inga, using the abbreviation for the Witness Protection Program run by the United States Marshals Service.

"Yes."

"I've been told by one of their agents that your first husband's father will be joining you and Phoebe," she said.

Joining them in witness protection, as if it were a dinner reservation, instead of a one-way ticket to a government-funded vanishing act.

If convicted, Jackson would be in prison for a long time, but possibly not a life sentence. That truth and the fact that both his brothers would be out from behind bars even sooner was all the impetus she needed to continue with plans to enter the Witness Protection Program.

"Yes." If she spoke without moving her mouth very much, the pain was tolerable.

She didn't know how much time Grandpa Orrick had, but he could at least spend it with them. She had hoped he'd accept and was thrilled with his enthusiasm. With his wife and son gone, he had nothing to hold him in North Carolina and it seemed he had missed them as much as they had missed him.

That was another thing Jackson had stolen from them. Time.

Elana closed her eyes, battling the throbbing ache of her bruised skin. Her heartbeat seemed to pulse through every nerve ending in her face.

"Well, I'll let you rest. Marshals will be by to go over relocation plans. When you leave the hospital, you'll be moving from our care to theirs."

Elana opened her good eye and lifted a hand. Special Agent Inga stepped forward and took hold.

"Thank you," whispered Elana.

"No, thank you for helping us bring Raelyn's killer to justice." She paused, likely thinking, as Elana did, that closure would be another heartbreak for her family. "And for your bravery in facing Mr. Belauru. I know I couldn't have done what you did."

"Yes, you could. For your child, you could."

Inga released her.

"You take good care of her and have a good life, Elana."

"Thank you."

She'd have to come back for Jackson's trial, but that would be the last time she ever set foot in Florida.

THIRTY-FIVE

January 2023

Elana walked along red-colored sidewalks past neat brick buildings. Here the palm trees were familiar, but the various cactuses, arranged in the planter beds, were not. And the air was different, dry, and scented with clay. The heat radiated like a blast furnace causing the moisture on her skin to instantly evaporate. At times, she almost missed the moist, wet blanket of humidity of a Florida summer. But both she and Phoebe loved the blue mountains surrounding the city and the stark beauty of the desert national park. Who would ever guess that cactuses in Tucson, Arizona, grew as tall as palm trees?

She was Mia now, Mia Sweet, and her daughter was Paige. Their new identities took some adjustment, but it was a small price to pay for not having to look over her shoulder or constantly scan the faces of strangers for some glimpse of Jackson.

Her ex-husband was in prison, having already been convicted of attempted murder and sentenced to serve fifteen years. The missing persons cases and murder were yet to come to trial.

Mia and her daughter had quietly disappeared five months ago, changing identities, and celebrating their first Christmas in the neat three-bedroom brick house, roofed with red ceramic tile, and fronted by five-foot rust-colored adobe walls with the new members of their family.

At first, the Marshals Service had refused to allow them to keep her favorite of Jackson's dogs. But Special Agent Inga had insisted and so the three of them were here together, along with a German shepherd puppy they had adopted and a stray cat that had adopted them.

Chase liked this location, too, especially dashing after squirrels and lizards in the walled backyard and their long walks with the new puppy.

Unfortunately, her former father-in-law had not made the trip with them as planned because his condition had worsened, and he had elected for hospice. She and her daughter had seen him often before their departure. The marshals had told her that he'd died a few days after they'd left for Arizona.

Now Elana watched her daughter grow and flourish. Funny how the life she'd thought would be best for her little girl had suppressed her daughter nearly as much as it had Elana.

Being able to choose her own clothing as she entered third grade, Paige had shown a dislike for the pastel colors Jackson insisted on, preferring bold bright primary hues of red, blue, and yellow.

And she was loud now, singing and dancing and ramming around with her new friends. Back in Bald Cypress, Phoebe had been quiet and serious. Why hadn't Elana noted that her daughter understood Jackson's control over them both and acted more like a shelter animal than a happy little girl?

Now, well established in their new life, they were safe.

Breathing deep of the dry air scented with sage, she let her shoulders relax. Everything was different now. She had enrolled in the university here, majoring in law and social justice, with ambitions to get a degree and work in the organization where she now volunteered with a legal aid service.

After dropping Phoebe safely at her new elementary school, she walked over to the political sciences building. Once inside, she presented her ID to the campus security guard. Then she tucked the new identification back in her bag, smiling at the name: *Mia Sweet* and her image printed.

She waved at several fellow co-eds, familiar now after orientation. She was nearly a decade older than the freshman with whom she would share her Introduction to Political Science class. But she found that a T-shirt, flip-flops, and a backpack did wonders to make her fit right in.

January. A new year.

She met one of her recent friends outside the lecture hall.

Lisa Naha was a slim Native American from the Hopi people in New Mexico, who had looked as lost as Elana on day one. She hitched her tote higher on her shoulder and threw back her curtain of dark hair.

"Hey there!" said Lisa and glanced around at all the waiting students. "Big class, huh?"

They were chatting when her professor from Introduction to Logic spotted them. Troy Carson was close to Elana's age, with a winning smile and thick sandy-colored hair. He was smart and confident. She'd felt a connection right on the spot. He waved a hand at them and made a beeline in their direction.

"Who's that?" asked Lisa, clearly interested.

Who wouldn't be?

Troy had a certain charisma, captivating his entire class.

Before he reached them, Elana leaned toward Lisa and quickly explained how they'd met.

"Oh, a professor," Lisa said, teasing. "Very nice."

He had an easy walk and carried a satchel over one shoulder.

"How'd he know your schedule?" asked Lisa.

"We were chatting after class. He was helping me get oriented. Thought I was a transfer student because I'm older."

"Hmm," said Lisa, narrowing her eyes.

"Hi, Mia. Thought I'd find you here," Troy said. He nodded at Lisa and then spoke to Elana. "I brought you something."

He held out a waxed paper bag with the logo from a local bakery and she accepted the offering, her brows lifting in surprise.

"You did?"

Had he come here looking for her? Elana smiled, flattered at his attention.

"It's a chocolate croissant. You said you loved chocolate."

And Troy remembered she'd mentioned that detail.

"I do." She accepted the bag.

He grinned, showing a confident smile. Something about it seemed lupine.

"That's very sweet," she said, peering into the bag at the flaky, golden treat.

He pointed a finger at her. "*Sweet!* Good one. Very clever."

She flushed at the compliment and Lisa looked from one to the other, her expression showing curiosity as she picked up on the vibe.

Elana made introductions and Troy chatted until the lecture hall doors swept open and the students began to stream in.

"Well, I'll see you in class, Mia. Maybe we could grab coffee afterward."

She nodded and thanked him again for her breakfast.

Lisa turned to watch him go.

"He's cute."

Elana hummed a noncommittal sound as they headed into the hall.

"Seems perfect," said Lisa.

"Yes. He does." She looked back the way she had come. Though dissimilar in appearance, the professor reminded her of another perfect man.

Together they headed up the risers to settle in empty seats. Elana tore the croissant in two pieces offering Lisa half.

Lisa accepted the piece, leaning closer, whispering, "So, are you going to meet him later?"

"I'm not sure." Something about that professor gave her pause. Or was she just gun-shy after her marriage to Jackson?

The professor dimmed the lights as they munched. With the taste of chocolate lingering in her mouth, Elana drew in a breath and let it go as the class and her new semester began. There were a few moments in your life when you recognized new beginnings. Here she was, savoring the moment, because from here on, everything would be different in the best possible way.

A LETTER FROM JENNA

Dear Reader,

I want to say a huge thank-you for choosing to read *The Ex-Wives*. If you enjoyed Elana's story and want to keep up to date with all my latest releases, just sign up at the following link. Your email address will never be shared, and you can easily unsubscribe.

www.bookouture.com/jenna-kernan

I hope you loved *The Ex-Wives* and if you did, I would be very grateful if you could write a review because your honest opinion helps new readers discover a book you enjoyed.

As you discovered from this story, Elana missed several red flags that might have indicated a potentially abusive partner. Finding herself the victim of domestic abuse, she feared what might happen if she asked for help. Eventually, she found the courage. Sometimes it is hard to seek help, but help is available.

Domestic abuse is never the victim's fault.

If you or someone you know is in immediate danger, get help now.
US: call 911
Canada: call 911
United Kingdom: call 112, 999

Ireland: call 112, 999
New Zealand: call 111
Australia: call 000 (112 on mobile)

Get more help here:
United States: The National Domestic Violence Hotline at 1-800-799-7233 (SAFE)
Canada: ShelterSafe to find a helpline of a shelter near you.
United Kingdom: Women's Aid UK at 0808 2000 247
Ireland: Women's Aid at 1800 341 900
New Zealand: Women's Refuge crisis line at 0800 733 843
Australia: 1800RESPECT at 1800 737 732

I love hearing from my readers—you can get in touch on my Facebook page, through Twitter, Goodreads, or my website.

Be well. Stay safe and happy reading!

Jenna Kernan

www.jennakernan.com

facebook.com/authorjennakernan

twitter.com/jennakernan

instagram.com/jenna_kernan

bookbub.com/authors/jenna-kernan

ACKNOWLEDGMENTS

Though it would be nice to claim full credit for this story, no novel reaches a reader without the work of many people.

My husband, Jim, provides me with boundless support and love while also helping me keep at least one foot on the ground. This is especially important when the characters in my head hold conversations or when the time slips away from me. He helps me get that other foot back down and it is always such a joy to come back to the earth and to him.

I'm a middle child, perhaps the most talkative and loudest of the bunch. Comes with the territory of never being first or last at anything. Thank you to my older siblings for showing me how it is done and my younger one for letting me do it first, from time to time. And thank you for making the occasional fuss over me.

Special thanks to my agent, Ann Leslie Tuttle, of Dystel, Goderich & Bourret, for not only handling business but offering navigational advice on steering a course through the treacherous waters of publishing.

I am grateful to my savvy editor, Ellen Gleeson, for her critical eye and her mysterious superpower that allows her to see both what does not belong in a story and what is missing. I'm so lucky to have her editing my work.

The entire Bookouture team again earned my appreciation for the amazing cover, promotion campaigns, packaging, and marketing for this book. Thank you all for everything you do to make my work shine. I appreciate you all.

This book, like many, is available for early reviews. Of course, I hope for glowing comments, but when early readers spot problems, I listen and make critical revisions. I know that their honest opinions make books better. Fingers crossed this book doesn't need changes, but what a gift to know in advance what the most ardent and preceptive readers think!

Many thanks to the many writing organizations for educating, encouraging, and championing writers while meeting the extra challenges of doing so during a pandemic. Thank you to Sisters in Crime, Gulf Coast Sisters in Crime, Mystery Writers of America, Mystery Writers of Florida, Thrill Writers International, Writers Police Academy, Authors Guild, and Novelist, Inc.

Finally, I am grateful to you for reading this story. It means the world to me. Thank you!